A Marquette Time Travel Novel

Odin's Eye

Tyler R. Tichelaar

Author of *Haunted Marquette, Kawbawgam,*
and *The Marquette Trilogy*

To Dan and Jim,
Wherever they may be.

"Everybody loses someone that they love, and no matter how badly they want to, they can't get them back. And in spite of that, they find a way to go on. That's everyone's history."

— Lucy Preston, *Timeless* TV series

Contents

A Note to the Reader

Odin's Eye is the ninth novel I have written set in Marquette and the greater Upper Peninsula of Michigan. It is a stand-alone novel, meaning it is not necessary to have read my earlier novels to enjoy it. That said, readers of my past novels may find pleasure in reconnecting with characters who seem like old friends, and new readers may be interested in exploring certain characters in *Odin's Eye* who appeared in previous books. Therefore, I have provided a list of characters that differentiates which ones are fictional creations and which historical personages as well as which novels they previously appeared in. I have also included a family tree of Neill Vandelaare, the main character in this novel, for reference since his ancestors were all characters in previous novels.

Cast of Characters

Characters from previous novels have the abbreviated titles of those novels beside their names.

Novel abbreviations:

IP – *Iron Pioneers: The Marquette Trilogy, Book One*

QC – *The Queen City: The Marquette Trilogy, Book Two*

SH – *Superior Heritage: The Marquette Trilogy, Book Three*

NL – *Narrow Lives*

OT – *The Only Thing That Lasts*

SN – *Spirit of the North*

BP – *The Best Place*

TT – *When Teddy Came to Town*

W – *Willpower: A Play About Marquette's Ossified Man*

Fictional Characters

John/Neill Vandelaare – Our main character, who is suffering from amnesia when the novel opens. (*BP*)

Mrs. Bessie Bingley – Housekeeper to the Allens.

Carolina Smith – Wife to Judge Smith, who lives in the Henning House on Ridge Street. (*IP, OT, TT*)

Jane Smith Hampton – Carolina Smith's daughter. (*OT*)

Cordelia Whitman – Early Marquette settler and former owner of a boarding house. (*IP, QC, SN*).

Margaret Dalrymple – A teenage girl with a crush on Howard Longyear who was born in the Whitmans' boarding house. (*IP, QC, SH*)

Allison Hayes – Neill's sort-of girlfriend.

Derek Jackson – Neill's best friend.

Xander – A man who lives at Peter's Landing.

Jorgen – A friend to Xander.

The McCarey Family

       Patrick McCarey – A police officer. (*IP, QC*)

       Kathy McCarey - Patrick's wife (*IP, QC*)

       Frank McCarey - Patrick and Kathy's oldest son (*IP, QC*)

       Jeremy McCarey - Patrick and Kathy's second son (*IP, QC*)

       Michael McCarey - Patrick and Kathy's youngest son (*IP, QC, SH*)

       Molly Bergmann Montoni - Kathy's mother (*IP, QC*)

Harry Cumming – A ne'er do well who works at Getz's, married to Sylvia Whitman. (*IP, QC*)

Franklin – Butler to the Longyear family.

Martha – Housekeeper to the Longyear family.

Historical Characters

Dr. James Dawson – A doctor, married to Bertha Adams. (*W*)

Mr. Ephraim Allen – A Marquette businessman, a founder of the Huron Mountain Club, and father to Hugh Allen.

Hugh Allen – Son of Mr. Allen, friend of Howard Longyear.

Peter White – Marquette's grand old man, a banker, real estate agent, and town philanthropist. (*IP, QC*)

Chief Charles Kawbawgam – An Ojibwa and great friend of Peter White. (*IP, QC, SN*)

The Longyear Family

       John M. Longyear – Marquette businessman and millionaire, founder of the Huron Mountain Club

       Mary Beecher Longyear – His wife, a believer in Christian Science.

       Abby Longyear – Their oldest daughter.

       Howard M. Longyear – Their oldest son.

       Helen Longyear – Their second daughter.

       Judith Longyear – Their youngest daughter.

       John Munro Longyear, Jr. (Jack) – Their second son.

       Robert Dudley Longyear (Rob) – Their youngest son.

Henry St. Arnold "Santinaw" – A woodsman and Indian guide who works for the Longyears.

Louis Getz – Owner of Getz's Department Store.

The Jopling Family

    James Jopling – Marquette businessman from England.

    Bessie (Mather) Jopling – His wife.

    Mrs. Henry Mather – Bessie Jopling's mother.

    Richard Mather Jopling – James and Bessie Jopling's son.

The Adams Family

    Mr. Sidney Adams – A Marquette businessman. (*W*)

    Harriet Adams – Sidney Adams' wife. (*W*)

    Bertha (Adams) Dawson – Wife of Dr. Dawson, daughter of Sidney and Harriet Adams. (*W*)

    Will Adams – Sidney and Harriet Adams' adopted son who suffers from ossification. (*W*)

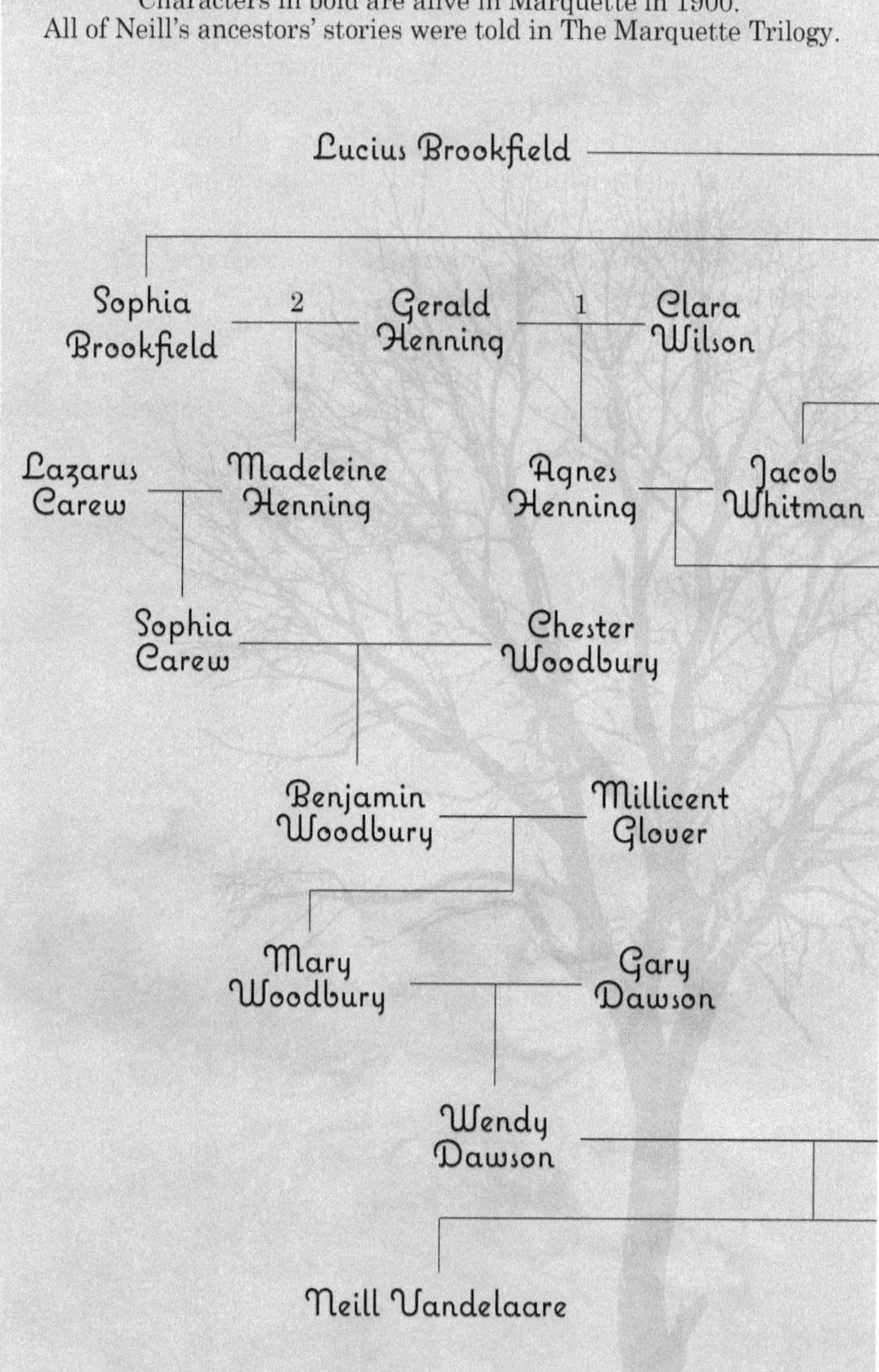

Characters in bold are alive in Marquette in 1900.
All of Neill's ancestors' stories were told in The Marquette Trilogy.
Lucius Brookfield
Sophia Brookfield
2
Gerald Henning
1
Clara Wilson
Lazarus Carew
Madeleine Henning
Agnes Henning
Jacob Whitman
Sophia Carew
Chester Woodbury
Benjamin Woodbury
Millicent Glover
Mary Woodbury
Gary Dawson
Wendy Dawson
Neill Vandelaare

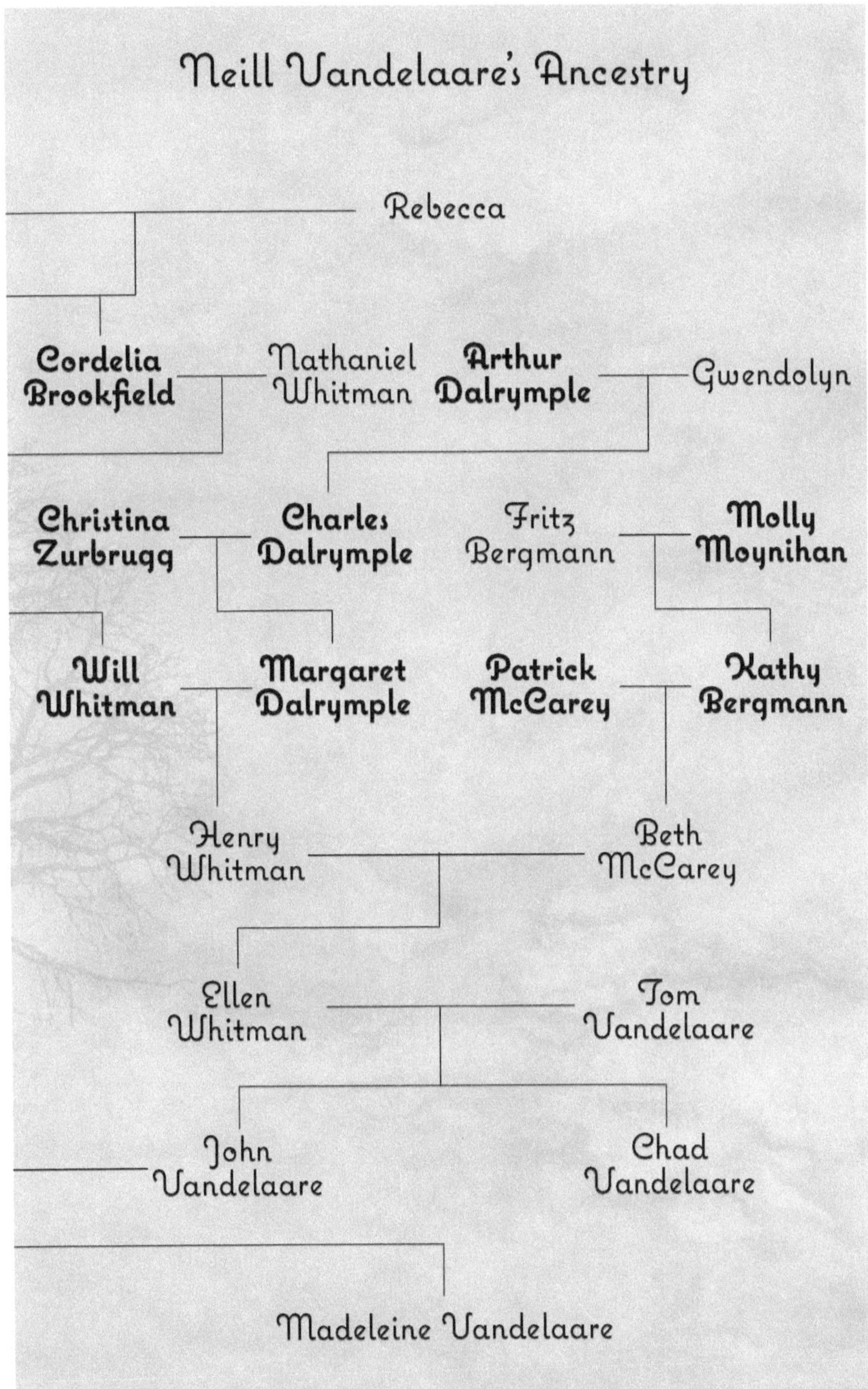
Neill Vandelaare's Ancestry
Rebecca
Cordelia Brookfield
Nathaniel Whitman
Arthur Dalrymple
Gwendolyn
Christina Zurbrugg
Charles Dalrymple
Fritz Bergmann
Molly Moynihan
Will Whitman
Margaret Dalrymple
Patrick McCarey
Kathy Bergmann
Henry Whitman
Beth McCarey
Ellen Whitman
Tom Vandelaare
John Vandelaare
Chad Vandelaare
Madeleine Vandelaare

Part I

Chapter 1

First, he heard voices, but he could not make out the words. He tried to open his eyes, but he was in that state of sleep paralysis where you try and try to open your eyes and wake yourself, but you just cannot—it feels physically impossible, as if the whole weight of the world is pressing your eyelids shut. You are half-awake, half still dreaming. He realized he had been dreaming, but he couldn't remember what his dreams were about. Nothing seemed normal. He couldn't understand why he couldn't just wake up.

Then he heard a voice, a female voice he did not recognize. "He's coming to, Doctor."

He felt a hand grabbing his wrist. A finger pressed on his vein. Someone was checking his pulse.

"I wonder what happened to him," said the female voice.

"We may know soon," said a male voice. It was close to his ear.

He struggled to open his eyes. He made an incredible effort, but he could not bring himself to do it. He felt like several minutes went by as he struggled, or was it hours? Suddenly, he had the terrifying feeling of falling, and he woke with a jolt and a shout.

"It's all right," said a man. "Just relax. You're safe."

His eyes now open, he found himself looking into the face of a bewhiskered man. They were not ordinary whiskers. It was a beard, a great bushy beard.

"How do you feel?" asked the man.

He took a moment to assess the state of his body. His back hurt. His arm hurt, and his head…. "Ow!" he cried out as he tried to move his leg.

"You have bruises," said the man. "Your muscles might be a little sore, but nothing serious. You were lucky. You took quite a tumble. Do you understand what I'm saying?"

"Where am I?" he asked.

The man—presumably the doctor—was saying something more, but his head was pounding so badly he didn't catch it.

What bizarre wallpaper—it was pink with swirls, like some Victorian nightmare. Where had that thought come from? It was Victorian. He knew that somehow.

"Where am I?" he repeated, looking at the doctor.

The doctor looked puzzled, surprised he had not heard what he had just explained.

"You're at the Allens' house," the doctor replied.

"Who?" he asked.

"The Allens," said the doctor. "Mr. Ephraim William Allen, his wife Mrs. Allen, and his four children live here."

"Oh." The names were not familiar. Did he know these people? Did the doctor somehow think he should? He couldn't seem to remember anything.

"Can you tell me who you are?" asked the doctor. "We couldn't find any card or wallet on you."

He stared at the doctor, suddenly feeling alarmed. "I'm…. I'm…." He could not remember his own name.

The doctor, apparently seeing how he was racking his brain, said, "It's all right. Don't strain yourself."

"Do you remember anything?" asked the woman.

He closed his eyes, hoping that would help. His head ached.

"Is he asleep?" the woman whispered to the doctor.

"Shh," the doctor replied.

He reopened his eyes and said, "I guess not. I don't know how I got here."

"You were found up at the Huron Mountain Club," the woman explained. "You rolled down a hill, or fell off a small cliff, something like that. Mr. Allen, my employer, had you brought back to Marquette, to his house."

"Marquette," he muttered. "That sounds familiar."

"Marquette, Michigan," said the woman. "It's a city on Lake Superior. You must know that."

He struggled with a memory of some sort—a big house made of stone. Was that where he was? He turned to his left. There was a window, but lying in the bed, he could not see anything out of it other than some trees and the top of a white wooden building, the gable of another house apparently.

"Is there a big…a…a long thing out on a lake here?" he asked, suddenly remembering something else, something the name of which he couldn't quite recall.

"Ye-es," said the woman. "There's a harbor. There are docks. Ore docks."

"Ore docks," he muttered. Then a sharp pang shot through his skull, making him cry out.

"Oh, you're giving him too much information, Mrs. Bingley," said the doctor. "He obviously has amnesia. We shouldn't strain him."

"But who is he?" asked Mrs. Bingley. "Sir, are you sure you don't know your own name?"

"My name?" he repeated, as if it were the most bizarre question in the history of the world.

"Everyone has a name," she said. "I'm Bessie Bingley, the Allens' housekeeper, and this is Dr. James Dawson. What's your name?"

He struggled with the thought. A name? He must have a name. He tried to remember. He grimaced from the throbbing pain in his forehead.

"Do you have a headache?" asked the doctor.

"Yes," he said, squeezing his eyes tightly to try to make the pain go away.

"Let's give you some aspirin powder," said the doctor. "Once it takes effect, it might be easier for you to remember."

The doctor pulled out a small bottle from inside his coat pocket and shook the pills into his hand. Mrs. Bingley poured a glass of water from a decanter on a small table. She gave the glass to him, and he struggled to push himself up to receive it. Then the doctor handed him the pills.

"Swallow those," said the doctor.

He did as he was told. He put them in his mouth and took a sip of water. Then he swallowed the pills and wondered how he had known how to swallow—automatic reflex, he figured. At least he had not forgotten that. Even the water had made him feel better, and he felt like maybe he could start to remember now since he was past the initial shock of waking in a strange place and being interrogated.

"Ask me some more questions," he said as Mrs. Bingley took back the glass.

"Are you sure you're up to it?" asked the doctor. "Perhaps we should just let you rest some more."

"Just a few questions," he replied. "I want to remember. I feel almost like I can, but something is blocking the memories."

"All right," said the doctor. "Do you know what year this is?"

"Um," he said, squeezing his eyes shut to concentrate better.

"Take your time," said Dr. Dawson.

He reopened his eyes and looked about the room. There was a photograph on the wall. It was black and white—it showed a harbor—three ore docks jutting out—but it wasn't the harbor he knew. The one in his memory had only one ore dock, a big reddish orange kind of thing—and it…it didn't seem to work from what he could recall.

"The year," the doctor repeated.

He looked at the doctor with that great bushy beard and those old-fashioned clothes, and then he looked at Mrs. Bingley, who had her hair up in a bun, and was wearing a white blouse and a long dress. It must be…but it didn't seem right that it could be that long ago….

"Nineteen…eighteen…nineteen?" he said, debating which century would be right.

"That's all right," said the doctor, as if not wanting him to strain himself. "We can come back to the year. Do you know who the President of the United States is?"

Without thinking, he began to say, "Joe Bi—" but then whatever made him remember left him and he could not finish.

"What?" said Dr. Dawson.

"I said, '*No I*'—no, I can't seem to remember," he said. But he had remembered for a second. Only, he had felt like there was something wrong about remembering that—about telling the doctor who he remembered as president.

"Is the name William McKinley familiar?" asked the doctor.

"Oh, sure," he said. The name was familiar. "Then it must be the year nineteen…no eighteen-ninety…."

"I'll make it easy for you," said Dr. Dawson. "It is a little tricky since the century just changed. It's 1900."

He felt shocked. It couldn't be. That year—1900—just did not seem right, not possible somehow, but how could he explain that to the doctor?

"It's 1900," the doctor repeated.

"Oh, right," he said.

"Do you know what month it is?" asked Dr. Dawson.

"Um," he said. "It's summer. I know that from looking out the window. I can see the leaves are bright green."

"It's July," said the doctor.

"Tomorrow is the Fourth of July," said Mrs. Bingley.

"Oh, okay," he said, some memories flashing through his mind. "The Fourth of July. Fireworks...."

"Yes, that's right," said the doctor.

"Do you think he's going to be all right, Doctor?" asked Mrs. Bingley.

"I think so," Dr. Dawson replied. "Sir, try to follow my finger." Suddenly, the doctor's finger was in front of his face, moving back and forth, and he slightly turned his head left and right while his eyes followed it.

"You seem to be fine," said the doctor. "You're alert and responding. You have a concussion, though, that may be causing some amnesia."

"Don't you remember anything?" repeated Mrs. Bingley.

He tried again. What was his name? It was like his name was behind a big black wall in his brain. He knew it was there. He just didn't know how to access it. He shook his head.

"Do you know where you're from?" she asked.

"Marquette," he said. He wasn't sure why, but he felt sure about that. After all, here he was in Marquette, so what would he be doing here if he weren't from Marquette?

"Are you sure?" asked the doctor.

"I think so."

"Well, that's a small clue anyway," said Dr. Dawson. "If you know that much, hopefully the rest will come back to you. But it's getting late. We should let you rest. Perhaps you'll feel better in the morning."

"Okay," he said, reluctant to quit trying to remember, but also feeling tired.

"It's nice to meet you, sir," said Dr. Dawson, standing up and then extending his hand. It took him a moment to realize what to do with the doctor's hand.

"You have a good, strong grip like a young man should," said the doctor. "I think you'll make a full physical recovery. Mrs. Bingley, I trust you have some clothes for him to wear tomorrow? Perhaps if he gets out of bed and can go for a walk in the neighborhood, he'll remember something."

"Oh, yes, I think Mr. Hugh's clothes will fit him. They must be about the same age. He'll be eager to see him too." She turned back to her guest and said, "They are all very concerned about you, sir."

"Don't let them in yet," said Dr. Dawson. "Perhaps he would take to Hugh since they're about the same age; maybe he'll even recognize him, but right now our patient needs a lot of rest."

"Yes, sir," she said. "Mr. Hugh told me he doesn't know him, but I'm sure he'll be happy to loan him some clothes. We destroyed his other clothes. You should have seen them. All burnt at the bottoms, most of his pants burnt completely away, and his shirt, why there was hardly anything left of the sleeves, though they didn't look burnt. The men said he was practically indecent when they found him. I would bet he was struck by lightning—that's what the men who found him thought—since there was no other explanation for how his clothes could have been half-missing like that."

"Do you remember anything like that?" Dr. Dawson asked his patient. "Lightning or having your clothes catch on fire?"

"No," he said, shaking his head, but he did remember some sort of burning smell—still, it was such a faint sensation that it didn't explain anything.

"Well, I'll leave you then," said Dr. Dawson. "I hope you feel better tomorrow. I'll stop by then."

"We'll keep an eye on him, Doctor," said Mrs. Bingley.

"Good night, Mrs. Bingley. I can see myself out," Dr. Dawson replied, collecting his bag from a chair and then nodding to Mrs. Bingley as he left the room.

"Are you hungry?" Mrs. Bingley asked, turning her attention back to her patient.

"Ravenous!" he said, suddenly realizing he was. And then he laughed, surprised he remembered such a funny, long word, and Mrs. Bingley laughed too.

"Well, you haven't lost your vocabulary," she said, "whoever you are."

He smiled.

"It feels awkward not to know your name," said Mrs. Bingley. "Would it be all right if I gave you a name until you remember?"

He shrugged his shoulders.

"Let me go get you some nice soup," she said, "and while I'm gone, you think about what name you might like to have."

"Okay," he said, wondering if he would even be able to remember any names.

"I'll be back in a few minutes then," she said. "Do you need any-thing else?"

"No, just some food," he replied since restoring his memory was beyond her powers.

Mrs. Bingley nodded and departed, shutting the door behind her.

His head still hurt a little. His eyes began to swim, and he felt a little faint, probably from hunger. But at least his headache seemed to be gone now. He tried to focus on items in the room. It was a small room. He realized he was in a twin bed. There was a small wooden table beside the bed and a lamp, but it was quite an old lamp—a lantern—kerosene probably. That's what they called them, he be-lieved. Strange anyone would have such a thing. He noticed some Victorian-looking sconces on the wall across from the bed with a mirror between them. How did he know they were Victorian? What exactly was Victorian? There were a few books on a shelf and a base-ball and a catcher's mitt and another bed—a twin bed like the one he was in. He wondered if this was the boy Hugh's room—his and a brother's? There was a wardrobe, with a door partly open and some clothes in it looking to be about his size. This wasn't the big stone house he had momentarily remembered when he first woke up. But he felt like somehow this house was also familiar to him. He tried to sit up a little, to look out the window, but he could only see a large white house across the street. That looked familiar too. He felt like he knew this place, yet he didn't.

"I don't even know my name," he said aloud, "though at least I know I should have a name. I'm not crazy. I don't feel crazy. I just can't remember...."

He pushed himself up into more of a sitting position, but the effort made his head hurt again. He closed his eyes to rest them and to quiet his mind; if he quit trying to remember, maybe then the an-swers would come to him. But all he could see in his mind was the room he was in. He couldn't seem to remember anything else.

After a few minutes, the door opened and Mrs. Bingley came in with a tray.

"Oh, good, you're sitting up," she said.

"Yes. I was trying to see if I recognized anything."

"Do you?" she asked, as she placed the tray on his lap.

"I don't know," he admitted. "That house across the street looks familiar to me."

"Which one?" she asked.

"The white, sort of long rambling one."

"The Breitungs live there," said Mrs. Bingley.

His face took on a puzzled look as he tried to remember why that name seemed familiar.

"Do you know them?" asked Mrs. Bingley.

"The name sounds familiar," he said, "but I can't envision any faces for the family."

"Well, you'll likely see them coming and going tomorrow. Perhaps you'll recognize them then."

"Maybe," he said, picking up his spoon.

"I hope you enjoy the soup. I made it myself, and Mrs. Allen baked the bread, and I bought you a nice glass of milk to wash it down. The doctor said not to give you anything that might be too rich for your stomach yet."

"This is fine," he replied. "Thank you so much." He doubted this scanty offering would satisfy his hunger, but he was more concerned with his craving to know his identity.

"Yes, Dr. Dawson thought since you've been unconscious for two days, we should slowly let your stomach get used to digesting food again."

"Two days!" he exclaimed. He felt deeply troubled by that news although he wasn't sure why. It wasn't like he had somewhere to go—well, he might, but where that somewhere was he did not know.

"Yes, two days," she replied. "They found you on Sunday, and now it's Tuesday. Tomorrow, the Fourth of July, is Wednesday."

He shook his head, trying to take this in.

"You look upset," said Mrs. Bingley.

"I just don't like to think I lost two days of my life," he replied, almost feeling like crying over it. "But I don't know why I should be upset. I can't remember what my life even consists of."

"There, there," said Mrs. Bingley, patting him on the shoulder. "You'll feel better after you've eaten, and if you need to, there's a bathroom at the end of the hall, and then if you get a good night's sleep, perhaps you'll be back to normal in the morning, Tom."

"Tom?" he said.

"Yes. You said I could come up with a name to call you. How does Tom feel?"

"I'm not a Tom," he replied.

"No," she said, frowning. "I kind of thought you looked like a Tom. Well, how about Harry?"

"No," he said, shaking his head.

"Bill?"

He frowned.

"Ike?"

"Definitely not," he said, smirking.

"Well, what name would you like until we come up with your real name?"

"I'd like my real name," he said, feeling irritated.

"But what is it? Paul, Charles, Fred, Frank, Lyman, Theodore...."

He shook his head at each suggestion.

"How about Nathaniel, or Martin, or Joseph?"

He frowned.

"Maybe James, or how about John?"

He didn't shake his head at the last name but mulled it over.

"I think John feels okay," he said. "I'm not sure it's my name, but it sounds familiar somehow. I guess I can answer to John until I remember my own name."

"John it is then," said Mrs. Bingley. "Well, I hope you have a good night, John. Just ring the bell there by the lamp when you're ready for me to come get your tray. I imagine Mr. Hugh or Mr. Allen will come in to visit you soon also."

"Okay," he said, looking over to the bedside table and seeing the bell. He had not noticed it before. "Thank you."

"I'll let you be now so you can eat. There's no end of work to do in this house, and your soup is going to get cold. Enjoy your dinner, John."

He smiled. He wondered why he had picked John. Was it his name? No, it didn't seem like it—he wished he could remember his name—but at least John was a name he liked, for whatever reason.

Mrs. Bingley now left, closing the door behind her.

John let out a big sigh and started to lift a spoonful of soup to his mouth, when suddenly the absurdity of his situation struck him.

"Holy cow!" he cried out. "Who are these people? Dr. Dawson, Mrs. Bingley, Hugh Allen, the Breitungs. And the year 1900—that seems strange too. I feel like I know these people—or at least their names are familiar—and yet, I know I've never met them before."

He looked out the window again and saw a horse and buggy going down the street. "That's funny," he muttered. "Where are the cars?" and then he found himself surprised to think he knew what a car was. He could see one in his mind's eye, but he didn't know how he knew what a car was or why it felt so out of place in the situation he found himself in. As he mulled over all these thoughts, he finished his soup. Eating it only seemed to make him hungrier. Then, almost instinctively—he wasn't sure later why he did it—he reached down to his pocket, as if to ensure he had something in it. Only, he discovered he had no pockets. For the first time, he realized he was dressed in some sort of hospital gown—no, it was more like a Victorian nightshirt for a man. Like Wendy's brother John wore in *Peter Pan*. He saw a cartoon character with a stovepipe hat on his head. Where had that thought come from?

But more importantly, where were his clothes? Oh, Mrs. Bingley had said they were all burnt up and in rags. But why had she thrown them out? They might have helped him remember. Whoever he was, he was sure he had never been in a Victorian nightshirt before. He felt like he was play-acting by wearing it. If only he could remember who he was and where he should be, and even what he normally wore.

"How will I ever find out?" he asked aloud. "What if no one in this town even knows who I am? How will I ever find out then?"

Then it occurred to him that even if Mrs. Bingley had disposed of his clothes, maybe he'd had some personal possessions she'd saved that might trigger his memory. He was just about to reach for the bell to call Mrs. Bingley back when the door opened.

Chapter 2

"WELL, HOW'S OUR PATIENT?" ASKED a bearded man. He appeared to be in his late forties with just the slightest touch of gray to his otherwise brown beard.

"Okay," John said, wondering to whom he was speaking. "I'm feeling better."

"I'm Mr. Allen," said the man, stepping out of the doorway and into the room, and thereby revealing behind him a young man of about John's age. "And this is my oldest son, Hugh."

"Hello," said John, nodding to Hugh. "I can't tell you who I am, but Mrs. Bingley and I agreed on calling me John for now."

"She told us you don't remember who you are," said Hugh, stepping forward to shake John's hand, "but I'm glad you're awake at least."

"Yes," said his father. "That must have been quite a fall you took. You must have rolled right down that hill and over a little cliff. You were unconscious when Hugh and Santinaw—he's one of our guides up at the Club—found you."

"I—I don't remember. I must have fallen, though, since I feel some pain and bruises. But my appetite doesn't seem to have suffered at least."

"That's good," said Mr. Allen.

"This is your house, right?" asked John. "Thank you for taking me in."

"You're welcome," said Mr. Allen, sitting down in the chair to John's right that had been previously occupied by the doctor.

"Am I throwing you out of your room?" John asked Hugh.

"Oh, no," said Hugh, walking over to sit on the bed across from John. "I have my own room. This is my younger brothers' room—Philip and Winthrop share it, and then I have a sister, Margery. They're all still up at the Huron Mountain Club with my mother.

Just Father and I came back to Marquette with you so you could see the doctor. So anyway, no one is being thrown out of their room or bed."

"I'm afraid I've been a lot of trouble to you all," said John. "You're so very kind."

"It's the Christian thing to do," replied Mr. Allen. "But what can you tell us about yourself? Do you remember anything at all?"

"I think I recall some things," said John, noticing as he turned his head back and forth to speak to them that Mr. Allen and Hugh were both looking at him with deep curiosity. "I seem to remember the harbor—that picture on the wall looks familiar to me, at least, and I recognize the name of Marquette. I think I must be from Marquette. I mean, how else would I have gotten here?"

"But you were found up at the Huron Mountain Club," said Mr. Allen. "Do you know what you were doing there?"

John shook his head. "No, the name seems familiar to me, but that's all."

"The Huron Mountain Club is a private hunting and fishing club north of Marquette," Mr. Allen explained. "I'm one of the members. It's a private club—private property, so you had no business being there unless you worked there. I know you're not one of the members or I would have recognized you. There are a few people who work there that I don't know just because I'm in town so much, but no one up there who saw you seemed to know who you were."

"Neither Santinaw nor I ever saw you before," Hugh piped in.

"That's strange," said John. "I mean, I'm not sure why since I can't remember, but I'm pretty sure I'm a law-abiding citizen, not the kind to go trespassing. Maybe if I went back up there, I might see something that would help trigger my memory."

"Perhaps," said Mr. Allen, raising his eyes as if considering the suggestion. "But I think you better rest for a while before we try returning up there with you."

"You don't remember your name?" asked Hugh.

"No," John repeated. "Mrs. Bingley suggested she call me John, and that name seemed familiar to me, but I'm not sure it's my real name."

Mr. Allen frowned. "So, no guess then what your last name is?"

John thought for a moment. Funny; he hadn't even wondered about that. He tried to think what it might be, but nothing came to him. "No," he finally said in defeat. "I can't even be sure my first name is John; it's just the one that stood out when Mrs. Bingley listed off a bunch of names for me."

"That's too bad," said Mr. Allen. "Well, you've only been awake for a little while. You were in a coma for a couple of days, so we can't expect everything to come back to you right away. Have you been out of bed yet?"

"No," said John, "although now that I've eaten, I do feel like I need to use the bathroom."

"I can show you where it is," said Hugh, standing up.

"Do you think you can walk?" asked Mr. Allen.

"I think so," said John, pulling back the blankets and looking at his legs. After a second, he moved them sideways over the edge of the bed.

"Do you need a hand?" asked Mr. Allen, standing up and putting his hand on his arm. Meanwhile, Hugh walked around the bed to help if needed.

"I think I'm okay," said John, slowly standing up. He did so successfully and then took a step. "My leg's a little stiff, but I think I'll be all right."

Hugh reached out and put his arm around John's back so he could lean on him as he half-stumbled to the door. They were about the same height, which made it easy for John to lean on him, but once they got a few steps to the door, John said he thought he could manage by himself.

Hugh backed up and let John lean a hand on the wall. Then he led him down the hall to the bathroom. Mr. Allen followed behind to catch John if need be.

"You're walking fine," said Hugh. "If you eat a little more to get your strength back, maybe you can go to the parade with us tomorrow."

"The Fourth of July parade?" asked John.

"Yes. We were going to spend the Fourth up at the Club, but with you to look after, we figured we'd stay here for the parade."

"You can go, Hugh," said Mr. Allen, "but I think John should stay home to rest. I can stay with him."

"No," said Hugh. "Mrs. Bingley will do that."

"She has tomorrow afternoon off," Mr. Allen reminded him.

"Oh," said Hugh. "Well, it won't be any fun going by myself."

"What about Howard?" asked Mr. Allen. "Isn't he coming home tomorrow?"

"No, not until Friday."

"Oh," said Mr. Allen.

"I'd like to go to the parade," said John as Hugh stopped in front of the bathroom door. "I might be up to it. I seem to be able to walk fine."

"Well, here's the bathroom," said Hugh.

"Can you manage on your own?" asked Mr. Allen.

"I think so," said John.

"I'm going to go bring your tray down to Mrs. Bingley then," said Mr. Allen. "Hugh, you stay and wait outside the door in case he needs anything."

"Thank you, sir," said John.

"Don't mention it," said Mr. Allen, and he returned down the hall.

"Just yell if you have trouble in there," said Hugh. "I'll wait out here for you."

"Thank you," said John before entering the bathroom and closing the door behind him. Until that moment, as he faced the bathroom, he had not really considered the look of his surroundings. Now he was greeted by dark purple and brown Victorian wallpaper that made the room look as small as a closet rather than like a bathroom. There was an old tub—nothing close to a shower. The sink had strangely shaped faucets and a large basin. A mirror hung above the sink, but there was no medicine cabinet. To the side of the mirror was a shelf with several items on it. And then there was a toilet. John was relieved to see it was a flush toilet. For a second he had feared he'd have to use a chamber pot. Still, it all looked very old-fashioned.

He turned around to sit down, pulling up the nightshirt. He was kind of alarmed to find he had no underwear beneath it.

"What happened to me?" he asked himself. Somehow, he knew none of this was normal for him. He was embarrassed to think Hugh was outside the door, listening to make sure he didn't fall. John felt a bit dizzy when he stood up, but at least he did not feel weak. He flushed the toilet and washed his hands, and then taking a look in the mirror, he saw he had some stubble. He usually shaved every day—funny that he remembered that. He was too tired to shave right now, though.

"Is everything okay?" Hugh asked as John opened the door.

"Yes," said John. "I'm a little dizzy, but I don't feel weak."

"That's good," said Hugh. "You've been in bed two full days so you probably just have to get used to being on your feet again."

"I look awful," said John.

"I don't think so. You're not pale anyway," said Hugh, stepping out into the hall so John could start down the hallway. John didn't grab ahold of the wall this time so he could see if he had the strength to walk back to the room himself. "You look healthy and strong to me," Hugh said as if trying to give him confidence. "Do you remember how old you are?"

"No," said John.

"I think you must be my age or a little older. I'm eighteen, although I don't have much of a beard coming in yet."

"That's what I mean," said John. "I look awful. I usually shave every day."

"You're lucky," said Hugh. "My friend Howard shaves every day. He's a year older than me, so maybe you are too."

"I don't know," said John. "Do you have a razor you can lend me?"

"Sure," said Hugh.

"I won't shave today, though," said John. "I think I need to lie back down."

By now they were back at the bedroom. John turned and walked toward the bed, happy to see it again.

Hugh, without asking, put his hand on John's arm to steady him as he sat down. Then he helped him scoot back a little and John lay down. Hugh pulled the blanket over him.

"Do you need anything?" asked Hugh. "Can I do anything for you?"

"No, I'm fine," said John. "You're very kind, and please tell your father how grateful I am."

"We're happy to help," said Hugh, sitting down in the chair by the bed. "I hope you get better and we can find your family or at least figure out who you are."

"You don't recognize me at all?" asked John.

"No," said Hugh. "I just graduated, and I don't remember seeing you at my school. But maybe you went to school out east somewhere like my friend Howard. I wish he went to school in Marquette because I only get to see him in the summers and on break, and now he's going to college at Cornell, but I'll be going there this fall. Howard's on the rowing team and I hope to make the team too."

John didn't say anything. Nothing that Hugh was talking about was familiar to him.

"Do you think you went to school in Marquette?" asked Hugh.

"I don't know," said John. "I wish I could remember. I seem to think I went to college."

"Do you go to the normal school?" asked Hugh. "If you're a year older than me, perhaps you were studying to be a teacher?"

"I don't know," said John, who felt his eyes wanting to close.

"Well, we'll get to the bottom of it," said Hugh. "We'll see how you feel in the morning. Maybe then you'll remember something. You were walking just fine."

"Thanks," said John. "I think I just have to sleep. I don't mean to be rude."

"Not at all," said Hugh.

"Maybe I could have a glass of water. I feel kind of warm."

"It is a warm day," said Hugh. "It was about eighty today, though it's cooling off now that the sun is going down. I'll go get you a glass of water. I'll be right back."

John closed his eyes after Hugh left the room. He was just drifting off to sleep when he heard, "Here you go."

"Thanks," said John, opening his eyes but not getting up.

"Did I wake you?" asked Hugh.

"Not yet."

"Are you thirsty now?"

John struggled into a sitting position and then took the glass Hugh handed him, but he only drank a little, too tired to want to have to get up and use the bathroom again right away.

"Well," said Hugh, once John handed him back the glass, "I'll let you sleep then. Have pleasant dreams and here is to hoping you remember everything in the morning."

"Thank you," said John as Hugh set the glass on the table. Then his host left the room, closing the door behind him.

In another minute, John was sound asleep.

Chapter 3

THE SUN BEAMING THROUGH THE window caused John to open his eyes. Then he jolted awake at the sight of the unfamiliar room. Then he remembered he was in the Allens' house and suffering from amnesia. "Do I really have amnesia?" he wondered aloud. At least he could remember that he had lost his memory. But again, he could not remember his real name.

A sunbeam across his bed declared it a beautiful morning. He could hear birds chirping outside and the faint sound of voices below him.

I might as well get up, he thought. He didn't want to just lie there until someone came to wait on him.

Swinging his feet over the edge of the bed, he realized he felt a lot stronger—more vigorous and normal—today. His legs and back didn't hurt like yesterday. A little more sleep had helped to reinvigorate him. He didn't even have a headache.

"It's going to be a great day," he said aloud, "and I'm going to get the answers I need."

Standing up, he felt a little pain in his leg; he could see a bit of a bruise there, but other than that, he felt like his old self, whoever that old self was.

Then he looked at the chair by the bed and saw that someone had set some clothes there. He knew Hugh or Mrs. Bingley must have brought them in while he was sleeping, and they must be for him.

John walked over to the clothes and picked them up. They seemed so out of style for some reason—long brown pants, long underwear, a long-sleeved button-up shirt, a vest, and a suit jacket. Why, it had to be seventy degrees outside! It was obviously the height of summer, and even though Marquette never got too warm—strange that somehow he knew that—he had a feeling he would sweat to death if he had to wear these while walking about town. And long under-wear! He'd never worn long underwear in his life, just jeans and T-shirts and—wait, how did he remember that?—and shorts. He had a feeling no one here wore shorts.

"How is this possible?" he muttered. How could he remember clothes so different from these in his hands? Was he remembering his real past or was his mind playing tricks on him? What was it the doctor or Mrs. Bingley—one of them—had said about his clothes—that they were indecent—like the bottoms of his pants had been burnt off? But those boys in his memory—why their shirt sleeves barely covered their biceps. Would Mrs. Bingley have thought that indecent? He had a feeling Mrs. Bingley was a bit of a prude.

Still, it was all so strange. He wished he could remember. He also wished he knew how he would manage to survive wearing all these hot clothes—especially the suit jacket. He hated wearing suits. He couldn't remember exactly when he'd ever worn one, but the thought made him feel all itchy and prickly, uncomfortable and irritated.

Still, he had nothing else to wear, and if he wanted to get an-swers about who he was, first he had to get dressed. He pulled off the nightshirt, struggling a bit to find his way out of it. Then, taking a deep breath, he picked up the long underwear and tried to figure out how to get into it. After he got one leg in, he nearly tripped while trying to get the other in, but he managed. It fit okay but kind of stuck to his skin in places, making him uncomfortable. At least it was much lighter than he had expected, and it only went just below the knee, not as long as he expected. Still, it would definitely absorb sweat and maybe make him sweat.

I'm going to be miserable wearing this, he thought, *but what else can I do?* He pondered not wearing underwear, but he feared someone would somehow notice and think him indecent. Given that he was a guest in this house and had nowhere else to go until he figured out who he was, he had better just suffer through it.

When he noticed the underwear had little buttons at the fly, he thought, *Well, at least no Victorian boy ever had to worry about getting stuck in his zipper.* Then he had that strange feeling again. If he knew what a zipper was, why did these clothes not have zippers? *Am I somehow in the past? Not in my own time?* The thought both intrigued and scared him. *Remember last night when I thought about cars?* he reminded himself. He knew what cars were, but he had a feeling he would not see any today. After all, it was 1900. He knew cars were invented just about that time, but he doubted there would be many, or any, in Marquette.

Could I be from another time? Is that why everything seems so strange? he kept asking himself as he buttoned up his shirt. *But how did I get here then? Did time traveling cause me to lose my memory? Maybe it's like in that TV show with the weird transportation system—what was it called? I can't remember, just that someone would say, "Beam me up, Scotty." Only I guess I didn't get beamed up properly—maybe some of my brain cells got left behind in my own time when I came here.*

All kinds of images were now floating through his head. Someone named Mr. Spock with his pointy ears, a television set, automobiles. He shook his head and looked out the window. Yes, still the same old city street. He saw a man on an old-fashioned bicycle ride by, and there was a horse pulling some sort of cart. It was crazy to think he could be from the future, but if he wasn't, where were these futuristic, scientific-type images in his mind coming from? *Maybe I read about such things,* he thought, *in H. G. Wells or Jules Verne or somewhere.* That he even knew that those authors were from about this time made him think he knew more about the future than he could fully recall.

If I didn't come from the future, how could I know these things? Am I just crazy? What year am I from? He didn't know the answers, but somehow he thought the TV show he'd remembered with Mr. Spock in it was from the 1960s. And then the 1960s made him think of… *hippies…. Am I a hippie? Is that the time I'm from?*

Shaking his head again, John sat down on the bed to put on his socks. Then he pulled on the trousers.

A vest, a suit, and a tie remained.

"I have no idea how to tie that," he said, picking up the tie. It was a strip of cloth ribbon, not a bowtie and not a long tie, much less a clip-on. He decided he would leave it off. *I can just say I couldn't remember how to tie it. But I can't say I think I'm from a future time when they didn't have ties like that; they'll think I really am crazy. Better that I just play up the fact that I have memory issues. I don't want to be locked up in an insane asylum because I think I time traveled.*

Once dressed, John felt ready to venture out of his room. He headed for the bathroom, hoping not to meet anyone until he had a chance to relieve himself and see if he could find a brush or comb so he could fix his hair. He was glad not to hear anyone moving about upstairs, though he could definitely hear voices downstairs.

After using the toilet, John washed his hands. He was pleased to find someone had placed a razor and a towel on the cupboard for him—and also a comb! He would have preferred a brush, but he would make do. He fought with his hair for several minutes. He had quite the bedhead, especially after not combing his hair for a few days, but after applying a lot of water to it, he made it look fairly flat and presentable.

His face was another story. There was the razor, but he didn't see any shaving cream. He didn't dare put that blade against his skin without shaving cream—after all, this was no Gillette Mach 3—funny he remembered the name of his razor. This was a simple straight razor, like you'd see a barber using in an old movie. But he also recalled those barbers lathering up their customers.

John shrugged and thought, *I guess I'll have to ask for some shaving cream.* He was sorry if the Allens wouldn't like his scruff this morning. He didn't like it either. He'd always shaved, never grown out his beard because after a couple of days, it would feel itchy and scratch his neck when he lowered his chin. But there was no helping how he looked until someone showed him how to use that razor properly or at least gave him some shaving cream. *Actually, I look kind of sexy,* he thought, gazing at himself in the mirror. He was, after all, young and handsome. He seemed to recall girls liking him. One in particular came to his thoughts though he couldn't remember her name, just her face. Still, women in this time would probably think he looked like a roughneck. He hoped the Allens would understand. Hugh seemed easy-going; if he told him he couldn't remember what to do, maybe Hugh could teach him how to shave 1900-style.

Taking another deep breath, John opened the bathroom door, feeling as ready as he could be to face the day.

He started down the hall, realizing he didn't even know his way around the house, which was a fairly good size. Fortunately, when he turned to the right, he saw the stairs and started down them. He came into the front entry hall and followed the voices until he reached the dining room.

"There you are," said Hugh. "I was just going to check on you."

Hugh and his father were seated at the table. Mr. Allen had the newspaper open in front of him. Hugh had been buttering his toast when he entered.

"I'm glad to see you are up," said Mr. Allen. "How are you feeling?"

"Good," said John. "Normal."

"Do you remember who you are yet?" asked Hugh.

"No, I'm afraid not," he said, suddenly feeling a tad weak and looking toward one of the four empty chairs at the table.

"Go ahead and sit down," said Mr. Allen. "Mrs. Bingley, can you bring another place setting for our guest?"

Mr. Allen had called through an open door, and in a moment, Mrs. Bingley popped out her head.

"Good morning, John," she said. "I'll have breakfast for you in just a minute. Would you like some coffee?"

"That would be wonderful!" said John, who could smell it brewing. He felt like he hadn't had coffee in ages. The memory of it surprisingly came back strongly.

John sat down at the table across from Hugh. Mr. Allen was to his right at the table's head.

"How did you sleep?" asked Hugh.

"Like a rock," said John.

"Do you feel up to going to the parade with us?" Hugh asked.

"I think so," said John.

"It's about a five or six block walk and down the hill to Washington Street, which is part of the parade route," said Mr. Allen. "You would have to walk all that distance."

"I think I can make it," said John. "What time is the parade?"

"Two o'clock," said Hugh.

"Well, once I get some food in me, I'm sure I'll feel stronger, but we can see how I feel then."

"Mrs. Bingley will be going to spend the day with her own family after breakfast," said Mr. Allen. "If you didn't go to the parade, would you be all right staying here alone?"

"Oh, yes," said John, "but I'd like to go to the parade."

"Good," said Hugh. "It would be strange to be the only kid there since my brothers and sister usually go with us, but this year we all decided to go up to the Club for the week."

"I'm sorry I ruined your trip up there," said John.

"Not at all," said Hugh. "It's only a few days, and now I can go up with Howard on Saturday."

"If you're sure you're feeling all right," said Mr. Allen, "I'll head back up to the Club tomorrow. Mrs. Allen will be missing me and not want to have her hands full taking care of the children by herself."

"How many children do you have?" asked John, trying to remember what they had told him the night before.

"Four," said Mr. Allen, "though Hugh here is hardly a child anymore. He's eighteen."

"Well, I'm used to being grouped with the others," said Hugh, though his face showed pleasure in his father considering him an adult. "I am the oldest, though."

"Philip is seventeen," said Mr. Allen. "Winthrop is fifteen, and Margery is eleven. They are almost all adults themselves, or think they are, but they can still be a handful."

"John and I will be fine," said Hugh. "You go ahead, Dad."

"I'm very grateful for all your kindness," said John, "but you don't even know me. I feel like I'm imposing on you."

"Nonsense," said Mr. Allen. "You stay until you remember who you are and then we can reconnect you with your family."

Mrs. Bingley now entered with John's coffee cup in one hand and a plate filled with scrambled eggs and sausages in the other.

"Thank you," said John, taking the plate from her while she set down the cup.

"I hope you have a good appetite," she replied. "I have pancakes on the stove."

"My gosh," said John.

"Mrs. Bingley makes the best pancakes," said Hugh. "Even the Longyears' cook can't match them."

"The Longyears?" said John, cutting up his sausage. "That name sounds familiar."

"It does?" said Hugh. "Do you know them?"

"I don't know, but I recognize the name."

"Well, my best friend Howard is a Longyear," said Hugh.

"The Longyears are one of the wealthiest and most prominent families in Marquette," said Mr. Allen.

"They're also among the founders of the Huron Mountain Club," added Hugh, "along with Peter White and Horatio Seymour."

"I think I've heard of Peter White too," said John, eating a bite of his sausage.

"Well, everyone in Marquette knows who Peter White is," said Hugh.

"It's likely you are from Marquette," said Mr. Allen, "if you recognize so many local people's names."

"But I've never seen you before," said Hugh. "Since you must be close to my age, I would think I'd recognize you."

"I know; it's strange," said John. "I wish I could remember something."

"And you don't know what you were doing up at the Club?" asked Mr. Allen.

"No," said John. "I don't understand it. I think you said I must have hit my head falling off a cliff."

"We found you lying on Mount Huron. You had obviously fallen down the hill some distance. You also looked like your clothes had been scorched off you. We thought perhaps you'd been hit by lightning."

"I don't know," said John, shaking his head. "I don't remember any of that."

"I do think," said Hugh, "that if you returned to where the incident happened, maybe you'd remember what happened to you."

"Maybe," said John, setting down his fork and staring out the window for a second to the house across the lawn. "Would you take me up there?"

"I think you're too weak today," said Mr. Allen. "We should wait to see what Dr. Dawson says."

"You can go up with me and Howard on Saturday," said Hugh.

"I was hoping I'd remember something before Saturday," John replied.

"Don't worry," said Mr. Allen. "You can take as long as you need to remember."

"I feel like…like the memory is there, but there's a wall blocking it. If I could just get over the wall."

His head began to hurt. He took a sip of coffee; it was strong and sent a jolt to his senses, but it did not free his brain from the fog that had come over it.

The doorbell rang, and Mrs. Bingley could be heard muttering something from the kitchen.

"I'll get it, Mrs. Bingley!" shouted Hugh, jumping up. "Don't burn those pancakes!"

"Thanks, Mr. Hugh!" she shouted back while Hugh dashed to the front door.

"I wonder whom that could be," said Mr. Allen, his voice drowning out those in the front hall.

In a moment, Dr. Dawson appeared.

"I thought I'd come and check on my patient. I didn't expect to see him out of bed already," he said, stepping into the room.

"There he is," said Mr. Allen, gesturing with a sausage-filled fork toward John.

"How are you feeling?" Dr. Dawson asked his patient.

"I'm doing fine," said John, turning around in his chair. "Thank you."

He took Dr. Dawson's hand when it was offered to him.

"Well, you still have a firm grip," said the doctor, pulling out a chair for himself.

"Mrs. Bingley, can you bring Dr. Dawson a cup of coffee?" called Mr. Allen.

Mrs. Bingley didn't answer, but a second later, she appeared with a plate of pancakes.

"Good morning, Doctor," she said. "I'll be right back with a cup of coffee for you, and a plate also if you care to have some breakfast."

"Being a doctor," he replied, "I know not to overeat. I already had breakfast, but the coffee will be most welcome. Thank you."

"It looks like it's going to be a beautiful day for a parade," said Mr. Allen to the doctor as Mrs. Bingley returned to the kitchen.

"Yes, it does," he replied before turning to John. "So, sir, have you remembered anything?"

"No, not much," he replied.

"John seems to know the Longyears' name and that of Peter White, and he thinks he's from Marquette," Hugh stated.

"John? Is that your name?" asked Dr. Dawson, looking at him curiously.

"No. I mean, I'm not sure, sir," said John. "Mrs. Bingley thought I should have a name to make it easier to address me, so we decided on that one."

"I see," he said. "Thank you, Mrs. Bingley."

"I thought he looked like a Tom myself," said Mrs. Bingley, setting down his cup of coffee, "but he said no."

"Well, John's a fine name," said Dr. Dawson. "But do you remember anything else?"

"No. But some things seem familiar to me, like this street in front of the house."

"Ridge Street?" asked Dr. Dawson.

"Yes, I feel like I know it, but at the same time, it doesn't quite seem like how I remember it. I mean, that big white house across the street I seem to recognize, but not the giant tall one next to it."

"The white one is the Breitung home," said Dr. Dawson, "and the tall one next to it belongs to Nathan Kaufman."

"Do you know those names?" asked Hugh.

"I'm not sure," said John. "Kaufman sounds familiar."

"Well, everyone knows Nathan Kaufman. He was mayor not long ago," Mr. Allen replied. "In any case, I think we can be pretty sure you're from Marquette, if not a resident of Ridge Street."

"No, that seems unlikely," said the doctor. "I think we'd all recognize you then. I live on Ridge too, just down on the next block."

"Well, at least you have a good appetite," said Mr. Allen, as John began to work on his eggs.

"Yes, I'd say that's a sign you're in good health," said Dr. Dawson, "but when you finish eating, I'd like to give you a quick examination."

"Okay," said John. "I noticed I do have a bruise on my leg, and I had a little trace of a headache this morning, but otherwise I feel fine."

"He's going to walk downtown to the parade with us," said Hugh.

"Do you think that would be all right, Doctor?" asked Mr. Allen.

"I think so," said Dr. Dawson. "It's not that far. Shouldn't be too much of a strain other than walking back up the hill, but let me make my examination before we decide."

John soon had his breakfast finished. He was craving a pancake, but he didn't eat any so as not to keep the doctor waiting, and he also didn't want to upset his stomach by eating too much when all he'd had in three days before now was the soup last night.

Dr. Dawson then asked him to go into the parlor. John sat down in a comfortable chair that had doilies pinned to it. Dr. Dawson pulled up a footstool and sat next to him. He pulled out a stethoscope from his medical bag and listened to John's heart. He had John follow his finger with his eyes, and he tested John's reflexes.

"I'd say you're a very healthy young man," Dr. Dawson pronounced.

"Great!" said Hugh, who had been hovering in the doorway.

John laughed. "You seem happier that I'm well than I do."

"Well, like I said," said Hugh, "I want you to be able to go to the parade."

"If you feel up to it, go ahead," said Dr. Dawson, putting his stethoscope back in his bag. "Perhaps Bertha and I will see you there—Bertha is my wife. Mr. Adams' daughter."

"Give your in-laws and Mrs. Dawson our best," said Mr. Allen, also now appearing in the parlor doorway. "And Will, of course."

"I will do that," said Dr. Dawson.

"Thank you, Doctor," said John, feeling relieved. At least now he didn't have to worry he had something seriously wrong with him.

Dr. Dawson said his goodbyes. John rejoined his hosts in the dining room and had another cup of coffee. Mrs. Bingley came to clear the table so she could do up the breakfast dishes before she left to join her family in time for the parade.

"I was just going to hire some young girl to help Mrs. Allen around the house," Mr. Allen told John when Mrs. Bingley had disappeared into the kitchen, "but Mrs. Allen thought it best we hire an older, married woman so there would be no nonsense with the boys. They are at that age."

John looked over to Hugh, who blushed at the remark.

"You can never be too careful," said Mr. Allen. "Just last year one of our neighbors' sons got the maid in trouble."

"I would never do that," said Hugh. "I believe in morality."

"I'm glad to hear it," said Mr. Allen. "I'm very lucky, John, in my children. They are upstanding young people. Of course, I'm very careful about whom I let them associate with."

"Howard and I," Hugh proclaimed proudly, "have both pledged not to associate with the opposite sex except in public and to avoid all impure thoughts. His mother, Mrs. Longyear, makes him keep a journal, and he lets her read it whenever she wants—well, not so much now that he's at Cornell—but that way he knows she's watching over him."

"That seems very wise," said John, thinking what a horrible invasion of privacy it would be if his mother did such a thing. His own mother—who was she? John knew he must have one....

"I thought about keeping a journal too," said Hugh, "but Mother said she didn't have time to be reading it every day."

"Your mother is a busy woman," said Mrs. Bingley, returning to the dining room to collect the coffee cups, "and she knows you're a good boy."

Hugh blushed again.

"Do you think you have any vices?" Mr. Allen asked, staring at John.

"No, I don't believe so," said John, surprised by such a direct question. "As far as I know, I do not drink or smoke or tell dirty jokes," he said, the words seeming to recall a rhyme or song he knew—something about a bus driver, but it wouldn't all come to him.

"Well, so long as you're staying under this roof, I expect you to live a good Christian life," Mr. Allen said. "Clean living is the best way."

"Yes, sir," said John, feeling awkward about the lecture. "Speaking of clean living, I would like to shave off this beard, but

I'm not sure my hand is steady enough. Maybe Hugh could help me."

Mr. Allen laughed. "Hugh barely has a whisker yet."

"I do so," said Hugh. "I shave every Saturday night so I look presentable to the Lord when we go to church Sunday morning."

"Well, John, if you want to trust him with your chin and cheeks, you go right ahead," said Mr. Allen, picking up his newspaper.

"I'll be happy to help you," said Hugh. "Let's go upstairs now."

John followed Hugh up the stairs to the bathroom. There Hugh found a razor and got out some "shaving soap." John was surprised, having always used shaving cream, but he found it made a nice lather. Having shaving cream had been his biggest concern—he hadn't been quite sure the Victorians had it—shaving soap certainly was messier than the shaving cream he seemed to remember, but it did a good job regardless. Hugh stood behind him and used the straight razor, guiding his hand until John got the hang of it. It was probably the longest shaving job since he had begun shaving, but in the end, John was pleased with the results.

"You're almost as handsome as Howard," said Hugh, admiring their shared work, "and you have more of a beard. But I think you must be the same age."

"I think I'm nineteen," said John. "I'm not sure why, but it seems like it."

"Yes. You seem a tad taller and older than me. Howard will be nineteen in September, but I won't be until next February. What time is it getting to be?" Hugh stepped out of the bathroom to go look at the clock in his bedroom. "Oh, we have lots of time until the parade still," he said from the hall. "Do you want to go outside and play catch?"

"Sure," said John.

In a few more minutes, they were outside in the cool of the late morning. They found a shaded spot on the lawn beside the house. The day was quiet since it was a holiday, and while Hugh said hello now and then to someone walking by, for the most part, as they tossed the ball, he talked all about his friend Howard and the letters Howard had written to him from Cornell. Howard was on the rowing team and Hugh hoped to be on the rowing team too when he went to Cornell in the fall.

"Dad wanted me to go to the University of Michigan," said Hugh, "but Howard got his dad, Mr. Longyear, to talk to my dad to convince him. Dad says it's too expensive, but Mom helped talk him into it. I promised to study hard. I didn't want to go to the University of Michigan since I wouldn't know anyone there."

"No one in your class is going there?" asked John, tossing the ball back to his new friend.

"No one in my class is going to college, just me," said Hugh. "Most of the boys can't afford to. They're going to start working right away. A lot of the boys I went to school with when I was younger are already out working. Many left school after eighth grade."

"Oh," said John, seeming to remember not many people went to college in 1900.

"Have you remembered anything about college?" asked Hugh. "You said you thought you went."

"No, I still can't remember," said John.

"Maybe you go to school out east somewhere. Hey, maybe you even go to Cornell and Howard will recognize you when he gets home. I mean, maybe you're one of the Club members' sons, which is why you were up at the Club. Not too many people in Marquette can afford to send their children to college. But most of the Club members have the resources."

"Maybe," said John, "but if I was somehow connected to the Club, I would think someone would have recognized me."

"True," said Hugh, "but there has to be a reason you were up there." He threw the ball kind of fast, causing John to reach quickly for it.

"Can we stop now?" asked John after he stumbled and failed to catch the ball Hugh had just tossed to him. "My head is starting to hurt a little."

"Yeah, you better sit down and rest a little so you're not too worn out to go to the parade."

"Boys!" Mr. Allen called out the window. "Mrs. Bingley made some lemonade before she left. Why don't you come inside and have some to cool off before we head downtown."

"Coming!" shouted Hugh.

John was relieved to go inside. Hugh was a nice boy, but John had to admit he was getting a bit tired of hearing him sing the praises of Howard Longyear. True, it would be a relief if Howard recognized him, but Howard wasn't coming home until Friday, which was two days away. John didn't want to wait that long to learn who he was. Hopefully, someone at the parade would recognize him and solve the mystery of his identity.

The Allen House

Chapter 4

AN HOUR LATER, HUGH, JOHN, and Mr. Allen departed out the front door. John noted Mr. Allen didn't even bother to lock it, which rather surprised him since Mrs. Bingley had already left, but he didn't draw attention to it.

Once they had walked down the driveway, they turned to their right and started west down Ridge Street. John felt like his head was spinning. He could swear he had often walked down this street before, but somehow it all seemed different. It was surreal, like he'd stepped into an alternate reality. The trees seemed too short, the houses taller than he remembered, and when they got to the corner of Ridge and Pine Streets, he was surprised to see a large vacant lot. Surely, there should be a building there.

"This is where my high school was," said Hugh. "It burned down last winter."

"Really?" said John. "That must have been scary."

"It was. It happened right in the middle of the school day, but everyone got out safely."

Hugh launched into a long story about the fire, how everyone inside had been alerted to it, how all the students had gotten out of the building, and then how he had been enlisted by the firemen to help put it out.

"It was a total loss," Mr. Allen chimed in. "A shame really, but plans are in place to build a new school soon."

They continued down the street to a sandstone church on the corner of High Street that looked familiar to John.

"Do you go to church?" Mr. Allen asked John.

"I—I don't know. I can't remember," said John.

"We're Presbyterian," said Hugh. "This part of Marquette is like the city church district. That's St. Paul's," he said, gesturing to the church they were passing, "and that one up there is the Methodist

Church and the one over there is the Baptist Church. We go to the Presbyterian church just down the street from the Baptist Church. You'll see it when we turn the corner."

When they reached the corner of Ridge and Front, John had a strange feeling. He was sure he had been here before. He was having déjà vu, and he seemed to recall walking across this street and entering a large building on the other side, but he did not see a large building there, just a house—it was a good-sized house but not like the large stone building with pillars he envisioned but whose name he could not remember.

"We have to go this way," said Mr. Allen, turning left to lead the way down the hill past the Baptist Church.

"How are you feeling?" Hugh asked John. "You're not tired or dizzy are you? I mean from walking downhill?"

"No, I feel fine," said John. "I'm excited to see the parade."

By now, they were entering into a crowd of people all lined up along the street to wait for the parade. John did feel fine physically, but mentally, he was starting to feel like a wreck. Mr. Allen and Hugh knew several people in the crowd whom they said hello to. They introduced him to a couple of neighbors as "our friend John." John kept hoping one of these people would say something like, "You're not John. You're my neighbor Matthew," or "John? You're not John. Your name's Ethan, and you're my cousin," but no one said any such thing. Surely someone in this town could help solve the mystery of his identity.

Everything felt so overwhelming. He had so much to take in, and it was all so unfamiliar and familiar at the same time. He wanted to walk slowly so he could try to focus on each building and each person's name and try to sort them in his brain, to catalogue them—no, to do a computer search; he got a sudden image of looking at a lit-up screen and typing in a name—the vision was there for a flash and then disappeared, replaced by an image of an old card catalogue—how would he ever make sense of it all? He knew all these flashes of images must be memories of some sort, but he could not quite make the connections to say what they were. Surely, there were no computers in this time. Was he like some sort of prophet able to see the future rather than someone from the future? When would he have answers to this dilemma?

As he walked down the street, he suddenly tripped.

"Are you all right?" asked Hugh, reaching out to steady him.

"Yes," said John, realizing he hadn't been paying attention to where he was walking and the sidewalk had just been uneven. "I just—I just can't get over that giant building there with the clock. It's a bank, isn't it?"

"Yes, the Savings Bank," said Hugh. "Our neighbor, Mr. Kaufman, is the bank president."

"I'm sure I've seen it before," said John. "It looks familiar, but a lot of these other buildings don't. I'm sure I'm from Marquette, but this doesn't quite look like the Marquette I seem to remember."

"Perhaps you lived here when you were a child, and then you just came back before you lost your memory," said Mr. Allen. "That's possible. That bank's been here a good ten years now so you might remember it from years ago, but some of these other buildings are newer."

"Maybe," said John. "I wish I could remember."

"Let's head down Washington Street to find a good spot to watch the parade," said Mr. Allen. "It looks less crowded on Washington than Front, and the parade will turn this corner anyway."

"Okay," said Hugh, and John readily followed. They walked a distance past many businesses where the crowd was extremely thick until they came to the next street corner. There on the block across the street was a giant building with a great red dome. John was sure he'd seen that building before, but never when it looked so bright and new. Still, the building next to it, right on the corner—the one with a tower, rather puzzled him.

"Oh, Dad, it's starting!" a little girl along the sidewalk screamed at the top of her lungs, jumping up and down. John had to laugh at her enthusiasm. Looking up the road, he could see a policeman riding a horse down the street, followed by a group of people carrying a large American flag that somehow looked unfamiliar, like some of the stars were missing.

"This seems like as good a spot as any," said Mr. Allen.

The trio stood behind a group of children, who were seated on the street curb. John couldn't help thinking how very subdued the parade seemed—no loud noisy trucks, no motorcycles, no firetrucks blaring sirens, nor vans playing rock music. His head began pounding—what was he remembering?

He quit looking at the horses and the floats and began to scan the faces of the people across the street, trying to see if anyone looked familiar. He prayed someone would recognize him and call out his name—a name that wouldn't be *John*, though he knew that name was somehow connected with him—a name that would identify him, spoken by someone who knew who he really was.

But soon the gaily colored floats attracted his attention with all their flowers and elaborate details. *They don't make them like that anymore*, he thought, though not sure why he thought so.

"Why, hello?" said a voice at his side, and suddenly, John felt hope rise up in him. Was this someone who knew him?

He turned, only to be disappointed that it was just Dr. Dawson.

"I see you made it," said the doctor. "How are you feeling?"

"Fine," said John, "but a little frustrated that I still can't remember anything."

"Well, be grateful for your health," said the doctor. "As long as you have that, there's hope the memory will come back."

"Yes," said John, though he didn't feel very hopeful. "I appreciate your help."

"I'll come by and see you again in a day or two," said Dr. Dawson.

"We'll be going up to the Club on Saturday," Hugh told him. "As soon as Howard gets home."

"All right," said the doctor. "Well, I'll stop by Friday if I can, John, or if you need me, Hugh and Mr. Allen know where to find me."

"Thank you, sir," said John.

"I better be going now. I got called to see a sick patient as soon as I got home from your house, so I'm here late and looking for my family. Have you seen them?"

"No, I'm afraid not," said Mr. Allen.

"Well, I'm sure they're around here somewhere. Happy Fourth of July!"

The doctor tipped his hat as they all said goodbye, and then he disappeared into the crowd.

"He's a nice man," said John.

"Yes," said Mr. Allen. "And a good doctor."

"His wife is lucky to have married a doctor," said Hugh. "Her brother Will is a complete invalid, and she and Dr. Dawson take very good care of him."

"Oh, Dad, look!" screamed the little girl who had been so excited when the parade began.

The object of her enthusiasm was a clown on a unicycle, who was pretending to be about to fall off. Everyone laughed at the clown's antics, and then Hugh, looking down the street, said, "There's Peter White!"

John's ears perked up as he saw the white-bearded man in a carriage and sporting a top hat. John felt deeply interested in Peter White, though he wasn't sure why.

"Who is he again?" he found himself asking.

"Who is Peter White?" said Hugh, half-laughing. "He's Marquette's most famous person. He owns the First National Bank and the Peter White Insurance Agency. He's done all kinds of things for Marquette, like founding the library and putting roofs on churches and funding the Father Marquette statue. You said his name seemed familiar last night."

"He sounds very important," said John, overwhelmed by all this information. "But who's that with him?"

Seated in the fancy black carriage across from Peter White was a man in a suit, hat, and spectacles who looked quite elderly.

"That's Chief Kawbawgam," said Hugh. "He's the chief of the local Chippewa Indians. He lives out at Presque Isle Park. He and Peter White are good friends."

"Yes," added Mr. Allen. "They met in 1849 when Marquette was founded. When Peter arrived here with Robert Graveraet to found the town, Chief Kawbawgam greeted them and let them all sleep in his wigwam."

"Oh," said John. "I think I remember something about 1849. Was your family here then too?"

"No," said Mr. Allen. "I came to Marquette in 1880. We're newcomers by comparison."

"I have this feeling," said John, "that my family's been here a long time. I wish I could just remember who my family is."

Chief Kawbawgam now turned and looked directly at John, and John suddenly felt himself overcome with emotion. The chief's noble profile and the slight wave he gave to the crowd—they, well, the whole thing just seemed so surreal. John felt it was such a significant moment for him to see this old Indian chief. He felt this deep longing to tell someone he had seen Kawbawgam, but whom would he tell? He felt like he was going to cry. He felt overwhelming loneliness, mixed with frustration and confusion, not to know whom he belonged to. He knew he wasn't alone. Hugh and Mr. Allen were being so kind to him, but they weren't his family. Did he belong to anyone?

As the parade continued, John tried to keep a stiff upper lip, hoping no one was looking at him as he struggled to hold back tears. He was relieved when the Marquette City Band went by, marking the end to the parade, and Mr. Allen said, "Well, I guess that's it."

"Let's go to Stafford's for ice cream," said Hugh.

"Oh, no," said Mr. Allen. "The place will be packed with people. Some other time."

Hugh frowned but did not argue.

"Besides," said Mr. Allen. "Mrs. Bingley made us a blueberry pie."

"She did?"

"Yes, it was meant to be a surprise," said Mr. Allen.

"Well, I am surprised," said Hugh. "Mrs. Bingley is the best. Do you like blueberry pie, John?"

John could already taste the pie. "Yes," he said. "Blueberry pie is one thing I have not forgotten."

The three turned and started down the street, but rather than walk all the way down Washington, they went up the hill on Third Street to get away from the crowd sooner. It was a rather steep hill and two blocks up to Ridge Street, but even though John worried he might not feel up to the climb, Hugh's chattering kept him distracted from feeling dizzy or as lonesome. Hugh was telling him all about last Fourth of July and how he and Howard Longyear had bought their own firecrackers when he exclaimed, "We didn't even buy any firecrackers this year, Dad!"

"Yes, we did," said his father. "At least I did, but they're up at the Club. I'm sure your brothers and sister will be enjoying them this evening."

Hugh looked downcast at this but must have decided it was best not to complain. John, however, felt bad that he was the reason Hugh could not enjoy the holiday with his siblings.

They walked in silence now as they turned onto Ridge. Not until they were again at the corner with the churches did Hugh speak, suddenly becoming animated when he saw a fancy carriage coming up Front Street.

"It's Peter White again!" said Hugh.

Sure enough, it was Peter White and Chief Kawbawgam.

"Ephraim!" Mr. White called out to Mr. Allen. "Is that boy your mystery patient?"

"Yes," said Mr. Allen, stepping up to the carriage. The driver had pulled it over to the side of the road. The horses waited patiently while Mr. White talked to them. "He can't remember his name," Mr. Allen told Mr. White, "so we're calling him John."

"Hello," said Mr. White, extending his hand to John.

"Hello, sir," said John, inexplicably feeling like he was encountering royalty. He knew Mr. White was important, but he was surprised by how reverent he felt toward the old man as they shook hands. Meanwhile, Chief Kawbawgam and the Allens exchanged nods and "hellos."

"I'm having a barbecue this evening," said Mr. White. "Why don't you all come and join us? I'm sure you must be lonely since the rest of your family is up at the Club."

"That's very kind of you, Peter," Mr. Allen replied.

"Good. Come around five o'clock."

"We will," said Mr. Allen. "Thank you."

"Well, I need to be getting Charley back home," said Mr. White. "See you at five." Then he told the driver to drive on.

"Wow!" said John, although not sure why.

"Mr. White was very interested when he heard you had been found up at the Club," said Mr. Allen. "He came by earlier yesterday before you woke up."

"Really?" said John.

"Oh, yes. I guess we're all rather curious about you. It's not every day someone gets struck by lightning and can't remember his name."

"Yeah," said Hugh. "And those clothes you were wearing were really strange."

"They were?" asked John as they continued down Ridge Street, Peter White's carriage still visible farther up the street.

"Yeah, they were like a swimming suit or something, the pants were so short."

"I thought they were half-burnt off," said Mr. Allen.

"I don't know," said Hugh. "They looked to me like they were made that way."

"I'm sure I had long pants on," said John. "I would never wear anything unseemly."

He knew it was a lie—he thought he must have been wearing shorts since it was summer—but he was not ready to start telling people he might be from the future. The less he said about that, the better. The last thing he wanted was to find himself in some sort of mental hospital. Yet, given that he could remember things from his own time, but not his name made him wonder if he belonged in one.

"Your shirt was different, too," said Hugh. "Like an undershirt."

"I wonder if you were attacked and your clothes stolen," Mr. Allen suggested.

"Maybe," said John. "I really don't know. I wish I did. Anyway, it's kind of Mr. White to take an interest in me."

"Yeah, and he always has a big feast when he has a party," said Hugh, "complete with Peter White Punch!"

"Which you are not to be drinking," Mr. Allen told his son.

"I'm eighteen now," said Hugh.

"And you're also living under my roof. No one in my household will be drinking any alcohol."

"Yes, Dad," said Hugh.

John was glad when they reached the Allens' house. He was starting to feel overwhelmed by everything and knew he would need to rest if he were going to the barbecue later.

"Can I lie down for a little while?" asked John as they went up the steps to the front porch. "I feel kind of tired now."

"Of course," said Mr. Allen. "In fact, a nap sounds rather attractive to me. How about you, Hugh?"

"I hate napping," said Hugh. "I'll go for a walk or something."

"I envy the energy you have," Mr. Allen replied as he opened the front door.

Chapter 5

JOHN DID END UP NAPPING a little, though he was less tired than just needing some time alone to figure out what he should do—to figure out how he might get his full memory back. But even lying on the bed and thinking was exhausting for him, so ultimately he did fall asleep. One thing was certain—he had no idea who he really was, and he had no idea how to find out other than to keep hoping someone would recognize him or that more of his memories would somehow be triggered.

He didn't know how long he had been asleep when a knock on the door woke him.

"Are you awake?" asked Hugh, calling through the door.

"Yes, you can come in," said John, sitting up. He had slept lightly anyway.

"Are you feeling up to going to the barbecue?" asked Hugh, coming in and sitting down on the chair.

"Yes," said John. "I'm actually excited to go. For some reason, Peter White seems very familiar to me."

"Well, everyone in Marquette knows Peter White," said Hugh. "You're bound to find him familiar if you are from Marquette."

"Maybe," said John. "Anyway, I guess he didn't recognize me. But maybe someone at his party will."

"Hopefully," said Hugh. "If not, maybe we should go down to the *Mining Journal* and have your picture put in the newspaper to see if anyone can identify you."

"Maybe," said John, but he didn't like the idea. He did not want to become a spectacle.

"Well, Dad said to tell you we're going to leave in about fifteen minutes."

"Okay," said John. "Will I look okay? I mean, Mr. White is really rich, isn't he? Does he expect me to dress up?"

"No, I think what you have on is fine, though you're a little wrinkled, but once you put your suit jacket on, you'll be fine."

"Okay," said John. "It's just so warm."

"It is summer," said Hugh.

"No, I mean wearing a jacket."

"You can't go to the party without a jacket," Hugh replied.

John grimaced.

"Don't you like that jacket?" asked Hugh. "I gave it to you because it's a little big on me, and I don't think any of my other jackets will fit you."

"No, I like it," said John, not wanting to be rude. "I just have to use the bathroom."

"Okay," said Hugh. "I'll meet you downstairs. I hope you're hungry. Mr. White always throws a banquet."

John waited for Hugh to leave. Then he got out of bed, sighing at the thought of putting back on the hot jacket, but he first went to the bathroom and fixed his hair to make sure he looked presentable. Then, he returned to put on the jacket and went downstairs.

"Ready to go?" asked Mr. Allen, getting up from his chair in the parlor when he saw John coming down the stairs.

"Yes," said John. "I feel bad going empty-handed, though."

"Oh, don't worry. Mr. White won't even notice. He's just happy to have a party."

"Where's Hugh?" asked John.

"He's outside waiting for us."

John waited for Mr. Allen to come out into the entryway, and then he went outside and Mr. Allen followed him, again not bothering to lock the door.

Hugh was standing on the sidewalk and looking down the street toward Mr. White's house.

"He must be having quite the shindig," said Hugh. "I already saw Dr. Dawson and his wife go by, and I can hear a lot of voices."

"I imagine he's invited everyone in the neighborhood," said Mr. Allen.

They started down the sidewalk, crossing the street when they came to the corner. As they continued on, a large two-story sandstone house with a tower in the front stood before them.

"Is that Mr. White's house?" asked John, thinking it looked familiar.

"No," said Mr. Allen. "The Smiths live there."

"Who are they?" asked John, stopping to stare at the house.

"Judge Smith and his wife," said Hugh. Then, in a lower voice, he added, "They aren't very pleasant people."

Mr. Allen laughed, then stopped himself and said, "Hugh, if you have nothing nice to say, don't say anything at all."

"Sorry," Hugh muttered. "Anyway, Mr. White's house is on the next block. Let's get going before all the food is gone."

John stood and stared at the house for another second until Mr. Allen also grew impatient and started down the sidewalk.

Somehow, John thought, *I think I know that house. I feel like I've even been in it.*

By now, they could see a party out on the lawn of the White house. Quite a crowd had gathered, probably a few dozen people, including several children. As they approached, Mr. Allen was immediately greeted by people he knew. John was introduced to so many people that soon his head was swimming. Finally, Mr. White came forward and they all thanked him for inviting them. Then Mr. Allen introduced John to Mr. White's daughter and her husband, Mr. and Mrs. George Shiras III. There was also a Mr. Jopling, Peter White's son-in-law, whose wife had passed away. Children were running about the lawn, including the Shirases' children. John was introduced to guests with last names like Kidder and Mather and Spear, many of whom seemed somehow to be related to Mr. White. John couldn't help feeling like many of their names were familiar. He even thought he recognized a couple of the people he met, but none of them acted like they knew him, though several asked him questions about himself and wished him luck in finding his family. Hugh was a true friend to John, staying by his side throughout the party. He introduced him to people and gave him details when no one was listening of who was who in the community, where they lived, who they were related to, and why they were important. But as the evening wore on, John felt like his brain was a muddle of names and details, and beneath it all, he felt a growing void of loneliness from fear he never would meet anyone he knew.

By the time they left the party, John's head ached even though he hadn't imbibed the famous Peter White Punch. However, the walk home and the fresh air helped a little. Hugh, feeling antsy since it was a holiday, suggested they play games when they got home. Mr. Allen said he was too tired and going to bed, but Hugh and John played several rounds of checkers until midnight. It had been a good day to celebrate America's freedom, but John went to bed wishing he could find freedom from his confusion.

The next day, John slept until 10 a.m. When he woke, he found Hugh and Mr. Allen downstairs having breakfast. Hugh had only just gotten up himself. Mr. Allen remarked that he never would have been allowed to be so lazy when he was a boy, but John seemed to remember that teenagers typically slept late. Mr. Allen asked the boys what they would do all day since he was returning to the Huron Mountain Club to rejoin the rest of the family. He had agreed to let Hugh and John stay home until Howard came to town tomorrow, and then the three boys would come up to the Club on Saturday.

"I'm eager to go up to the Club," said John. "Maybe if I'm there, I'll remember something about what happened to me or why I was there in the first place."

"That's possible," said Hugh.

"Would you rather come with me today?" asked Mr. Allen. "I'm going up there with the Shirases. Howard and Hugh plan to canoe up there, but that might be too strenuous for you."

"No, I'm feeling fine," said John, "and I kind of like the idea of paddling on Lake Superior. I'm not sure if I ever have."

"You can't go with Dad," Hugh told him. "I don't want to be left alone all day. Stay and I'll keep you entertained. I can show you all around Marquette, and maybe you'll see something to jog your memory."

"Actually," John said, as Mrs. Bingley placed his breakfast before him, "I keep thinking about that big sandstone house we passed yesterday on the way to Mr. White's house."

"You mean Judge Smith's house?" asked Mr. Allen.

"Yes," said John. "I feel like I know that house well, like I've been inside it."

"You should see Howard's house," said Hugh. "It's sandstone too. The Smiths' house is like a carriage house compared to it."

"Hugh," said Mr. Allen, frowning.

"Well, it's true," said Hugh. "Mr. Longyear is probably even richer than Peter White. They have the biggest house in Marquette—sixty-five rooms. They even have a bowling alley."

"Really?" said John. "Where is it?"

"On the block kitty-corner from Peter White's house. I can't believe I didn't point it out to you yesterday. But I'll show it to you today, and we can probably go inside it on Saturday when we go to see Howard."

"I'll look forward to that," said John, "but I don't think I have a connection to the Longyears. I think the Smith house, though, might have some connection to my past."

"Well, I don't know," said Mr. Allen. "The Smiths only have a daughter, Jane. She recently married a Mr. Hampton and just had a baby."

"John might be the Smiths' nephew or some other relation," said Hugh.

"Hmm," said Mr. Allen. "I know Mrs. Smith has a brother, Mr. O'Neill, but he has two daughters—I can't remember their names, though they're probably around your age."

"O'Neill," said John. "That name sounds familiar."

"The O'Neills were originally from South Carolina," said Mr. Allen. "They've lived in Marquette since they were children, some time before the Civil War, but you can still hear a bit of an accent when you speak to them, though I think Carolina Smith likes to exaggerate hers."

"She's something else," said Hugh.

"Hugh," said his father, "what did I just tell you yesterday about not saying anything unless—"

"I know," Hugh said. "If you have nothing nice to say, don't say anything at all, but you know I'm right." He turned to John and whispered, "She's rather a witch."

"Hugh!" said Mr. Allen, and he picked up his newspaper and gave Hugh a swat with it, but John could tell from the look in his eye that Mr. Allen was amused.

"Ow!" shouted Hugh, pretending to be hurt but actually laughing.

"Do I need to come in there and make someone stand in a corner?" called Mrs. Bingley from the next room.

Mr. Allen laughed. "No, Mrs. Bingley. I'll behave myself."

She appeared in the doorway with a coffee cup in her hand and a smile on her face. John could tell she was just like one of the family, the friendly grandmother figure as much as the housekeeper.

"I hope you'll keep these two boys in line once I'm gone, Mrs. Bingley," said Mr. Allen. "I'm not too worried about John here, of course."

"I'll keep an eye on them," said Mrs. Bingley.

"Well, I better be going. I don't want to keep the Shirases waiting," said Mr. Allen, and he stood and headed upstairs to his room.

By the time Hugh and John finished eating, Mr. Allen was back downstairs and opening his wallet to give Hugh some money in case of an emergency.

"Thank you, sir," Hugh said politely. "Give my love to Mom and everyone else. I'll see you all on Saturday."

Father and son hugged and then John shook Mr. Allen's hand and wished him a safe trip.

"Next time I see you, John," said Mr. Allen, "I hope you'll know your real name."

"You and me both," said John.

Mrs. Bingley gathered up the breakfast dishes after Mr. Allen left, while Hugh asked John what he wanted to do. John didn't quite feel up to traipsing around Marquette so early. Hugh wanted to show him all the sights, but John suggested they wait until the afternoon.

"I know," said Hugh. "I got a new book for my birthday I haven't read yet—Mark Twain's *A Connecticut Yankee in King Arthur's Court*. How about we read that?"

"How can we both read it?" asked John.

"Well, we can read it aloud and take turns doing the characters' voices."

"Okay," said John, thinking it sounded like fun.

Hugh led him to the back of the house, which John hadn't been in yet. A small room there had a couple of comfy old chairs and a few shelves of books. John felt immediately drawn to the books, like they were old friends. He scanned the shelves, finding the novels of Dickens, a full set of Sir Walter Scott's Waverley novels, and various books on flora and fauna and American history.

"Here it is," said Hugh, pulling the Twain novel off a shelf. He sat down in one of the chairs and motioned for John to sit down in the other and pull it next to his. Then he opened up the book, and in a few minutes, he was reading aloud to John.

John listened, thinking Hugh had a good reading voice. He was soon caught up in the story of Hank Morgan, who after being hit on the head, found himself in King Arthur's Camelot. John could not help thinking how Hank's predicament was somewhat similar to what he was experiencing—only Hank had not forgotten who he was when he time traveled. John was feeling more and more certain that he had time traveled. Otherwise, why would he have mental images of TV screens and cars? He only wished he understood why he could remember such trivial things but nothing about who he was.

They had a pleasant morning, taking turns reading from the book. Then Mrs. Bingley fixed them lunch. After lunch, Hugh asked if John was ready to go walk around town.

"Sure," said John, "but I have a feeling it's not going to help my memory."

"You won't know until we try," said Hugh. "If you are from Marquette, someone or something is bound to trigger a memory for you."

"I hope so," John replied, but he was doubtful. He was starting to think that the places in Marquette he did recognize might be because they still existed in the future he was from. Those he didn't recognize had probably been torn down before his time. He wasn't sure what time he was from, but he knew it must be a hundred or so years in the future if the clothes he seemed to remember wearing were any indication. He wished he could talk to Hugh about all this, but he was afraid he would only freak out his new friend.

The boys set off down Ridge Street, taking the same path they had the day before to Front Street and then down the hill to Washington Street. The streets were somewhat deserted, but the businesses were open, and they walked into a few stores. Hugh used some of the money his father had given him to buy them ice cream at Stafford's Drug Store since his father had refused to let them go there the day before. John hoped Mr. Allen had intended for Hugh to enjoy the money, even though he had said it was for an emergency. John thought the ice cream had a strange taste and texture, not at all the kind of ice cream he seemed to remember tasting before, but Hugh gobbled it down. Then they walked farther down the street, past what Hugh said were the post office and city hall, the buildings with the tower and the red dome that they had stood in front of yesterday to watch the parade. They walked another block past the French-Canadian Catholic Church and then turned down Fourth Street to walk past a rather grand brick house in a fenced-in yard. "That's the Harlow House," said Hugh. "Mr. Harlow was the founder of Marquette. He's dead now, but his family still lives there."

"What's that big church up there?" asked John, pointing up the street.

"That's St. Peter's Cathedral," said Hugh. "It's a Catholic Church. I don't know why the Catholics have to have the biggest church in

Marquette. The Catholics are mostly poor because the church expects them to give it all their money."

"And what's that building?" asked John, pointing to one across the street.

"That's the courthouse and that other one is the jail."

As they turned left, Hugh said, "This is Baraga Avenue. It used to be Superior Street, but they renamed it to honor Bishop Baraga; he's the founding bishop of the Catholic Church here in the Upper Peninsula."

They walked past hotels and saloons and more businesses and then reached Front Street and crossed it to go down to the harbor. John was surprised to see three big wooden docks and several boats, including a large boat up against one of the wooden docks that Hugh explained was an ore boat.

"Oh, iron ore," said John, surprising himself by the comment.

"That's right," said Hugh. "There are iron mines west of here in Negaunee and Ishpeming and thereabouts. They ship the ore on trains out here to the harbor, and then the boats take it south to other cities where it's made into steel."

"Oh," said John. "I think I knew that somehow, but I didn't expect to see so many docks and all these railroad tracks."

"There are lots of railroads around here," said Hugh. "That's Dad's business—railroads."

"Oh, I didn't know that," said John.

"Yes, he's the treasurer for the DSS&A."

"What's that?" asked John.

"The Detroit and South Shore. It was the Detroit and Mackinac originally. Dad came to Marquette because he got his job with the railroad. I was just a baby when we moved here."

"Oh, where were you from originally?"

"Dad was born in Salem, Massachusetts, home of the witch trials and all that you know."

John laughed, but mainly because he was happy to remember that he had heard about the witch trials.

They walked along the harbor and shoreline until the road started to turn to the left, circling around the large hill upon which Ridge Street was built. Eventually, they came to the foot of Ridge Street.

"This is all the bottom of the Longyears' property," said Hugh. "They own everything all the way to Cedar Street at the top of the hill."

"Really?" said John. "Is that their house?" He pointed at a giant stone mansion on top of the hill.

"Yes," said Hugh.

"It looks huge."

"It is. Sixty-five rooms, like I said, and it's on three acres. They have something like two-dozen servants."

"They must be very rich," said John.

"Millionaires," said Hugh.

"I would think so," John replied.

As they started up the hill, John was glad to see the stone stairs built along the sidewalk. Somehow, they seemed familiar to him. He was certain he had walked up these steps before, but he did not really recognize the landscape. The Longyear Mansion was built on beautifully landscaped property. "They hired some famous land-scaper," said Hugh. "I can never remember his name, but he de-signed Central Park in New York."

"Frederick Law Olmstead," said John.

Hugh, who was going up the steps in front of John, stopped to turn around and stare at him.

"How did you know that?"

"I don't know," said John, feeling as puzzled as Hugh's face looked. "It just came to me. I feel like I've walked up these steps before and like the Longyear Mansion is familiar to me too."

"Really?" said Hugh. "Well, perhaps you do know the Longyears. We'll see tomorrow when Howard comes, but I know all his brothers and sisters, so I can tell you that you're not one of them. Besides, they're all up at the Club like my family is. That's why Howard and I are going up there on Saturday, with you, of course."

"I'm looking forward to meeting Howard," said John as they continued up the hill. "He sounds like quite a fellow."

"He is," said Hugh. "He's really smart, and he's really good too. He has impeccable morals, like a knight in shining armor."

"Really?" said John, thinking that was quite some praise.

"Well, a modern-day version. I mean, he doesn't have any armor or anything, but he can ride a horse well, and he's just—well, a gen-tleman. I guess that's what I mean. He's not perfect, but he's pretty close to it."

"You think very highly of him, don't you?" said John.

"Yeah. I don't get to see him as often as I would like since he's always gone away to private schools and all, but even though his family has so much money, he treats me like I'm just as good as him and he writes me letters and always asks me to go camping in the summer. We're really good friends. I'm glad we'll both be at Cornell this fall."

By now they had reached the top of the hill and were walking past the Peter White house. John was feeling rather exhausted after the long walk and was hoping Mrs. Bingley might have made up a new batch of lemonade for them.

However, they were not to arrive home yet. As they reached the next block, they saw Peter White walking toward them on the opposite side of the street. He saw them and waved, and then started across the street as if to speak to them.

"Beautiful day, isn't it?" said Mr. White.

"Yes, sir," said Hugh.

"Have you had any luck remembering anything yet?" asked Mr. White, coming to a stop and addressing John.

"I still can't remember my name," said John, "but I'm sure I must be from Marquette or have been here before."

"Have you seen anyone you know?" Mr. White asked.

Peter White

"I feel like a lot of people I've met are familiar to me, including you, sir."

Mr. White looked at him, as if searching for something in his face. "I honestly don't think we ever met until yesterday."

"I...I especially," said John, feeling suddenly almost like his life depended on his saying so, "feel like I have some sort of connection to that house there."

He pointed at the sandstone house a block up the street.

"The Smiths' house?" asked Mr. White.

"Yes, sir. I'm sure I've been in it before, maybe even lived in it."

"That seems odd," said Mr. White. "The Smiths have lived there for many years—longer than you've been alive I would say."

"Still, I—I would love to see the inside of it. Maybe my parents were friends with them or something? I just feel like if I could go inside it, something in my memory would be triggered and I'd find the answers."

Mr. White developed a thoughtful look. John and Hugh stared at him in anticipation of what he would say next.

Finally, after inhaling deeply and exhaling out of his nose, and kind of shaking his head like it was against his better judgment, Mr. White said, "Well, I know the Smiths. I'll tell you they are not the friendliest people, but Judge Smith has always been cordial to me for business reasons. Why don't we go over there now to see if they recognize you."

"Really?" said John. "You would do that for me?"

"Sure," said Mr. White. "I can't imagine what you're going through feeling so lost. They might not appreciate you showing up on their doorstep unannounced, but they know me, so that might help explain things to them."

"That would be great!" said Hugh. "My family doesn't really know them, but everyone respects you, Mr. White."

"You'd be surprised," said Mr. White, half-laughing. "I know a few people in this town who would rather cross the street than speak to me, but let's see what we can do."

The portly old gentleman turned and started across the street, followed eagerly by John and Hugh.

In another minute, they were standing in front of the Smiths' house.

"Let me do the explaining," said Mr. White as they went up the front walk.

"Okay," said John.

Mr. White went up the steps and rang the bell while John and Hugh stood on the walk. It was an excruciatingly long moment, and Mr. White was just about to ring the bell a second time, when the door was opened by a young woman with a baby in her arms.

"Why, hello, Jane," said Mr. White. "I wasn't expecting to see you. How is your precious little boy?"

"Hello, Mr. White," she replied. "He's fine. I was just going to put him down for his nap."

"I'm sorry. I won't keep you long, but I do wonder if you or your parents could help us in some way."

Jane raised her eyebrows, looking doubtful. "What do you mean?" she asked.

"Jane, this is a young friend of mine, John, and Hugh Allen, your neighbor from down the road. John, Jane here is the Smiths' married daughter, Mrs. Hampton. She and her husband are living with her parents while they are having their own home built."

"It's a pleasure to meet you," said John, bowing his head slightly.

"It's nice to meet you," Jane replied. "What can I do for you?"

"Well, it's rather an odd request," said Mr. White. "You see, John has had an accident—he hit his head and has lost his memory. He was found unconscious up at the Huron Mountain Club. Some memories are starting to come back to him, but he can't quite remember his last name or who his family are. Yesterday, when he walked by your parents' house, however, he felt strongly drawn to it, like he's been in it before."

"Oh," said Jane, twisting her lips as if doubtful.

"I take it you haven't seen John before?" asked Mr. White.

"No, I'm sorry, but I haven't," she replied.

"We were wondering—"

"Jane, what are you doing answering the door!" shouted a woman from inside the house. "Where is Lucy? What do you mean opening the door like a common servant, and with the baby no less? Who is it anyway?"

By this point, Mrs. Smith was at Jane's shoulder. Jane stepped aside so her mother could see their visitors.

"Oh, Mr. White," said Mrs. Smith, her tone instantly changing from one of irritation to gratification. "How are you? What can we do for you?"

"Hello, Mrs. Smith," he said, tipping his hat to her.

"*Carolina,*" she replied, insinuating they were old friends.

"Carolina," Mr. White repeated, and then he told her what he had just told Jane about John's memory issues. As Mr. White spoke, John did not listen so much as watch Mrs. Smith's face. At first, he wanted to see if she recognized him—she did look oddly familiar to him—but then he saw her phony smile slowly turning into a frown. Her chest also began to heave and her eyes became fiery.

"So, if it's not too much of an imposition," Mr. White was concluding, "John was hoping he could just walk around your downstairs to see if anything triggers his memory."

Mr. White's last words fell into an atmosphere of palpable tension. Silence reigned for a few seconds as Carolina Smith inhaled deeply. Then rage worked its way up her throat, and John could see her starting to shake as she spit forth, "Mr. White, I am astonished by your nerve!"

"We don't mean to impose," Mr. White replied, "but we hoped you would understand, given that it is a peculiar situation."

"Peculiar indeed," Carolina Smith snapped. "To imply that this urchin should have any connection to our family!"

John thought *urchin* a bit misdirected. He was not Oliver Twist, after all, though perhaps in the same situation of not knowing his parentage.

"We don't mean to offend," said Mr. White. "I'm sure John is a perfectly respectable young man. He has very good manners. He just simply can't remember—"

"Because he's an impostor," Mrs. Smith stated. "I know exactly what he is trying to imply. I'm rather surprised by you, Mr. White. I have always taken you for a man of good sense, but I can see this charlatan has completely taken you in."

"I'm not a charlatan," said John, feeling called on to defend his honor.

"John is just trying to find out who he is!" protested Hugh.

"Please, boys," said Mr. White, turning to them to implore them to let him handle the matter.

"If he's not a charlatan, I don't know what else he could be," Mrs. Smith replied. Then she turned her attention directly to John. "I assure you my husband is a God-fearing Christian who never would have had any interest in whatever kind of dance hall hussy your mother may have been. You can look elsewhere for fools to play your manipulative, gold-digger games on."

"Carolina!" exclaimed Mr. White.

"Mrs. Smith," said John, too desperate to learn the truth to fear her wrath, "you completely misunderstand me. We never meant to imply anything improper."

"I will thank you all to leave my property now," said Mrs. Smith.

"Carolina, be reasonable," said Mr. White.

"Jane, shut the door," her mother commanded.

Jane looked uncomfortable, and silently mouthed, "I'm sorry," to Mr. White as she started to close the door.

"Carolina, just listen to me one minute!" Mr. White shouted.

Carolina pushed the half-closed door back open and stuck her head out. "You listen to me one minute, Mr. White. This is libel! That's exactly what it is. My husband is a judge, so don't think I don't know the law. If I hear one more word of this, not only will you be hearing from our lawyer, but I can assure you we will close our accounts with your bank and your insurance agency. Good day, sir!"

As the door slammed, John could not help a giggle over the completely baffled expression on Mr. White's face.

"I don't think it's very funny," said Mr. White, as he walked down the steps.

"I'm sorry," said John, "but if you had seen the look on your face."

"I don't think it's funny either," said Hugh. "That woman is… is…a witch!"

"Shh, she'll hear you," said John.

"I hope she does," said Hugh. "She's no Christian woman."

Mr. White laughed as they started down the front walk. "I have to admit," said Mr. White, "I don't know what she has against dance hall hussies, except maybe that they have more class than she does."

"Her daughter seemed nice," said John.

"Yes," said Mr. White. "Jane is a good girl. I think it must be the influence of her aunt, Kathleen O'Neill, because she certainly didn't inherit the milk of human kindness from her parents."

Mr. White turned and started walking toward his house. The boys accompanied him, even though the Allens' house was in the opposite direction.

"I'm sorry, John," said Mr. White, "that you didn't get the answers you sought."

"I'm kind of relieved," John replied. "I still feel I'm connected to that house somehow, but I sure don't want to be connected to its owners. I don't know why I feel such a connection."

"I don't know either," said Mr. White. "Like I said, the Smiths have been living there since before you must have been born."

"But Mr. White," said Hugh, "they weren't the first owners of that house, were they?"

Mr. White stopped and turned around to look at them. "No, that's true; they weren't. They bought the house from the Hennings, who built it. I was good friends with Gerald Henning. The Hennings moved away after their daughter drowned in Lake Superior. It was a terrible tragedy."

John felt again like he was experiencing déjà vu. "Their daughter?" he said, seeming to remember something about a drowning. "What was her name? Wait..." he said as Mr. White was about to reply. "Was it Madeleine?"

"Yes. How did you know that?"

"I don't know," said John. "I think...I'm not sure, but I think Madeleine is my sister's name."

"Your sister!" exclaimed Mr. White.

"I don't know why. I just have this strange feeling I have a sister named Madeleine."

"But you can't be more than twenty," said Mr. White. "Madeleine Henning would have died before you were born, and well..." He stopped in his tracks and looked like he was pondering something for a minute. "No, I don't think it's possible Madeleine Henning was your sister," he finally said. "You see, Madeleine's mother, Sophia, she must have been fifty at least by the time Madeleine died. She would have been well past childbearing years when you were born."

"Oh," said John, feeling downcast.

Mr. White, seeing the expression on John's face, put his hand on his shoulder. "I'm sorry," he repeated. "I wish I had answers for you. It is strange that you knew Madeleine Henning's name, but her drowning was a great tragedy. Anyone who was alive in Marquette at the time would remember it. Perhaps you just know the name for some reason, kind of like you feel you recognize me."

"Yeah," said Hugh. "Even I know about Madeleine Henning drowning. Mr. Henning came back to Marquette to visit a few years ago. My father met him on a business matter, and I remember him telling me about it, so maybe your parents told you about it."

"Maybe," said John, though he felt doubtful.

"I'm sorry I couldn't help you get any answers," said Mr. White, "but it's suppertime now, so I should head home. Mrs. White doesn't like to keep dinner waiting."

"Thank you, sir," said John. "I appreciate your trying."

"You boys have a good evening," said Mr. White. "Keep your chin up, John. The answers will come. Just trust the good Lord to bring them to you when he's ready."

"I'll try," said John.

"Good night, sir," said Hugh.

Mr. White tipped his hat to them and then proceeded toward his home. John and Hugh turned around, and after crossing the street to avoid walking close to the Smiths' house, headed home to supper.

Chapter 6

Mrs. Bingley had supper almost ready for the boys when they returned, so they quickly washed up and then sat down to a hearty meal. John's spirits were a bit down so he didn't feel that hungry at first, but watching Hugh devour his food with vigor cheered him up a little.

"I really appreciate all you're doing for me, Hugh," he said.

"I'm happy to help," said Hugh. "Besides, it's kind of fun trying to solve this mystery about who you are."

"I wish Mrs. Smith had seen it that way," John replied.

"Oh, don't worry about her," said Hugh. "No one in Marquette likes her. She thinks she's the leader of society, but most people laugh at her behind her back."

John didn't feel comforted by this fact.

"Of course, if you end up being related to her somehow," said Hugh, "I'm sorry to say anything nasty about her."

"I don't think I could be," said John. "Not closely related anyway, but I still feel very connected to that house."

"What if you lived in that house in another time, like from the future?" said Hugh.

John nearly fell out of his seat at this remark. Was Hugh serious? "What do you mean?" he asked, starting to wonder if he should be completely honest with his friend about some of his memories.

"I'm just joking," said Hugh. "You know, like in *A Connecticut Yankee in King Arthur's Court*. Hank Morgan hit his head and woke up in Camelot. Perhaps the same thing has happened to you."

"But isn't Hank Morgan dreaming in the book?"

"I don't know," said Hugh. "Maybe, but maybe not."

"Well, if I'm dreaming, then you wouldn't be real."

"I'm pretty sure I'm real," said Hugh. "I mean, I have memories of all kinds of things that happened to me before you ever came into my life."

"That's true," said John, "so I guess I can't be dreaming."

"But wouldn't it be wonderful if we could time travel back to Camelot?" asked Hugh.

"Sure," said John, and Hugh then engaged him in a conversation about all the adventures they could have if they visited King Arthur's time. John let Hugh do most of the talking, still too preoccupied with his own concerns to get too excited about a fantasy. Still, it kept them entertained until Mrs. Bingley came in to clean off the table so she could get home to her own family.

The boys were just about to go outside to play catch when the phone rang. Hugh jumped up to answer it. A moment later, he said, "Sure. I'll get him," and hollered, "John, it's Mr. White! He wants to talk to you."

John felt surprised, but he quickly got up from his chair and took the phone from Hugh.

"Hello," he said.

"John," said Mr. White, "my brilliant wife just reminded me that there might be someone in Marquette who can help you."

"There is?" asked John, beginning to tremble with anticipation.

"Yes," said Mr. White. "Remember how I said the Hennings moved away, but Mrs. Hennings' sister, Cordelia Whitman, still lives in Marquette? It's possible you belong to her family."

"Do you know her?" asked John.

"Not as well as I used to in Marquette's early days," said Mr. White, "but her son Jacob married Gerald Hennings' daughter by his first wife. The daughter was named Agnes. She and Jacob are both deceased now, but they had several children, including a couple of boys, and I think those boys might be about your age. You could be one of Cordelia Whitman's grandsons."

"Do you think so?" asked John.

"I don't know," said Mr. White. "I haven't seen those boys in years now, but it's possible, or if not, since you feel so connected to the Hennings' house, maybe Cordelia will recognize you."

"That would be wonderful," said John.

"Well, I'm too tired to go this evening," said Mr. White, "but tomorrow if you could meet me at my bank at five o'clock when the workday is over, we could go over to Mrs. Whitman's house to visit her. I'd ring her up, but she apparently doesn't have a telephone."

"I really appreciate it," said John. "Thank you."

"You're welcome. Just meet me in the lobby of the First National Bank. Get there a few minutes before five and then we'll go visit Mrs. Whitman."

"Thank you, sir. I'll be there," said John, although he wished he could go that minute. "Thank you so much."

"I can't promise anything," Mr. White reminded him, "but we won't know unless we try."

"Yes. Thank you again, sir."

"You're welcome. Have a good evening," said Mr. White and he hung up.

"What was that about?" asked Hugh, staring eagerly at John. For a moment, John didn't reply because he was distracted by what to do with the phone.

"Put the phone back on the receiver," said Hugh.

John looked at the phone hanging on the wall and realized the metal clasp at the top was where he was supposed to hang the part he had just listened with. That was how you hung up this phone. Just like he'd seen in movies. Weird. He knew he'd never used a phone like this, but he couldn't remember what kind of phone he had used.

"Are you okay?" asked Hugh. "You look strange. What did Mr. White say?"

"I'm fine," John replied, and he quickly told Hugh what Mr. White had said. "Will you go with me tomorrow?" asked John. "I don't even know where the bank is."

"Um," said Hugh, thinking, "no—because Howard is coming tomorrow. He's coming on the late train so he will probably be contacting me about that time. I should stay home in case he calls or comes by."

"Oh," said John, sitting back down at the table and feeling a little disappointed.

"But the bank is down at the bottom of Front Street. It's easy to find," said Hugh. "You can go while I wait for Howard and then tell me about it when you get home. I'll ask Mrs. Bingley to make us a supper of cold cuts. That way you can eat when you get home so she doesn't have to wait for you, and then we can go up to the Club with Howard on Saturday."

"Yes," said John, "unless Mrs. Whitman knows who I am. Then I might have to go find my family instead."

"Well, I hope she has answers for you," said Hugh, "though it's been fun having you around, and I've been looking forward to you going up to the Club with me and Howard and to introducing you to my brothers and sister."

"I would like that," said John. He did want to visit the Huron Mountain Club since it had been the scene of his accident. "Maybe I can still go. We'll just have to wait and see." But waiting was so hard. He had so many questions he wanted answered, and now it seemed like they might be answered, but to wait until five o'clock tomorrow to find out was extremely hard.

"Come on; I thought we were going to go play catch," said Hugh.

"Okay," said John, and he followed his friend outside.

About four-thirty the next afternoon, after a day spent with Hugh reading more of *A Connecticut Yankee in King Arthur's Court* and then helping him pack some things to go up to the Club, John headed to the First National Bank to meet Peter White, and hopefully, get answers about his true identity.

Hugh had told John that Mr. White's bank was at the bottom of the hill on the right. It was several blocks down Front Street. John stared at the old sandstone storefronts as he walked downhill, feeling déjà vu again about the experience. Just as he reached the bottom of the hill, he crossed the street to the bank's side when out of the corner of his eye, he noticed the building across the street. "Getz's Clothiers—Grand Opening" proclaimed a large banner across the storefront. *Hmm*, John thought. *If I had any money, I would go in there and buy some clothes so I wouldn't have to wear Hugh's.* But he realized he had no money, and no job. If Mrs. Whitman didn't recognize him and take him in as one of her grandsons, he wondered how long the Allens would let him live on their charity. Would they or maybe Mr. White help him find a job so he could support himself? He wasn't even sure what he could do. Did he have any skills? Could he go work in the nearby mines or on the docks? Certainly, college was out of the question; he might be Hugh and Howard Longyear's age, but he did not have the money their parents had. But he didn't have to think about that yet; hopefully, Mrs. Whitman could help him, and if not, going up to the Club tomorrow might give him the answers he sought.

John had now arrived at the large sandstone bank on the corner of Front and Spring Streets. He walked up the few steps and opened the door, then stepped inside. In the lobby were a couple of men making deposits before the business day ended.

First National Bank, corner of Front of Spring Streets

"Sir, we are about to close," said a young man, calling to him from a teller's window.

"I'm here to see Mr. White," John replied. "He's expecting me."

"I'll see if he's available," the young man replied. "Your name, sir?"

"John."

"And your surname, sir?" the man asked.

John tried to think how to reply—he didn't want to risk being thrown out for not knowing his own last name—but fortunately, a door in the back opened right then and Mr. White stepped into the lobby.

"Oh, John!" he said. "Perfect timing." Hat in hand, he looked ready to depart for the day.

"Good night, Mr. White," said the teller, seeing that his employer knew the stranger.

"Good night, Fred," said Mr. White, putting on his hat as he crossed the lobby. "I trust," he said to John, "you found your way here without any problem."

Lobby of the First National Bank

"Yes, sir," John replied. "Hugh gave me good directions." He stepped forward to open the door for Mr. White.

"I'm always glad when Friday comes," said Mr. White, crossing the threshold. "Not that the bank isn't open Saturday, but it's only a half-day, and at my age, I can usually afford to stay home, even though something always seems to need my attention."

"I can well imagine," said John as they stepped outside.

"Now," said Mr. White, turning to climb the hill, "Mrs. Whitman lives just off Front Street a few blocks past Ridge. We should have time to talk to her before dinner. Hopefully, we'll catch her at home since she doesn't have a telephone. She must be pushing eighty now and probably doesn't believe in such new contraptions. If I weren't a businessman, I wouldn't mind doing without it myself. Today, people can just ring you up and bother you at all hours of the day and night, even after business hours. It can become a bit tedious."

"I understand," said John, feeling like he'd had the same thought at some point.

"I've known Mrs. Whitman nearly fifty years," said Mr. White as they walked past Getz's. "She wasn't one of Marquette's first settlers, but came a few years later. It's amazing how Marquette has grown since those early days—such progress." He looked about him at the three-story buildings lining Front Street. "It's amazing really.

And while I know I had a big hand in building this city and creating all of its success, sometimes I do hanker for those early days. Why, when I was your age, all of this hill was just a bunch of trees. My house was the first built up on the Ridge and that wasn't until 1868. There were just a few houses, a machine shop, a forge or two, and a couple of stores those first years. The post office was run out of Amos Harlow's house, and the church services were held in houses too, and, of course, the Indians had their wigwams. Back then, they lived right down here along the lakeshore with all of us Americans."

"Really?" said John. "I would have liked to have seen that."

"Some of the best sleep I ever got," went on Mr. White, pausing a second to tip his hat to acquaintances as he passed them—and it seemed almost everyone was his acquaintance—"was sleeping on the ground in Charley Kawbawgam's wigwam in those early days. His wife could cook a fine venison stew, let me tell you. Nothing fancy like these French cooks some of my neighbors have these days, but when you're an eighteen-year-old boy who's been paddling on Lake Superior for hours, you don't want any of that namby-pamby food. You want some good old meat."

John's stomach curdled a bit. He didn't think he'd ever tasted venison—it didn't sound too appealing. He knew hunting had always been a big pastime in the U.P., but it seemed like the younger generations were largely content to get their food…at the grocery store. He had a sudden flash in his mind of a long aisle in a store, with a row of glass doors—the freezer section. *Where did that thought come from?* he wondered.

"Are you all right?" asked Mr. White since John had nearly come to a standstill.

"Yes, I—I just didn't want to get hit by that wagon trying to get across the street before the streetcar comes," said John. They were now at the corner of Washington and Front and the streetcar was turning to cross before them.

"I don't blame you," said Mr. White. "Those things still make me nervous. I suppose I could ride one home, but I walk up this hill every day regardless—other than in winter sometimes when it's too slippery—but in the summer I walk up it—it's good for my health."

Once the streetcar had moved past them, they crossed the street and continued up the hill, past the Union National Bank and the Presbyterian and Baptist Churches, until they reached the top. John saw the Methodist Church on the corner and commented, "I feel like I've been in there, or I have some connection to that church."

"You do?" said Mr. White as they walked past it. "That might be a good sign. The Whitmans and Brookfields were among the founders of that church. Mrs. Whitman's mother, old Rebecca Brookfield, she was a staunch Methodist, trying to convert everyone in Marquette's early years. Can't say I was ever too fond of her, but I liked her husband, Lucius. He had a good sense of humor, and he was a hard worker too. He was well into his sixties when he came to Marquette, and he worked in the forge with Amos Harlow. Funny, they seemed like really old people to me then, but I'm probably several years older now than they were back then."

John felt like these names were familiar to him—Lucius and Rebecca Brookfield. Could they be his relatives? He hoped Mrs. Whitman could tell him.

"Almost there," said Mr. White, turning left down a side street. "It's that house on the other corner."

They walked down the block, John admiring all the old-fashioned homes. Well, they were probably relatively new, built in the last decade or two, but for some reason, he felt they were old-fashioned. In another minute, they arrived at a fairly modest two-story home with an iron fence around the yard.

Mr. White turned up the walkway, then stepped onto the porch and knocked on the door.

"I hope she's nicer than Mrs. Smith," John couldn't help saying.

Mr. White turned and smiled at him. "I guarantee she will be," he replied.

They could faintly hear someone moving about inside. Mr. White seemed patient. After all, he had said Mrs. Whitman was about eighty.

After another minute, Mrs. Whitman opened the door. She was the stereotypical old lady, a bit tall but somewhat bent over, with her gray hair in a bun and a long dark dress. *Bugs Bunny*, thought John. He had an image of an old woman he was sure he'd seen in a Bugs Bunny cartoon—whatever that was.

"Why, Peter!" she said. "I never would have expected to see you."

"Hello, Cordelia," he replied. They obviously knew each other well. "How are you?"

"Oh, still kicking," she said. "I was just thinking it would be nice to have some company. Won't you come in?"

"Thank you," he said. "I've brought a guest with me, as you can see."

"Hello," said Mrs. Whitman, turning to look and smile at John.

"Hello, Mrs. Whitman. It's a pleasure to meet you," he said, putting out his hand for her to shake. "My name is John."

She didn't take his hand—maybe her eyesight wasn't good enough to see it, or maybe Victorian old ladies didn't shake hands? Instead, she turned and walked down the hall.

"Let me get us some tea," she said. "Go have a seat in the parlor. It won't take me but a few minutes."

"Oh, we don't want to trouble you," said Peter.

"Nonsense," she replied. "I always have tea around four, but I'm afraid I must have dozed off. Why, it's already past five," she said, staring at a clock in the hall. "I'll just put the water on to boil."

"All right," said Peter, and removing his hat, he led John into a little parlor off the hall while Mrs. Whitman disappeared into a kitchen at the back of the hall.

Mr. White took a chair and John seated himself on the sofa. John felt awkward, not knowing what to say, but Mr. White drew his attention to a collection of photographs on the mantelpiece.

"That's Cordelia's family," said Mr. White. "See if any of them look familiar to you."

John got up and walked over to the mantle. There were several photos, but he didn't see anyone in them he recognized. One fellow in a big bushy fur coat looked like a wild man. "Who is this?" he asked, pointing to the picture.

"Oh, that's her brother," said Mr. White, standing up and walking over to him. "I can't remember his name now. He was an Indian scout and everyone thought him dead for years, and then he showed up out of the blue one day with his son. His son married Cordelia's daughter, Edna. They live out West somewhere. Oh, this is Edna and her husband," said Mr. White, looking at a photo of a man and woman together. "Hmm, I don't see any of Jacob and Agnes, though. Jacob was Cordelia's son—the one I said died. And Agnes, his wife, was the Hennings' daughter. The Hennings are the ones who built the Smith house."

"Yes, I remember," said John. He wasn't likely to forget any of these details since they might help solve the mystery of his identity.

"The water will boil in a few minutes," said Mrs. Whitman, returning into the room. "I'll hear it when it does."

She sat down in a chair and said, gesturing toward the mantle, "That's all of my family."

"Yes, I was just telling John who they are," said Mr. White, returning to his chair. John wanted to linger by the photographs, but he didn't want to be rude, so he sat down on the sofa.

"I just got a letter from Edna yesterday," said Mrs. Whitman.

"How is she doing?" asked Mr. White.

"Fine. Busy, of course."

"And how are her children?"

"They're fine. The boys are all grown now, you know, but Celia's only eleven. She's the youngest."

"Where have the years gone?" asked Mr. White.

"You tell me," said Mrs. Whitman.

Mr. White sighed, then said, "Cordelia, we've come to visit because John here has a dilemma that we were hoping you might be able to help us with."

"Oh, well, I'll be happy to help if I can," she replied.

"It's rather a difficult situation to explain," said Mr. White.

Mrs. Whitman gave John a puzzled look. John waited for Mr. White to explain further, but when he did not, John told her, "You see, I've had an accident. I hit my head, and now I'm having difficulty remembering things. I'm not even sure that John is my real name."

At that moment, the kettle whistled.

"Oh, hold that thought," said Mrs. Whitman. "I'll be right back."

John waited in silent agony as she struggled to her feet and then plodded her way to the kitchen. Then he looked at Mr. White and frowned.

"It's all right," said Mr. White. "Just be patient."

"I'm trying," said John, half-whispering, "but it's hard. Obviously, I'm not her grandson or she would have recognized me."

"That's true," said Mr. White.

At that moment, someone knocked on the front door.

"Oh, who could that be?" shouted Mrs. Whitman from the kitchen.

"I'll get it for you, Cordelia!" Mr. White said.

He stood up and stepped into the hall. John remained seated, continuing to feel uncomfortable.

A second later, John heard a female voice exclaim, "Oh, Peter White! I mean, Mr. White. I—I apologize, sir; it's just I didn't expect to see you. You gave me the shock of my life!"

"I'm sorry," said Mr. White. "Are you looking for Mrs. Whitman?"

"Yes, please," said the female visitor. "I didn't know you were a friend of hers, Mr. White."

"I've known Cordelia for years," said Mr. White. "Won't you come in? She's in the kitchen making us tea."

John heard the door close, and then a young woman appeared in the parlor doorway.

"Who is it?" Mrs. Whitman shouted from the kitchen.

"It's Margaret, Mrs. Whitman!" the girl shouted back. "Margaret Dalrymple. My mother sent me over with some strawberry preserves she made for you."

"How sweet of her. I'll be right there," said Mrs. Whitman. "Do you want to stay for tea, Margaret?"

Margaret turned to look at Mr. White, as if unsure, but when he smiled encouragingly at her, she called back, "Yes, please!"

"Have a seat. I'll be right there!" Mrs. Whitman replied.

"Come into the parlor, Miss Dalrymple," said Mr. White.

"Thank you, sir," she said.

John stood up as Margaret entered the room. He wasn't sure why, but it seemed the proper thing to do. After all, she was a young lady—maybe in her mid-teens.

"Miss Dalrymple, this is my friend John," said Mr. White, introducing her.

As Margaret approached him, she raised her hand and held it in front of John's face.

John was surprised by her movement, but then he half-laughed, realizing what she expected, and taking her hand, he pressed it to his lips. Margaret giggled. "Oh, a gentleman," she said.

"Please, be seated," said John. He waited until she sat down on the sofa beside him, and then he also sat down.

"Well, I never thought I'd be having tea with Peter White!" Margaret gushed.

Mr. White had just returned to his chair when Mrs. Whitman entered the room, so he popped back up—rather quickly for a man his age. John followed suit, wanting to show his manners, although he felt all this bobbing up and down for the ladies was a bit tiresome.

"Let me help you with that," said Mr. White, stepping over to take a heavy tray from Mrs. Whitman. It contained a teapot and four teacups. "Allow me," he said, placing it on the coffee table.

"Margaret, will you pour please?" asked Mrs. Whitman.

Margaret scooted to the sofa's edge and reached for the teapot. She filled each teacup and handed them around.

"I left the preserves on the table in the hall," Margaret told Mrs. Whitman.

"Please thank your mother for me," said Mrs. Whitman.

"So, how do you two ladies know each other?" asked Mr. White.

John was wondering the same thing and also why he felt like he knew Margaret.

"I've known Margaret since the day she was born," said Mrs. Whitman. "She was born in my boarding house."

When John looked at Margaret, he saw her cringe.

"I helped to deliver her," Mrs. Whitman continued.

"Mrs. Whitman!" Margaret exclaimed, as if the old woman had said something indecent.

"Mr. White knows the facts of life," said Mrs. Whitman. "And I'm rather proud to say I had a hand in bringing such a pretty young lady into this world."

"My parents do have a nice, elegant home now," Margaret said to Mr. White. "The boarding house was just temporary when they first moved to Marquette."

"I know your father," said Mr. White. "He has a loan with my bank."

Margaret looked like she wanted to crawl beneath the sofa at this revelation of her family's financial situation.

"Oh, Margaret, don't take things so personally," said Mrs. Whitman. She turned to Mr. White and said, "Margaret likes to give herself airs, but she's really a good girl."

Margaret grimaced and then sipped her tea so that the cup would hide the embarrassment showing on her cheeks.

"Now, young man, I'm afraid I forgot your name," said Mrs. Whitman to John, "but please continue with your story."

"I'm John," he told her.

"I've always liked the name, John," said Margaret. "It's such a strong, noble-sounding name. Just like in that novel by Mrs. Craik, *John Halifax, Gentleman*."

John ignored this superfluous declaration and continued. "As I was saying, I've been having some memory issues. I can't seem to think of my last name. I'm sure I'm from Marquette, but I'm not sure who my family is."

"Oh my," said Mrs. Whitman. "That must be rather frightening for you."

"Yes," said John.

"John seems to think," Mr. White said, "that he has some connection to Gerald and Sophia's old house, but when we went there,

Carolina Smith…well, she didn't know him at all, so that made me wonder if he might have some connection to your family, Cordelia. Obviously, he's not one of your grandsons, but…."

"No," said Mrs. Whitman. "I just saw Will and Clarence yesterday—those are the only grandsons I have in Marquette. Will would probably be close to your age, John. My other grandsons, Edna and Esau's boys, all live out West. I haven't seen them for a few years now. And I'm afraid, John, I don't think I've ever seen you before."

"That's what I was afraid of," said John, frowning, and then he sipped his tea to hide his disappointment.

"It's so romantic, though," said Margaret. "Not to know your own identity—it's just like something out of a novel."

"What do you remember?" asked Mrs. Whitman.

"Nothing too…too definite," John replied, not thinking he should share his grocery store freezer section memory, much less that of the cartoonish old-lady. He really wasn't that surprised that she didn't know him. He was becoming more and more convinced that he had somehow time traveled to 1900. If only he could remember what year he had come from….

"Mr. White," said Margaret, suddenly changing the subject. "Do you know Howard Longyear? I just saw him downtown. He came in on the train."

"Yes, I know Howard," said Mr. White. "I heard he was coming home from out East this week."

"Howard goes to college out there," Margaret said, turning to John. "He's very smart—and very handsome and only a few years older than me, but I do think a husband should be older than the wife anyway; don't you agree?"

"I…I hadn't really—"

"Do you go to college?" asked Margaret, cutting him off.

"I—I'm afraid I don't know," said John. "But I've been staying with the Allens. Hugh Allen is a good friend of Howard's. We're going up to the Huron Mountain Club with Howard tomorrow."

"Ooh, you're so lucky," said Margaret, her eyes glowing. "Howard is so rich too. The Longyears live in the finest house in Marquette. I hope to be invited to a ball there someday."

Mrs. Whitman laughed and looked at Mr. White, who ignored Margaret's indirect disparagement of his own fine home.

"The Longyears do have a big house," said John, remembering Hugh showing it to him.

"If you get to go inside of it," said Margaret, "tell Howard that your friend Margaret would like a grand tour of it. It's got dozens and dozens of rooms. It's the grandest, most elegant home in all the Upper Peninsula. Oh, I would give anything to see the inside of it."

"I'll mention it to Howard if I get a chance," said John.

"Oh, then I'm sure he'll invite me," said Margaret, "because he's such a gentleman, I'm sure."

"In case you haven't figured it out," Mrs. Whitman told John, "Margaret is sweet on Howard."

"Oh, Mrs. Whitman!" exclaimed Margaret. Upset to have her obvious secret revealed, she jumped to her feet, tipping her teacup and slightly splattering her dress. "Oh, I have to get home to supper now!"

"Oh, Margaret, don't run away," said Mrs. Whitman. "I was just teasing you a little."

"No, I really must go," Margaret replied. "But I don't think it's at all polite to make such common insinuations about the most eligible bachelor in Marquette. I simply respect Howard because he's a college man now."

"I see," said Mrs. Whitman, struggling to keep a straight face.

Mr. White stood, made a little bow to the lovesick girl, and said, "It has been a very great pleasure to meet you, Miss Dalrymple."

"The honor has been all mine, Mr. White," she replied and curtseyed. "Wait until I tell my mother I had tea with the Honorable Peter White."

John also stood up, but he did not say anything, hoping to avoid a repeat of the hand-kissing.

"Be sure to thank your mother for the preserves," Mrs. Whitman said as Margaret showed herself out.

"I will!" Margaret called over her shoulder as the door shut behind her.

Mrs. Whitman smiled. "That girl," she said, shaking her head and staring at Mr. White meaningfully as he resumed his seat.

"She's still young," said Mr. White, returning to his seat. "And she is pretty. Give her another year or two and I'll bet she turns the heads of plenty of young men, maybe even Howard Longyear himself."

"She's sixteen now," said Mrs. Whitman. "If she doesn't have sense yet, I'm not sure she ever will, but she is a good girl. She obviously likes young gentlemen, but I am sure her mother raised her right, so I don't worry about her getting herself into trouble."

John suddenly felt a little dizzy. Was it the green tea? Maybe he had stood up too fast when Margaret left. Why was he still standing?

He felt déjà vu again, like he had met Margaret Dalrymple before. Or was he just feeling disappointed that he wasn't Mrs. Whitman's grandson?

"So, I guess you can't help me," he said, sitting back down and addressing Mrs. Whitman.

"I wish I could," said Mrs. Whitman. "It must be very difficult not to remember who you are, but don't give up hope. Someone in Marquette will know who you are. It's not that big of a town; almost everyone knows everyone else here. I don't get out as much as I used to, so I don't know many young people anymore, Margaret being an exception, so don't be too disappointed that I don't recognize you."

"Well, thank you for your time, Cordelia," said Mr. White, getting to his feet.

"I'm sorry I couldn't help," Mrs. Whitman repeated, struggling to get up from her chair.

"No need to see us out," Mr. White replied, "but thank you for the tea. I'd stay longer, but Mrs. White hates when I am late for supper."

John braced himself and stood up, glad to see that his feet felt stable under him. Being a gentleman overcame any concern about his health, so he said to Mrs. Whitman, "Let me carry this back into the kitchen for you," and he collected the teacups and set them on the tray, then he carried it down the hall, setting it by the kitchen sink.

"Thank you!" Mrs. Whitman called after him, surprised by how quickly he had moved.

John returned a few seconds later.

"Ready, John?" asked Mr. White.

"Yes, sir," he replied.

By now, Mrs. Whitman had gotten to her feet. "Thank you both for coming. It's always a pleasure having callers. Feel free to stop by any time. Like I said, I don't get out much anymore, so I always enjoy having company."

"I don't know what John's future holds," Mr. White replied, "but I'll be sure to come by and visit you again soon, Cordelia. There aren't many of us left who remember those first years in Marquette, so we need to stay in touch."

"That's too true," said Mrs. Whitman. "The only other person I see from those early days now is Mrs. Montoni."

"Thank you again, Mrs. Whitman," John said, giving her a little bow.

"You're welcome, and good luck to you," Mrs. Whitman replied.

She walked them to the door and stood there until they had walked out of sight.

Chapter 7

"That was disappointing," John admitted once he and Mr. White were back on the sidewalk and out of Mrs. Whitman's hearing range. "I was hoping she would know me."

"I know," said Mr. White, "but think of it this way—every possibility you eliminate gets you closer to the answer."

"I hope that's true," said John, frowning over how difficult it all was.

"Don't be so down in the heart," said Mr. White. "Perhaps you're too young to realize how many ups and downs there are in life, but in the end, let me tell you, it's all a great adventure. Even the bad things help to shape whom we become, as you will realize when you look back at them later. Someday you'll be grateful for this experience. Why, when I was your age, I had nothing but the coat on my back. I was eighteen when I came to Marquette, and all I had was a determination to make something of myself. Before I knew it, I was helping to build a city, running the post office, founding a bank and an insurance agency, and selling real estate. Just imagine where you might be in ten or fifteen years. You might own a bank yourself."

"I don't want a bank," said John. "I just want to find out who I am and whether I have a family."

"Don't worry," said Mr. White. "That will happen. If it hasn't yet, it's only because there are things you're meant to learn from this experience."

"I hope that's true," John repeated, but he thought it easy for Mr. White to spout off platitudes when he had never lost his memory.

"Trust me, far worse things can happen than losing your memory. Try having three of your children all die within the same week."

John nearly stopped as he turned to stare at Peter White's face. "You mean...?"

"Yes, three of my children—they all died in the same week in 1873, of diphtheria. Morgan was twelve. Sarah was nine, and Mark was three. All three died between April 25 and May 2. My niece also died that week. You have no idea the pain and anxiety and horror my wife and our other daughters went through during that time. We'd already lost our son Kirtland as a baby in 1872. He was just shy of eleven months. My two remaining daughters, Frances and Mary, grew up and married and had children, but Mary died just four years ago. She was only thirty-seven. Of my six children, only one is still alive. So yes, I know what pain is, and I also know that despite it all, there is a God with a reason for everything we go through."

"I'm so sorry for your loss," said John, seeing the pain written across Mr. White's face. "I don't think I could go on if I had a child who died. I wish I had your faith."

"Sometimes you have no choice," Peter White replied. "You can choose to have faith, or you can choose to despair. In any case, young man, I suggest you see your current predicament as an adventure rather than give way to despair. Even if things seem upside down right now, they will turn around eventually. Be patient and persevere. There's a favorite poem of mine by Henry Wadsworth Longfellow you should read called 'A Psalm of Life.' The last stanza is:

> Let us, then, be up and doing,
>   With a heart for any fate;
> Still achieving, still pursuing,
>   Learn to labor and to wait.

For me, that pretty much sums up what life is about. Laboring until God tells us it's time to do otherwise. On this earth, there isn't time to do much other than labor. Some days just trying to survive is a labor, like it might seem to be for you right now, but there can be no harvest unless the labor takes place first." Mr. White paused and took a deep breath. "Well, I've lectured you long enough. Here we are back at your friend's house, and I understand you're going up to the Club tomorrow with Howard Longyear, so perhaps that is why you didn't get the answers you sought today. They may come to you tomorrow at the Club, and if not, there'll be a reason for that too. In any case, I wish you all the best."

"Thank you, Mr. White. I do really appreciate all your interest in me."

"Being interested in our fellow humans is what we're supposed to do," said Mr. White. "Isn't that what Jacob Marley told old Ebenezer Scrooge? I may be a good man of business, but ultimately, 'mankind is our business.'"

"That sounds familiar," said John.

"Good. If you know your Dickens, I'd say there's hope for you yet." Mr. White smiled and tipped his hat.

John extended his hand. "Thank you, sir. I do feel better."

"You're welcome. It was my pleasure to try to help," said Mr. White, and then he crossed the street and headed home.

John had barely stepped inside the door when Hugh came tearing down the stairs into the front hall.

"Where have you been?" he demanded. "I didn't think you'd ever get home."

"I went to see Mrs. Whitman," said John, surprised by his reaction.

"I know. I just didn't expect you to be gone so long," said Hugh. "Did you get any answers?"

"No," said John. "She never saw me before."

Hugh frowned. "Too bad," he said, "but no time to worry about that now. Howard wants to get an early start in the morning, so we're going to go spend the night over at his place. Come upstairs and help me finish packing. We're going to have supper with him too and should have left by now."

Ten minutes later, the boys were carrying a couple of huge satchels down the street. They turned when they got to Cedar Street and then again at Arch until they reached the gate into the massive property of the Longyear Mansion.

John, who already knew the Longyears had a large home, was not at all ready for the sight before him now that he was so close to it. The mansion was situated on the middle of the hill, just above the main slope, and nestled among a landscaped and terraced yard that sloped down toward the lake.

"Wow," said John. "It's like a palace almost."

"I know," said Hugh. "Wait until you see the inside."

The Longyear Mansion

Hugh led him through a small pedestrian gate, but John also noticed a larger gate made for vehicles that opened out of a curved sandstone wall. From there, the driveway split with the left leading to the basement service entrance under a terrace on the west side of the mansion while to the right the drive led to the covered front porch.

John felt overwhelmed just walking up the driveway toward the porch. The entire house was three stories tall, and John was not even that surprised when Hugh told him it contained an elevator. Because the mansion took up an entire block, every side of it had been built to be a front façade. Numerous chimneys jutted out of the roof. On one side was a stone arched area for cars to drive through to drop off guests. Its roof was covered to prevent anyone having to disembark in the rain or snow. A tower stood on the other side of the arch, which John later learned enclosed a playroom for the children. The whole house, built of raindrop sandstone native to the Marquette region, was elegant. Adding to its dignity were shrubs and vines growing up the tower, and trees and flowers galore. Hugh pointed out where a twenty-five-foot marble drinking fountain would soon be installed.

"It's like the home of an English lord!" said John.

"Almost," said Hugh.

John almost expected to be greeted by a line of servants in black, the women wearing white aprons. Where had he seen such an image? He did not think he'd ever been to England himself. The house did seem somewhat familiar to him, but it was so awe-inspiring that he could not imagine he had ever lived in it himself.

Hugh was just about to go through the arch to knock on the door when someone shouted, "Hugh! Over here!" Looking to the right, John saw a young man about his age in a suit jacket. He was tall and slender but strong-looking and waving at them.

"Howard!" cried Hugh, elated to see his friend. He rushed over to the porch and climbed the stairs, and soon the two friends were giving each other a hearty hug. John followed Hugh, but waited at the bottom of the steps while Hugh said, "It's so great to see you, Howard! It's been months."

"I know," said Howard, his hand on Hugh's shoulder. "But we have all summer now to go camping and enjoy ourselves, and then in the fall, we'll go to Cornell together."

"I hope so," said Hugh, "but let me introduce my new friend, John."

"Hello," said Howard as John came up the stairs. Howard extended his hand and said, "Welcome. I understand you're going up to the Club with us."

For a moment, John took in Howard's blue eyes and curly brown hair and felt a bit overwhelmed by the boy's handsome face and obvious charisma. He liked him instantly and could see why Hugh practically hero-worshiped him.

"Yes," said John, "it's very kind of you to let me go with you."

"Of course," said Howard, squeezing his hand before letting go. "We can always use another paddler."

"Paddler?" said John.

"Yes, we'll go up in my canoe tomorrow morning," said Howard. "It's a long trip—about ten or eleven hours, so we want to leave early, like 7 or 8 a.m."

"Okay," said John, wondering if he was up to that much paddling. But he was not going to argue; he had no other way to get up to the Club, and he dearly wanted to find out if being there would trigger memories that might give him answers to his identity.

"As I said on the phone," said Hugh, "John had an accident up at the Club and can't remember who he is. We're not even sure his name is John."

Howard Longyear, circa 1898

"Do you remember anything?" asked Howard.

"Not much," said John. "I have fleeting images in my mind. I feel certain I'm from Marquette, but I can't remember my family or where I grew up. A lot of things look familiar to me, but others seem different, and I have no idea why I was up at the Huron Mountain Club."

"No one up there recognized him," added Hugh. "Dad and I brought him to Marquette to see Dr. Dawson, but he seems to think John is fine physically. He doesn't know how to help his memory."

"Interesting," said Howard, looking curiously at John. "I don't know if you know this, but I'm a Christian Scientist, and we believe the body is capable of healing itself. If you can't remember something, then you must be blocking your memory for some reason, perhaps to protect yourself. I'm sure there is a way to gain it back. Do you have a headache?"

"No, not really," said John. "The first day after I woke up—Wednesday I think—I sometimes felt a little dizzy or had a slight headache, but yesterday and today I've been feeling fine."

"Headaches are easy to cure," said Howard. "Usually it just has to do with massaging your temples a little or changing your thoughts."

"What about regaining memory loss, though?" asked Hugh.

"That may be a bit more challenging, but I'm sure it can be done," said Howard. "We can consult Mary Baker Eddy's works."

"Who's that?" asked John.

"The founder of Christian Science. She's written many books on health and wellness and spirituality. Health all has to do with trust in God and our connection to the divine. I'm sure there are answers in her books, though we may not have time to look for them before we head up to the Club, but my mother is up at the Club. I'm sure she will know what to advise."

"Do you really think so?" asked John.

"Yes. If she doesn't, she'll find the answer. If she has to, she'll contact Mrs. Eddy herself to get it for you. But come inside now; supper is ready and I'm starving."

Howard turned and patted Hugh on the shoulder as a way to urge the boys into the house. John willingly followed, not really sure he understood or believed in the Christian Science philosophy Howard was spouting, but the young man's charismatic positivity appealed to him.

John felt even more encouraged when he stepped inside the mansion to see the finest and most elaborate furnishings he could imagine. He stopped and stared, finding it hard not to say, "My gosh."

Howard and Hugh were already across the room, but Hugh stopped and turned back. "Are you coming?"

"Yes," said John, catching glimpses of silk-covered sofas, expensive rugs, and gold-framed pictures. "I just never saw a living room like this."

"Living room?" said Howard. "This is the sitting room."

"Oh," said John. "Like a parlor?"

"I guess," said Howard, "but we call that the drawing room. This room is less formal, just for the family. The drawing room is on the other end of the house."

"There's a reception room, too," said Hugh. "Howard can give you the tour after supper."

"Come on; I'm starving," said Howard, again turning and leading them into a hallway.

The hall had a room off of its right, which Hugh said was the breakfast room, and then they passed a staircase and entered a large, octagonal-shaped room that was two stories high and capped by a huge dome. "Wow!" said John.

"Isn't it beautiful?" said Hugh.

Longyear Mansion main entrance

"Yes," said John. "It's like something you would see in a library or courthouse."

"It's Tiffany glass," said Howard of the glass dome, which was decorated in a beautiful floral pattern of yellow, blue, and green glass that reminded John of Easter and spring.

"I could spend all my time just in this room," said John, looking around at the ferns and the arched walls of the second floor.

"Well, not right now, though," said Howard. "Dinner is served."

John had to force himself to stop staring at the ceiling so he could follow Howard back into another bit of the hall before they entered the dining room, which, being built into a side tower, was a hexagonal shape.

A long table greeted them, with place settings for three on one end. Howard took his place at the head of the table with Hugh and John each sitting to his side. Only after John sat down did he realize they were not alone. A butler—John thought that's what he must be—came forward to pour drinks for them, and two young women came in bringing plates of food.

"Nothing fancy I'm afraid," said Howard.

John thought it plenty fancy. It was some sort of steak, as well as mashed potatoes with gravy, and peas and carrots.

"We have a chocolate soufflé for dessert," said Howard.

The boys were asked if they wanted coffee, water, or lemonade. They all agreed to lemonade since it was summer and too warm for coffee.

"We usually have more elaborate meals," Howard said, as if apologizing for the meager fare, "but it being summer and my family being up at the Club, some of the servants have time off, and I didn't want to trouble them too much since we'll only be here this evening."

"It's more than plenty," said John, appreciating Howard's good manners and obvious desire to please just as much as he appreciated the free meal.

Once the servants had departed, the boys began to eat while Howard questioned John more on his memory loss. Hugh explained that they thought John might have been struck by lightning, though John said he thought he would remember that if it had happened.

"Then why were half of your pants and shirt gone?" Hugh asked.

"I don't know," said John, although he felt so overly warm in the clothes Hugh had given him that he suspected he was used to wearing less heavy and cumbersome garments. He had images of people wearing far less clothing in his head, though he couldn't remember the correct terms for the garments he envisioned. Sometimes he wished they would all quit asking him questions when he had made it clear he didn't have answers to them.

But Howard was struck by the novelty of John's situation and continued to question him.

"Do you believe in God?" asked Howard. "I know it may be an unexpected and personal question, but I am a firm believer, and being a follower of Christian Science, I know illness is just a symptom of a spiritual problem."

"I haven't thought much about God," said John, "other than wishing he would give me back my memory."

"He will," Howard replied, "but you have to help him by figuring out why it may be blocked."

"I told you Howard was smart," Hugh interjected. "He knows so much. He just has a different way of looking at things than most people."

John could see that, but he wasn't sure he liked the idea that his memory loss might be his fault.

"So what have you been doing lately, Hugh?" Howard asked, changing the subject.

"Oh, just enjoying the summer. I've been showing John around town. We started reading *A Connecticut Yankee in King Arthur's Court* together. It's funny because the main character, Hank Morgan, gets hit on the head and kind of loses his memory and is transported to Camelot—kind of like John—at least the getting hit on the head part—he's had a bit of a concussion."

Howard smiled and said, "John, you're not from the future like Hank Morgan, are you?"

"I doubt it," said John, not wanting Howard to think him crazy.

"It would be amazing, though," Howard said, "to travel through time like that. Imagine how we would benefit if someone from the future came and told us about things that had yet to happen, or what technology they will have then. Can you imagine what the future will be like a hundred years from now? Perhaps we will have time machines then like in H. G. Wells."

"That would be cool," John admitted.

"Cool?" said Hugh. "Are you cold? I think it's warm in here."

"No, I mean 'neat.' I would like that."

"Neat?" said Hugh. "The whole house is clean."

"Of course it is," said John. "I'm sorry. I'm not making much sense."

"Yeah, your words seem confused," said Hugh. "Are you sure you're feeling all right?"

"Maybe I still do have a bit of a concussion," said John to cover for his more modern slang—somehow he knew the words he had spoken were called slang. "My head does kind of hurt a little."

"Do you need to go lie down?" asked Howard.

"No. I'm okay. I'm just talking too much," said John. "Once I eat, I should feel better." John turned his attention to his plate, deciding it was best if he not say much more until he got to know Howard better. He didn't want to be thought crazy, especially if Howard was going to bring him up to the Huron Mountain Club.

"Howard, what would you do if you could go to the future?" asked Hugh.

"I don't know," said Howard. "It's hard to imagine being in the future. I think I'd rather go there than the past, though, but if I did go to the past, I'd be like Hank Morgan and try to help people with the knowledge I had from the future, and if I went to the future, I'd want to come back to this time to help people with what I had learned."

"But…" John found he couldn't keep his mouth shut at this remark, "but wouldn't you be afraid that you might change the past?"

"That's exactly what I would want to do," said Howard. "To make things better. Life was a lot harder a hundred years ago than it is now."

"But what if you messed up something?"

"Like what?" asked Howard. "How could I? Say I went back to 1800. I would know more than most people then, so I could make things better. I could warn them about—oh, all kinds of things. If I went to 1865, I would warn Abraham Lincoln not to go to Ford's Theatre, for instance, or in 1871, warn the people of Chicago about the fire, or for that matter, warn people in Marquette about the fire from 1868 that burned down the town. Imagine the lives I could save. Imagine if I knew how to build an automobile and went back in time and taught people how to do it a whole century before they were invented."

"I don't know if that would do much good," said Hugh. "My father says automobiles are a passing fad. No one in Marquette even has one."

"But if you did that," John told Howard, "you would disrupt industry."

"I would improve industry," said Howard. "Why, automobiles are only in their infancy. Think how much better they will be a hundred years from now. Why, they'll probably be able to drive themselves then."

"That's a scary thought," said Hugh.

"And think also about all the things we could learn that have been lost. What if I went to June 1, 1870, just days before Charles Dickens died. I could ask him how he planned for *The Mystery of Edwin Drood* to end so it wouldn't be left unfinished. Or what if I could go way back to Ancient Egypt? Think about the things we could learn that the Egyptians knew but that have been lost to us."

"Like what?" asked Hugh.

"Like all kinds of things. Like how they built the pyramids. I've always been interested in ancient cultures and languages—just imagine all the lost writings that haven't come down to us. Think of the Bible—there are books referenced in it that have been lost. What if I could go back and get copies of those books and bring them to the present? Just think how the world would be different today if all that knowledge hadn't been lost."

"Yeah, but who could read those books?" said Hugh. "They'd be in an ancient language."

"I could read them," said Howard. "I'm good with languages. You know that, Hugh. I can write sentences in twenty-three different languages, including hieroglyphics and cuneiform."

"Really?" said John, finding that hard to believe.

"I can," said Howard. "They might be simple sentences, but I'm proficient with languages, and anyway, I would ask some rabbi in ancient Israel to teach me how to read the language so I could translate it when I brought it back to twentieth-century America."

"You seem like you've thought of all this before," said Hugh, impressed with his friend.

"Not really, but I am interested in languages like I said," Howard replied.

John thought Howard seemed like a very bright young man. He was intelligent but also likeable because he was enthusiastic about what he knew rather than simply trying to show off. John could see why Hugh liked him. As Hugh and Howard continued to talk, John began to wonder if he had any friends he was as close to as Hugh and Howard seemed to be. He tried hard to remember anyone he might have known. Now and then in the last few days, he had seen faces in his mind that seemed familiar to him, but he couldn't quite place who they were. One face kept recurring, the large face of a young man about his age, a man who looked big and strong, but not necessarily intellectual. John felt like he knew this man well, though he looked nothing like him, so he figured it must be a good friend, not a brother or his father or anything. He could not for the life of him bring up an image of his father or mother. A couple of female faces kept appearing, though. One of a girl a few years younger than him who might be a sister, but the other seemed closer to his age, like maybe a girlfriend. He wished he could remember. It would be so nice to have a girlfriend, even better than a smart best friend.

"I told you how smart he is, didn't I, John?" Hugh said, interrupting his thoughts.

"Yeah," said John, realizing he had missed part of the conversation.

Howard smiled. "John, you look like you're really tired."

"I am," said John. "I was hungry, but now that I've eaten, I feel like I need a nap."

"Don't you want a tour of the house first?" asked Hugh as Howard rang the bell for the servants to collect the dishes.

"We'll have dessert now, Franklin," Howard told the butler.

"Very good, sir," Franklin replied and departed again.

"I don't really need dessert," John was about to say when the maids returned with plates of chocolate soufflé that John knew he could not resist.

As John ate, he felt like he was drifting asleep, but he enjoyed the soufflé regardless.

Once dessert was over, Howard offered to give them a tour of the house. John willingly followed, all the while longing for a bed, but nevertheless, he was impressed by what Howard told him was Chippendale furniture and Ming vases, plus the family portraits and the overwhelmingly massive size of the house. Finally, when they were upstairs, Howard said, "This is one of the guest rooms. It has two twin beds. Do you two want to sleep in the same room?"

"Sure," said John. "Then we can be sure we're both awake in time."

"We'll get up at six," said Howard. "It takes about ten hours to get up to the Club by canoe, so if we leave about seven-thirty or so, that will give us a little extra time in case the waves are rough and it's harder-going. Then we'll be there in time for supper."

Six a.m.? John thought that sounded horrible, but he was too tired to argue.

They said goodnight, and soon John was crawling into bed.

"I'm so glad you're here, John," said Hugh, as he turned off the light. "I think Howard really enjoyed talking to you."

"Really?" said John. "I enjoyed talking to him."

"He likes you; I can tell," said Hugh. "He doesn't warm up to too many people because so many people are shallow and unintellectual, but I think he's really fascinated by your predicament."

"He and I both," said John, "but hopefully I won't have a 'predicament' much longer. Hopefully I'll find answers up at the Club."

"I hope so, John," said Hugh. "Whoever you really are, I'm sure I'll still like you. Well, good night. We'll have lots of time to talk tomorrow."

"Good night, Hugh, and thanks for everything."

Chapter 8

THE BOYS WERE UP JUST after 6 a.m. They dressed and ate, and by a little after 7 a.m., they were ready to head down to the harbor.

They each had a satchel with some clothes and other personal items. Howard also had a box of flowers to bring his mom to plant at their cabin at the Club.

Howard led them down the driveway, then turned west rather than east toward Lake Superior.

"I thought we were going to the harbor," said John, thinking they should go down the hill to the lake.

"We'll take a shortcut down the Hundred Steps," Hugh explained as they followed Howard.

The Hundred Steps? Where had he heard of that before? John didn't know, but he thought it best just to follow along. He found himself enjoying the early morning sunshine. Everything looked bright, fresh, and summery, and the large Victorian houses in the neighborhood could have been taken from an idealistic Americana painting. John felt like he knew this world well, and yet he didn't since it had never before been quite the picturesque perfection it was this morning. As they walked along Cedar Street, he asked Hugh who lived in each house, so Hugh rattled off the names of the Joplings and then the Kidder family on the corner of Ridge. Across the street, John recognized Peter White's house and Hugh explained Mr. White's son-in-law's parents, the Shirases, lived next door. But there was no time for a proper tour, for Howard was moving with the speed of a gazelle despite his arms being loaded with his satchel and mother's flowers. The other boys briskly followed him. They knew they had a long day ahead of them if they were to get to the Club in time for supper. John was glad they had sandwiches in their satchels since supper was a long time off.

Soon they came to Spruce Street and then crossed Ridge and walked down a path between two houses—one belonging to the horrible Carolina Smith—and to a giant wooden staircase that extended all the way down to the road that wound along the harbor.

"Boy," said John, "whoever built this staircase sure had his work cut out for him. I can see why it's called the Hundred Steps."

"It's a great timesaver," said Hugh, "so you don't have to walk all the way over to Front Street to get down to the harbor."

"It's a heck of a hike up, though," said Howard, calling over his shoulder as he led the way down the stairs.

John felt elated by the view of the lake breaking through the heavily leafed maples, oaks, and various bushes thickly rooted along the hillside. Even though the trees mostly blocked his view, John still found everything beautiful this morning, especially since he felt oddly hopeful he would soon know who he was. It would be too late when they arrived at the Club to trek to Mount Huron where he had been found, but in a little more than twenty-four hours, he would be there and, hopefully, his memory would be jogged; every second that passed now he thought might be bringing him closer to answers. Maybe just the sight of the cabins at the Club would trigger his memory.

"Do the two of you regularly canoe to the Club?" he asked his new friends.

"Yes, we do it every summer," said Hugh.

"And it's about a ten-hour trip?" asked John. "You must be strong paddlers."

"We are," said Hugh. "Well, I'm fair anyway, but Howard is on the rowing team at Cornell. You should feel his muscles. He's as strong as Hercules."

Howard laughed. "I wouldn't go that far. Maybe just as strong as Theseus. Anyway, Hugh will be trying out for the rowing team this year, so he'll soon catch up with me."

"I hope I make the team," said Hugh.

"We'll practice a lot this summer to get you ready," Howard promised.

"It sounds wonderful," said John, "to spend the summer rowing on the lake."

"Well, you're welcome to join us," said Howard, almost halfway down the Hundred Steps now with Hugh and John each about half-a-dozen steps behind.

"Yeah, even if you find out who your folks are," said Hugh, "I want us to stay friends."

"What if I'm—well, working class and have to work?" asked John. "I don't know if I'm the kind of guy who goes to college."

"You thought you did before," said Hugh. "And you seem smart."

"I feel like maybe I do go to college," said John. "But I'm sure I never went out East."

"I think you must go to Northern Normal," said Hugh. "If we don't find answers for you at the Club, we'll go talk to President Kaye—he's the president at the normal school."

"What's the normal school?" asked John, who recalled Hugh mentioning it before, but he wasn't really clear what it was.

"The teacher's college!" said Howard. "Northern Normal. It just started up in Marquette last year. They're still constructing the buildings north of town."

"Hmm," said John. He wished he could remember. The name Northern seemed familiar. "What do you study at school, Howard?"

"Forestry mainly," Howard replied. "My father owns a lot of land, and as the oldest son, I'll end up managing it all someday, so I want to learn the best way to use our resources. Plus, I love being out in the woods."

"Sounds like a good idea," said John. "I love being in the woods too."

"Perfect," said Hugh. "You'll have to go camping with us this summer."

John liked the thought of that. Whoever he was, he hoped Hugh and Howard would stay his friends when he found out. He hoped his family had the resources to allow him to live the life these boys did, but he realized they were ultimately very privileged. Few people had the kind of wealth Howard Longyear enjoyed, and even Hugh had a fine home. John had seen some of the smaller houses in Marquette, and for all he knew, his family lived in one of them, or were farmers rather than having business interests like Hugh and Howard's fathers.

Soon they were at the bottom of the stairs and making their way along the harbor. John felt in awe of the giant wooden docks and all the industrial chaos of the lakeshore. He took in everything from the boats to the railroad cars and the dock workers as they walked past them. Not far from one of the docks stood a little boathouse, and once they arrived in front of it, Howard drew out a key and unlocked the door. Then Howard and Hugh entered the building and started to pull out a canoe. It was green, and John was surprised to see it was made of canvas, though he wasn't quite sure why he was surprised. Thinking the canoe looked like a giant pea pod, he had to repress a smile.

"Grab that end," Hugh told John, who quickly followed directions. He marveled at how light the canoe was. He wondered whether it would be able to support the weight of three college-age boys.

Once they had the canoe clear of the door, they set it down while Howard locked the boathouse.

"John, grab it and we'll slide it down into the water," said Hugh.

John did as he was told, with Hugh helping to push the vessel. Meanwhile, Howard picked up his box of flowers and carried it down to the shore. Once they were at the lake's edge, Howard told John and Hugh to get in the canoe while he held it. Hugh took the flowers from Howard and set them in the canoe's center before he got in the front. Then he told John to sit in the middle since it was more important to have the best paddlers in the front and back and John was a bit unsure how strong a paddler he would be. Once his two friends were seated, Howard pushed the canoe into the water. Then he hopped in the back when only a few inches of the canoe still touched the beach. Once inside, all three boys got their paddles in hand and pushed against the sandy bottom of the lake to launch themselves forward.

In a few seconds, they were floating offshore. They swiftly began paddling to avoid getting too close to the docks or the other boats out in Iron Bay.

"We're going to head toward the breakwater!" Hugh called over his shoulder to John. "Then we'll paddle around it and out into open water."

"Okay," said John. He felt like he had easily gotten the rhythm of paddling, although Howard and Hugh's paddling was clearly stronger and may have been compensating for any weakness on his part. He was amazed by how quickly they made it around the breakwater, but once they had gotten past it, the waves grew stronger.

"The water's kind of rough," said Hugh.

"Yeah," said Howard. "It's going to be a tough forty miles."

Forty miles, thought John. *My arms are going to fall off before then.*

But they didn't have to paddle too hard. John was surprised by how quickly they were moving through the water. Before long, they were coursing around Lighthouse Point, which was sort of at the bottom of Ridge Street, where a red lighthouse looked out over the bay. John was struck by how tall and majestic the lighthouse looked from out on the lake.

"Is any of this familiar to you, John?" Hugh called over his shoulder.

John gazed at the tree-lined shoreline, but he did not recognize anything. There was little to see other than the natural surroundings—beautiful pines, maples, oaks, and birches rising up along a sandy shoreline. Once they were past the lighthouse, any evidence of the city quickly disappeared. But soon they were coming up on some giant rocks out in the water.

"No," John finally replied. "I don't remember all these rocks at all."

"We call them Picnic Rocks!" Howard shouted. The wind was making it a little hard to hear now.

"Let's go out into the lake a bit more so we don't hit them," said Hugh, although the wind itself seemed to be blowing them away from the rocks.

John could not get over what a deep blue the lake was, or how the canoe rocked about in the waves. He had to focus on paddling to keep them from floating off course, but he found he was enjoying the experience. He was sure they must have gone a couple of miles already. Forty miles might not be so bad after all.

"How long will it take again to get there?" John asked, hoping he misremembered what they had told him.

"We'll be there by sunset," Howard said.

"Sunset!" exclaimed John.

"Yeah, three miles an hour is about average," said Howard. "Perhaps a little more if the waves cooperate, but longer if they don't."

"I thought you said we'd be there in time for supper?"

"Well, supper leftovers more likely," said Hugh, "but don't worry. We have plenty of food in our satchels."

John did the math—three miles an hour divided into forty miles was…just over thirteen hours.

"What time is it now?" he asked.

"About ten minutes to eight," said Howard after looking at his watch.

"We won't get there until nine o'clock then!" John exclaimed.

"That's still a good hour before the sun really sets," said Howard.

Gee whiz, thought John. *Haven't any of these people ever heard of a motorboat?* Then he realized the question was really: How had he heard of a motorboat? He wondered if they would stop for a lunch break, but he didn't dare ask. He didn't want to complain. He'd paddle for two days if it meant finding out exactly who he was. He just hoped his arms didn't fall off before they got to the Club.

Soon they were paddling out into Lake Superior to make it around Presque Isle Park. "Mr. White got the government to give the city this park," Hugh told John. After a few minutes, they skirted around the breakwater. Some people were out walking on it and waved to them and they waved back. A minute later, they were passing by the tall imposing cliffs on the park's east side.

The waves were picking up now, a strong wind coming from the west, and the boys ceased talking, needing all their energy to make it around the little peninsula the locals called "The Island." John did not need to have all this explained to him—somehow he knew it instinctively. He was sure he had spent many a day on Presque Isle; he had never seen it from the shoreline—at least not since he'd lost his memory—but he recognized it regardless.

"We have to get out farther to avoid the Black Rocks!" Howard shouted to John and Hugh a few minutes later. The wind was blowing hard now, making the boat roll up on substantial waves and then down into a gulf again. Some of the water was splashing into the canoe, and for a minute, John was a little afraid they would tip over. He saw the Black Rocks off to the right—they were hard to miss since they were like a large plateau dock jutting out into the lake. While the rest of the island was covered with trees, the Black Rocks were exposed and apparently volcanic so that nothing grew on them. John momentarily wondered why they were so bare, but then he had no time to think further about it. The waves were becoming brisk and difficult to thwart, and every muscle in his body seemed to be straining itself to paddle the canoe as spray began to assault his face.

"Keep going, boys!" shouted Howard as they slowly tried to force their way around the Black Rocks. The wind was growing stronger now, and while they were heading west, the wind was blowing against them, fighting their every stroke, slowly pushing them backward.

"The wind's too strong!" cried out Hugh, and then suddenly, a great gust came up and shot them backward into a roaring wave.

John felt the canoe tipping sideways as a wave came over its side, but somehow they righted themselves, and for a moment, he felt relief that they were safe, but then he heard and felt a horrible jarring sound.

"Ouch!" he shouted, for he could feel something poking from beneath his feet.

"Watch out!" warned Howard.

And then there was a sort of grating sound.

"We hit the rock!" Howard yelled.

The wave had washed them right up onto the edge of one of the Black Rocks. They started to turn sideways, riding up the wave, but when the wave withdrew, it left them for a second in mid-air; then suddenly, the canoe tipped forward, causing them to plunge into the lake and the canoe to flip over.

For a moment, John was too stunned to realize what had happened. Then he found himself underwater. Although he felt panic coursing through him, he knew if he could get to the rocks, he would be safe, so with all his might, he pushed himself upward to the water's surface.

Once he broke the surface, John shook his head to get the hair out of his eyes, and then he opened them. The canoe was there, right in front of him, still capsized. He looked around and saw Howard about six feet in front of him.

"Flip over the canoe!" Howard shouted. "I'll go find Hugh!"

John did what he was told. He didn't know how he knew what to do, but fighting against his internal panic, he managed to flip the canoe over, as if it were second nature. It had some water in it, but that could be dealt with later. It would still float for now. It didn't seem to be damaged in any way. With great skill, John pulled himself into the canoe, and he was relieved to find one of the paddles had been trapped inside it. He quickly grabbed the paddle and started heading toward Howard.

Where was Howard? He had seen him a second ago, but now he didn't see him anywhere.

"Howard!" he screamed. "Howard, where are you?"

A few seconds later, John saw a head above the water and started paddling toward it. He wasn't sure if it was Howard or Hugh, but he was coming to their rescue.

"Howard!" he cried.

"Over here!" a voice shouted. It was Howard. But he had his back to John. Why didn't he turn around and swim toward him?

John paddled with all his might, and in a few seconds, he had breached the gap between them, which had somehow grown to fifty feet.

"Howard!" he shouted as he came up behind him.

"I can't find him!" cried Howard. "Help me look!"

"What do you mean?" screamed John, suddenly letting the panic overtake him. "Where is he?"

"I don't know!" cried Howard. "Hugh! Hugh!"

John began paddling in circles, trying to look in every direction. Then he saw Howard go under.

"Howard!" he screamed. John jumped to his feet, which almost tipped over the canoe. He struggled to regain his balance and fell back into the canoe. He wanted to get out, to dive into the lake, to try to find Hugh and Howard, but whenever he tried to stand up, he fell back into the canoe as the waves continued to wreak havoc with it. Finally, he was able to sit up and get the paddle back in the water.

"Howard!" he cried, suddenly seeing Howard surface.

"I don't know where he is!" cried Howard. "Oh, please, God, where is he?"

"Howard, get in the canoe!" John shouted, and he frantically began paddling toward him.

Howard was screaming Hugh's name and spinning in circles, swimming and diving underwater and making John very nervous that he would lose sight of him again. After a minute that seemed like an hour, John managed to poke Howard in the back with his paddle. Howard was too frantic to listen to him, but he felt the paddle and spun around, grabbing onto it, apparently hoping it was Hugh before he realized what it was. He grabbed the paddle so hard he nearly yanked it from John's hand until John screamed, "Howard! Get in the canoe!" Then John began to move the paddle up in his hands until he was close enough to grab Howard's hand and firmly place it on the side of the canoe.

"Get in the canoe!" he again ordered Howard.

"I have to find him!" Howard screeched.

"We can see better from inside the canoe," John replied. He leaned down and began to pull at Howard's shirt to try to get him into the canoe.

"Hugh! Hugh!" screamed Howard one last time before, probably out of exhaustion, he let John half-lift him into the canoe.

"Help me," John demanded, and finally Howard pulled himself up into the canoe, rolling into it really, and collapsing into the puddle on the bottom of it. But he only lay there a second before he was up and screaming Hugh's name again.

"I don't see him anywhere," said John. "We have to go get help."

"What?" asked Howard, not understanding.

"Howard, there's the other paddle," said John, spotting it about twenty feet away and quickly paddling toward it. "Grab it, Howard!"

Howard was beginning to regain his senses now. He saw the paddle and reached for it.

"Where is he?" Howard cried out as he began to paddle with John.

"I don't know," said John. "We have to get help. Quick. We'll paddle back to the breakwater." He started to turn the canoe around in the direction the wind was blowing. Howard didn't help paddle or even seem to know what John was doing. He just kept staring out at the lake and shouting "Hugh!"

The wind was blowing so strongly it sent the canoe speeding along the lake in the direction the boys had come from. John knew if Hugh had gone under, he would be drowned by now, but he hoped the waves had somehow driven him to the shore. It was only a few minutes before they came around the side of Presque Isle and saw the breakwater again. When the people on the breakwater saw them and waved again, Howard half stood up and began screaming, "Help! Help! Man overboard! Help us!"

What happened next was afterwards largely a blur for John. The men on the breakwater quickly moved into action, one running to the beach where there was a boat. Another ran to the caretaker's house where they sent up the alarm. John and Howard paddled back toward the Black Rocks to find the caretaker on the other side of the island launching a boat. They soon were joined by a group of sailors—later John would learn it was Captain Cleary's Life-Saving Team. Several other boats from the Lower Harbor made their way to the area to search.

But after several hours, all hope of finding Hugh Allen alive had died.

The grief and agony that followed cannot be described. Howard sent word to his parents at the Huron Mountain Club, who personally went to the Allens' cabin and gave them the bad news. Mr. and Mrs. Allen and their three remaining children returned to Marquette with the Longyears that evening in Mr. Longyear's boat, *The City of Marquette.*

Searches continued for several days to find the body. The incident had happened on Saturday, July 7, but not until a week later, on July 14, was Hugh's body found between the Black Rocks and Middle Island Point. Mr. Allen was in the boat with those who found Hugh.

John and Howard were among the many who attended the private memorial service for Hugh at the Allen home. Mr. Allen had told John he was welcome to continue to stay with them, but John felt it best not to intrude on the family's privacy. The Longyears were kind enough to let John stay with them during all this time. Howard promised he'd still get John up to the Club, but no one was in the mood to go again until after Hugh's memorial service.

Devastated by the loss of his friend, Howard also realized his own life was nearly lost, and he repeatedly thanked John for saving him. "I would have drowned if you hadn't made me get in the canoe," he said. "I would have worn myself out with exhaustion from trying to find Hugh." He then broke down into a torrent of tears while John wrapped his arm around him. Howard cried out, "Why? Why did God have to take him?" "I don't know," was all John could say. Once Howard wiped his tears and drank some water to relieve a throat sore from sobbing, he was calmer and said, "I know he's with the Lord. I know death is just a transition into another form of life and someday I'll see him again, but I will miss him so much until then, and now his poor family has to go on without him."

John did everything he could to comfort Howard. He had not known Hugh well, but he had grown to really like him in the few days they'd spent together, and he recalled how Hugh had hoped their friendship would continue.

Despite their grief, John found himself growing fond of the Longyears. As he got to know them better, he found himself fascinated by Howard's wealthy, entrepreneurial father, appreciative of his kind mother (though she did talk too much about Christian Science and was prone to giving him unlikely solutions for healing his memory loss), and Howard's friendly brothers and sisters. There were five other Longyear children—Abby was a year older than Howard at twenty, Helen was fifteen, Judith thirteen, John Jr. (Jack) ten, and Robert Dudley (Rob) was four. While they had all known and liked Hugh, they could not sit and mope all day, so they enlisted John in their sedate games and many conversations. Howard and John even finished reading *A Connecticut Yankee in King Arthur's Court* together in the evenings.

Finally, on Monday, July 23, three days after Hugh's memorial service, the Longyears decided it was time to return to the Huron Mountain Club for the week. Howard, however, refused to take the canoe. "I'll go back on the water eventually, but not yet," he said. And so the entire family went up in Mr. Longyear's boat, *The City of Marquette*.

During these two weeks between Hugh's drowning and the trip to the Club, John often felt like he was in a haze. He wanted to get answers to his dilemma, but he did not want to pressure anyone, and sometimes he felt so comfortable with the Longyears that he almost forgot he was not part of their family or that any mystery existed about who he was. Still, he knew he could not live on their charity forever. The morning they set out for the Club, he decided if he did not find answers there, he would look for a job in Marquette so he could support himself, even if it that meant just living in a rented room in a boarding house.

"My dad will find you a job in one of his businesses," Howard told John when John expressed his intention to Howard.

"No," said John. "Your family has already done more than enough for me."

"Nonsense," said Howard. "You're smart; he could make you a clerk. Do you have good penmanship?"

"I don't know," said John.

"Let's see," said Howard, and he told John to write out a sentence on a piece of paper, and then Howard wrote the same sentence. John's penmanship looked terrible by comparison. It looked more like printing than the beautiful cursive flourishes of Howard's hand. John didn't think he'd ever been taught to write like Howard did. It was all the more reason he wanted answers to his situation.

He began to think again that somehow he did not belong to this time. Traveling up to the Club on *The City of Marquette* added to this belief. He could not believe how long the trip took, although four-year-old Rob was delighted by how fast they were going, and Mr. Longyear said they were making good time. John wondered why he felt so impatient. Was the journey really that slow, or did he just want answers?

Longyear Cabin

Chapter 9

WHEN THEY REACHED THE CLUB, John was rather surprised. He had expected rustic cabins, but instead, he found a large wooden clubhouse and a cluster of numerous log cabins around it along the banks of the Pine River. The Longyears' cabin, though certainly no mansion, was larger than many a house in Marquette, save for those along Ridge and Arch Streets. It was two stories with an upstairs that jutted out over a porch and contained several bedrooms. *If this is roughing it*, John thought, *I'm not going to complain.*

John was given a room to share with Howard and his younger brothers, Robert and Jack, who were a little rambunctious given their age and excitement to be up at the Club. Howard was still feeling very melancholy after losing Hugh, but he tried not to let it affect his siblings' fun. They had also known Hugh, but they had not been close to him like Howard.

They were all tired by the time they got to the Club, but Mrs. Longyear, with the help of Abby and Helen, fixed a simple meal for everyone. Mr. Longyear built a bonfire, and they spent the early evening watching the sunset. Not long after dark, they all agreed they were ready to turn in. Soon John found himself in bed, exhausted yet unable to sleep in anticipation of visiting where he had been found unconscious a few weeks earlier. So far, the Huron Mountain Club had not triggered any memories for him, but he was hopeful that would change when Howard brought him to Mount Huron tomorrow. When John finally did fall into a restless sleep, his dreams were filled with half-remembered people and places that looked nothing like what he had been experiencing in 1900 Marquette.

John woke early, but only because it was impossible to sleep for long in a cabin full of Longyears. The younger kids were up and running about with the dawn. Even though John heard Jack telling Rob to try to be quiet as he got dressed, Rob refused and soon was shaking John, wanting him to get up and go outside to play with him. Rob was adorable, but John didn't know how the family kept up with his four-year-old energy. John was just crawling out of bed when Howard entered the room. He had apparently been up for quite a while.

"Breakfast will be ready in a few minutes," Howard said. "How'd you sleep?"

"Not too well," said John. "I'm anxious I guess."

"I don't blame you," Howard replied. "I got up early and went to talk to Santinaw, the guide who was with the Allens when they found you. He said he can guide us to where you were found."

"Can I go too?" asked Rob.

"No, I'm afraid not, buddy," said Howard. "It's several miles away. Too far for you to walk."

"Really?" said John. "I'm surprised I would wander so far from this little village of cabins."

"Mount Huron is a bit of a hike," said Howard. "But if we set out after breakfast, we should get there well before lunch. We'll pack a basket to bring with us."

"Great," said John. "I really appreciate it. I can't thank you enough."

"Rob, come on now," said Howard, reaching out and taking his little brother's hand. "Let's give John his privacy so he can get dressed."

"All right, but I want to sit next to John at breakfast," Rob replied, letting his big brother lead him out of the room. Middle brother Jack quickly followed them, leaving John alone. He looked out the window to see it was a sunny summer day, but whether it would turn out to be a beautiful day for him remained to be seen.

A few minutes later, John joined his hosts at the table. He was still wearing the clothes Hugh had given him when he first came to

Marquette. Howard had given him a clean nightshirt and he had bathed while at the Longyear Mansion, but he had not wanted to ask for new clothes—he felt he was imposing on the family enough—and they had all seemed too distracted by Hugh's drowning to think of getting him anything new to wear.

Interior of the Longyear Cabin, Huron Mountain Club

The moment John came to the table, Howard looked him over and said, "You can't wear those clothes out hiking. You'll sweat to death. I have some clothes I can loan you. We're about the same size, I'd say."

"Thank you," said John, feeling he should protest, but he was so warm he didn't have the heart to do so.

Abby and Judith both asked him how he had slept, and Rob kept trying to get him to eat more. Mr. and Mrs. Longyear, who had taken an interest in his memory issues, asked if being at the Club was triggering any fresh memories for him. John felt nervous and claustrophobic from all the questions. At the Longyear Mansion, the family was rarely all gathered together except at meals, but here, even though the cabin was large, they were all packed together into the room. He was relieved when breakfast was over and the family all started picking up after themselves—"camp style" as Mrs. Longyear called it. "Although we have servants," she said, "I wasn't raised with them, so it's kind of a relief to wait on ourselves once in a while."

"I understand," said John, who didn't mind at all carrying his dishes to the counter. He was about to offer to help wash them when Howard said, "Come to my room, John, and we'll get you some better clothes."

"Okay," said John and followed him upstairs. Once there, Howard pulled out a light shirt from his dresser and some less formal pants that looked like they'd been on many a hike.

"These will do," Howard said. "Hurry up and change. Our guide should be here any minute."

The words were hardly out of Howard's mouth when Mr. Longyear shouted upstairs, "Howard, Santinaw is here!"

"Hurry up," Howard repeated and left John alone in the boys' bedroom.

John was beyond grateful to rid himself of the hot shirt and jacket he'd been wearing. If he'd had to go hiking wearing a jacket, he probably would have died of heat exhaustion before he ever reached Mount Huron. He was glad to see these Victorians were not completely unreasonable, even if a bit repressive, in their clothing choices.

In less than two minutes, John had shed the clothes Hugh had given him and put on Howard Longyear's duds. Then he reappeared in the kitchen.

"You look like you could climb the Alps now," Abby remarked.

"Thanks," said John.

"Howard is outside," Mr. Longyear told him.

"Okay," John replied. "Thank you again for breakfast. I guess I'll see you all later."

"Yes, we'll see you by suppertime I'm sure," said Mrs. Longyear. "Good luck with trying to remember something."

"Thank you," said John, and then he joined Howard outside. He found his friend waiting with a bushy-bearded, middle-aged man who looked part Native American.

"John, this is Henry, but we all call him Santinaw. His last name is really St. Arnold, but he's part French so pronounces it Santinaw."

"I'm pleased to meet you, Santinaw," said John, giving the man a handshake and feeling like he was meeting Grizzly Adams—where had that name come from?

"You don't remember me?" Santinaw asked.

"No," said John. "I think I was completely unconscious, but I'm grateful to you for finding and rescuing me."

"When we found you, you opened your eyes and muttered some words," said Santinaw, "so I thought you might remember."

"No, I'm sorry, but I don't. Do you remember what I said?"

Santinaw shook his head. He was a big, strapping fellow. John could see the gray in his beard and thought he might be sixty, but he doubted Santinaw's age had given him any trouble in helping to carry him back to the cabins, even if it had been a few miles.

"Anyway, I'm very grateful," John said.

"Glad you're better," said Santinaw.

"Well, let's get going," said Howard.

"Howard!" Mrs. Longyear called, sticking her head out the door.

"What?" Howard asked, sounding annoyed.

"You forgot your lunch." She held out a big picnic hamper to him.

"Jumping Jehoshaphat, Mom! There's enough food in here for an army."

"Well, hopefully for three men anyway," she replied. "You all have a good time." She nodded at Santinaw, who nodded back to her. "Be careful too," she added. "After you boys nearly drowned, I don't need any more close calls."

"We'll be careful, Mom," Howard said, tears springing to his eyes as he remembered Hugh's loss.

"Poor boy," said Santinaw as Mrs. Longyear returned back inside. John and Howard knew he was referring to Hugh, and sadness descended on all of them at the thought of their lost companion.

"Well," said Howard, after a moment, "let's get going. It's a long walk."

They traipsed off toward the woods on a well-trodden trail, but by the time Howard and John finished talking about how they wished Hugh were there with them, the trail had faded into nothing. John soon realized he could easily get lost in these thick, wooded hills, but Santinaw, who was leading the way, clearly knew where they were going.

The boys talked among themselves as they trekked through the woods. Santinaw did not say much. He was friendly enough, but John realized this woodsman had little in common with him and Howard. John wondered what it was like to be part Native American, part French-Canadian, and work as a wilderness guide—and to work for rich white people who entertained themselves by escaping to the woods away from their mansions, banks, and real estate businesses.

It was a pleasant day for a hike. Only about seventy degrees and not overly humid. The shade from the trees kept them cool despite their physical exertions. It was a long walk, but John was enjoying being outside.

"I wish life could always be like this," he told Howard. "I love being in the woods. I think I feel better today than I have since I lost my memory. I think the woods are the reason."

"Nature is definitely invigorating," said Howard. "Being in God's creation has healing properties. Hugh loved to be out in nature. Perhaps his spirit is here with us."

"I hope so," said John.

"You don't seem anxious now about seeing where you were found," said Howard.

"Maybe I am a little," John replied. "I just hope it triggers some memories in me, but I'm starting to worry less about that. I feel like if the answers are meant to come, they will. The last few weeks have been kind of frustrating, but today, somehow I feel like I'm on the right path."

"I know Hugh told you this before," said Howard, "but I want to reiterate it. Whoever you turn out to be, John, I hope we can still be friends. I've grown to be rather fond of you."

"Thanks," said John. "I've enjoyed getting to know you too. You've been very kind. Hugh sang your praises before I ever met you, and I'm really honored to be friends with someone so thoughtful, intelligent, and good-natured."

"Thank you," said Howard, choking on his words a bit. "I miss Hugh so much, but it helps that you remember him too, so I don't want to lose you also."

"We'll stay in touch, no matter what I find out," John replied, hoping that would somehow be possible.

"What do you think you'll do once you figure out who you are?" asked Howard, clearing his throat to compose himself again.

"I guess that depends on who I am," John replied.

"I know one thing," said Howard. "Now that Hugh is gone, I'm going to do everything I can to be the best person I can be. Hugh had his whole life before him, so I'm going to value every moment I have and try to make it up to him by succeeding at things he won't be able to do."

"If anyone can do that," said John, "I know you can. I think you were Hugh's hero, Howard—like the big brother he never had."

"Thanks," said Howard. "I just want to make Hugh proud now, wherever he is."

"You will," said John.

They walked in silence for a while then, both boys pondering what the future might be while Santinaw led the way.

The hike was becoming a bit more difficult since there was no trail, but the gorgeous day made it feel effortless. The sun was shining, the trees were at their peak of green summer lushness, and not a cloud could be seen. John wondered if heaven might be a great, untouched forest in Upper Michigan.

Santinaw began to be more talkative now, drawing their attention to a porcupine that scurried up a tree to avoid them. Then he told them stories about some of his hunting trips. Finally, he said, "We're almost there. Just around this bend."

They followed Santinaw around a clump of birches and then past some underbrush. Suddenly, Mount Huron rose before them.

"It was over this way we found you," said Santinaw. He led them around the bottom of the hill, slowly half-climbing it in a somewhat circular fashion. The terrain was a bit rocky, so the boys had to go a little slower to keep their balance, but Santinaw went up the hill effortlessly. They were nearly to the top when he stopped and pointed.

"Right there," Santinaw said. John saw a little outcropping of rock on the hill, more like a ledge that dipped down than a true ravine. It was not far from the mountain's summit, twenty feet or so. John walked over to investigate it.

"Let's go to the top, Santinaw," Howard said. "There's a great view from up there."

Santinaw followed Howard up the mini-mountain, both of them realizing John might need a moment alone to try to remember anything.

John looked about the place where he had been found, but he could recall nothing. "I must have been unconscious by the time I got down to this point," he muttered. He saw nothing to jar his memory—just dirt, rocks, moss, little saplings, and berry bushes.

"John, the view is wonderful. Come on up!" shouted Howard.

John frowned, disappointed that nothing was coming back to him. He felt for a moment like he was going to cry—the earlier feeling that he was on the path to discovery had deserted him. He instantly felt a deep anxiety and fear that he might never know who he really was.

"Come on, John!" Howard shouted again.

"I'm coming!" John called. He turned and started up the mountain, realizing his last hope was that the view from the summit might trigger some memory.

He was just beginning to see the summit when Howard exclaimed, "Hey, what's this?"

John reached the top of the mountain in time to see Howard bend over to pick something off the ground. "It looks like some sort of rock," said his friend.

John was too far away to see the object.

"Santinaw, what is it?" Howard asked, handing the object to him. "It's like slate or something."

"Looks like some strange black glass," said Santinaw upon turning it over. "I've never seen anything like it before." Holding it seemed to make him nervous, so he handed it back to Howard.

"It looks like something man-made, but how?" asked Howard. "It's so unusual."

John was beside him now and could see Howard was looking at the flatter side of the rectangular object.

"There's a couple of circles on it," said Howard. "I think this one's made of glass, like it's a button or something." He tried to press it but nothing happened. "What do you think it is, John?"

He passed the item to John, who now saw it clearly for the first time. As the object touched his hand, John instantly felt like he was going to vomit. The long, black object, about five or six inches long and two to three inches wide, sent off a jolt in his brain that caused him to jerk back his head.

"Are you all right?" Howard asked him. "Did it give you a shock?"

"No," said John, shaking his head. "I...I remember."

"You do?" said Howard.

"I know what this is," said John. "It's...it's...."

But he stopped. How could he explain? How could he ever make them believe this was a type of telephone? It looked nothing like the telephones they knew.

But it was a telephone. It was his cell phone!

"Oh, my God!" he exclaimed as a flood of relief and surprise washed over him.

"What is it?" asked Howard, impatiently.

But John ignored them. He was pressing the button on the back. Howard had tried to press the camera lens, not the actual power button. "Yes!" John shouted as he turned it over and saw the screen light up. The battery hadn't died yet. Look at that—22 percent charged, even after nearly three weeks of just lying out here in the middle of nowhere. "Oh, my God!" he repeated.

"What is it?" Howard repeated.

"Just give me a minute," said John, not wanting to be distracted. "It's all coming back to me." He pressed an icon on the screen that opened up the app for his contact list. He quickly scrolled down the list, but too fast because the scroll bar flew to the end of the list, so he had to backtrack. There it was—"Mom." He could call Mom. He remembered his mom, and he remembered his dad. His parents were John and Wendy—John wasn't his name; it was his dad's name. His name was—he was Neill Vandelaare! Neill Vandelaare! And his parents were John and Wendy Vandelaare...and he had a sister too, Madeleine. They must all be beside themselves with worrying over him.

Neill pressed the little phone icon to dial his mother.

"No network available," popped up on the screen.

"No," he muttered and tried again.

"No network available."

"There's no signal," he said. "But how could there be?"

"What are you talking about?" asked Howard.

"There can't be any signal," Neill said, although he knew Howard wouldn't understand. Howard had never heard of a cell tower. How would he have? How could there be a signal in the year 1900 when the technology to make a cellular phone call didn't exist yet? Not only could Neill not make a phone call, but he wouldn't be able to text his parents or send them an email. This phone was useless to him.

Neill had all the answers he had sought now. He knew who he was. He remembered he had been living in 2021, working at the Huron Mountain Club for the summer, when he'd lost his memory. He had been born in 2002 and was nineteen. And somehow he had been transported back to the year 1900. And now he had no way to get back to his own time, and he missed his family and friends and....

It was all too much. He felt like he was going to break into tears.

Embarrassed, Neill turned away from Howard and Santinaw, and while staring at the phone, at the name "Mom" on the screen, he walked a few feet forward across the top of Mount Huron.

He nearly collided with something, just seeing it dimly above the line of his phone. Looking up, he asked, "Hey, what's that?"

An oblong stone balanced on two other stones stood before him.

"It's a dolmen," said Howard. "No one knows how it got here."

Neill felt intrigued by it. Who could have built it? The slab of rock on the top must weigh hundreds of pounds. Who could have lifted those rocks to put them in place?

Neill reached out to touch it, and….

Now it was Howard and Santinaw's turn to shout, "Oh, my God!"

Neill had vanished.

Part II

Chapter 1

"WHERE AM I?" ASKED NEILL when he opened his eyes.

"Oh, you're awake," said a woman. "You're in the hospital."

Neill turned toward the voice and saw she was dressed in light blue scrubs and reviewing some sort of chart by a sink. She must be a nurse or doctor.

"How did I get here?" he asked.

"You had an accident," she replied, walking over to the bed. "How do you feel?"

She looked at some sort of monitor rather than at him as she spoke.

"I—I feel fine," said Neill. "What happened? Why am I here?"

"We don't know what happened," she replied. "You were found lying out in the woods at the Huron Mountain Club. The doctor thinks you were struck by lightning."

"Oh, my God. This can't be happening," Neill muttered. He felt like Bill Murray in the movie *Groundhog Day*.

"What year is it?" he asked.

"Oh, my," she replied. "Are you having memory issues? I better go call the doctor."

"No, it's okay," Neill replied. "But what hospital is this?"

"UP Health System."

"Oh, yeah," he said.

"You know where that is?"

"Sure," he said. "It's in Marquette, Michigan."

"That's right. Do you remember the year now?"

"Two thousand and…Two thousand and…twenty?"

"Close enough," she replied. "It's 2021. Do you remember that?"

"Yes," he said.

"Do you know who the President of the United States is?" she asked.

"Yes, Joe Biden."

"Good," she said.

"What day is it?" he asked.

"Sunday, July 25."

Neill thought for a moment. It had been July 24 when he had gone to the dolmen, so it made sense he would wake up the next day, though today would be a Wednesday in 1900. It had been a few days before the Fourth of July when he had first traveled to 1900. If three weeks had passed since then, he clearly hadn't dreamt all of it.

"Um...." He felt awkward saying so, but he needed to be alone to think. "I have to use the restroom."

"All right," she replied. "Let me just remove these."

She pulled back a blanket covering him, and he saw some giant Velcro-like pads wrapped around his legs—he knew they were to prevent blood clots because his father had worn them when he'd been in the hospital for a ruptured appendix a few years earlier. He also realized now that he was hooked up to an IV.

Once freed from the leg pads, Neill sat up in the bed.

"Can you walk?" asked the woman.

"Yes," he said. "Where's my phone?"

"Right there on the table," she replied. "It's locked, so we couldn't access it to call your emergency contacts. I'm afraid we don't know who you are."

"Oh," he said. He picked up the phone and swung his legs over the bed.

"What about this?" he asked, referring to the IV.

"You can walk with that to the bathroom and use it for support."

Neill didn't want the IV, didn't feel he needed it, but he had to pee and didn't want to argue. He stood up, grabbed the IV bag on wheels with the hand not holding his phone, and headed to the bathroom.

"Wait, sir," said the nurse. "Can you tell me your name?"

"Neill Vandelaare," he replied.

"Can you spell it for me?" she asked, returning to the counter to grab his chart.

He did so and she wrote it down.

"Do you have any family you want us to notify for you?" she asked.

"No. I'll call them on my phone," he said.

"We'll still need emergency contact info," she replied.

"Okay," said Neill, "but I really have to use the bathroom first." He bounced a bit as if he could not hold it any longer. He didn't want to tell her any more information until he'd had a few minutes to absorb what had happened to him. Had he really dreamt that he had traveled back to 1900? Maybe he'd been lying in this hospital bed all this time.

"All right," the nurse finally said, after a moment of hesitating and Neill's eyes pleading with her to let him pee.

Neill pushed the IV into the bathroom with him and shut the door behind him.

"I'll go get the doctor and see if I can bring you some food," the nurse called through the door.

"Thanks!" he replied as he pulled the IV out of his arm, not feeling at all like he needed it.

But he did really have to pee, and more importantly, he had to call his parents. There was no way could he have traveled through time. He knew he had been working at the Huron Mountain Club for the summer. He must have had some sort of accident there and been knocked unconscious, then dreamt it all—like Dorothy in the movie version of *The Wizard of Oz*. But if that was the case, wouldn't whoever had found him at the Club have known him? Why hadn't the nurse known his name?

Well, he'd get answers soon enough.

Neill relieved himself, then unlocked his phone and scrolled through his contacts until he came to his parents' landline. He hit the phone icon and waited for it to ring.

"The number you have dialed is no longer in service," said an automated voice.

"That's weird," he muttered. He knew he hadn't dialed wrong since the number was saved in his phone. He scrolled down to his mom's listing and tapped the button to call her cell phone.

"Hello," answered a man.

"Hello," said Neill. "Who is this?"

"Todd," said the man.

"Todd who?" asked Neill.

"Who wants to know?" asked the man, sounding irritated.

"I'm looking for my mom, Wendy Vandelaare," Neill replied.

"Dude, I ain't no one's mom."

"But this is her number."

"You must have dialed wrong."

"No, I dialed…" and Neill read off the number saved in his phone.

"That's my number, but I've had it for at least five years now. Don't know any chicks named Wendy."

Neill felt like an idiot. But he knew it was the right number. He knew he'd dialed it many times.

"Thanks anyway. Sorry to have bothered you," he said and disconnected.

Then he scrolled down to his dad's number.

"Come on, Dad; pick up," he muttered as he listened to it ring several times.

"You have reached Jared Applebaum," said a recorded voice.

"No way!" Neill shouted and hit disconnect. What the hell was wrong with his phone? Who the hell was Jared Applebaum? He knew he had dialed his dad's cell.

"This can't be happening," he told himself.

Afraid even to try, he dialed his sister Maddy's cell.

"This number is out of service," said an automated voice.

"Shit!" How was this possible?

Neill looked up at the top of the phone's screen. The battery warning light was blinking. Less than 10 percent of battery life left.

"Damn it!" he said.

He stood up and set the phone on the counter, then washed his hands. He looked at himself in the mirror. The hospital gown wasn't flattering, but he looked healthy enough—no sign of a bump on his head or any wounds. He lifted up the gown and scanned his body. No real bruises. He didn't feel like he was crazy, but it made no sense that none of his family's phone numbers worked. He had to get answers.

Neill returned to his hospital room. The nurse hadn't come back yet. Where were his clothes? He had to get out of here. He had to go find his family.

Neill spied the closet and opened it. The only item inside was a white plastic bag with "Personal Belongings" written on it. He grabbed the bag, brought it over to the bed, and opened it.

"Oh, no," he said. He pulled out the shirt Howard Longyear had given him, along with the trousers, weird old-fashioned underwear, and shoes no one in the twenty-first century would ever wear. "This can't be happening," he said, feeling like crying, but he knew he didn't have time for that if he wanted to get out of here.

"It's going to be okay," he told himself as he pulled off his robe and started to dress himself in what would look to others like some sort of historical reenactment costume. "It's okay because I'm back in my own time, so I'll be able to get this all sorted out."

Neill put the weird underwear and socks on. He pulled up the pants. He was buttoning the shirt when the nurse returned with the doctor.

"What are you doing?" she asked. "You can't go anywhere."

"How are you feeling?" asked the doctor. He was short man, and well past sixty. Neill knew neither he nor the nurse would be strong enough to hold him.

"I feel fine," he said, hurriedly sticking his feet in the old-fashioned shoes and wiggling them on while still buttoning the shirt. "There's been some mistake. I don't belong here. I'm sorry for your trouble."

"There has been some sort of mistake," said the nurse. "We can find no record of any Neill Vandelaare. Are you sure that's your name?"

"No," he said. "I'm not sure of anything anymore. Excuse me!"

Before they could stop him, Neill rushed past them, forcing them to step aside. Once in the hall, he had no idea how to get out of the hospital. He just randomly turned right and ran down the hall, skirting around someone in a wheelchair and an empty hospital bed, until he saw a bank of elevators on his left. All the elevator doors were closed. No, he didn't have time to wait for an elevator. Already, he could hear the nurse running down the hall after him. He ducked back into the main hall and ran around a corner past the nurses' station.

"Sir!" a nurse screamed in surprise, but Neill ignored her. He continued down the hall until he saw an exit sign above a door. He quickly opened it and practically leaped down the stairs. He saw through the window that he was only a few flights up. He should be able to get out before anyone notified security.

Neill was at the bottom of the stairs before he knew it. The door opened into a lobby. He ran through the door and lobby, dodging hospital visitors headed for the elevators. A man was being pushed inside the building in a wheelchair. Neill impatiently stood and waited for the disabled man and his assistant to get through the door. Someone shouted, "Sir! Wait!" but at that moment, Neill's path became clear and he bolted out the door. In a second, he was running through the parking garage and out into the parking lot.

At first, he didn't know where he was going. He soon came to the road and realized he was running west on Baraga Avenue. He should be running the other way—home was east, near the lake—but he wasn't going to go back toward the hospital now. He ran like he had never run before, wanting to get away before anyone came after him in a vehicle. Soon he had run past a couple of businesses and reached McClellan Avenue. He turned to the right and ran down the little hill. When he got to the corner of Washington Street, he saw the bike trail. Realizing he would be less visible on that than the main road, he headed down it, soon finding himself behind McDonald's and the other business buildings where he was hopefully out of view. Only then did he slow to a walk to catch his breath.

In front of him, Neill could see the towers of St. Peter's Cathedral. He knew if he kept walking toward the lake, he would be heading in the direction of home, and down here on the bike trail, he would not garner much attention. He didn't want to be too noticeable, though he knew his clothes made him stand out. He just wanted to get home so he could try to make sense of all this.

"Just stay calm," he told himself. "You'll be home in another twenty minutes or so."

He felt very anxious. As he walked swiftly, he thought about how he would explain everything he had experienced to his parents. He felt relieved that his memory was intact after what he had experienced. Had he really been back in 1900? It seemed completely impossible. Again, he thought he must have dreamt it all—but usually dreams quickly fade, while his memories of 1900 were extremely vivid. Then a bicyclist approached him, slowing down to look at him oddly.

"Hello," Neill said to the woman as if nothing were unusual, but she just stared at him as she passed.

At first, Neill thought she was the odd one, but then he remembered what he was wearing—proof it had not been a dream. It had to be eighty degrees out—it was July and felt typically humid. The biker had been in shorts and a biking shirt, with short sleeves, showing more skin than cloth, and yet here he was dressed head-to-toe in warm clothes—clothes that had been summer wear in 1900, but no one in 2021 would be caught dead in such garments on a hot summer day.

I can't wait to change, Neill thought, visualizing the shorts and T-shirts in his dresser drawer at home.

But most of all, he couldn't wait to tell his parents and sister everything that had happened to him. He knew it would be hard for them to believe—he was still trying to believe it—but he had never been one to lie or make up things, so they were bound to believe him after a while—and they would be delighted by everything he had to tell them about the historical experience he'd had. Why, he had slept in the Longyear Mansion and met Peter White and seen Marquette in the old days. His parents were history fanatics who lived in a historical home in Marquette's most historical residential neighborhood. Why, he had even met nasty old Carolina Smith, who had once owned the house he lived in.

"Oh, my God!" Neill exclaimed. "I had tea with my own ancestors." It was true—Margaret Dalrymple was his great-great-grandmother. His father would be thrilled to know he had met her. Neill's father had only been a small boy when Margaret Dalrymple Whitman had died, and he often spoke of her because she was rather a celebrity in family history. And Cordelia Whitman, she had been his…he had to think a minute…his great-great-great-great-grandmother. Margaret had married Cordelia's grandson, Will Whitman, making them both Neill's ancestors.

How amazing it had been, but sadly, because he'd had a concussion and couldn't remember who he was all the time he was in 1900, he now realized he'd lost the opportunity to ask Cordelia and Margaret all the countless things he and his parents would love to know about them. *If I'd only known who I was then, I could have completely enjoyed the experience of being back in the past. I would have walked all over Marquette taking notes and interviewing people and looking up people everyone would want to know more about—I could find out what Mayor Nathan Kaufman did that was so horrible his wife Mary divorced him posthumously, and whether the famous author Constance Fenimore Woolson had ever really visited Marquette, or Mary Todd Lincoln for that matter, or all the other mysteries of Marquette history that my parents are always speculating about. Why, my McCarey ancestors would have been alive then, too, and I didn't even get to see any of them. My dad has always wondered where my great-great-grandpa, Patrick McCarey, came from—was he really a rebel who escaped from Ireland like family legend claims?*

Neill almost wanted to cry at the incredible opportunity he had lost. He was relieved to be back in his own time, but he almost wanted to go back to 1900 right now so he could give his family a better report.

Maybe I can go back again, he thought, although he wasn't sure he wanted to risk that. Nor did he know how he could. But he felt inundated now with memories of what had happened to him. Not only was touching the dolmen at the Club the last thing he remembered from 1900, but now he remembered it was the last thing he had done before he woke up in 1900. He had gotten a summer job at the Club, and on his day off, he had gone hiking by himself and found the dolmen he had heard existed on top of Mount Huron. He remembered touching it, and then suddenly feeling different, and then he had realized his shorts were on fire, like he'd been struck by lightning, or like somehow being transported through time had caused him to catch on fire. In panic, as he had tried to smother the flames, he had tripped and fallen and his cell phone must have fallen out of his pants when he rolled down the mountain—it wasn't much of a mountain, but enough that he recalled falling rather rapidly. And then he must have hit his head and been rendered unconscious. That was when Santinaw and the others at the Club had found him and carried him to the cabins, and then the Allens had brought him to Marquette, where he had finally regained consciousness.

I could go back to the dolmen to try to get back to 1900, Neill thought, *only it could be dangerous. I'll have to talk to a scientist, maybe a professor at NMU, and convince them of what happened to me, and then a study can be done about how it could be possible that I time traveled. I may have just discovered how people can time travel!*

The possibilities that lay before him now seemed incredible, but at the same time, Neill was tired and starving and just wanted to get home.

By now, Neill had begun to pass through the bike trail's tunnel, where it went under Seventh Street, and a few minutes later, he was at Fourth Street and entering downtown. As he crossed the street, he couldn't help looking behind him where the historic Harlow house sat beside the remains of an old railroad trestle. It had belonged to the town founder. And up the hill, he saw St. Peter's Cathedral—he never could get used to the illiterate-sounding change to St. Peter Cathedral—and over to his right was the Marquette County Courthouse.

Oh, he loved Marquette. He was so glad to live here and to be back in the twenty-first-century city he knew and loved, as amazing as it had been to see the Marquette of 1900.

Neill continued along the bike trail that led through the downtown area until he reached Front Street. At first, he thought he must just be exhausted because, suddenly, he felt very strange again, like something was wrong. *Why do I feel anxious and worried?* he wondered, but then he remembered no one had answered his phone calls. He dismissed the thought, telling himself the time travel had somehow messed up the electronics in his phone. He'd just buy a new one—he would deal with that later, but first he wanted to get home. But somehow, he still felt troubled, like something was wrong that he couldn't quite put his finger on.

He looked out at beautiful, big Lake Superior as he turned up Front Street. It kind of grounded him to see that beautiful lake— he loved Lake Superior, loved waking every morning and looking out at it—*even though I nearly drowned in it a couple of weeks ago,* he thought. *Was it two weeks ago, or 121 years ago?* He wasn't sure. But he was certain that there on his left as he started up the hill was the block where VAST, the insurance company, had its office. The modern building stood where once had been the First National Bank, the building where he had gone to meet Peter White in 1900, right across the street from Getz's. *It's a shame they tore that bank down, or did it burn down? I can't remember.* But as Neill turned to walk up Front Street, he saw up ahead the beautiful, impressive, white First National Bank that Louis Kaufman had built in the 1920s, said to be the most expensive building per square foot ever built at the time, complete with its beautiful gold doors. Neill remembered now that it had not been there when he was in 1900, though at the time, he hadn't been able to recall why that corner of downtown had seemed strange to him. But now he knew because everything was back to normal.

And there was the old Savings Bank building with its clock tower, standing as bold and proud in 2021 as it had in 1900. Neill was glad to see it, and he paused to admire the decorative sculpturing of its sandstone walls as he waited for the traffic light to change at the corner of Washington so he could cross the street.

As soon as he got the "walk" signal from the traffic light system, Neill looked both ways and then started across the street. As he did so, though, he saw the lake again.

What the heck? he thought, feeling jubilant and liberated from worry. Rather than walk up Front Street, he decided to take the scenic route home by turning down Washington to the lake. He would walk on the bike trail through the Lower Harbor's Mattson Park, along Lakeshore Boulevard to Ridge Street. It would take a few minutes longer to reach home that way, but then he could continue to enjoy the view of the lake on this beautiful day.

Neill's celebratory mood continued as he looked up to see people enjoying eating on the patios of Sol Azteca and Iron Bay, two of his favorite Marquette restaurants. He remembered that the pandemic was almost over. Half the population was now vaccinated. Summer in Marquette was returning to normal. Life seemed worth celebrating.

But then something far more shocking than a pandemic happened.

Neill had barely turned to look to his right when his stomach felt like it had dropped into his knees.

"Oh, my God!" he exclaimed. He was staring out at the harbor, out at a great void, a great emptiness, a great vacancy that made him want to cry.

"No!" he almost screamed. "What happened? Where is it?"

People passing him looked at him with surprise.

"What—what happened?" he asked them.

They ignored him, though looking at him strangely because of his clothes, then hurried past.

Neill quickly realized his strange clothes must have made them think he was crazy. He almost felt like he had to be crazy because how else could he explain that the old iron ore dock that had stood in Marquette's Lower Harbor for ninety years was completely gone? There wasn't a trace of it—not its pilings or anything resembling it. He had only been up at the Huron Mountain Club for a few weeks— there was no way, even if someone had finally torn down the old dock, that it could have vanished this quickly. Why, for years some people had complained that the dock was an eyesore, but most residents wanted to preserve it, and several elaborate plans had been proposed for its renovation, including turning it into a botanical garden or a condominium. The city had allowed it to stand, partly because the cost of tearing it down was prohibitive, but also because most people thought it iconic, symbolizing Marquette's important role in the nation's iron ore industry.

But now it had completely vanished!

"What happened to the ore dock?" Neill demanded of a middle-aged man coming up the sidewalk toward him.

"Ore dock?" said the man. "What ore dock?"

"The giant ore dock that used to stand here in the harbor," Neill said.

"Oh, that," said the man. "Why that's been gone since I was a kid. You couldn't possibly be old enough to remember it."

Neill just stared out at the water in disbelief, completely speechless.

"Have a nice day," said the man, and he quickly turned to go eat at Iron Bay, perhaps also thinking Neill was a little crazy.

Neill couldn't believe his ears. He stood there gawking out at the lake until he realized some people were standing across the street staring at him; they seemed uncertain whether they should cross the street and get close to him. Embarrassed, Neill turned left and started walking alongside the condos until those gawking at him had crossed the street. Then he also crossed the street and jogged down to the bike trail.

This all looks normal, he thought. *The park looks like it always has.*

Neill felt a strange urgency to get home now. Despite his fatigue and hunger, he started jogging down the bike trail through the park. All the while, he kept looking back, even jogging backward, to where the harbor stood vacant of its ore dock. How could it have just disappeared so fast? And what did that crazy man mean by saying it had been gone since he was a kid?

Neill soon jogged past the boathouse that housed the Lake Superior Theatre, and then he came to the Coast Guard building and the Marquette Maritime Museum—there was nothing abnormal about any of this. After looking both ways, he crossed the street and began walking up Ridge Street's hill, heading for home.

And that was when he had his next shock.

All the houses he had known as being along the right side of the street were gone. Instead, there was an elaborately manicured and terraced lawn, and as his eyes made their way up the hill, perched near the top and dominating the beautifully landscaped terrain was an enormous sandstone mansion.

"No way!" Neill exclaimed.

Neill didn't need to be told whose house it was. But he was astonished. Yes, he was walking up the historic stone steps that had been there since the days of the Longyear Mansion. He had walked up them countless times. But until now, he had never seen the actual Longyear Mansion.

"No way!" he exclaimed again as he got closer to it. "No way is it possible."

Had someone decided to move it back to Marquette? But even if that were the case—which seemed extremely unlikely—it could not possibly have been moved and rebuilt in the few weeks since he had been at the Huron Mountain Club.

There's no way they could have moved it, he told himself. He knew back in 1903 people would have also said a sixty-five-room mansion could not be moved, but it had been moved back then—moved by railroad car to Brookline, Massachusetts—when the Longyears had decided to move and take their sumptuous home with them. Neill's own great-great-great-grandfather, Charles Dalrymple, Margaret Dalrymple's father, had been among the men hired to take it apart, stone by stone, labeling each piece so it could be reassembled in Massachusetts. Then, when the fragmented house had arrived in Massachusetts, the family had decided to reassemble it in a different, more modern configuration and add more rooms to it. The entire process had been a near-miracle of engineering ingenuity at the time and was even featured years later on *Ripley's Believe It or Not*.

Now, as Neill reached the top of the hill, he stopped and stared. *Look at that house just towering there! How is it possible? And even if someone did move it back to Marquette from Massachusetts, what did they do with the houses that used to be here?* Neill knew his Marquette history very well from listening to his parents. He knew after the Longyear Mansion was moved that the Longyears' daughters, Abby and Helen, had each built a house on the property, and so had Charles Schaeffer, a friend of the family they had sold property to. Why, by Neill's time, those large houses had been standing there for about a hundred years. How could they have possibly been moved, plus the smaller houses farther down the hill, and this giant mansion put back where it had once stood more than a century ago?

I have to get home, Neill told himself, suddenly panicking. He took off running down the street, so agitated that he didn't even notice the Peter White House was still standing. He had visited that house just days before, but in the year 1900. Had Neill spotted it, he would have been equally astonished since he knew it had been torn down in the 1940s and replaced with a smaller, more modern home. But Neill was far too anxious to get home to stop and regard any other changes that existed along Ridge Street.

Chapter 2

NEILL SLOWED DOWN AS HE got to the front walk of his family's home. The large sandstone house—not a mansion—but substantial in size—the grandest in the neighborhood in some estimations until the Longyear Mansion had been built, and the grandest after the Longyear Mansion had been moved—stood before him. And he longed to be inside it and with all his family.

Not thinking twice, Neill went up the walk, up the couple of steps, and opened the front door. Or rather, he tried to open it, but he found it locked. He did not have his key—he remembered leaving his keys in his room at the Club when he had ventured out to find the dolmen, so he had not had them with him when he was transported to 1900, and he did not have them now. He thought about walking around to the door off the porch, but instead, he knocked on the door, expecting his sister or one of his parents to appear any second and let him in.

Instead, after a few seconds, a strange man answered the door.

"We don't want any solicitations," said the tall, middle-aged man, looking down on Neill, who stood on the step below.

Neill didn't know what to say at first. He didn't know this man. Finally, he managed, "Who are you?"

"Who am I?" asked the man. "I'm the owner of this house."

"The owner?" said Neill.

"That's what I said," said the man. "What do you want?"

"I'm looking for my parents," said Neill. "They live here. This is their house."

The man looked vexed. "What is this, some sort of joke?" he asked. "I don't know your parents. I live here with my wife and daughter."

"My parents are John and Wendy Vandelaare," Neill replied. "They've lived here for more than twenty years."

"Never heard of them," said the man. "Either you have the wrong house or you're nuts. I've lived here since 1999."

The man started to shut the door.

"Wait!" shouted Neill. He pressed against the door to stop it from closing.

The man flung the door open and shouted, "Get the hell out of here or I'll call the police!"

Neill stepped back, shocked by the man's response.

"But I—but I just—"

"But I…" mocked the man, and then he slammed the door in Neill's face. Neill could hear him sliding back the bolt.

Neill stood there for a minute, not knowing what to do, until a curtain was pulled back and he saw the man glaring through the window at him.

Neill felt so baffled that he backed up, nearly falling down the couple of steps. Then he turned and walked back to the sidewalk, certain the man was still watching him.

I better go before he does call the police, thought Neill. *But where are my parents? They wouldn't have moved without telling me.*

He didn't want to believe it; he didn't want to tell himself it was possible, but he was beginning to think he had not returned to his own time. The nurse at the hospital had said it was the year 2021, and she had agreed with him that Joe Biden was president, so he had to be in his own time, but then, why were some things so different?

Then he had a frightening thought. *Am I dead?* He had a strange feeling that he was like George Bailey in *It's a Wonderful Life*, experiencing what life would be like if he had never lived. "No!" he shouted, shaking his head furiously back and forth to erase the thought. "I can't be dead. People wouldn't be able to speak to me."

Neill continued down the street in a stupor, staring at the sidewalk, not knowing what to think or do. Only after he heard some kids shouting as they played did he look up, and then turning toward the kids who were running around in a yard, he saw a giant Victorian home where he knew a much more modern, ranch-style house had been built long before he was born.

What's happened? he wondered. It was all too much to take in. He had to accept now that he was not back in his time, at least not the time he had known. Suddenly, he began looking all about him, trying to determine what was the same and what else had changed in this neighborhood where he had lived all his life—a neighborhood he knew as well as he knew his own name.

Within another block, he discovered that the Pine-Ridge Apartments building that soared up several stories at the corner was not there. Instead, a beautiful turn-of-the-century sandstone building rose before him.

"The Howard-Froebel School!" Neill exclaimed. "But they tore that down in the 1960s to build the senior citizen high-rise." Marveling at the beautiful building with two long wings and little towers on each of its corners, he walked closer until he saw a sign in front of it, proclaiming it was the "Longyear-Froebel Art Museum."

"Art museum?" he said. "I always heard it was a school." He also thought it weird it was named Longyear-Froebel, not Howard-Froebel.

Something really weird is going on, he told himself. *It's like I'm in some kind of alternate reality.*

Neill was starving and sweating after all the running he had done, but he didn't know what to do about it. He hated these old clothes he was wearing, but obviously, he couldn't go home and change. And he had no money. He had to eat something, but he didn't have any credit cards on him either. He had no way to get back to the Huron Mountain Club since he didn't have a car, and he didn't know how to find his parents to get a ride there.

Then it struck him—his best friend, Derek. Derek would come pick him up. Derek could probably loan him some clothes too. Derek was a big guy, several inches taller than Neill, but one of his T-shirts and his shorts would probably fit him. Digging into his pants pocket, Neill retrieved his phone and pressed the button to turn it on.

The screen lit up, but a warning on the screen said his battery only had 1 percent of life remaining. Neill knew if he tried to use it, his call might not go through, or if it did, he could be disconnected early in his conversation.

"Damn it!" he said. He wasn't one to swear, but this situation was getting ridiculous. He had no phone charger, and even if he had one, he had nowhere to plug one in. Well, there was the Peter White Public Library just a block or so in front of him. It would have outlets free for use, but he would still need a charger.

But Derek didn't live that far away—he had a tiny one-person apartment in an old house just off Fourth Street. Neill would go there. Certainly, Derek would know where his parents were, or at least help him find them.

His stomach growling, Neill kept walking past the library parking lot. He crossed Third and then Fourth Street, and turned up the street. He felt exhausted after all the walking and running in these hot old clothes, but he knew in another minute, his problems would start to get solved.

Only, when he got to Derek's apartment, Derek turned out not to be home. No one answered when he knocked on the door multiple times.

Now what do I do? he wondered. Maybe Derek was at work. But it was Sunday, wasn't it? Or Monday? He wasn't sure. It had been Sunday when he had gone with Howard Longyear to the dolmen, but.... Oh, his head was starting to hurt. Why couldn't Derek be home?

Neill collapsed on the steps to think for a minute. Should he sit here until Derek came home? But what if Derek didn't even live here? Neill looked up the mailbox. "Yes!" he almost shouted. Derek's name was on it. He was in the right place. But where was Derek and how long would he have to wait for him? The only other option he could think of was to go see his friend Allison, but she lived way over by Seventh Street. That was another three blocks away and he was tired. No, he'd sit here for a little while and hope that Derek showed up, and if not, he would go over to Allison's house. One of them was bound to help him. After all, Derek was his best friend and Allison and he were good friends; they had even gone to prom together. Neill had often thought about asking her to be his girlfriend, but he wasn't sure Allison felt that way about him, or that he felt that way about her. Still, all three of them would do anything for each other. So, he would sit here and wait for Derek while he cooled off a bit—at least the house's front steps were in the shade—and if Derek didn't come home by the time he got his energy back, he'd go find Allison.

Chapter 3

A s Neill waited for Derek to come home, he wondered if his friend had missed him or even realized he'd been missing. After all, he had been in 1900 for nearly three weeks. Even in 2021, there were no telephone lines up at the Huron Mountain Club and cell phone coverage wasn't so great, so he doubted anyone would be too worried if he didn't contact them while he was there, but after three weeks, his parents would have expected to hear from him. He had promised to write letters to Allison, but Derek was no letter writer so he might not suspect anything and be surprised to see him.

Derek was doing an internship that summer through Northern Michigan University's forestry program, so he had probably been too busy to try catching up with his friend anyway. Allison was busy too; she'd gotten a job at a clothing store in the Westwood Mall, but she was also involved in some summer plays—a big deal to her since she was a theater major and there had been no plays performed for more than a year because of the pandemic; fortunately, life was slowly getting back to normal now that so many people were vaccinated, even if Michigan had been one of the states hardest hit by COVID-19.

As a history major, Neill found himself interested in both of his friends' careers. Derek's interest in forestry related to local history since the Upper Peninsula had a long and proud history of logging, and Allison was often in historical dramas. Her senior year of high school, she'd starred as Cecily Cardew in the classic play *The Importance of Being Earnest*.

"It's so fun to escape into a character," Allison had told Neill just before he had left for the Club. "Real life is just too boring sometimes, don't you think?"

"I don't know," Neill had said. "Sometimes I rather like boring after all the turmoil of this past year since my uncle Chad died unexpectedly and then the pandemic began."

"I know; no one wants that kind of trauma," said Allison, "but don't you want to have a great adventure? I mean, you love history. Wouldn't you love to experience it for yourself? I can't go back in time, but by being in a play, I get to feel how people in history might have felt. As an actress, I can imagine what it's like to have been a silent movie star like Norma Desmond or to have lived in the eighteenth century like in *She Stoops to Conquer*. I can experience all that. It's like I get to live many different lives. Technology aside, by comparison the twenty-first century isn't all that interesting."

"I wouldn't say that," said Neill. "I can see how your own time can get boring and other times can become attractive by comparison, but I'm not sure any other time is better than our own."

"How can you say that?" asked Allison. "Look at this horrible pandemic, and the race riots and protests lately and how the country is so politically divided these days."

"I doubt living during the American Revolution or the Civil War was any better," said Neill, "and this pandemic, terrible as it is, is nothing compared to the bubonic plague. It doesn't do us any good to romanticize the past because if we really experienced it, I think we'd find we'd rather be in the present."

"Not necessarily," said Allison. "A lot of things about the past were better. Just think about clothes today. I mean, no one has any class or style anymore. Girls rarely even wear dresses."

"A lot of women would say that's a good thing," replied Neill. "A sign of women's equality."

"Well, I believe I can be feminine and still be the equal of a man," Allison stated. "If I had my way, I'd dress like Cecily Cardew every day."

"Sure," said Neill, "but Cecily was worth 130,000 pounds, remember? That's like twenty million dollars today. She was rich. Not everyone could afford to dress like that back then. What if you had been a scullery maid then? You'd be wearing gingham or something worse that was years old."

"Whatever," said Allison. "I'm glad you know your history, Neill, but sometimes you're lacking in imagination."

At that moment, Derek had arrived so they could all go out to lunch. When Allison had asked him if he would like to live in the past, he had said, "I don't know."

"Oh, come on," said Allison. "At least one of my two guy friends has to have some imagination."

"I have imagination," said Neill. "I can imagine how hard it would be."

"Then at least one of my guy friends has to be adventurous."

"I'm adventurous," said Derek. "I guess I'd be willing to live in the past."

"I still think life was a lot harder back then," said Neill, "and we'd all be in for a shock if we visited it."

"I don't know about that," said Derek. "I'm strong. I think I could hack it. At least I wouldn't have to deal with people always texting and calling and emailing me and then getting mad when I don't respond right away. Sometimes a man just wants a little peace, not something beeping and buzzing at him constantly. That's why I like being out in the woods. Too much crazy technology these days for my taste."

"You act like you do belong in the past," Neill replied, "and since I'm the one who texts you the most, I'll take that as a personal insult."

Derek punched Neill in the arm.

"Ow!" said Neill.

"You're pretty soft," said Derek. "I don't think you could hack it living in the past. You'll have to come over to my parents' cabin and help me chop wood this summer to toughen you up a little."

"Yeah, well," said Neill, "I think you'd get sick of chopping wood if you lived in the 1800s. They didn't have any weight rooms back then, you know. And you'd be eating food full of lard all the time. Those abs you're so proud of wouldn't last long."

Derek was rather proud of his abs. He was a big guy, 6' 4" and 240 pounds of muscle. Although he'd never been into sports, he enjoyed working out and showing off his strength. But what Neill had always admired most about Derek was that, despite his size, he was a gentle person, never a bully. He felt safe with Derek, who had already respected him for his intelligence. Since they had been kids, the two of them had complemented each other, from teaming up on science projects to buddying up for activities at summer camp; they were the perfect mix of brains and brawn.

Allison had been a nice complement to their friendship also, like a sister to them both. The three had developed a good rapport, especially during high school, and they had always looked out for each other, staving off any suggestions that Derek was stupid just because he was big, that Allison was "loose" because she was in theatre, or that Neill was just a know-it-all. They all had each other's backs and knew none of the accusations were true. They were three good friends who had enjoyed each other's company. They had even all gone to prom together, though technically Allison had been Neill's date. But none of them were too interested in dating yet, being focused on their studies and career goals and just wanting to enjoy their youth while it lasted.

Recalling all this now, Neill realized how much he missed his friends. He felt cooler now and was tired of waiting for Derek. He looked at his cell phone to check the time, but the battery had gone completely dead. He estimated he'd been sitting on Derek's porch for half an hour. Since Derek was in the forestry program, he might be out driving around in a truck anywhere in the UP, so Neill figured he might as well give up waiting.

I hope Allison will be home, he thought. He figured it had to be getting on toward mid-afternoon. It was possible she would be at work at the mall, but she only worked part-time so he might be lucky and find her.

The thought of seeing Allison excited Neill. The conversation he had just recalled seemed ironic now. How would she react if he told her he had actually been to the past? Once she got over not believing him, he knew she'd be jealous. *She's bound to ask me a million questions about the fashions the ladies were wearing*, he thought, though he couldn't remember much about them, other than that they wore long dresses. Neither Mrs. Bingley nor Mrs. Longyear's clothes had been anything too fancy that he recalled, but they had also been wearing everyday clothes, and Mrs. Bingley was a housekeeper. Mrs. Longyear would have been in Cecily Cardew's social class, but she seemed fairly down to earth and had been at home with the family, not out in society, while he was visiting them. Howard's sisters' dresses had been fairly plain as well. Still, the Longyear Mansion had certainly been ornate, and Neill knew Allison would enjoy hearing about how it was decorated.

More importantly, Allison might know something about where his parents were.

Feeling new hope, Neill stood up and started back down the street.

Chapter 4

How do you tell your two best friends you've time traveled? As Neill walked toward Allison's house, he began to wonder if Allison would believe him. Given that she was a theatre major, she might accuse him of wearing a costume rather than actual clothes from 1900, and even of trying to play a joke on her. Oh, well, even if she did, maybe she would take him to Meijer to buy some jeans and a T-shirt so he'd quit looking so ridiculous and feeling so excruciatingly hot. He hated to borrow money from her, but he was sure she'd let him. She could put it on her credit card, and then once he found his parents, he could pay her back before the bill was due. *And,* he thought, *Allison has always been level-headed, even if she can be a bit dramatic at times. Maybe she'll help me make sense out of all this.*

Allison lived with her mom just off Seventh Street, over near Park Cemetery, so Neill turned down Michigan and headed west. When he came to Sixth Street, he turned north and started toward Allison's house, then turned again and was almost to Seventh when he saw her house.

"At least it looks the same," Neill said as he approached the house. He had almost been afraid it wouldn't be there since other things had changed. Thankfully, everything about Allison's house looked normal.

Neill went up to the front door and knocked. He waited a minute, but when no one answered, he knocked again. And again. No answer.

She must not be home, he thought. For a moment, it occurred to him that she might not even live here given the other strange things he had experienced today, but he looked at the mailbox and clearly saw her last name, Hayes, written on it. *Thank God. She does live here. But where is she?*

He realized Allison and her mom—her father had died years before in a car accident—were probably both at work since it was the middle of the day. Her mother worked in some office at NMU, but he wasn't sure exactly where. He didn't feel like walking back downtown to try to find Allison if she was at work, and if he did, he might miss her anyway if she took a different route home.

Well, all I can do is wait, Neill thought. He was about to plop himself down on the front step when he saw movement to the left. Turning, he noticed a neighbor looking out her window at him. Given his weird clothing, Neill didn't want to draw too much attention to himself—someone might just call the police, believing he was a vagrant or some sort of kook.

I'll come back in a little while, he thought. As he started to walk away from the house, he looked down the street and saw the gate around Park Cemetery. Not knowing how else to pass the time, he decided to go walk in the cemetery. *No one will notice me there*, he thought. *There's hardly ever anyone in the cemetery.*

Neill felt like maybe he wasn't thinking clearly anymore. He didn't know when he had last eaten. The nurse had said it was July 25, but it had been July 24 when he, Howard, and Santinaw had gone to the dolmen, which meant he hadn't eaten in more than twenty-four hours now. In any case, he felt hot and weak. As he walked toward Seventh Street, he undid the buttons on his shirt cuffs and rolled up his sleeves. At least he could get some relief from the heat. He realized he was also thirsty. Fortunately, the cemetery had some water faucets so people could water the flowers they planted on their loved ones' graves. He thought there might even be a bench somewhere so he could sit down. He just knew he needed a quiet place to rest and think about what he should do. He would go back to Allison's house in a little while since he was sure she would help him, but he had so many questions that a little quiet, alone time might help him make better sense of things.

After walking along Seventh Street a short way, Neill crossed the street and walked through the cemetery gates. He turned to the right and walked up the hill toward the caretaker's house and garage and the little parking lot. Then he turned to his left and started walking around the pond, past the Peter White obelisk and the little mausoleum where some of the White descendants were buried. Given how he and his parents were history buffs, he'd made many trips to the cemetery with them to visit famous people's graves, as well as those of his own ancestors, the earliest of whom had come to Marquette when it was founded in 1849.

Neill paused for a moment and circled back to look at some of the graves. It was so weird to see Peter White's final resting place. The Marquette pioneer had died in 1908—113 years ago—and yet just a couple of weeks ago, Neill had been talking to him. Mr. White had been full of life and energy then. Now to know he was dead seemed overwhelming, and Neill felt like crying, but he knew he was partly just exhausted and needed to rest.

Not wanting to draw attention to himself, he kept walking, looking for somewhere to sit, or maybe he would just lie down in the grass if he didn't find a park bench. The old Breitung mausoleum was to his right, which looked just like it always had, and to his left, Neill could see the imposing Greek temple-shaped Kaufman mausoleum. *At least everything seems to be normal here*, he thought. He knew he would notice if anything major had changed since he'd visited the cemetery so many times. He'd always loved it here, but because his parents were Catholic, they would be buried in Holy Cross Cemetery, not Park Cemetery, and they'd already bought extra plots for him and his sister if they wanted them. His grandparents would be buried there too. They had bought plots next to where Uncle Chad had been buried.

Then Neill realized he had not thought about his grandparents all day. A couple of years ago, they had sold their house and moved to the Tourville Apartments behind Jilbert's Dairy. He could go to them for help if need be—though that would be an even farther walk. But he'd try to connect with Allison first. His grandpa wasn't in the best of health, and his grandmother's eyesight was going, and neither of his grandparents drove anymore, so Neill didn't think they could help him much; plus, he didn't want to upset them with his strange story, even though they would probably know where his parents were. He knew they were still mourning the loss of Uncle Chad, who had unexpectedly dropped dead of a blood clot after breaking a bone in his foot. It had happened just a couple of months before the pandemic began. He and Uncle Chad had been close; in fact, his uncle had helped him get his summer job at the Huron Mountain Club. Neill missed Uncle Chad every day.

Neill kept walking through the cemetery, deciding he'd walk toward the grotto. He thought he remembered seeing a park bench back there, and since the grotto was hidden from view behind a hill, he could sit there quietly and think.

But then a gravestone caught his attention. It was a huge, imposing stone. Not an elaborate mausoleum, but still a good five feet tall and elaborately carved. Across its top was written "Longyear."

I don't remember seeing that stone before, Neill thought. He had thought all the Longyears were buried out East since they had moved their house out there. But then Neill stepped close enough to read the names on the stone:

Howard Munro Longyear   Margaret Dalrymple Longyear
1881—1965   1884—1976

Married 1903

"Howard married Margaret..." Neill muttered, not completely understanding. Then he exclaimed, "No way!" It was too much to wrap his brain around. It was...it was impossible.

"But...but..." he said to himself. "But Margaret married my great-great-grandpa, Will Whitman, and in 1903 too. How can this be possible? How could she have married Howard?"

Neill almost felt like he was going to faint. His knees buckled and he collapsed on the grass. He sat there, staring at the stone in shock.

Chapter 5

THERE WAS NO DENYING IT. Here was a gravestone attesting to the fact that Howard Munro Longyear had married Margaret Dalrymple. She should have become a Whitman, but instead, she had married a Longyear.

Hard as it was to wrap his head around it, Neill realized this must mean his great-great-grandparents had never been married.

"And if Margaret didn't marry Will," Neill said aloud, "then they couldn't have had a son named Henry, and if Henry didn't exist, then...." He went through the mental gymnastics of the generations in his family tree between Henry and himself, but no matter how he looked at it, the result was the same. "If Henry wasn't born, then I wasn't born, and then my parents also wouldn't have been born...well, my father anyway. My mother wasn't descended from Margaret. But if my father wasn't born, my mother couldn't marry him, so she probably never moved here from Montana. But I exist. I must have been born. I'm here, aren't I?

"How could this have happened? How is it possible? I mean, I liked Howard," he told himself. "I have nothing against him, but he couldn't marry Margaret because he...."

And then it really hit him. It hit Neill so hard he felt like he was going to vomit, and he had to stand up so the rising gas in his stomach could settle. He reached out and supported himself against the gravestone as he realized the horrible thing he had done.

"But it wasn't a horrible thing!" he cried out to the Universe. "It isn't fair. I saved Howard's life! I saved his life. I would have saved Hugh's too if I could. How can that be wrong?"

It was all making sense now. It was why Marquette was different. It was why his parents did not seem to exist, and it was why he had seen the Longyear Mansion at the top of the hill on Ridge Street. It was all because Howard Longyear had not drowned, and so the Longyears had never moved their house to Brookline, Massachusetts.

"Howard didn't die," Neill muttered. "And it's all my fault." It sounded ridiculous, but it was his fault—at least, he was responsible for it. He remembered now what he couldn't remember when he had been trapped in 1900. Howard Longyear and Hugh Allen had drowned in Lake Superior on a summer day in 1900 when they had been canoeing up to the Huron Mountain Club. The story was well known in Marquette by everyone who loved local history. When the boys had failed to arrive at the Huron Mountain Club, Mr. and Mrs. Longyear had been frantic. They had sent the rest of their children home to Marquette while they had walked the Lake Superior shoreline all the way back to Marquette looking for the boys. Eventually, the boys' bodies had been found and buried in Park Cemetery. Mrs. Longyear, completely grief-stricken, had wanted to honor her son by creating a memorial park named after him on the property below their house. Only, one of the railroads—Neill couldn't remember which—wanted to run its tracks through the land where Mrs. Longyear wanted to build her park, and in the end, the city had sided with the railroad. The grieving mother had been furious with the city, and the family had packed their bags and gone to Paris. And there, riding down the Champs-Élysées in a carriage, Mr. Longyear had suggested to his wife, perhaps half-jokingly, that they move their house to Massachusetts. She had taken the suggestion seriously and decided that was exactly what they would do, and so Marquette had lost the grandest house it had ever seen.

One of the men hired to disassemble the house had been Neill's ancestor, Charles Dalrymple, a carpenter in Marquette, and working for him had been another ancestor, Neill's great-great-grandfather, Will Whitman. And one day, Charles' daughter, Margaret, had come to the Longyear Mansion to bring her father his lunch, and that was when she had met Will Whitman. And before long, Margaret and Will had fallen in love and gotten married, and the rest was history.

"Or not," said Neill, talking to himself to make sense of it. "It isn't history now because Margaret and Will didn't get married, and so my parents don't exist, and I shouldn't either. And they didn't get married because they didn't meet at the Longyear Mansion because it didn't get moved. And the mansion didn't get moved because Howard Longyear never drowned. And Howard never drowned because I saved his life."

Neill felt like crying with frustration. "Oh, what do I do now?" he exclaimed.

Of course, at that moment, some sweet lady who had come to plant flowers on a loved one's grave heard his cry and walked over to see if he was okay.

"I'm fine. Thanks," he said and quickly walked away, ignoring the stares of a couple of people who were out to get their exercise by walking in the cemetery.

Beginning that day, unknown to Neill, rumors would spread that a tall young man in clothes dating from about 1900 had been seen in the cemetery. Some speculated it was the ghost of Howard Longyear. It would even make its way into a book about hauntings in Marquette. But that is another story.

Neill, completely beside himself, began walking back toward the cemetery entrance, stumbling over tree roots and nearly tripping over an ancient flat gravestone he did not see. By the time he made it back to the cemetery gates, he felt far more horror than if he had simply seen a ghost.

He was only distracted from his despair when his stomach growled loudly. He was starving. Wiping tears from his face, he told himself he had to focus now on finding someone who could help him.

Leaving the cemetery, Neill turned onto Seventh Street and walked again to Allison's house.

Please be home, Allison, he silently prayed. He wasn't sure how Allison could help him, but he knew he had to talk to someone who would listen to him; hopefully, someone who would believe him and help him make sense out of it all.

Chapter 6

W HEN NEILL WAS ABOUT HALF a block from Allison's house, he saw her car come down the street and pull into her driveway.

Thank God, was his first thought, soon followed by, *What happened to her?*

As the young woman got out of the car, he saw she was the right size to be Allison, but her hair, which had always been a dark brown, had been died black with a splotch of red in it. She was wearing black fish-net stockings, and that wasn't the only thing that was black. Her shorts, if you could call them shorts—Neill didn't actually know the proper descriptions for most female attire—were also black, as was the blouse she had on, and when she turned around, her eyeshadow was black too. The only thing not black, other than the red splotch in her hair, was her nose ring.

"Hello, Allison," he said when she noticed he was staring at her. *She must be in a play*—Rocky Horror *perhaps*, Neill thought.

"Hello yourself," she said. "Do I know you?"

Neill had done some quick thinking as he returned to her house. He knew that since he had apparently never been born in this new version of the present, Allison might not know him, and if he started off by telling her he was a time traveler, she might slam the door in his face. He was relieved that he had caught her alone and outside. That way he could speak to her before she could escape inside.

"You do and you don't know me," he said as she shut the car door.

"What?" she asked, sounding irritated.

"I have a strange story to tell you," he replied, "about how you should know me, but the truth is you don't know me. I don't want you to think I'm a total kook, though, so let me first tell you something that will make you trust me."

Allison eyed his strange clothes. God, he wished he could find other clothes.

"Are you some sort of actor?" she asked. "You theatre people are always so overly dramatic."

What? She's in theatre herself, thought Neill, quickly trying to overcome his shock to get to the point. "No, I'm not in theatre," he said. "Allison, I'm in some trouble—a situation that is very hard to explain—and I don't expect you to understand it. I promise you I'm not a criminal or anyone you need to fear—but I do hope you will help me. I know you are a kind and good person, so please, no matter how outlandish what I have to say seems, please take pity on me."

Allison laughed out loud and replied, "You're a sweet talk-er—I'm a 'kind and good person'? Shit. I don't think you do know me."

Neill had feared his speech might make her bolt; instead, he seemed to be amusing her.

"Please listen to me," he said. "I'll prove I do know you. I have a very strange story to tell, but first I'm going to tell you something I don't think you've ever told anyone but me so you will know I'm being truthful. Are you following me so far?"

"I don't know what kind of game you're playing," said Allison, "but I'll tell you two things: One, you wouldn't be the first asshole I kicked in the nuts if you try anything, and two, my boyfriend is six-foot-four and very strong."

"O-kay," said Neill, wondering what had happened to the Allison he knew. She'd been too much of a lady to use words like "asshole" and "shit," much less to go around kicking guys in the nuts. And was she serious about the boyfriend? She had to be refer-ring to Derek.

"Allison," he said, "I promise I'm a safe person to talk to. You're practically the last person I would ever try to hurt. You see, we're actually friends, or should be. We knew each other once under very different circumstances—in another time actually."

"You've got to be shitting me," she said, clutching her car keys and arranging one so it pointed out at Neill like a weapon she was ready to use if needed. "I don't go in for all that reincarnation crap."

"It's not crap," he said. "I'll explain it all to you the best I can, but first, just so you know I'm telling you the truth, let me tell you that in that other time when we knew each other, you told me a secret that you said you'd never told anyone else. I'm going to tell you that secret now so you know I'm not lying to you. Please don't be scared that I know this. It will seem strange that I do, but I promise you I mean you no harm."

She rolled her eyes like she was running out of patience but said, "Shoot!"

"Okay," he said, feeling extremely nervous, realizing this was his only chance. "Allison, you told me once that you blamed yourself for your father's death."

Allison's eyes grew wide.

"You told me this," Neill continued, quickly spitting out his words before she could turn and walk away, "one night after we had watched *The Sixth Sense* together. You told me you had only been six when your father died, and that that day, he had been mad at you for dawdling in the morning so you had missed the bus, and then you had been too afraid to tell him you had to go to the bathroom, so you peed your pants in the car and he had to bring you home to change. He was really mad because now he was going to be late for an important meeting. After you got your clothes changed and he brought you back to school, he headed to Ishpeming for his meeting and got struck by another driver at an intersection. You thought God had killed your dad to punish you for being a bad girl. You believed that for a really long time until one night you started crying really hard, and when your mom asked you what was wrong, you told her you had done a really bad thing, but you wouldn't tell her what because it was so horrible. So your mother told you to pray to God for forgiveness, and when you did, you felt God forgave you and even made you feel that it wasn't your fault but had simply been your dad's time to go."

As Neill had been speaking, Allison's eyes had been growing wider and wider.

"Where did you come up with that?" she asked when he had finished. "Who told you that?"

"You told me," said Neill. "It's true, isn't it?"

She got a strange expression on her face, like she was trying to find the right words to reply.

"Sort of," she finally said.

"Sort of?" he asked.

"Well, yeah, my dad died and all that, but I never prayed to God. I don't believe in God. If God existed, he wouldn't have taken my dad. I was just a little girl. Little girls piss their pants. It wasn't my fault he died. It was God's—if God exists."

"Oh," said Neill. "I'm sorry. You mean you—you never healed from your dad's death?"

"Would you have?" she asked, getting angry. "Fuck, who told you that story? Did my mom tell you that, or does your mom know my mom or something?"

"No," said Neill. "I'm telling you I've known you for many years. We were best friends in high school, you, me, and Derek."

"Derek? You know Derek?" she asked, raising her pierced eyebrow. "Did he tell you that? I don't remember telling him about it, but maybe I did some time when we were drunk or high."

"I do know Derek," said Neill, "but like you, he doesn't know me because I knew him in another time—an alternate reality."

"An alternate reality?" She rolled her eyes in disbelief.

"Yes," Neill said. "A time that is very similar to this one but slightly different. See I—well, it's a long story. I'll be happy to tell you—and Derek too—the whole thing, but please, I desperately need you to help me."

"Help you?" she said. "What kind of help?"

Neill sighed with relief. She was actually listening to him.

"For starters," he said, "I need some decent clothes, and I need something to eat. I haven't eaten in…two days I think."

Allison looked him up and down.

"Are these your clothes from another time?" she asked.

"Yes," he said, hoping she was starting to believe him.

"What time did you come from?"

"That's the thing," Neill replied. "I came from 1900, but I belong in this year. Somehow I got stuck in 1900, and I accidentally did something there that changed the future because now I'm back in 2021, but a lot of things are different from what I remember. Worst of all, I can't find my parents. I don't even know if they exist in this time."

"But you knew me in this time?" she replied, trying to make sense of what he was saying.

"Yes, at least in the version of 2021 I came from."

Allison peered into his eyes; he could tell she was wondering if he was crazy. He didn't blame her. He felt crazy himself, but he said, "Please believe me."

"What if I don't?" she asked. "What will you do then?"

"I don't know," he replied, trembling at the thought. "I guess I'll just leave you alone. Just, please, don't do anything drastic like call the police. I'm completely harmless, and the last thing I need is to be stuck in a psych ward when I have to figure out how I can go back and fix the past."

"I wouldn't call the police," said Allison, seeming to hesitate. "See, I know what it's like to be in a psych ward. The fuckers are all crazy in there. I wouldn't wish that on anyone."

"Do you believe me then?" he asked.

"I'm still trying to figure that out," she said.

"Is there anything I can say to convince you? I'm willing to answer any questions if you promise to keep this just between us."

"You know that's what stalkers and narcissists say, right? Not to tell anyone."

Allison pulled out her phone.

"What are you doing?" he asked. "You said you wouldn't call the police."

"I'm calling Derek. If you are some sort of psycho, he needs to know what's going on, plus you said he's your friend from this alternate reality too."

"Yes, he is," said Neill. "We can tell him."

"I can't promise you he'll believe you," Allison said as she held the phone up to her ear and let it ring. "The mother fucker can have a temper."

Neill didn't know what to say. What had happened to her, dropping the f-bomb practically every sentence, and talking about Derek that way when he'd always been like a big brother to her?

"Hey, dumbshit," she said into the phone when Derek answered, "get your ass over here when you get off work and bring a couple of pizzas."

She walked away from the car and into the yard as she continued to speak so Neill couldn't eavesdrop. He waited, wondering since Allison was so changed, what Derek would be like. He couldn't imagine the Derek he knew putting up with anyone talking to him so disrespectfully, but neither could he have ever imagined Allison as a Goth chick with a potty mouth.

After a few minutes, Allison walked back toward him while putting the phone in her pocket.

"He's getting off his shift at Rocket's in a few minutes. Said he'd bring us some pizzas."

"Rocket's Pizza?" said Neill. "Is that where he works?"

"I thought you knew him. You should know he works there. He's a freakin' manager."

"Oh," said Neill. "In my time, he and I had both worked at Rocket's one summer, but then he got an internship in the forestry program at NMU."

"That dumbshit at NMU? He's not smart enough for college."

"Oh," said Neill.

"I am," said Allison, "but it's tough, you know, working and going to school."

"I understand that," said Neill. Then he dared to ask, "But if Derek is a dumbshit, why are you dating him?"

"Why do you think?" she said.

"I don't know," said Neill. "We were all just friends in school. We even all went to the prom together, but none of us was interested in dating each other."

"Hmm," she said, her eyes running up and down Neill like she was undressing him. "You are kind of cute. I can see where I might have gone to the prom with you. Derek can get jealous, though, so you better not say that to him."

Derek, jealous of him? Neill didn't like the thought. He knew he wouldn't want to be on Derek's bad side.

"So," said Allison, "if Derek is going to NMU in this alternate universe or whatever you call it, what do I do?"

"You go to NMU too," he replied. "You're a theatre major."

"Ha!" She laughed out loud. "You're shitting me—a theatre major." She reached into her purse and pulled out a pack of cigarettes.

"You smoke?" said Neill, in surprise.

"Yeah, you want one?" she asked, holding the cigarette pack toward him.

"No thank you," he said. "I take it you're not a theatre major in this world."

"No," she said. "I dropped out of NMU to make some money first. I'm a waitress. Got a couple of jobs. Have to pay the bills you know, especially since my mom's afraid to leave the house since the pandemic started."

"Oh," said Neill. "Where is your mom now?"

"She's inside," said Allison. "Balled up in the sheets in her bedroom. She's too afraid she'll get COVID or I'll give it to her, and she won't get vaccinated because she believes all that shit about the government planting microchips in us. She kind of had a nervous breakdown last fall when it started to get really bad in the U.P. She was working from home, but she got fired because she wasn't doing her work. I'm working my ass off to keep a roof over our heads."

"I'm sorry," said Neill. "That has to be really tough."

Allison didn't reply, just blew smoke through her nose.

"I'll have to bring her a piece of pizza, but she won't come downstairs to talk to us or anything. Once Derek gets here, we'll go in, but we'll wait out here until then just so you don't try any funny stuff."

"Okay," Neill replied, coughing as the cigarette smoke drifted into his face.

"Sorry," she said as he waved it away.

"It's okay," said Neill. "I think I'm coughing just because I'm so thirsty. I haven't had anything to drink in hours."

"Oh," she said, taking a last puff off her cigarette before smooshing it out on the step. "I tell you what. If you promise not to move, I'll go in the back door and come back with some water for you. While I'm in the house, I'll look out to see if you're still out here. If I find you've followed me to the back door, I won't be coming back out."

"I won't move. I promise."

She looked into his eyes, checking for sincerity.

"Sorry. You can't be too careful these days. Anyway, I'll be right back." Allison started to slowly walk backward, keeping an eye on him. She finally went around the side of the house to the back door. Neill didn't move. He waited, and after a few seconds, he heard her open and close the back door. A minute later, he heard it open and close again, and then she returned with a plastic cup with water and ice in it.

"I figured it was so hot you might like some ice," she said.

"Thanks," he replied, gratefully accepting the cup and quickly drinking half of it. Then he got a brain freeze and had to stop for a minute.

"Drink it too fast?" she asked, sitting back down on the step.

He nodded while trying to wait out the freeze.

"I hate when that happens," Allison said. "Well, Derek isn't known for being fast, so while we're waiting, why don't you sit down and tell me more about how you did this time traveling thing?"

Neill hesitated a moment, but his legs were tired after all the walking he'd done, so he sat over on the far edge of the steps from her. He wasn't sure he wanted to tell her all of his story and then have to repeat it to Derek, but he figured if she had changed so much, he had no idea how hard Derek would be to convince. If he got Allison to believe him, it might be easier to convince Derek, and he knew he desperately needed their help.

"Okay," Neill began. "It all happened when I got a job for the summer up at the Huron Mountain Club...."

Chapter 7

BY THE TIME DEREK ARRIVED in his truck with the pizzas, Allison was half-convinced Neill really was a time traveler.

"It's a lot to be asked to believe," she said, "and I'm not sure yet I do believe you, but we'll see what Derek thinks."

Neill could hear the doubt still in her voice, but he felt he was making progress. He stood up and looked hesitantly at his best friend as he got out of the truck. Allison, however, ran across the street to where Derek had parked and gave him a big kiss. Derek managed to hold the pizza boxes out to avoid dropping them while their lips met. It gave Neill a chance to look at his friend. He appeared the same—same large body, same height, wearing shorts and a T-shirt that said, "Rocket's Pizza." Nothing as unusual as Allison's clothing choices. Neill felt hopeful.

"Derek, this is Neill," said Allison, walking back across the street with her boyfriend. She took the pizza boxes from Derek as Neill offered Derek his hand to shake.

"Hi, Derek," said Neill. "It's a pleasure to meet you."

"That remains to be seen," said Derek, ignoring Neill's gesture. "Allison says you have some crazy story about knowing us."

"Yes," said Neill. "I'll be happy to share it with you."

"He's got me half-convinced," said Allison.

"I'm starving," Derek replied. "Let's go inside and he can tell us while we eat."

Neill couldn't argue with that. His stomach was rumbling from not having had food in so long. He felt dizzy just standing up because he was so hungry.

Allison led them around to the back door. Once they were inside, Neill asked if he could help with anything. Allison started to tell him where the plates were, but he was already opening the cupboard.

"How did you know where they were?" she asked, shocked.

"I told you," he replied. "We're friends. I've been eating at your house for years."

"That's just weird, dude," said Derek, sitting down at the table.

"Yeah, it is," said Neill.

"It gets even weirder," Allison told Derek. "Anyway, what do you want to drink?"

"A beer," said Derek.

Neill was surprised. They were all underage.

Allison wasn't surprised. She opened the fridge, pulled out three Budweisers, and set them on the table. Neill didn't drink, but today, he wasn't going to argue. It might help relieve the incredible stress he felt about his situation. He hoped it would also help these odd versions of his friends to relax and be receptive to what he had to say.

"So, Neill," said Derek, opening a pizza box, "you expect us to believe you're some sort of time traveler, hey?"

"Be nice, Derek," said Allison. "He's had a really rough time of it."

Neill was surprised by her remark. Was he making headway with her? He noticed she wasn't dropping f-bombs anymore—maybe she had just been defensive over meeting a stranger, and now she was starting to warm up to him a little.

"It's okay," Neill told Derek. "I wouldn't blame you if you didn't believe me, but I sure hope you will because I need your help, and I don't know who else I can turn to."

"And why did you come to us?" asked Derek, putting pizza on the plate Neill handed him before sitting down.

"Because you're my two best friends," said Neill.

"That's a weird thing to say when we never met you before," Derek replied.

"I know. It's weird for me too," said Neill, taking a slice of pizza, "because I know you both so well and yet you don't know me at all."

"What do you know about me?" asked Derek.

"I know all kinds of things," said Neill. "For example, I know that you broke your leg falling out of a tree when you were eight."

"That never happened," Derek replied.

"No?" said Neill, feeling confused. "We were climbing a tree, and I was up above you and...."

Neill got a strange look on his face.

"What is it?" asked Allison, sitting down next to Derek and across from Neill.

"It's weird," said Neill, "but I guess Derek is right. He wouldn't have fallen out of that tree and broken his leg when he was eight because I wasn't there to climb the tree with him. He was always kind of nervous about climbing trees, but I had talked him into it."

Allison laughed. "He is a bit afraid of heights."

"Hey," said Derek. "I'm a big guy. The bigger they are, the harder they fall, and I don't like falling."

"You don't mind being tackled in football," said Allison, taking her first bite of pizza.

"That's different," said Derek, "and anyway, I'm usually the one who does the tackling."

Neill didn't know what to say. Derek had never played football in his time. "I wish I knew how I could convince you both," he finally said.

"Why don't you tell Derek how you got here in those funny clothes," said Allison.

"Yeah, what are you, a reenactor up at Fort Wilkins or something?" Derek asked.

"No, these are the clothes I was wearing while out hiking in 1900 when I got transported back to this time."

"Back?" said Derek.

"Yes, somehow I accidentally time traveled from 2021 to 1900, and then somehow, I did the same thing again, only back to this time. But when I got here, a lot of things were different because I—well, I only just realized this, and I'm not even sure I understand it, but I somehow changed history when I was back in 1900. I changed it so severely that it meant I was never born, and neither were my parents, grandparents, or even great-grandparents, which is why you now don't know me in this time."

"That's pretty intense, man," said Derek, so surprised he set down the pizza crust he was chewing.

"Yeah, it really is," said Neill. "It's pretty scary for me, and that's why I need your help. I need to get back to 1900 so I can fix it, though I have no idea how I'll do that."

"You don't know how you'll get back?" asked Allison.

"I'm not totally sure, but I know what happened that caused me to travel to the past and then back to the present, so I think the same way will work. I'm just not sure if I do go back, I'll be able to undo what I already did. And even if I can, it's a moral quandary."

"How's that?" asked Derek, halfway through his second piece of pizza.

"Well, see," said Neill, and he paused to sigh over the thought of the weighty problem, "I inadvertently saved someone from drowning, and by doing that, I changed the past. This person was supposed to drown, and now, I have to go back and let him drown I guess, but at the same time, if I don't save him, isn't that morally wrong—like committing murder? Still, if he doesn't drown, my great-great-grandparents will never meet, and then I will never be born."

"That's some weird shit," said Derek.

"You didn't tell me that part," Allison added.

"Well, I'm still kind of piecing it all together," Neill replied. "It's all so surreal that I keep thinking this is all a dream, but I know it's real. I know because I woke up wearing these clothes, and my parents are missing, and...."

Neill couldn't help himself. His eyes began to tear up a little at the thought he might never see his parents and sister again.

"Fucking sucks," said Allison to show her sympathy for Neill's plight.

"But," said Derek, "none of that makes sense because if you weren't born, you wouldn't be here now."

"Hey," said Allison, "that's true. Derek, sometimes you're not such a dumbshit."

He elbowed her playfully. She retaliated by smacking his arm so hard he dropped his pizza.

"Fucking bitch," he said.

"Whatever," she said. "I was paying you a compliment."

Neill was speechless. How could they treat each other this way? He missed the familiar, supportive versions of his friends. He felt his lip quivering and wondered if he should leave the room before he started crying.

"Hold on, man," said Derek, looking at him. "Don't get emotional. We have to figure this out logically. You need to convince me you're telling the truth. Crying like a girl isn't going to do it for me."

Neill inhaled, feeling a stir of anger, but he decided not to let it get the best of him. "It's okay," he said. "I don't blame you for being skeptical, but I promise you I'm not trying to manipulate you with tears or in any other way. I'm just overly tired and hungry and overwhelmed. You have to admit it's a lot for a person to take in."

"It's okay, Neill," said Allison. "Have another slice of pizza."

"Yeah, Allison is paying," said Derek.

"Am not," she replied.

"You think I'm made of money?" Derek asked. "I don't get to live at home with my mom."

"Oh, whatever," she replied.

"Guys," said Neill, wondering if he'd made a mistake coming to them, "this isn't helping."

"I have a lot more questions," said Derek, reaching for more pizza, "before I decide to help you. I'm not even sure how you think we can help."

"Neill," said Allison, "why don't you start over and tell it from the beginning. I get what you're saying, but it takes a little longer for things to sink into Derek's thick skull."

Derek didn't retort, just mawed down his pizza.

"Okay," said Neill, knowing he was being honest so there was no reason to hold back anything. "It's weird, but I think it all has to do with a dolmen."

"A dolmen? What's that?" asked Derek.

"It's kind of like a—well, like an altar. It's a giant stone set on some smaller stones. They were created by ancient people in places like England and Ireland."

"Like Stonehenge, Derek," Allison explained.

"An altar like for human sacrifices?" asked Derek.

"No, I don't think so," said Neill, "but yeah, maybe like Stonehenge. Anyway, the dolmen is up at the Huron Mountain Club. It's not a stone circle, nothing fancy like that. Just three large rocks with another large one sitting on top of them. Anyway, I had heard it was there and went to see it, and when I touched it, somehow it transported me back to 1900."

Neill went on to explain how he had woken up in 1900, and then he told about all the events that had happened to him in that time before he had returned to the dolmen and experienced the strange time traveling again, followed by the shock of waking in 2021 to discover that several things about Marquette had changed. By the time he had finished his tale, all the pizza was gone, he had finished his beer and switched to water, and Allison and Derek were on their third beers.

"I have to piss," said Allison when Neill finished. She got up and left the room.

"That's crazy, man," said Derek. "I mean, moving the Longyear Mansion across the country like that—that would be almost impossible, especially over a hundred years ago."

"I know," said Neill. "But I swear it happened. It even made *Ripley's Believe It or Not.*"

"I don't know much about local history," said Derek, "but I'm pretty sure Howard Longyear lived to an old age, and his family is still living in that house. I had a job mowing their lawn one year when I was in high school."

"So you believe me?" asked Neill.

"Dude, it's unbelievable," said Derek, "but yeah, I mean, I want to. You'd have to be a real psycho to make up all of this kind of stuff. Unless you've just been watching too much *Dr. Who.*"

"Actually, I've never seen that show," said Neill.

"Doesn't matter. I want to believe you," said Derek. "It would be cool if it was true, but it is far-fetched."

Neill sat back in his chair. He had eaten six pieces of pizza and was now starting to feel sleepy.

"Thank you for the pizza," he said politely.

"No problem," said Derek.

"So, Neill," asked Allison, returning to the room. "What will you do now?"

"Yeah, let's say I did believe you," said Derek. "How would we help you?"

"Well, for starters," said Neill, looking at Derek, "I don't have any clothes. Could you lend me some, Derek, and then give me a ride up to the Huron Mountain Club so I can go back to the dolmen?"

"Man, you know that's private property," said Derek. "They'll never let us in there. And for all I know, even though you seem sincere, you might still be nuts, so I'm not going to risk it."

"I assure you I'm not nuts," said Neill, although he privately admitted he wasn't fully convinced he wasn't. "I wish I knew how to convince you I'm telling the truth."

"Derek," said Allison, "could you at least give him some of your clothes? Or we could take him up to Walmart so he can buy some and not look like a total freak."

Derek kind of wrinkled up his lip. "Yeah, I guess I—"

"Wait! I know!" said Neill, and he pulled out his cell phone.

"Know what?" asked Allison.

"How I can convince you I'm telling the truth, only, no, I guess that won't work after all." As Neill spoke, he swiped his phone, but only a black screen greeted him. His phone was completely dead.

"What, man? What were you thinking?" asked Derek.

"I thought my phone might still have a little life left to it," said Neill, frowning, "but it looks like the battery has totally died, and I don't have a charger."

"So?" asked Derek. "How would the phone help?"

"I have pictures on it," said Neill, "of me with you guys. There's one of the three of us at high school graduation, and one of Allison and me at the prom."

"The prom!" said Derek. "I took her to the prom."

"Yeah," said Neill, slowly, "because I wasn't around. We, well, we all went together as friends."

"What the fuck is this?" asked Derek, clenching his fist. "You better not be trying to put the moves on my woman."

"Derek, calm down," said Allison. "I'm not *your woman*. You don't fuckin' own me."

"You don't get into this," said Derek, turning to her. "This is between men."

"Oh, shut up," said Allison, slapping him in the head, "or you won't be getting any tonight."

Neill wanted Derek to calm down too. He knew Derek must have a good seventy pounds on him. Neill didn't remember Derek ever being aggressive other than with a few jerks in high school, whom he had intimidated enough for them to leave him alone. But he and Derek had always been friends, always had each other's back. This version of Derek and Allison was shocking to say the least. *Maybe I was a positive influence on them before*, Neill thought. *Is this what they're like because I wasn't in their lives?*

"I don't need him talking about dating my woman," Derek told his girlfriend.

"I'm not *your woman*,'" Allison replied. "Yes, we're dating, but I haven't seen a ring of any kind yet."

"We're nineteen!" said Derek.

"So?" said Allison. "That's my point. We're too young for you to get so territorial. Besides, I wouldn't date Neill anyway. He's not my type."

"I never said we dated," said Neill, trying to calm both of them down. "Just that we were friends and went to the prom as friends."

"God, we sound like a bunch of losers," said Allison, "going to the prom as friends."

"I wish I could show you the pictures," said Neill.

"Maybe you can," said Allison. "Let me see that."

She reached across the table and took the phone out of Neill's hand.

She turned the phone over, then said, "It's the same brand as mine. My charger should work on it. Hang on."

She got up from the table and disappeared down the hall.

Derek gave Neill a look that silently said, "She's my woman."

"Derek, I'm a nice guy," Neill told him. "I know that if I end up staying in this time, we'll end up being best friends. Please give me a chance."

"I don't need any more friends," said Derek. "I have enough."

"Here it is," said Allison, returning with the phone in her hand and a charger plugged into it. She set the phone on the kitchen counter and plugged the charger into the wall socket.

"Is it working?" asked Neill after a few seconds.

"Looks like it," she said. "It says two hours and eighteen minutes to a full charge."

"I'm not waiting that long," said Derek.

"Aren't you going to stick around?" asked Allison. "I was just kidding about later tonight. You know you can stay over."

Derek looked torn.

"It probably won't take that long," Neill told him. "Once it's 10 or 20 percent charged, I should be able to access the photos."

"I'll stay," said Derek, "but not because I want to see the stupid prom picture. I'm just not leaving my woman alone with Marty McFly here."

"What does that mean?" asked Neill.

"You know," said Derek. "Michael J. Fox's character in *Back to the Future*. He traveled back in time in that movie."

"Oh, I never saw it," said Neill.

"Maybe it didn't exist in your time," said Derek.

"Well, it does," said Neill. "I've heard of it, and I know who Michael J. Fox is. I saw a few reruns of *Family Ties* when I was a kid."

"Maybe we should go get Neill some clothes while we wait for his phone to charge," said Allison.

"I'm not worried about his clothes," said Derek. "I want to know where he's going to sleep."

"I don't know," said Neill, raising his eyebrows at the thought. "Could one of you put me up?"

"I have an apartment of my own," said Derek, sounding like that made him a big shot. "You can stay with me and we can get some clothes when we go back to my place."

"Derek, you have a one-room apartment and you don't even own a decent couch," said Allison.

"Well, he isn't staying here alone with you," said Derek. "I can tell you that."

"My mom is here," said Allison. "She'll make sure nothing happens."

"That zombie," said Derek, grimacing.

"I appreciate your kindness, Derek," said Neill, before he and Allison could go at it again. "I would be happy to stay with you."

"It's not kindness that motivates me," said Derek.

"Well, fine," said Allison. "Neill can get clothes later when he goes to your place. What should we do then while we wait for the phone to charge?"

"I want to hear more about how this time traveling works," said Derek, sitting back in his chair.

"I don't know what else to tell you," said Neill. "I told you I think it has something to do with the dolmen on top of Mount Huron."

"Where's Mount Huron? You didn't mention that before," said Derek.

"It's at the Huron Mountain Club," said Neill. "It's the biggest mountain in the area. You can see it from Lake Superior if you're out on the lake."

"You can," said Derek, crinkling up his forehead in thought. "Then I imagine we could walk there from Lake Superior's shore. I mean, if we had a boat."

"Why would you want to do that?" asked Allison.

"So we wouldn't have to try to go through the gate at the Club," said Derek. "We can just land on the beach and then walk inland to this dolmen."

"But how would we do that?" asked Neill. "I mean, where would we get a boat?"

"I have a kayak," said Derek. "It holds two people."

"Would you really do that for him, Derek?" asked Allison. "Kayak along the lake so he can get to the dolmen?"

"Maybe," said Derek, "if he can convince me he's telling the truth. I want to see those photos first."

"Fair enough," said Neill. "I would really appreciate that. Could we go up there tomorrow?"

"No," said Derek. "I have to work all day tomorrow, but I have the next day off."

"Okay," said Neill, "if you don't mind putting me up for a couple of nights."

"You don't mind too much, do you, Derek?" asked Allison.

"No," he replied, turning to Neill. "I'm not sure I believe your story or trust you, but I don't have anything worth stealing in my apartment, so I can trust you that far anyway. And you seem smart enough to know that a guy your size shouldn't mess with a bigger guy like me."

"Thanks," said Neill. "Actually, it's fine if it's the next day. I could use the time to go to the library."

"What's at the library?" asked Derek.

"I want to know more about Howard Longyear and basically everything about Marquette's history in this time since it's apparently very different from in my time."

"Different how?" asked Allison.

"Well, like that the Longyear Mansion wasn't moved, but other things too, like the Howard-Froebel School on Ridge Street is—"

"You mean the Longyear-Froebel School," said Derek. "I went there for elementary. But it's an art museum now."

"That's just it," said Neill. "In my time, it was known as the Howard-Froebel School because it was partly named for Howard Longyear after he drowned, but the school was also torn down, back in the 1960s I believe, and a giant high-rise senior citizen center was built there."

"The only high-rise senior home around here is Snowberry Heights," said Allison.

"Yes," said Neill, "but in my time, there was also Pine-Ridge Apartments."

"No one would build a high-rise on Ridge Street," said Derek. "The homeowners would be all up in arms."

"Right, you would think so," said Neill, "but in the past I came from, it wasn't until after they built it that the neighborhood was named a historical district to prevent similar buildings being built there."

"Interesting," said Allison. "What else is different?"

"Well," said Neill, "I've only seen a little of Marquette in this time so far. The new hospital appears to be the same, and you have a bike trail like in my time, but the ore dock in the harbor is missing in your time. In my time, they left it standing. It was unused for years, but everyone felt it was iconic of Marquette's past, so people kept talking about turning it into condominiums or a museum or a botanical garden or something."

"Weird," said Derek. "Why would you keep an ugly old ore dock?"

"Yes, it's all really weird," said Neill, thinking it best not to waste time defending the star of the Lower Harbor, "especially when you've seen the ore dock and all these other things with your own eyes, and now you see that they aren't there, or in the case of the Longyear Mansion and the school, they are there when they shouldn't be."

"It is weird," Allison agreed. "But I guess I don't know enough about Marquette history to explain why things are so different."

"That's what I want to find out," said Neill. "I'm pretty sure it all has something to do with Howard Longyear not drowning. I want to find out more about him. Maybe I can find answers at the library."

"Allison, check the phone," said Derek. "It should be charged enough now for us to see those photos. The way this dude is talking, I'm starting to get really curious."

Allison must have been equally curious because she jumped up to check the phone. "It's only at 12 percent," she said.

"That should be enough," said Derek. "It should only take a few minutes to show us the pictures, and then we can plug it back in so it can finish charging."

"All right," said Allison, unplugging the phone. She handed it to Neill and then sat back down.

Neill didn't say anything. He was too nervous. These photos could make or break the deal. He quickly swiped his phone to open it and then clicked on the camera icon. He began swiping through photos. He was glad he hadn't gotten a new phone in a couple of years and had never gotten around to downloading the photos to his computer and erasing them on his phone. First he found the prom pictures. There was only one of him and Allison. He hesitated to start there, but it would take another minute or two to swipe to the graduation photo Derek was in, and he wanted to prove he was telling the truth before the phone died.

"Here," he said, holding out the phone for both to see. "Allison and me at the prom in 2019, our junior year. We were going to go together in 2020 too, but prom got canceled because of the pandemic."

"Oh, my God!" said Allison, seeing herself in the photograph with Neill's arm around her. "I look good!"

"That's not the dress you wore," said Derek, his eyes wide. "I remember your dress was white and off the shoulders."

"Yeah," said Allison. "I'd never wear a poofy pink dress like that, that's for sure."

"How do we know you didn't photoshop these pictures?" Derek asked, leaning across the table to take the phone and look closely at it.

"I didn't," said Neill.

"How could he, Derek?" asked Allison. "We never met him before."

"He could have downloaded our photos from Facebook and manipulated them," Derek replied.

"He couldn't have manipulated this one," said Allison. "It would be impossible to change my dress and makeup and all that, plus I look skinnier in this photo."

Derek looked confused and set down the phone. Neill grabbed it and quickly swiped to the graduation pictures.

"Here, Derek. Here's a photo of you and me in our graduation caps. Remember, there wasn't a ceremony because of the coronavirus, but we got together anyway and drove around in a car parade with a bunch of other students in your truck honking our horns."

"Fuck, I didn't graduate," said Derek, "so I don't know how you photoshopped this one."

"You didn't graduate?" said Neill in surprise.

"No. Got into a fistfight with the shop teacher my senior year and got suspended so I dropped out. I might go back to get my GRE, though."

"Oh," was all Neill could say. He felt so sad to think what his friends' lives were in this time.

"You can believe what you want, Derek," Allison said, plugging the charger back into the phone, "but I don't see how he could photoshop these pictures. I believe you, Neill."

She looked at Derek, waiting to see how he would respond. Derek inhaled and flared his nostrils. Then he looked Neill in the eye and said, "If I find out you're lying, I'm going to hurt you."

"I'll make sure you don't need to do that," Neill promised. "So, does this mean you'll help me?"

"Yeah, I guess," said Derek.

"Thank you," said Neill. Finally, he felt things might work out. He had no idea how he would get things back to how they had been, but at least two people now believed him and were willing to help.

Chapter 8

Neill, Allison, and Derek talked until almost dark, and then Derek and Neill said goodnight and promised to talk to Allison tomorrow. The boys got into Derek's truck and drove to his one-bedroom apartment, upstairs in an old house off Fourth Street.

Derek found a spare blanket and pillow for Neill so he could sleep on the couch. Best of all, he let Neill take a shower and get cleaned up. He also had a spare razor he gave Neill, which Neill was thrilled with—a Gillette Mach 3. No more dangerous razor blades from 1900. And Derek had an extra toothbrush and real, honest-to-god Crest toothpaste, not the icky hog-bristle brushes with disgusting bicarbonate of soda Neill had been forced to use at the Allen and Longyear homes. Derek had even recently bought a new package of boxer briefs and not worn a couple of pairs yet, so he gave them to Neill. Derek was bigger than Neill, but also in good shape with a small waist, so they fit Neill perfectly as did the shorts Derek gave him. Derek also found an old T-shirt from high school he had outgrown that fit Neill.

"It's such a relief to have normal clothes again," said Neill when he emerged from the bathroom.

"Yeah, you never would have caught me in those heavy clothes you were wearing," Derek replied.

"I really appreciate everything you've done for me," said Neill, sitting down on the couch next to his pillow and the folded up blanket.

"No problem," said Derek, turning off the TV, which he'd been watching while Neill got ready for bed.

"It feels like old times," said Neill, "me spending the night at your place."

"I wouldn't know," Derek replied, getting up from his chair. "It's really weird to think we're friends in an alternate time. You seem like an okay guy, though, despite my first impressions. Anyway, I'll see you in the morning."

"Good night," said Neill.

After spreading out the blanket, Neill crawled under it and prepared to sleep. It wasn't the most comfortable couch, but Neill was grateful to have somewhere to sleep at all after the scary day he'd had. Still, he had so much to come to grips with that he found at first he couldn't sleep. It was all so surreal to be back in his own time, only to find it so altered. To discover his family didn't even exist in this time was a shock he still wasn't over, but perhaps even stranger was to see how different Allison and Derek were, as if he didn't know them at all. He'd never heard a four-letter word come out of Allison's mouth before, and this Derek was rougher, and also somewhat lacking in self-esteem from the way Allison treated him. He hadn't even finished high school. Neill hated to think it, but his friends were, well, kind of losers. How could they be so vastly different in this time?

Is it because they didn't have me around to be their friend? he wondered. It was a rather arrogant thought, but Neill remembered he had been there to comfort Allison when she was depressed and to encourage Derek when he had self-doubt. Neill also remembered all the things they had done for him over the years that perhaps had helped them become gentler and kinder. *I wish I had been around when they were younger to help them,* he thought. *They're helping me now, so I think they're still good people at heart.* Maybe he could help them now, but he wouldn't be staying around to do so, not if he could get back to his own time or somehow go back to 1900 to fix things. If he could do that, he wouldn't need to help them because time would change back and this version of them would have never existed. He hoped that was true, but how he could make that happen, he had no idea. What if he couldn't travel back in time again? What if he was wrong about how touching the dolmen had transported him? After all, other people must have touched the dolmen and not been transported through time. Just thinking about it was enough to give anyone a headache.

And if it doesn't work, he thought, *I'll be stuck in this time forever. Then I will be friends with Derek and Allison again, but they'll be these different versions of Derek and Allison. I won't be able to go back and change them, but maybe they'll become better friends with me over time.*

Neill thought back to when he and Derek had become friends. It had happened in first grade. A girl in their class had decided to make a list of which of her classmates were good and which were bad. Soon, almost every kid was making their own good or bad list, and those who weren't making lists were trying to convince people to put them on their good lists. When Neill made his list, he asked Derek, "Derek, how do you spell your name?" Neill thought there was a C in it. When Derek spelled it for him, Neill wrote it down under the Bad column. "Don't put me on the bad list," Derek had said. "I have to," Neill had replied. "Why?" asked Derek. "Because you burp," said Neill, adding, "Good people have good manners." Derek hadn't replied to that, but Neill had never forgotten the look of shame on Derek's face. Embarrassed, he had stuffed the list in his desk without a word.

The next morning before the teacher called the class to order, a boy named Sam took Neill's chair and wouldn't give it back to him. When Neill tried to grab the chair, Sam pushed him down. Before Neill knew how to respond, he saw Sam fall on the floor beside him. Then Neill saw Derek towering over him and Sam. "Don't you ever take Neill's chair again!" Derek warned Sam. Then Derek reached down and pulled Neill to his feet. "Tell Neill you're sorry," Derek demanded of Sam. Sam, too stunned to know what to think, managed to gasp out, "I'm sorry, Neill." "You better be," said Derek. "People with good manners don't take things that aren't theirs. Neill has good manners. He could teach you a thing or two."

The teacher now entered the room, so Sam quickly got to his feet and everyone went to their chairs at their tables.

"Thanks, Derek," said Neill when they sat down in their adjacent desks.

"Do I get to be on the good list now?" asked Derek.

"Yes, definitely," said Neill, and he pulled his list out of his folder. He erased Derek's name from the bad list and replaced it with Sam's. Then he wrote Derek's name in big letters at the top of the good list.

From that day on, Derek had seemed enthralled to be hanging around Neill. He clearly admired and respected Neill for his intelligence and good manners, and he tried to copy a lot of his behaviors. As for Neill, no one dared to pick on him again since Derek, the biggest guy in the class, was his best friend. They became inseparable after that, often spending the night at each other's houses. Derek was a frequent dinner guest at the Vandelaare home and both of

Neill's parents were glad for the friendship between the boys, even referring to Derek as "our third child." Neill's sister Madeleine had looked up to Derek as a big brother, and he had treated her like a princess, not even minding when she acted annoying. Derek had no siblings of his own, and his parents did not give him the attention Neill's parents gave to their children, so Derek happily became an extension of the Vandelaare family.

Now, lying on Derek's couch, Neill felt sorry for this alternative Derek who had never had a best friend. He also felt sorry for himself that his friendship with the Derek from his own time might be completely over. Even if he and Derek became best friends in this altered time, it would never be the same since they would not have a shared past. And the same was true with Allison.

Restraining the tears he felt, Neill tried to comfort himself by thinking, *It will all work out somehow. It has to.*

In the morning, Derek and Neill got up and had breakfast together. Neill again thanked Derek for letting him stay there and also for feeding him.

"I'm so sorry," Neill said, "that I don't have any money or any way to repay you."

"Well, if you are lying to me about all this time traveling stuff," Derek replied, "or we get you to the Huron Mountain Club and find this dolmen thing doesn't work, then I'll get you a job at Rocket's so you can pay me back."

"That's funny," said Neill, "because you and I worked at Rocket's in my time before I got a job at the Huron Mountain Club and you got your forestry internship."

"Weird," said Derek. "I do like to be outside, though. I imagine a forestry internship would beat making pizzas, even if I am a manager now."

"I hope the time travel thing does work," said Neill, "but if it doesn't, will you let me stay with you until I can get my own place?"

"Probably," said Derek, smirking, "so long as you don't make any moves on Allison."

"I won't. I promise," said Neill. "She's a great girl, but like I said, we were never more than friends."

"Make sure it stays that way," said Derek, before lifting his cereal bowl to his mouth to swallow the last of the milk.

Neill had to laugh a little. Some things had not changed.

"What?" asked Derek.

"Nothing," said Neill, focusing on his cereal.

"Hey, did you mean it when you said Allison is a great girl?" asked Derek.

"Sure," said Neill. "We were always close friends."

"Yeah, in your time," said Derek. "But she's different in this time, isn't she?"

"Yes," said Neill.

Derek stood up, looking like he wanted to say something more, but then he stated, "Well, I better get going. The delivery truck comes this morning. What will you do while I'm at work?"

"I'll go to the library," said Neill. "I want to see what I can learn about Howard Longyear and anything else in Marquette's past that is different from in my time. It probably won't help me get back to my own time, but I am curious about how Howard would have turned out if he did live."

"Okay," said Derek, handing Neill his apartment key. "I don't have a spare one, so just be back before five so I'm not locked out."

"I will," said Neill, putting the key in his pocket. "Thanks!"

"Oh, and…" said Derek, seeming a bit hesitant as he pulled out his wallet, "I don't have much food in the fridge, so here's some money so you can buy some lunch."

He handed Neill a twenty-dollar bill.

"Thanks, man," said Neill, wishing he didn't have to take it, but knowing he would need to eat. "I'll pay you back somehow, though I'm not sure how."

"Don't worry about it," said Derek. "If your incredible story is true, this may turn out to be the most interesting thing that ever happened to me."

Derek laughed and Neill laughed back, though he wasn't sure what was so funny. For all he knew, the dolmen might not work this time. He hoped he wouldn't have to disappoint Derek by being made to look like a liar, and worse, being stuck in this alternate time and never seeing his family again.

"Okay. I better go," said Derek, slipping on his shoes.

"Have a good day at work," said Neill.

"Thanks, bye," Derek replied, and he was out the door.

Neill finished his breakfast and used the bathroom. Then he walked to the Peter White Public Library, which was only a few blocks away. He was glad to see, as he approached the building from the back, that it didn't look like it had changed at all.

Being a bit of a nerd since his parents were history geeks and his father an author, Neill knew his way around the library. He immediately walked upstairs to the Michigan history section, thinking he would find a book about Marquette there to see if he could find the answers he sought.

After a couple of minutes perusing the shelves, he found Tyler R. Tichelaar's *My Marquette: Explore the Queen City of the North, Its History, People, and Places.*

"Cool," Neill whispered. In his own time, he had actually known Tyler Tichelaar. The author and Neill's father were good friends, both being members of the Upper Peninsula Publishers and Authors Association and the Marquette Regional History Center. Neill had even read parts of *My Marquette* since his parents owned a copy. He recalled it had a large section on Marquette's historical homes. He hoped it would tell him what he wanted to know about the Longyear Mansion. It might even tell him something about the Robert O'Neill Historical Home, the home Neill had grown up in. His father had inherited the house in trust for his lifetime from Mr. O'Neill with the stipulation it be operated as a historical home with public tours a couple of days a week. Neill was curious to find out how the un-pleasant man he had met yesterday had come to own the house in this time.

Neill took the hefty book off the shelf and carried it to a near-by table. He sat down and eagerly opened it, turning to the Table of Contents to find out on what page the entry on the Longyear Mansion began. Once he found the right page, he began to read:

The Longyear Mansion
536 E. Arch

Although the Longyear Mansion's official address is 536 E. Arch, it encompasses the entire 500 block between Ridge and Arch Streets and consists of three acres. It is, without doubt, the finest home Marquette has ever seen.

The mansion was built by John M. Longyear, who came to Marquette from Lansing, Michigan, where his father was a congressman and judge. Longyear arrived in 1873 and worked as a landlooker, someone looking for profitable property who estimated its worth. In addition, he would become involved in developing the mineral wealth on the Gogebic Range in Upper Michigan and the Mesaba Range in Minnesota. Later, he would be involved in founding a mine on an island off Norway, resulting in the town of Longyearbyen being named for him.

Longyear's contributions to Marquette would include serving as mayor, funding the Marquette Opera House, donating the land where the Peter White Public Library was built, being a founder of the Huron Mountain Club, and helping to start Northern Michigan University, resulting in Longyear Hall being named for him. Despite these many contributions, Longyear is best remembered in Marquette for his impressive sandstone mansion.

After living in a couple of different Marquette homes, none of which met with his satisfaction, Longyear decided in 1890 to begin building the famous Longyear Mansion, which would not be completed until 1892. D. Fred Charlton, who had already built many fine homes in Marquette, was hired as architect for what would become his masterpiece. Literally, tons of the local Jacobs quarry's raindrop sandstone would be used at a cost of $500,000. The home would have sixty-five rooms, leaded glass windows, parquet floors, an octagonal entry that rose up to a Tiffany stained glass dome, a library, music room, and a basement containing a bowling alley and billiard parlor. The elegant gardens were designed by famous landscape artist Frederick Law Olmsted, who would also design New York's Central Park and numerous other landscaping projects across the nation. When the Longyear family moved in at Christmas 1892, the home had the distinction of being the first in Marquette to use electric Christmas lights. Marquette had never seen such a home and likely never will again.

"I know all this," Neill muttered, feeling frustrated. But then his eye caught the name of Howard in the next paragraph. He knew if he had not changed the past, the next part of the story should have detailed how Howard had drowned and how his parents, grief-stricken, had wanted to build a park to him below their property, but the city had allowed the railroad to run its tracks through the proposed park, causing the Longyears to leave Marquette and take their mansion with them. Instead, that entire part of the story was missing and the entry just jumped ahead to Mr. Longyear's death.

When John M. Longyear died in 1922, he left his mansion to his son, Howard Longyear, with the provision that his wife could continue to live in it the remainder of her life. Mrs. Longyear would die in 1931. After that, the mansion's new mistress was Mrs. Howard (Margaret) Longyear. Howard and Margaret Longyear continued his parents' practice of hosting several social events a year at the mansion. Margaret became the leader of Marquette society. She was deeply involved in charitable causes, especially during the Great Depression and World War II. She was a promoter of women's suffrage, a member of the Women's Federated Clubhouse, served on the library board, and was also involved in the First Christian Science Church.

Howard served as mayor of Marquette three times. He took an early interest in preserving Marquette's heritage, along with his sister Helen Longyear Paul. They were both active in the Marquette County Historical Society and were proactive in preserving many of Marquette's architectural treasures, including the Longyear-Froebel School and the Peter White House, which they bought from the family and donated to the Marquette County Historical Society. They established the Marquette Historic Trust to raise money to help businesses and private citizens receive grants to preserve their historical buildings or provide upkeep to them as needed. Consequently, unlike many other cities along Lake Superior, most of Marquette's original sandstone architecture has been preserved to be enjoyed by future generations. Howard and Margaret's legacy was as significant as those of Howard's parents, Peter White, the Harlows, and other pioneer contributors to Marquette. Howard died in 1965 and Margaret in 1976. They had three children and left the house to their son Howard, Jr.

Howard, Jr., born in 1910, continued his parents' roles as benefactors and visionaries to the Marquette community. Like his father and grandfather, he served as mayor of Marquette. He also saw incredible growth of the Longyear businesses, as well as prosperity for the many employees who worked for them. As a result, by the second half of the twentieth century, Longyear, Inc. became the biggest employer in Marquette County, and it continues as such today as it leads in innovations for handling its many assets, from mining and forestry to technology and modern forms of entrepreneurship. Howard strongly believed in beautifying Marquette and was instrumental in helping to clean up the Lower Harbor, including removing the ore docks when they were no longer used.

Howard, Jr. never married, so when he died in 1998, he left the house to his nephew, John Beecher Longyear, son to his brother, Allen Longyear. John Beecher did a major renovation of the Longyear Mansion in the early years of the twenty-first century, in many ways restoring its late Victorian charm. John Beecher Longyear continued to head up the Longyear businesses until his retirement in 2005. Although today he lives in Florida, he frequently still visits Marquette. Today, the company's CEO is his son, Joshua Longyear, who also resides in the Longyear Mansion of his ancestors.

Joshua and his wife Patricia frequently open their home for garden parties and home tours, ensuring that the mansion has remained a focal point of Marquette's social activities. It is fair to say no visit to Marquette is complete without a glimpse of it.

"Interesting," said Neill. And it was interesting. He was especially happy to hear that his great-great-grandmother, Margaret Dalrymple, had shined as a society hostess in Marquette, as well as done many good things. He was surprised, though, that she had become a Christian Scientist, given that he had always understood she was a staunch Baptist; obviously, she had decided to change religions to suit her husband. Neill knew Howard's mother, Mrs. Longyear, had been a strong believer in Christian Science. In fact, he seemed to recall in his own time that when she had died, she had left the mansion in Brookline, Massachusetts to the Mary Baker Eddy Foundation since Eddy had been the founder of Christian Science. But in this time, instead of inheriting it herself, Mrs. Longyear had been passed over in her husband's will so that the house would go to Howard. Neill didn't know what he thought about all that. But the history of the Longyear family did not matter that much to him; what mattered is that Howard had lived and married Margaret Dalrymple, thus messing up his own family's history.

Neill now paged through the book until he came to the entry on his parents' house: the Robert O'Neill Historical Home. The history began as he knew it, describing how the house had been built by the Hennings, then sold to Judge Smith and his wife. It had been inherited by the Smiths' grandson, Mark Hampton, who had died in World War I and left the house to his wife Eliza. Eliza had then married Robert O'Neill, who had outlived his wife. In Neill's timeline, Robert O'Neill had then left the house in trust to Neill's father, John Vandelaare, largely because Neill's father was a descendant of the Hennings, the original owners. And that inheritance had, in fact, been why Neill had been given his name—in honor of Mr. O'Neill. But in this version of 2021, the history was a little different. The entry in *My Marquette* stated:

> When Robert O'Neill died, his family sold the house to Brad Tousignant, who is the present owner. Mr. Tousignant has done a lot of work to restore the house's sandstone façade. He also built a modern-looking garage beside the house which raised the ire of his neighbors until he had it resided to better match the sandstone mansion beside it.

I didn't even notice the garage, thought Neill. Of course, he realized *My Marquette* had been published in 2011 and was ten years' old now, so perhaps the garage had been torn down since the book's publication.

Neill sat back in his chair and wondered what to do now. What was he to make of all this? He thought about paging through the rest of the book to find out what else was different in Marquette, and he did flip over a few pages, but he felt too overwhelmed by what he had already learned to find out if anything else had changed. Plus, why page through a book when he could walk around Marquette to see the changes for himself? He could always come back to the library to read the book later. Right now, he felt he needed some fresh air to clear his mind. Just the fact that he had time traveled was enough to drive a person bonkers. He just couldn't understand how it was possible since he obviously wasn't the first person to have touched the dolmen. It had been there for hundreds of years, and several people at the Club had told him about it. No one had ever been reported missing who had gone to see it, so why had it had such a strange effect on him? Maybe it wasn't the dolmen that had caused him to time travel, but given that he had touched it both times, it seemed to be the common denominator.

Suddenly, Neill had an idea. He flipped through more of *My Marquette* until he came to the entry on the Huron Mountain Club. Maybe the dolmen would be mentioned there. If Howard Longyear had seen him disappear when he touched the dolmen in 1900, it might be in this history book written in 2011. But, unfortunately, after a few minutes scanning the chapter on the Huron Mountain Club, Neill found no mention of the dolmen.

Sad, confused, and feeling overwhelmed, Neill turned and stared out the window for a while. The library was perched on the top of Front Street's hill so he had a view that overlooked the downtown. After a few seconds, he began to notice a few buildings that were different from his own time. Should he walk around Marquette to see what else was different? What good would that do him? It might just depress him more, though he was happy that the historic buildings had been preserved. What he needed to figure out was how to get back to 1900. Then he could change things back to how they should have been so he could return to his own time and find it normal again. But all that presented a moral quandary, for how could he right the past unless he let Howard drown? If he went out in that boat with Hugh and Howard again and it overturned, could he purposely not row to their rescue? Could he intentionally watch them drown? He doubted he could. He would never be able to live with the guilt. But if he didn't let them drown, he'd have to live with the guilt of destroying his own family, however unintentionally he had done it.

He seriously missed his parents and sister now. How was it possible they did not exist, yet he still existed? It was too hard to wrap his head around that. It was so unfair that he was in this situation. None of it was his fault. What kind of person would have let Howard drown? Even if he hadn't lost his memory and had recalled that Howard was supposed to drown, he couldn't have let him. And it wasn't his fault that he had been transported back in time. How was he to know touching the dolmen would do that? Why was he the dolmen's victim?

Neill began to feel like he was suffocating while sitting there thinking about it all. He knew he thought best when he was out walking. Getting up from the table, he picked up *My Marquette* and carried it back to the shelf. It was almost lunch time and Derek had given him money for food, so Neill decided to walk downtown and find something to eat. That would give his brain a little break. Really, there was no reason to keep stressing over it; nothing could be done until tomorrow when Derek took him back to the Huron Mountain Club.

Chapter 9

NEILL LEFT THE LIBRARY, EXITING out the front door onto Front Street. He then started down the hill, wondering where he should eat. Usually, he would go to Sol Azteca or Iron Bay near the harbor, or The Vierling on Front Street, or maybe Donckers or the Delft Bistro on Washington Street. But he wondered how many of those places still existed. He had walked by Iron Bay and Sol Azteca yesterday and seen people there—that had been when he'd discovered the ore dock was missing—but the thought of looking out at the empty harbor again rather depressed him, so he turned right onto Washington. He decided he'd try the Delft Bistro, which was only half-a-block away, but as soon as he turned onto Washington, he got another shock. The Delft Bistro was in the building that had once been the Delft Theatre, and the theatre's marquee had been an iconic part of Marquette's downtown for nearly a century, but it was no longer there. In fact, the street looked bare without it.

"That really sucks," said Neill, unable to curb his frustration. He started down the south side of Washington Street to see if the restaurant would even be there. He passed several shops whose names he recognized, but when he came to Donckers, it looked to be just a candy store without a restaurant above it, and beside it, the Delft Theatre appeared to be all boarded up.

In disgust, Neill continued down the block, passing a few storefronts until he came to a place called Superior Sandwiches. It looked like some sort of deli, and it did not appear to be busy. Curious, Neill opened the door and stepped inside. Against the back wall was a glass counter with some potato and bean salads inside it and a few other items. About a dozen tables with chairs were strewn about the room, but only a couple of them were occupied by patrons.

"Hello," said a girl. When Neill looked up from the counter to return her greeting, he was shocked to find Allison staring at him.

"Oh, hello," he replied.

"What are you doing here?" she asked.

"Uh," said Neill, distracted by being surprised that her employer didn't require her to remove her nose ring, "I just thought I'd get some lunch. Derek didn't have much food in his fridge, so he gave me a twenty to get something to eat."

"Well, that's enough cash to eat in this dump," said Allison.

Neill repressed a laugh and looked around to see if the other customers had heard her.

Returning his attention to her, he said, "Okay. What's good here?"

"The pastrami sandwich is edible."

"Pastrami sounds great," said Neill.

"It comes with a pickle and chips."

"Perfect," said Neill, "and can I get a Coke too?"

"Sure. It's your choice to rot out your gut."

Neill didn't reply, but he had to wonder who in their right mind would employ Allison.

She rang up his order, took his money, returned his change, and gave him a plastic number for his table. "Have a seat and Jordan will bring it to you when it's ready," she told him.

Neill assumed Jordan was the coworker, the one busy doing something over in the corner. Neill felt like he should be friendly and say something more, but he found Allison's attitude off-putting, so he just said, "Thank you," and sat down at a table.

Usually when Neill found himself waiting, he'd pull out his phone and check his email. Since Allison had charged the phone yesterday, he realized he could try to check it. In fact, he was surprised to realize he hadn't thought to do so before. Not that he expected to get any email given he was in a different time, but he could at least pass the time by surfing the internet.

When he opened the email app, a bunch of spam filled his inbox. He quickly scanned and deleted them, but then when he got to the end, he found an email from Allison.

"No way," he said. "Is it possible?"

Filled with hope, he clicked on it.

It was dated from two weeks ago, the day he had disappeared.

> Hi Neill,
>
> Hope you're doing well. Any big plans for the Fourth of July? I wish you could be here, but I understand you need to work. Derek promised to take me to the fireworks.

I hope they don't decide to cancel them at the last minute because of the coronavirus. We'll be sure to stay away from everyone, even though we've both been vaccinated.

Not much else to say. Just working and trying to learn my lines for my Shakespeare role at the boathouse later this month. So glad we can perform plays again. Hope you're doing well. Write when you can. I know you don't have good reception there.

Happy Fourth.

Love,

Allison

Love, Allison—Neill almost had to laugh. He couldn't envision the Allison at the lunch counter ever signing a letter like that.

He wondered how he had managed to get Allison's email. He thought she must have sent it before he had touched the dolmen that day so that it had already loaded on his phone before he had time traveled, but when he looked at the date on it, he saw she'd sent it at 4:18 p.m. on July 3. That was the day he had woken up in the Allen house, so it meant she sent it after he had time traveled. Was it possible the email had gone through to his phone despite his time traveling? Apparently it was! Now he wished he hadn't deleted all that spam since it had been at the top of his email list and must have come in after Allison's message. It would have confirmed he could get his email in this alternate time. But if that was possible, could he also send one to his own time? Did he dare try?

"What's stopping me?" he muttered, and he furiously began typing a reply to Allison's message.

Dear Allison,

This is going to sound crazy, but I am in another time. It's hard to explain, but I found that dolmen at the Huron Mountain Club that I told you I wanted to find. It's on the top of Mount Huron. When I touched it, I somehow time traveled back to 1900. I know that's hard to believe, but please believe me because it's absolutely true. You know I'm not one to make up stuff. Anyway, it's a long story, but when I got to 1900, I had lost my memory and didn't realize what I was doing. I ended up meeting all kinds of famous people like Peter White, and I was even a guest of the Longyears. But during that time, without realizing it, I ended up changing the past. Then when I found the dolmen and touched it again, I ended up back in 2021, but because I changed the past, the 2021 I'm in is really different, and I don't know how to get back to the version of 2021 I'm actually from. But I know it still exists because you emailed me from it! I don't know if that makes sense. I'm still trying to figure it out myself.

I know this is all hard to believe, but please believe me. I need you to help me. I just don't know how you can. Maybe you can find a really smart professor at NMU, like in the physics department, who can understand this and figure out how to get me back to my own version of 2021. I'm going to try to use the dolmen again tomorrow and go back to 1900 to try to fix things, but if you get this, please write me back asap.

P.S. Please don't tell my parents. I don't want to alarm them.

Love,
Neill

Neill hit send just as Jordan appeared with his food. Shutting off his phone, he thanked Jordan, set the phone down next to him, and began to eat his sandwich. But now his brain was spinning. He had considered telling Allison he had met a different version of her in this time, but he had been afraid that would freak her out too much. He really hoped she got his message. If she did, then maybe he shouldn't go to the dolmen but wait until she could talk to a physics professor to see if they could help him. That said, maybe he could just go talk to a physics professor himself. But who would believe him? And it was summer, so most professors wouldn't just be sitting in their offices at the university waiting for some nutcase who thought he was a time traveler to show up. Maybe it was best just to eat his sandwich and then see if Allison wrote him back. He'd had enough people thinking he was a nutcase lately without talking to some professor he didn't even know.

At least today he seemed to fit in. No one gave him strange looks as he sat eating or paid any attention to him. He was so grateful to be wearing shorts and a T-shirt and not those awfully warm old-fashioned clothes he'd had on yesterday. Of course, he'd have to put them back on if he was going to try to return to 1900 tomorrow. But now he thought maybe he wouldn't have to time travel anymore except back to his own time—maybe Allison could find some answers for him. But that seemed like a stretch. He hoped she would believe him, but even if she did, it wasn't like the professor would immediately know how to get him back to his own time. Time travel was just a theory, and the professor might know nothing about it and have to consult their colleagues, and of course, everyone's first thought would be that it was all a hoax and try to claim Allison or he had manipulated the emails, even if he was able to keep emailing her. And if he took pictures with his phone of things like the Longyear Mansion to prove he was in an alternate version of 2021, people would just think he was photoshopping them.

Neill's heart began to sink into his stomach as he realized how impossible it would be to get anyone to believe and help him. Yes, Allison and Derek seemed to believe him now, but they were far from qualified to understand time travel—after all, he certainly didn't.

When Neill finished eating, he still felt hungry and he had a few dollars left, so he decided to go back up to the counter and order a piece of blueberry cheesecake. He figured he might as well eat well since, while Derek would likely feed him supper and breakfast, once he got back to the dolmen tomorrow and was transported back in time, who knew when he would eat again? Hopefully, he would be able to reconnect with the Longyears, but after Howard had seen him mysteriously vanish, chances were the family would tell him to stay away from them.

Jordan waited on Neill this time, taking his money and telling him he'd bring the cheesecake out to him. Neill had seen Allison take a couple of orders from new customers who entered, but then she had disappeared into the back. Neill wondered if she was avoiding him. When he returned to his table, he almost wished he hadn't ordered the cheesecake, fearing his very presence was making Allison uncomfortable. But then she appeared again with a plate holding his dessert.

"Here you go, one blueberry cheesecake," she said, setting it down. "Do you need anything else?"

"No, thank you," he said.

"Enjoy," she muttered. She started to turn away, but then stopped and said, "Neill, I get off at three if you want to come back. Maybe we can talk."

Neill was surprised but glad she wasn't avoiding him. "Okay," he said. "Derek doesn't get home until five anyway."

"Great. I'll see you then," she said and went back into the kitchen.

Neill enjoyed the cheesecake far more than the pastrami, probably because he now felt assured that Allison did want to be his friend. And Derek had seemed friendlier this morning. Neill knew what he had dumped on his new friends had been a lot to take in. Now that they'd had time to get used to the idea, maybe they were more inclined than before to help him. He suddenly felt hopeful again.

After he finished the cheesecake, Neill carried his plates over to a container next to the trash for dirty dishes. Since Allison was in the back, he simply left. He had a couple of hours until she would get off work. He figured he might as well just walk around and explore Marquette until then.

But when he got outside, he remembered his email to Allison. He quickly checked his phone, but he was disappointed to find his inbox empty. *Oh, well,* he thought. *She's probably working and might not reply until this evening.*

He decided just to relax and enjoy his walk. Suddenly, he felt less traumatized than amused by the changes between his time and this one considering what he now saw as he approached the corner of Fourth and Washington. St. John the Baptist's Catholic Church was standing there—he remembered his father telling him about it, and he thought it funny to find a flower shop where Little Caesar's should be. After exploring the downtown, he headed to the harbor, walking the bike trail up to Picnic Rocks and back. Regardless of which version of 2021 he was in, Marquette was still beautiful. Kids were still on the beach playing volleyball or swimming at McCarty's Cove. He saw an ore boat coming into the Upper Harbor, and he passed many people jogging, biking, skateboarding, or walking their dogs. There were condos along the lakeshore like he remembered, but also lots of trees and fresh air.

I guess if I had to, I could get used to living here, he told himself. *It's not that different from the Marquette I knew.* But when he returned to Superior Sandwiches, he was still hopeful he wouldn't have to stay in this time. He had thought when he'd get back to the deli that he'd have a few minutes to check his email before Allison got off, but Allison was already on the sidewalk waiting for him.

"What do you want to do?" she asked. "Do you want me to show you around town?"

"Actually," he said, "I've spent all afternoon walking around. I'm kind of tired now."

"Okay," said Allison. "My feet are killing me anyway. When did you say Derek was getting off?"

"Five," said Neill. "He told me to be home by then because he gave me his only key."

"Well," said Allison, "I walked to work this morning—parking downtown is terrible—so why don't we just walk over to the party store on Third and get some snacks. Then we can walk over to Derek's and wait for him."

Neill looked hesitant. "I don't think Derek would want me to be alone with you."

"Don't worry what Derek would want," said Allison. "Trust me; nothing's going to happen between us."

"Okay," said Neill. He felt a little insulted by Allison's tone, as if he were not desirable, but he had to admit he had no interest in her.

"Come on," she said. "I'm dying for a cigarette and I'm all out."

Neill followed her up Third Street and to a party store he had never seen before. As she told the cashier which cigarettes she wanted, he thought how he was not looking forward to an afternoon of her blowing smoke in his face. He'd rather touch a dolmen.

Chapter 10

After Neill and Allison got back to Derek's apartment, they made themselves comfortable. They ate the potato chips and drank the pop they had bought—though Allison had a Diet Coke so it wouldn't rot her gut. Neill was relieved that Allison had smoked her cigarette on the way to Derek's apartment and put it out before coming inside.

"So, are you ready to go back to the dolmen tomorrow?" Allison asked, plopping herself down on the couch. Neill wisely sat in the chair rather than next to her. He didn't want Derek to think anything was going on between them when he got home.

"I guess so," said Neill. "I mean as ready as I can be."

"Do you need to bring anything back with you?"

Neill shrugged his shoulders. "I'll put back on the clothes Howard Longyear gave me so I'm not out of place when I get back to 1900. I don't know what else I could bring. I wish I had some money, but it would cost a fortune to go buy coins and bills from 1900, and if I brought modern money, no one would take it. I'll just have to hope once I get there that I can find my way back to the Longyears' cabin and find someone who will help me."

"You seem pretty calm about it all," said Allison before taking a sip of her Diet Coke.

Neill laughed awkwardly. "I guess I am, at least compared to yesterday. I was about ready to have a panic attack when I realized how the present had changed. It's a little scary to think about going back in time again, but it's even scarier for me to think I'll never see my family again."

"You know," said Allison, "I'm still not so sure Derek and I should help you."

"Why?" asked Neill, raising his eyebrows. "Do you still not believe me?"

"No, it's not that," she replied. "You seem like too sweet and honest a guy to make up such a story, and you've given no other signs that you're a nutcase. No, what bothers me is if you go back and change the past to what you claim it was, where does that leave me and Derek? You say we're your friends in that other time, but we don't know that time. We only know this time. It would be scary for us to be in that strange time just like it is for you to be here."

"That would make sense," said Neill, "except that you won't know it's different because you won't have known this time or anything other than the time I came from. This time will have never existed."

"I hope you're right about that. Still, I can't see myself wearing a poofy prom dress."

Neill laughed. "It was only that one time. More of the present will be the same as this time than it will be different."

"But my father will still be dead in that time," Allison replied. "You yourself said he was dead in your time."

"Yes," he replied.

"I wish you could go back and change that," said Allison.

Neill had a hard time knowing how to reply. "I wish I could too," he finally said, "only I don't know how this whole time travel thing works. I only know when I touched the dolmen the first time, it sent me back to 1900 and the second time to 2021. To keep your father from dying, I'd have to go back to what, about 2005 or something?"

"2008."

"Yeah," said Neill. "I don't know how to control what year I can go to and…." He realized it as he spoke. "My biggest fear is when I go back to 1900, it will be just a few days after when I left 1900. And I think that's what will happen because when I came to 2021, it was the same date as the day I left 1900."

"So Howard will be alive anyway?"

"Yeah," said Neill, "and it will be after he should have drowned, in which case, how can I change what is already past?"

"Well, you could just kill him," said Allison, laughing.

Neill's face went white. Deep down, he had been fearing that was what he would have to do.

"I'm only joking," said Allison. "Actually, I don't see why you'd have to kill him. Just make sure he doesn't marry your great-great-grandma. That would ensure your family still existed, right?"

"Sure," said Neill. "I guess so, but it would still mean some things would be different like the Longyear Mansion would never have been moved."

"So what?" said Allison. "It would be kind of cool to have it still be in Marquette."

"Maybe," said Neill, but he wasn't sure what other implications might matter that he couldn't foresee.

"So," said Allison, focusing only on the major issue, "you just have to figure out how to keep Margaret from marrying Howard, right? Is Howard hot?"

"You mean attractive?" asked Neill. "Yes, I guess so. He's fairly handsome and athletic, and he's very intelligent. To hear Hugh talk, you would think he was Adonis and Einstein rolled into one."

"And what about your great-great-grandpa that Margaret's supposed to marry? I forget his name."

"Will Whitman," said Neill.

"Is he hot?"

"I don't know," said Neill. "The only picture I saw of him when he was young was his wedding picture. I guess he was handsome enough."

"But Howard has the money, and you said Margaret wants to be a high society lady."

"Yeah," said Neill, realizing now how difficult this could be.

"And how old is Margaret in 1900?"

"Um, I think she's sixteen."

"Sixteen!" said Allison. "Hell, I wouldn't get married at sixteen."

"Well, she didn't marry Will until 1903, so she'd have been nineteen then."

"What? You don't plan to hang out in the last century for three years to make sure they get married, do you?"

"No, at least I hope not," said Neill. "But how will I fix this? And how long will it take? Every day I'm in 1900 is time in 2021 I'm missing out on. What if I do have to stay until 1903? Then I might not get back to my own time until 2024. How will I explain being gone for three years?"

"I don't know," said Allison. "I think you'll just have to take it day by day."

"But what will I do to fix things?"

"Well, if you tell Margaret not to marry Howard, she'll think you're crazy," said Allison. "But Howard seems like a smart guy. Maybe you can explain it to him."

Neill didn't like that idea. He felt like he could trust Howard, but it would still be awkward.

"I think you'll figure it out as you go," said Allison. "No point in worrying about it until the time comes. First you have to get back there."

Neill knew she was right, but it didn't relieve the anxiety he felt and his continual wondering why this bizarre situation had happened to him.

"Or you could just stay in this time. I mean, I know you miss your family, but there's no guarantee you can fix what happened, and I'm sure 2021 is a better time to live in than 1900, even with the pandemic."

"It probably was a harder time in a lot of ways," Neill agreed, "but the Longyears had it pretty well made, not that anyone's life is perfect."

"What if Howard is freaked out to see you when you return?" asked Allison. "I mean, you did just disappear in front of him."

"I hadn't really thought of that," Neill replied. "It will be hard to befriend him again. Maybe instead I could find Will and work to get him and Margaret together without involving Howard."

"That doesn't sound easy. From my experience, playing matchmaker doesn't usually work."

Neill hadn't tried to play matchmaker, but he had to admit it didn't sound easy.

"I know it sucks to lose your family," said Allison. "But you would adapt in time if you did stay in this time. Trying to fix the past might just make a bigger mess of things."

"Maybe," said Neill, who didn't want to think about that possibility. "But what would I do in this time?"

"You'd figure it out," said Allison.

"Derek said he could get me a job at Rocket's," Neill replied, although he didn't feel enthusiastic at the prospect. He hadn't liked working there in the first place, which was partly why Uncle Chad had helped him get the job at the Club.

"Oh, fuck Derek," said Allison. "He's so small-minded. You could do better than work there."

"Don't you like Derek?" asked Neill. "You always seem to be putting him down. Why do you go out with him?"

"Want to know the truth?" asked Allison, grinning.

Neill didn't answer, not sure he wanted to know. Allison told him anyway.

"Size matters," she said, grinning.

"Seriously?" Neill frowned.

"Well, partly. He knows how to satisfy a woman's needs in that way, but once I finish college, I plan to find someone who has something going for him. Someone like you who is smart and a gentleman, not a slob."

"Thanks," said Neill, unsure where this conversation was going.

"I mean it, Neill. If you stayed in this time, maybe you and I could...." She looked at him suggestively.

"Allison," he said, "I think that would make Derek very angry."

"What do you care? He's not really your friend. Not in this time. You just met him, and he doesn't even seem to like you that much."

"He was just a little jealous at first," said Neill. "He is my friend since he's agreed to help me, and no offense, Allison, but I really do want to go back to my time, so it's not going to happen between us."

"Well, maybe it will in your time," she replied.

Neill didn't reply. He was relieved that Derek opened the door at that moment before he had to start fending her off.

"You're early," said Neill, hoping Derek hadn't overheard any of their conversation.

"Work was slow," said Derek. "I brought home a couple of pizzas."

"Cool," said Allison.

Derek looked at her as if to inquire what she was doing there, but he didn't ask and she didn't offer any explanations. She just got up, took the pizzas from him, and set them on the table. Then she went to the cupboard where she knew his plates were.

While they ate, Derek asked Neill what he had done all day, so Neill launched into a summary of his walk around town and all the things he had noticed were different between his own time and this one. Then they talked about their plans for tomorrow. Since Allison had to work, she wouldn't be going to the dolmen with them. Neill and Derek planned to get an early start as soon as it was daylight; they figured the earlier they went, the less likely anyone would see them sneaking onto the Huron Mountain Club's property. Derek planned to drive them up to Big Bay in his truck, and then they'd embark from there in his kayak, making their way across Lake Superior to Mount Huron so they could access the Club property from the lake rather than trying to get past the gatekeeper. Neill said he'd bring his 1900 clothes to change into before he touched the dolmen, but he asked if he could keep the underwear Derek had given him. No one would know if he was wearing Hanes boxer briefs under his old-fashioned clothes, and he never wanted to wear that overprotective Victorian underwear again.

Finally, Derek said they should get to sleep so they could get up early. He offered to drive Allison home, but she refused. He wanted to make sure she got home safely, but she told him it wasn't close to dark yet. When Derek continued to press her, Neill realized he was hoping to get some action with her at her house. Instead, Allison pushed him up against the wall to give him a good night kiss. What followed made Neill blush, and he turned away when he saw where Allison's hand went, but a minute later, she broke off the kissing and, with a laugh, said "Good night" and disappeared out the door.

"Cock tease!" Derek shouted, looking disgusted as the door closed behind her.

Neill, seeing the frustration on Derek's face, changed the subject by asking, "Do you mind if I go take a shower?"

Derek, looking like he needed a cold one himself, replied, "Suit yourself." Then he plopped into his recliner and grabbed the TV remote.

Neill went into the bathroom. By the time he got out of the shower, he could hear Derek talking on the phone. His voice was raised, but Neill could only make out a few words. He waited until it sounded like Derek was off the phone before he exited the bathroom. He was exhausted and looking forward to going to bed early so he could get all the sleep possible for the big day tomorrow.

But when Neill entered the living room, Derek said, "Can I talk to you?"

"Sure," said Neill, seeing that his friend looked upset. He feared Derek had changed his mind about taking him to the dolmen tomorrow. He sat down on the couch and waited for Derek to speak.

"Did Allison say anything about me today?" Derek asked.

"What?" asked Neill, surprised by the question. "No."

"Come on, man. Something happened."

"What do you mean?" asked Neill, wondering how he would defend himself if Derek started accusing him of cheating with Allison.

"I think she's hot for you," said Derek. "She's cheated on me before, and you're not an unattractive guy, so I'm not surprised."

"Man, I assure you nothing happened," said Neill.

"Did she hit on you?"

"No," said Neill. "Not really."

"Not really?"

Neill sighed. "Look, man, I don't want to cause a problem between you and her. I'm not interested in her. I just want to get back to 1900 and then back to my own time."

"So you turned her down?" said Derek. "That's why she was so pissy with me on the phone."

"What do you mean?" asked Neill, too curious not to ask.

"She told me she needed something more than a pizza delivery boy."

"That's rude," said Neill, "but I don't know that it has anything to do with me."

"She said, 'I want a gentleman like Neill, someone who's going somewhere in life.'"

Neill gave an awkward laugh and said, "I don't know where she thinks I'm going, other than back in time."

"I love her," said Derek. "I don't cheat. I don't abuse her. I pretty much do whatever she wants. Why does she have to treat me that way?"

As gently as possible, Neill replied, "Derek, I think the question is: Why do you let her treat you that way?"

"Because I love her," Derek said.

"Derek," said Neill, shaking his head, "I think you need to start loving yourself."

"What does that mean?"

"I mean, you seem like a nice guy for the most part. I don't know you that well, but I'm pretty sure you don't deserve a girlfriend willing to cheat on you. You're a big, strong, attractive guy. So what if you work at Rocket's? You can get your GRE and go to college and make something of yourself. If you did, I'm sure lots of girls would be interested in you."

"Yeah," said Derek, grimacing. "Whatever. I'm probably just tired. We should go to sleep."

"All right," said Neill. "Things always seem better in the morning."

"Yeah," said Derek, standing up. "Good night. I'll wake you up around five-thirty so we can leave as early as possible. It's daylight by a little after six."

"Okay," said Neill. "Good night."

Derek went into his room. Neill stood up, spread out his blanket on the couch, and found his pillow. Once settled on the couch, he closed his eyes, but his thoughts were full of Derek and Allison. He felt bad that his presence was causing trouble between them, but it seemed like they had already had problems before he arrived in their time. Still, he hated seeing his two best friends behave in ways that made them hurt each other or be miserable. They deserved so much better.

Hopefully tomorrow, Neill thought, *I can get back to 1900 and figure out how to fix everything. Once I do that, most things should go back to how they were. Derek and Allison should be their old selves again, at least, and even if the Longyear Mansion is still standing on Ridge Street, I'll have my family back. Well, except for Uncle Chad. Like Allison wishes with her dad, I wish I could bring him back.*

Neill and Uncle Chad had been close. Sometimes they had felt like the other was the only one in the family who truly understood them. But right now, Neill would have done anything to be misunderstood by his parents, if only he could see them again.

As Neill thought about his family, he slowly drifted into sleep, only to jolt awake when he remembered he had nearly forgotten something.

Sitting up, he reached for his cell phone on the end table. Quickly swiping it open, he touched his email app and waited for it to update.

After a second, he saw he only had one message. It read:

> Message undeliverable. We have tried but failed to send your message to ally49855@mqtmail.com. You do not need to resend this message. We will continue to try to send it for 48 hours. If we can still not send it, we will notify you.

A bunch of gibberish code followed that meant nothing to Neill.

Neill was disappointed but not surprised. "I didn't think it would really go through," he muttered, holding back a tear. He shut off the phone, set it back on the table, and lay back down. *Now I know for sure I have to go back to the dolmen,* he thought. Hopefully, tomorrow would be a better day.

Chapter 11

IN THE MORNING, BOTH DEREK and Neill were fairly silent as they drove up the Big Bay Road in Derek's truck, heading toward the Huron Mountain Club. Neill felt sleepy, but he was also anxious. Derek was quiet; Neill figured his friend was brooding over his relationship with Allison, so he thought it best not to interfere further.

Finally, they reached Big Bay and then drove to Lake Superior where Derek parked his truck. Neill went around the back of the truck and changed out of his T-shirt and shorts into the summer clothes Howard Longyear had given him. After putting on life jackets, they each grabbed an end of the kayak and carried it to the water. Neill was surprised Derek had life jackets—he seemed like a bit of a risk-taker, and Howard and Hugh had not had any; Neill wondered if life jackets had even existed in 1900—though, he knew they'd had them on the *Titanic* when it sunk in 1912.

In another minute, the two young men were paddling out onto Lake Superior, heading northwest toward the Huron Mountain Club's property. Neill felt so anxious that he thought he might hyperventilate. He knew he would shortly see the mountain rise up along the lake, and soon after, he hoped he would be back in the past so he could try to resolve matters.

"What are you going to do when we get there?" asked Derek, calling over his shoulder from the front of the kayak.

"Walk up the mountain and find the dolmen," Neill replied.

"I'll go with you," said Derek.

"You don't have to," said Neill.

"Well," called Derek, briefly turning around, "what if your magic rock doesn't work? I'm not going to leave you stranded there, so we might as well stick together until we're sure you've gone back in time."

Neill realized Derek was right. He didn't want to be stranded there.

"Okay," he said. "After all, you promised me a job at Rocket's if the time travel thing doesn't work out, and I'll need you to give me a ride to work."

Derek laughed and splashed him with his oar.

"Hey!" said Neill. "I don't want to arrive in 1900 looking like a drowned rat. These old-fashioned clothes don't dry out very quickly."

It was a sunny July morning, still cool on the lake. The sunshine was sparkling on the waves, creating a look of glittering diamonds. Neill almost wished he could just spend the day out on the lake. The beautiful morning lifted his spirits, and then the words of Tennyson's "Ulysses," a poem he had memorized to present as a dramatic monologue in high school drama class, came back to him:

> 'T is not too late to seek a newer world.
> Push off, and sitting well in order smite
> The sounding furrows;
> for my purpose holds
> To sail beyond the sunset, and the baths
> Of all the western stars, until I die.

Ulysses had yearned to continue adventuring into the unknown, to the Happy Isles or whatever lay beyond the ken of men. To have such an adventure was an intoxicating thought, but Neill knew he could not sail on—and if he did, it would not be beyond the sunset but just to Minnesota or Canada. And yet time traveling was a form of seeking a newer, or at least different world; even by returning to 1900, he would be entering a past that had never existed before because Howard Longyear continued to live in that past. Certainly, the situation was as complicated as any Ulysses had ever faced. Neill felt trapped between his own Scylla and Charybdis—whether to find a way to get his great-great-grandparents together, unknown to them and despite Margaret's attraction to Howard, or to risk never returning to his own time or seeing his family again. Like Ulysses, Neill knew all he could do was what his heart called upon him to do and to trust things would work out despite the risks. As Ulysses had known,

> It may be that the gulfs will wash us down:
> It may be we shall touch the Happy Isles,
> And see the great Achilles, whom we knew.

Neill knew misery might await him, but so might returning to his family. He would not give up until all the possibilities were exhausted.

"Is that it?" Derek shouted, waking Neill from his thoughts. Neill turned slightly to his left and saw Mount Huron rising up before him.

"Yes! That's it!" Neill called.

"Great. Let's find a good spot to stop," said Derek. "I don't see any 'No Trespassing' signs stating this is Club property, so we shouldn't have any problem disembarking along here."

They paddled closer to shore and then glided a bit with the waves until they found a small rocky beach where they could land without damage to the kayak.

Neill used his oar to paddle them closer to shore while Derek raised his ore out of the water and used it to make contact with a small tree and pull them in. Once Derek was close enough to grab onto the tree, he unbuckled himself and jumped out of the kayak. Before Neill knew what was happening, Derek's strong arms were pulling the kayak up onto a rocky little beach. Neill had to admire Derek; if he had lived back in 1900, he would have made an incredible wilderness man just like Santinaw.

In another minute, Neill was scrambling out of the kayak, getting his feet a little wet in the waves that lapped up onto the rocky beach. He was barefoot, but he had shoes stored in the kayak that he now removed. He found a large rock to sit down on, and then after wiping as much sand off his feet as possible, he tried to put on his shoes.

Derek was wearing sandals, which were a bit wet and not appropriate for climbing a mountain.

"Are you sure you don't just want to wait for me here?" Neill asked. "If I'm not back in half an hour or so, you can assume I've gone back in time."

"No," Derek replied. "I want to check out this magic rock and see you vanish before my eyes."

Neill was surprised Derek was willing to hike up the mountain, especially in sandals, but he was also a bit relieved.

"The dolmen really isn't that much to see," said Neill.

"I don't care," said Derek. "You said it was an ancient altar of some sort, so I'm curious."

"I don't know if it is an altar," said Neill. "Some people think the Vikings sailed through the Great Lakes, so maybe they built it. It might be a grave for one of their crew."

"Do you believe that?" asked Derek. "That Vikings came here?"

"I suppose it's possible," Neill replied. "We know they made it to Newfoundland."

"Well, let's go see it," said Derek. He bent down and picked up the kayak, flipping it upside down and then standing up with it on top of his head.

"What are you doing?" asked Neill.

"I'm taking the kayak with us," said Derek. "I'm not going to leave it for someone from the Club to find and confiscate."

"It's quite a hike up the mountain, though," Neill replied.

"Not for me," said Derek. And before Neill could say another word, Derek had started up the hillside.

"Don't you want me to carry one end?" asked Neill.

"Nah, I got it," said Derek. "It's harder for me to carry it with someone else since I'm taller than most people. It's not that heavy. Only maybe eighty pounds, so I've got it."

Neill was a bit amazed by Derek's endurance, but it turned out the walk wasn't too steep and the hillside largely barren, so there wasn't a lot of brush to tangle with. Neill was actually surprised to find he had a bit of a hard time keeping up with his friend. Derek certainly had stamina. The situation reminded Neill of an incident he'd read about when Marquette was founded. Peter White, who had arrived with Robert Graveraet, had described how easily Graveraet could carry a pack up a hill and how he had even offered to carry White up on his shoulders with the pack. Neill wondered now if maybe Derek was Robert Graveraet reincarnated. After all, if he could time travel by touching a dolmen, there was no reason why reincarnation wasn't possible.

"Are you coming?" called Derek, turning around to see Neill about twenty feet behind him.

"Yeah," said Neill, trying to rush up closer. "You sure you don't want help with that?"

"Nah, I got it," said Derek. "But if you end up not traveling back in time, I'll let you carry it back down." Derek flashed Neill a smile and then turned and kept climbing.

Neill didn't like the thought of that, but carrying the kayak down would at least be easier than trying to fix the past. He tried not to feel overwhelmed about the task before him and turned to gaze at the beautifully lush green trees and blue sky surrounding him, and the view of Lake Superior as they climbed higher. But it was difficult to enjoy the view when every minute brought him closer to learning his fate.

"Almost to the top," called Derek, beginning just slightly to pant.

Neill picked up speed, deciding he wanted to get there before Derek. He passed him just as they arrived at the summit. Immediately, he saw the object that would determine his future.

"Here it is!" he shouted. He turned and watched Derek stare at the dolmen for a minute. Then Derek lowered the kayak from above his head and awkwardly propped it under his arm.

"Is that it?" asked Derek, nodding toward the dolmen.

"Yeah," said Neill, stepping toward it.

"I thought it'd be bigger," said Derek, also stepping forward.

"It doesn't look that big," Neill admitted, "but I don't know how they even got it up here. That stone on top is huge. It must weight seven hundred pounds."

"Ahh," said Derek. "A couple of big guys like me could have easily carried it up here. Those Vikings you were talking about wouldn't have had much trouble."

Neill wasn't so sure about that. Lifting a stone was one thing; carrying it all the way up this mountain was another.

"Well," said Derek, stepping up next to Neill and putting one hand on his shoulder, while holding onto the kayak with the other, "let's see you do your thing."

"Okay," said Neill. But he did not move. He felt afraid. He also was surprised that Derek had touched his shoulder. Was Derek beginning to feel sentimental, like he was going to miss him?

"What's stopping you?" asked Derek.

"You are," said Neill. "You're holding onto me."

"Oh," said Derek, laughing. "Just resting after that climb. Sorry."

Derek removed his hand. Neill walked up to the stone and stared at it.

"So what do you have to do?" asked Derek. "Sing 'Bibbidi-Bobbidi-Boo' or something?"

Neill laughed. He'd already told Derek all he had to do was touch it.

Meanwhile, Derek had walked up beside him again. They both stared at the dolmen. It wasn't giant at all. It barely came up to their waists, and it couldn't be more than four feet across.

"Maybe it is an altar," said Derek, grinning, "for midget blood sacrifices."

"I don't think so," said Neill, nervously half-laughing. "Well, here goes."

Neill reached out his hand, but before he could touch the stone, Derek shouted, "Wait!"

"What?" asked Neill, pulling back his hand.

Derek put his hand on Neill's shoulder again. *Is he trying to hug me goodbye?* Neill wondered.

"Go ahead now," said Derek, one hand on Neill and his other arm still wrapped around the kayak's edge.

"What?" asked Neill, feeling confused.

"Touch the rock."

"But," said Neill, "you're touching me."

"Just do it," said Derek.

"But you don't understand," said Neill. "If you're touching me when I touch it, you might—"

"Just do it!" Derek shouted so loud it made Neill jump, and then Derek moved his hand from Neill's shoulder to grab Neill's hand.

Before Neill knew it, Derek had forced his hand down on top of the dolmen.

Part III

Chapter 1

A̲T FIRST, THERE WAS A flash of light, and for a second, Neill thought he smelled something burning. He feared his pants would be ruined like the first time, but then suddenly, he felt completely wet—drenched; he sensed resistance against his body—water—he was in the water—underwater. And he couldn't breathe. His mouth was filling with water. He was drowning!

In a panic, Neill opened his eyes to find himself in a dark sea. He looked about for any sign of light or Derek—where was Derek? Had he been transported with him?

Lifting his head, Neill saw the faintest light above him and prayed the surface was not too far. He furiously began pushing himself upward. How the heck had he ended up underwater? He didn't know. He only knew he had to get to the surface. His lungs were bursting for air, his head starting to ache, his eyes feeling like they were going to bug out of his head, and then as he reached up to propel himself to the surface, he felt his fingers meet air, and in another second, his head was above the water and he was gasping.

Neill treaded water, struggling to keep his head above the waves; he wished he'd never taken off the life jacket when he got out of the kayak, but who would have thought he'd need it on the top of Mount Huron? The waves were making it difficult not to swallow more water, not to mention just see. Water was everywhere in his line of vision. The waves were so high and moving so much he could barely see over them.

"What the heck?" he exclaimed, only to have a wave flood into his mouth. He went under again, then struggled to resurface, gasping for air and coughing madly. When he regained control, he still could not see anything but the lake. Was he in the middle of Lake Superior? How was that even possible? He tried to rotate himself to look around, and for a second, it seemed like the waves were starting to lessen, but he still couldn't see anything. Then he heard Derek shouting, "Neill! Over here!"

Neill kept turning around until, after a few seconds, he caught sight of his friend. Derek was inside the kayak and paddling toward him, only maybe ten feet away.

"Grab on!" shouted Derek, extending a paddle toward him.

For a second, Neill had a sense of déjà vu, recalling how he had rescued Howard with the canoe, but now he was the one being rescued. Swimming forward as fast as he could with the waves pushing against him, in a few seconds, he was able to grab the paddle. Derek quickly and almost effortlessly pulled him toward him until he could grasp Neill's hand. Then Neill hoisted himself up into the kayak. Struggling to keep his balance and coughing up more water, after a few seconds, Neill managed to slide his legs inside and get settled in his seat.

"Are you okay?" asked Derek.

Neill was coughing too much to speak, but he managed to nod his head.

"I'm so glad I found you," said Derek. "I couldn't hold on to you and the kayak, and I was afraid I'd lost you."

"Where are we?" asked Neill. "What happened?"

"Well, your magic rock certainly took us somewhere," said Derek, "but where I can't say."

Neill looked around. Water still surrounded them, but now sitting in the kayak, he was higher up and could see a bit farther without the waves blocking his view. There seemed to be an island, or at least a large rock, sticking out of the water maybe fifty feet from them.

"Head for the shore," he said.

"Here," said Derek, handing him a paddle. "Fortunately, I grabbed these before they could float away."

Neill didn't reply, just started paddling. As they approached the island, it became clear it was just a giant rock. There was no easy way to get onto it. They circled it, realizing it was rather pointless to try to land on it—it was definitely not inhabitable, just a few feet above water and no more than twenty feet wide.

"Look! There's another island over there," said Derek, pointing. Neill looked, but from a distance, it didn't appear to be any larger than this one.

"What the hell happened?" asked Neill.

"I don't know why we're in the middle of the lake," said Derek, "but I'm assuming this is Lake Superior. Good thing I carried the kayak up Mount Huron with us."

"But," said Neill, "what I don't understand is...oh, no!"

"What?" asked Derek.

Neill said nothing. He was staring at the giant rock they were circling.

"Derek," he said, trying to repress the tears he felt springing up, "every time I've time traveled, it was because of the dolmen, and each time, I apparently entered the other time where the dolmen was, so we should have arrived beside the dolmen when we entered this time."

"Yeah…?" said Derek, not getting Neill's point.

"So," said Neill, "we entered this time underwater. That must mean the dolmen is underwater in this time."

"What?" said Derek, trying to understand. "How is that possible?"

"It's possible if the lake level rose," Neill replied.

"But it wouldn't rise that high," said Derek. "That's got to be more than a thousand feet. I mean, it took us a good quarter of an hour or so to climb up the mountain."

"I know," said Neill. "Even in the rainiest years, the lake level has never risen that high, but…."

"But what?" asked Derek. Neill turned around in his seat and was met by worry on Derek's face.

"But if I did time travel," said Neill slowly, trying to gently break the news to Derek and himself, "it's possible we've gone back in time—a really long time—to when the Great Lakes were all one giant lake. The geologists had a name for it, but I can't remember what it was. But I do know all of the U.P. was underwater back then. That's the only explanation I can think of. We must be back in pre-historic times."

"No way!" said Derek. "What will we do?"

"Well, the dolmen must be below us," said Neill. "I think this rock must be Mount Huron—what's left of it, or rather an earlier version of it."

"But if this isn't the time we want, how do we get out of here?" asked Derek, sounding like he was going to panic.

"I don't know," said Neill, realizing if Derek was afraid, this situation had to be very serious. "I don't know what we could do. We could try to swim down and find the dolmen, but if we've gone that far back in time, I doubt we'll find it. Plus, the water is freezing. I mean, we must be thousands—maybe tens of thousands—of years in the past. The dolmen might not even have been built yet."

"There has to be land around here somewhere," said Derek.

Now Neill felt like panicking. What if there were no habitable land anywhere? "I don't know," he said.

"Let's go look for land," said Derek. "There has to be land. It can't be what you say. Somehow, we must have just randomly ended up somewhere on the lake." Derek furiously began paddling.

"Wait!" said Neill. "I agree we can't stay here. It's desolate and we have no food unless we figure out how to fish, but we need to take action methodically in case we have to find our way back here. Which way is the sun?"

They looked around and saw the sun still rising in the sky. "So that way is East," said Neill. "It has to be morning still since we've only been in this time a few minutes, and it was still pretty early in the morning when we left. Wait, let me check."

He reached into his pocket for his cell phone. But he came up empty.

"Shit! I don't have it. It must have fallen out of my pocket into the lake," said Neill.

"Shit!" said Derek. "And I left mine in the truck."

Neill felt like he was going to hyperventilate, but he managed to say, "It's okay. It's okay. I'm sure the sun has to be in the east. Let's head east, no southeast—that's the direction Big Bay and Marquette would be in. Maybe we'll come to something. Maybe we're not even near the Huron Mountains. Maybe these are just big rocks in the lake—kind of like Stannard Rock, with the lighthouse on it."

"But you just said we would have come out where the dolmen was," said Derek.

"I know," said Neill, feeling grateful to see the sun hit the kayak because he was starting to shiver from being wet. "I know what I said, but we don't know for sure. Like you said, maybe we just randomly ended up somewhere on Lake Superior. Let's head southeast and see what we find. Then at least if we find nothing, we'll know to come back this way."

"All right," said Derek. "I don't know what else we can do. The wind is blowing in that direction, so at least it will be easy paddling. I hope we find something soon or we're going to get awful hungry."

Neill hoped so too. He knew what a tremendous appetite Derek had.

"Maybe we'll run into some cavemen or someone who will feed us?" said Derek. Then he added as an afterthought, "Or someone who will want to feed on us."

"I don't think so," said Neill, trying to lighten the mood. "I mean, we might meet prehistoric people, but I doubt they'll try to eat us. More likely, they'll think we are gods and want us to rule over them."

"I wouldn't mind being a god," said Derek, "so long as I got fed."

"You're so tall, I'm sure they'll do whatever we say. I don't think cavemen were very big, though they were probably really strong."

"I'm not afraid of them," said Derek.

Neill didn't reply. He focused on trying to paddle in sync with Derek, hoping he was wrong about the time they were in and that eventually they would come across another boat or some land, or better yet, a familiar sight.

Neill was grateful the sun was coming out and it was turning into a beautiful day; the waves had calmed down also. But being in a kayak in the middle of the world's largest freshwater lake with no land in sight, and knowing Lake Superior could turn deadly without warning, did not make him feel very secure. Even being with Derek did not help. Derek was large and strong and could out-paddle most, but what good would that do if there was nowhere to paddle to? They wouldn't survive long if they did not find inhabitable land.

Soon their wet clothes were drying, and the waves were only gently lapping against the kayak, giving them no real trouble. Still, as the minutes slowly turned to hours, they both began to weary of paddling; sometimes Neill almost gave up and let Derek do the bulk of the work, and then he would realize Derek needed a rest and tried to paddle for both. They carried on this way, taking periodic short breaks for longer than either cared to guess at.

They did occasionally come upon something—something that would turn out just to be a large rock sticking out of the water or even a floating tree. At one point, they came upon a cliff that rose above them about twenty feet. It was rocky but had some small trees growing on the top. It was large enough that Derek said, "Hey, we could build a house on that."

"We may need to," Neill replied, "but let's keep going first and see what else we might find."

As they paddled past the rocky island, Neill dreamed of chopping down its trees to build a shelter and then spending his days out fishing from the rocks or in the kayak until he and Derek died of starvation or old age, depending on how long this deluge lasted. He also began to question whether they had gone back in time; instead, maybe everything had simply flooded. *Global warming!* he thought. *Maybe we're not in the past but in the future.* But he did not share his thoughts with Derek. He saw no point in frightening his friend, and they would have plenty of time to discuss all this if they ended up stranded in this mysterious aquamarine world for the rest of what would be their short lives.

Then Neill began to wonder why Derek had even come with him, and his curiosity made him unable not to ask.

"Derek?" he said, ceasing to paddle so Derek would hear him.

"What?"

"Why did you do it?"

"Do what?" asked Derek, but his tone made it clear he knew what Neill was asking.

"You know—why did you hold my hand down on the dolmen? You must have realized that if you were touching me when I touched it, you would get transported through time too."

Derek laughed. "I didn't want you to have all the fun."

"Fun?" said Neill. "Do you call this fun—being out here in the middle of nowhere?"

"Well, I thought we were going back to 1900," said Derek, turning around to look at Neill, "and I thought that might be fun. I feel out of place in this technology-filled world. I thought I might like to see what it was like in another time when men had to work with their hands and when being physically strong counted for something. I thought I might fit in better in that time. I'd rather be out chopping down trees than making pizzas."

"But what about Allison?" asked Neill. "Aren't you concerned that she'll be worried about you?"

"Allison doesn't really care about me," said Derek. "She'll figure out what happened and get over me fast."

"Still..." said Neill.

"Don't worry about it," said Derek. "It was my decision, and I had every right to go back in time if I wanted to. Besides, aren't you glad you're not alone? If I hadn't come with you, you probably would have drowned."

"That's true," muttered Neill, unable to stop himself from wondering if, like Howard, he had been meant to drown, only to have Derek mess with fate and change the future. Perhaps since he had made it so his family no longer existed, the Universe was intent on erasing him also. The thought made his head hurt.

And was Derek right? Did he really have the right to go back in time if he wanted to? Did either of them? Was it morally responsible to time travel? It wasn't natural—it was against the natural laws, wasn't it? But then again, if it were possible—and it clearly was—then it wasn't unnatural, just maybe unusual. Was it immoral? Probably if you tried to change time, but what if you did it only as an adventure, like Derek? Neill didn't know. He might be doing wrong just by trying to fix the unintentional mistake he had already made. All he knew was he was glad not to be alone right now.

"Yeah, I'm glad you're with me," said Neill.

"Thanks," said Derek. "I'm not so glad I came now, but it is what it is. Let's just keep going."

There was nothing else they could do. Neill realized any moral quandaries about time travel were irrelevant when they had to focus on survival. They had to keep going until they found some way to sustain themselves in this strange new world. *I guess,* Neill thought, *Ulysses would be proud of us. We've definitely set off "to seek a newer world." Or an older one that's new to us.*

The young men continued to paddle until the sun was well behind them, signaling it was early evening. Despite how boring it was to see nothing other than the occasional rock or little island—they had not even seen a bird or a fish in all this time—the day now felt like it was going by rapidly. Neill was starting to wonder what they would do if night fell before they found inhabitable land.

And then the strangest thing happened. Two round, almost pointy, brownish islands seemed to rise up out of the water only maybe twenty feet from each other. They looked like they were the exact same shape, like twin islands. But as Derek and Neill drew closer, they could see that beneath the lighter brown of the tops of the islands was a darker brown, and then what looked like some caves or something beneath them, just barely above the water's level. They looked like very narrow caves, but definitely caves. But they were so small. Did the water pass through them? No, they seemed a bit above the water, many feet above the water, and there appeared to be—what was it—wood or something—a dock? It couldn't be....

"Oh, no!" cried Neill. In all his worst nightmares, he never could have imagined this.

"What is it?" asked Derek. "What's wrong? Why are you so upset?"

"Oh, no!" cried Neill, and he began to cry. It was just way too shocking to take in.

"I don't understand!" shouted Derek, still trying to figure out what Neill was looking at.

"It's—it's!" Neill began sobbing. "It's St. Peter's Cathedral. Those are the towers of St. Peter's Cathedral. We're in Marquette, or rather, we're above Marquette. Marquette is underwater!"

Chapter 2

"N o way!" said Derek. He was so freaked out that he leaned forward and nearly stood up to get a better look at the cathedral towers. Then he started to lose his balance and realized he might fall out of the kayak.

"I swear that's what it is," said Neill as Derek sat down.

"I think you're right," said Derek, also recognizing the towers now as the evening light reflected off their blue-and-orange-colored domes. "Let's get a closer look. What is that wooden platform in front of the left tower? It looks like a porch or maybe a dock."

They paddled forward, and within a few more minutes, neither could deny they were staring at the towers of St. Peter's Cathedral.

Neill looked around, trying to spot anything else he remembered. The cathedral had always been one of the tallest buildings in Marquette and seated partway up a hill. The hill sloped down, then rose up again to where St. John the Baptist had stood, on the other end of Fourth Street. That hill was even higher, but straining his eyes in that direction, Neill could see nothing. It must be completely underwater. He slowly turned his head to the right until it made a nearly 180-degree arc so his eyes could encompass the whole downtown. Then he turned his head to the right, but both times, he had the same result—nothing rose above the water. Surely, if the top of St. Peter's was tall enough to be seen, part of the Landmark Inn or the AT&T building would have been also, but there was no sign of anything else.

"I don't like this," he muttered.

"What?" asked Derek.

"Let's land and look inside those towers," Neill replied.

"That's what I was thinking," said Derek.

They paddled up close to the dock, which turned out not to be wood but some sort of floating metal raft, strapped to the sandstone of the left cathedral tower. Derek got the kayak up close to the raft, and then Neill stood up and stepped onto it. Next, Derek got out and hauled the kayak up onto the raft, which was a good ten feet wide, the size of a small bedroom and large enough for the kayak and he and Neill to fit comfortably.

By the time Derek had the kayak on the raft, Neill was looking inside one of the tower's arched windows.

"Derek, there's some sort of open trap door in here, and a pair of stairs leading down from it."

"Really?" said Derek.

"Yeah, it's not wet or anything," said Neill, "so it doesn't look like the water's washed in here. The trap door is made of metal, like a submarine hatch or something, so whoever built it made it water-proof. It sure wasn't here in our time. I can tell you that."

Derek walked over and looked through the arched windows. "Cool," he said. "Let's go see what's down there."

"Are you sure?" asked Neill, not sure he wanted to know what was down there. He had a flashback of watching the Morlocks come up from the ground and chase Guy Pearce in *The Time Machine*. By now, he was convinced he and Derek had been transported far into the future. Who knew in what condition the world now was?

"Yeah, I'm sure," said Derek. "I mean, obviously humans did this, and we haven't seen any humans since we got here, so it's time to find some and learn what caused all this."

"But," said Neill, "how will we know if we can trust them? We don't know what this time is like."

"Please," said Derek. "It's Marquette. Most people don't even lock their doors here."

"Maybe not in 2021, though I think more lock them than you might think, but we don't even know what year this is. Times have probably changed."

"Do you think?" said Derek, laughing. "That's probably an understatement."

"I'm not going down there," said Neill. "I don't think it's safe, and what if while we go snooping around the cathedral, someone comes up these stairs and steals the kayak? Then what will we do?"

"Anyone who touches my kayak will have these to deal with," said Derek, raising clenched fists.

Neill knew Derek was tough—few men would dare challenge him—but was he tough enough to take on a Morlock?

"Jorgen, is that you?" shouted a male voice.

"Shit!" said Neill. "They heard us."

Someone was clearly coming up the stairs. They could hear his feet pounding on metal stairs.

Neill was about to suggest they hide, though where he had no idea, when Derek shouted, "Hello there!"

A head emerged—the head of a bald, thin man perhaps in his late thirties. Then his shoulders emerged and then his upper arms, and then he stopped on the stairs and stared at them.

"You're not Jorgen," he said.

"No, I'm Derek. And this is my friend, Neill."

"Are you making a delivery?" asked the man.

"Um, no," said Derek.

"Well, Jorgen usually comes on Thursdays in time for supper, so I thought you were him. Is he not coming?"

"We don't know any Jorgen," Derek replied.

"I don't understand," said the man.

"Neither do we," said Derek.

The man stared at Derek, then turned and looked at Neill; he obviously felt he wasn't getting anywhere with Derek. Meanwhile, Neill stared at him, assessing his T-shirt that looked like some sort of wicking material and was a deep blue, like a shirt you would wear while biking—not so futuristic or cheesy as the Star Trek type uniform he had been expecting.

"Can you tell us where we are?" asked Neill, thinking that a better question to start off with than asking what year it was. "We're kind of lost."

"This is Peter's Landing," said the man.

"And what exactly is Peter's Landing?" asked Neill.

"Where are you from that you don't know Peter's Landing?" asked the man.

"We're from Marquette," said Derek before Neill could think how to answer.

The man's head jolted backward. For a second, Neill thought he was going to fall down the stairs. "Did you say Marquette?" asked the man.

"Yeah," said Neill.

"I thought I was the last one," said the man. "Where have you been all this time? You—how old are you? You look quite a bit younger than me. I'm thirty-eight, and I was just a teenager when the deluge happened. You couldn't have been alive then, so how can you be from Marquette? Did your parents survive? Where are they? Where have you been living?"

"That's a lot of questions," said Derek.

The man stared at them, waiting for answers.

"I don't think we can answer your questions," said Neill, "until you answer some of ours."

"Why not?" asked the man. "What do you mean?"

"We're lost," said Neill. "We're from Marquette, but…."

Neill didn't even know how to explain it all. It had been hard enough to explain he was a time traveler to Allison and Derek, but at least he had kind of known them. This man was a complete stranger.

"We're from another time," Derek blurted out, making Neill cringe at his lack of caution. "We don't know what time this is, but we're from Marquette in the past."

"Ah," said the man. "That explains the fabric."

"Fabric?" asked Derek.

The man was looking at Neill, who was still wearing his 1900 outdoors clothes, but then he turned to Derek and said, "You look like you're from two different times."

"Kind of," Neill admitted. "It's a long story."

Just then they heard a motor—at first it was faint, but they all paused to listen as it became clear some sort of motorboat was approaching.

Derek turned to look and exclaimed, "Wow!"

What they saw resembled a landspeeder out of *Star Wars*, but on water. It had a sort of see-through pod over the top to protect its operator from getting wet.

"There's Jorgen," said Neill and Derek's new acquaintance.

In a few seconds—it moved very swiftly—the vessel pulled up to the raft. The pod automatically opened and a man became visible.

The man on the stairs now came up the rest of the flight onto the tower landing and looked out the window.

"Jorgen!" called the man. "Come in. We have two guests—they're time travelers. They arrived just in time for supper."

Chapter 3

"I KNEW YOU HAD GUESTS," JORGEN replied to his friend's statement as he tied his boat to the dock. "I've been following them on the scanner."

"What?" asked Neill. "You knew we were coming?"

"Yes," said Jorgen. "Not that I knew you were time travelers, but I saw you traveling in that—well, that primitive vessel, whatever it is, on my scanner." He stepped onto the platform and shook their hands through the window. "I'm Jorgen."

"Neill," said Neill, returning the handshake.

"Derek," said Derek, and then he turned to the man who had come up the stairs. "But we didn't get your name."

"Xander," the man replied. "Come on in. We have much to talk about."

Jorgen stepped through the window into the tower and began to follow Xander down the stairs but he stopped when Neill and Derek didn't follow. Seeing that Neill looked hesitant, Jorgen said, "It's okay. We don't bite. We're not space aliens."

"Are there space aliens in this time?" asked Derek.

Xander laughed. "I hope not. At least, we haven't discovered any yet. Are there in your time?"

"No," said Derek.

"What year is this?" asked Neill.

"2142," said Jorgen. "What year are you from?"

"2021," said Derek.

Jorgen's eyes took in Derek's clothes and then he turned to Neill. "And what year are you from?"

"The same as him," said Neill, "but I visited 1900, which is why I'm dressed like this."

"Sounds like you've had quite the adventure," said Xander. "I love a good story and haven't had any company in months, other than Jorgen. Come on down to the dining room. You can tell us all about it while we have supper."

"Cool," said Derek. "I'm starving!"

Jorgen and Xander smiled and then Derek started down the stairs after them.

"Thank you for the invitation," said Neill, following his companions. Normally, he would have protested that he didn't want to put anyone to any trouble, but he and Derek definitely needed some food, and even more, some explanations.

As a boy, Neill had been in St. Peter's Cathedral countless times. His grandparents, parents, and he had attended St. Michael's Parish on the other end of Marquette, but they had gone to St. Peter's on the odd weekend when the Mass time there was more convenient, as well as for Christmas concerts. Consequently, Neill was very familiar with the interior of the main sanctuary, with its beautiful mosaic of Christ and the apostles over the altar, its colorful stained glass windows, and its large red marble pillars. But he was not at all prepared for the dingy, dark gloom he found himself descending into. Of course, he was just going down a flight of stairs in a tower, but he felt like he was descending into the depths of the earth now that the cathedral was almost all underwater. There were no windows with light coming through them. Where windows had once been in the tower, only large, black window casings stood, blocking out any light. Neill also noticed the stairs had treads on them to prevent slipping, probably in case water spilled down the stairs if the lake's water level rose. Neill was anxious to learn more about the cathedral's recent history and current state.

When they reached the bottom of the stairs, Xander led them through the vestibule and past the doors that led into the main sanctuary.

"Can I take a peek?" Neill asked, unable to bear walking past the sanctuary without looking to see if it was still the same as he remembered.

"A peek?" repeated Xander.

"Can I look inside the sanctuary?" asked Neill, pointing to its door.

"Oh," said Xander. "I suppose."

Neill tried to open the door, but it was locked. Xander quickly entered a code that allowed the doors to slide sideways rather than open out, revealing that they had somehow been airlocked, again probably to secure the room from water entering it.

"We have to protect the sanctuary," Xander explained. "It's a historical artifact, you know."

As the doors opened, all that met their eyes was sheer blackness, but then Xander clapped his hands and fluorescent ceiling lights illuminated the sanctuary, making it as bright as an operating room. It was not the soft, gentle lighting Neill remembered. And what the light revealed horrified him.

"What happened?" he exclaimed. All of the large stained glass windows had been replaced with giant black window casings like he had seen in the tower windows. "Where are the windows?"

"Oh," said Xander. "Many of them broke during the deluge. The rest had to be removed to protect the building from flooding. They weren't built to withstand floods. We've preserved the few we could save downstairs."

"Wow, it's still amazing," said Derek. Not being Catholic, he had never been in the cathedral before.

Neill looked about, glad to see the pillars still stood and the mosaic in the front of the church looked the way he remembered it—its colors perhaps even brighter. But all the wooden pews were gone.

"I'm glad the mosaic survived," said Neill.

"Yes, we just had it restored about ten years ago," said Xander.

Neill looked around and saw that the statues of Joseph and Mary in the front of the church and the other statues along the sides of the aisles looked chipped and filthy. When he asked what had happened to them, Xander said, "Vandals and smoke from candles. We hope to restore them eventually too."

"What happened to the pews?" Neill asked.

"They rotted from being underwater," said Xander. "The whole church was submerged for several months before we figured out how to board up the windows and then pump out the whole place."

Now, in place of the pews were some modern rolling office-type chairs scattered around a few round tables. "We use it as a conference room now," Xander said. "Once a year, we have a memorial service here to remember those who died in the deluge. People come from all over the U.P. to attend."

Neill felt like crying. The whole thing was horrifying to him. He had always thought St. Peter's Cathedral the grandest church he had ever seen. *The Chicago Tribune* had once called it the most beautiful sandstone building in the world. Now it was a shell of its former glory. A monument to a past apparently long dead.

"I can't look anymore," Neill said, and he turned around to face the vestibule.

"What's wrong?" asked Derek, who thought the church quite impressive, not having had any expectations of what the sanctuary should have looked like.

Neill just shook his head as Xander closed the sanctuary doors.

Derek's stomach now growled and Jorgen laughed.

"You weren't kidding that you were starving," said Xander. "The kitchen is this way." He led them through a large room Neill remembered as a gathering hall people entered from off the parking lot. The elevator Neill remembered was still there. A minute later, they had descended into another hall that led into the cathedral's original basement. Neill remembered the basement well. He'd been to many a pancake breakfast and church bazaar there. It looked the way he remembered, but it was cluttered with all kinds of things seemingly randomly stacked about so that it looked more like a cluttered home basement than one belonging to a church.

"We've tried to preserve artifacts from Marquette's past here," said Xander.

A bust of Peter White stared at Neill from among what mostly looked like rubbish. Neill remembered the bust being inside the Peter White Public Library. He turned away, unable to bear the sight of more relics left from the devastation of his hometown.

"The kitchen is this way," said Jorgen. He led them through a narrow pathway between piles of furniture, stones, and books—Neill wondered how the books had not been destroyed during the deluge—and plastic boxes. Neill did not have the heart to ask what was in them.

"This way," said Jorgen, until they had crossed through the entire basement and come to the kitchen, which Neill also remembered.

They went through the kitchen door, and then Xander told them to have a seat at a table while he prepared supper. Neill and Derek watched him, and the process appeared simple. From a modern-looking refrigerator, he pulled out what appeared to be fancy TV dinners. He placed these in a cupboard with several shelves that looked like a giant microwave. Derek and Neill just sat and stared as he did all this, while Jorgen busied himself with getting them glasses of water. Neill would have killed for a Coke, but since no one asked what he wanted to drink, he thought water might be the only option.

"Here we go," said Xander, carrying the heated trays to the table and setting them down in front of everyone. Meanwhile, Jorgen had distributed glasses of water and forks and cloth napkins. Neill suspected paper napkins must now be a rarity, given that there were few trees around to turn into paper.

"What is it?" asked Derek, looking down at a long gray slab of something on his tray.

"Trout loaf," said Xander. "What else?"

"I was kind of hoping for a pasty," Derek replied.

"What's a pasty?" asked Jorgen.

"What's a pasty?" exclaimed Derek. "What kind of Yoopers are you?"

"Never mind," said Neill. "This will be fine." He did not like fish, but he was grateful to be fed. It turned out to be something like a tuna loaf, but made with trout, and kind of mushy, like it was partly composed of mashed potatoes and breadcrumbs or something else he couldn't identify and didn't want to ask about. Surprisingly, it wasn't half-bad given how hungry he was.

"Now," said Xander, once they were all seated at the table, "we have many questions."

"So do we," said Neill.

"First off," said Xander, "tell us how you got here from the twenty-first century."

Derek looked at Neill, his mouth full.

"All right," said Neill, "but will you promise in return to tell us exactly what this place is, what you are doing here, and what happened since our time?"

"We'll tell you what we can," said Xander.

"What does that mean?" asked Derek, his mouth now only half-full. "Are you like some government agents who are forbidden to share top secret information?"

Jorgen laughed. "Hardly," he said. "Xander means we don't know everything. After all, you want more than a century of information from us. That would be like us asking you to tell us everything that happened from 1900 to your time. Just discussing the World Wars and Great Depression in detail would take hours."

"True," said Neill. "The main thing I want to know is how Marquette, and apparently a lot of the U.P., came to be underwater."

"We can tell you that," said Xander, "but first, please tell us your story."

"We also want to know how to get back to our own time," said Derek, "or rather the year 1900. That's where we were trying to go."

"Oh, so you intentionally time traveled?" asked Jorgen, looking at them curiously.

"Yes, we were trying to," said Neill. "I'm surprised you're not freaked out by the fact that we did time travel. You seem to believe us."

"Why would we be freaked out?" said Xander. "People have been time traveling for several decades now. But you can only do so with a passport, and getting one of those is very difficult; you have to pass a whole series of security clearances and psychological tests to ensure you won't try to change the past."

"I see," said Neill.

"We promise to tell you everything we can," said Jorgen, "but first, please tell us how you managed to time travel because as far as we know, the technology wasn't developed yet in your time."

"That's true," said Neill. "It hasn't been. That's why we're kind of confused about how we got here. We thought we'd end up in 1900, but we really don't know how the whole thing works."

"Neill's the real time traveler," Derek added. "I just came along for the ride, so I'll let him tell you."

Xander noticed Derek's tray was already empty.

"Do you want more?" Xander asked.

"I'd love some," said Derek, "but it's kind of dry. You wouldn't have any salsa I could put on it, would you?"

"I don't know what salsa is," said Xander.

"I was afraid of that," said Derek. "How about ketchup?"

Xander stared blankly at him.

"Never mind," said Derek. "I'll explain what they are to you later."

Xander nodded, got up, and placed another tray of trout loaf in the microwave. He asked Neill if he also wanted more, but Neill said he'd had enough. It had been difficult just getting one plateful down.

A minute later, Derek had his second tray of food before him and Neill had begun his story. It turned out to be quite a long tale because he had to stop to answer questions and sometimes go back and retell things, and then Derek would chime in to mention something Neill had forgotten, followed by another clarifying question from Xander or Jorgen. But finally, Neill had told it all, ending with how they had arrived at "St. Peter's Cathedral."

"Peter's Landing," Xander corrected him.

"Yeah," said Neill. "I've finished my story now so you can begin yours by telling me when this place quit being St. Peter's Cathedral? Was it because of this 'deluge,' as you call it?"

Jorgen sighed. "It is rather a sad story."

Neill felt anxious but replied, "Still, I want to know." Deep in his heart, he feared the deluge had somehow resulted from his changing the past in 1900, although he suspected the climate change the world had been facing in 2021 might have also caused these changes. Maybe his coming to the future was not an accident but a chance to warn people of what could happen. But he was surprised by Jorgen's answer.

"The deluge," said Jorgen, "was the result of greed on the part of some people who wanted to mine beneath Lake Superior. The idiots caused an explosion underwater that made the lakebed shift, which caused a tsunami wave to sweep over most of the Upper Peninsula. The explosion was also like an earthquake and it caused a type of mini-mountain chain to build up around parts of the U.P., trapping the water inside it like a giant basin, especially in Marquette County where the ground collapsed, creating a type of crater for the lake to pool into."

"Holy crap!" said Derek.

"I don't really understand it all," said Jorgen. "I just know the results."

"So it wasn't global warming?" asked Neill.

"Well, sort of," added Xander. "The planet was getting warmer so the melting icebergs caused the water levels in Lake Superior to rise so that just made it worse."

"It must have been horrible to experience," said Neill.

"It was," Jorgen agreed.

"The worst part," said Xander, "is no one expected it. The tsunami that resulted from the mining explosions wiped out a lot of towns, including much of Marquette. People were trapped on the roofs of their houses even in higher elevations like Ridge Street, and most houses were underwater. Thousands died. The luckiest were those who owned canoes or kayaks and could stay afloat until help arrived. Only some of the strong stone buildings remained standing. Over time, most of the houses and other buildings' foundations rotted away. FEMA came, but that only made a bigger mess of things, and what was left of the US Government was too bankrupt to use federal funding to try to fix the land, especially when global warming had already put Miami and New Orleans and a lot of other cities under water. Most survivors from the U.P. moved south to more inland places like Kansas and Nebraska. I think I'm the only person from Marquette still in the area."

"But Jorgen is still here," said Neill.

"Yes," Jorgen replied. "I live over where L'Anse Bay used to be, on the hill where the Bishop Baraga statue still stands. My wife and teenage son live there with me, so I'm able to leave once a week or so while they keep an eye on things. We all have lookout stations along the lake to make sure the United States doesn't invade the lake. We're all technically Canadian citizens now. We're trained military—a national guard if you will—but mostly we work at preserving what we can of the culture and history here."

"Yes," said Xander. "We hope to turn Peter's Landing into a museum someday when things get better between the United States and Canada. There's a team of marine archeologists who come a few times a year to help me collect whatever we can preserve of Marquette's past. I expect them in a couple of days. That's why the basement is full of artifacts. There are all kinds of treasure hunters, though, out for personal gain—"

"Pirates really," said Jorgen.

"Yes," said Xander, "so I can't leave this station in case someone tries to steal what I've preserved."

"You must have thought we were pirates then," said Derek.

"I kind of feared you might be," said Xander. "I was trying to feel you out, and I had my laser gun with me, but you were obviously not armed in any way."

Neill was waiting for Derek to make a stupid remark like "I don't need guns. I have my fists" since he kept blurting out everything else. However, Derek was looking rather sleepy now that he'd stuffed himself with trout loaf.

"That's quite a story," said Neill. "It's really sad. I never would have envisioned such a terrible end for my hometown."

"Neither would I have," said Xander, "but Marquette wasn't what it had been in the good old days that you knew."

Neill no longer wanted to know what had happened to his hometown in the last century. Instead, he said, "I imagine you get lonely here. What do you do all day?"

"I have a groper," said Xander. "I go out groping and trying to reclaim items from the ruins of Marquette to preserve. Then I try to restore them, and I also monitor the lake levels for the government."

"What's a groper?" asked Derek.

"It's a type of underwater boat," Xander replied.

"I think they called them submarines in your time," said Jorgen, "only mine is more like the size of a—well, a minivan I think you called it."

"Oh," said Neill. "But isn't everything underwater ruined?"

"Not everything," said Xander. "And some things are worth saving. We have the Father Marquette statue here, minus its pedestal. It's in the basement and also the statue of Chief Kawbawgam."

"I never heard of a statue of Chief Kawbawgam," said Neill.

"No?" said Jorgen. "Peter White commissioned it after Chief Kawbawgam died. It was standing out at Presque Isle in your time and until the deluge."

"Sure, I've seen it," said Derek.

"Really?" said Neill. "My dad used to talk about how Peter White wanted to build a statue to Kawbawgam, but he told me Peter White died before it could happen."

"Peter White did die the year before it was erected," Xander replied, "but Howard Longyear finished raising the money to fund it after Peter White died."

"That explains it," said Neill. "In my time, Howard Longyear drowned in Lake Superior in 1900 when he was just shy of nineteen, so he never lived to help fund the statue."

"Howard Longyear drowned in your time!" exclaimed Xander.

"That's terrible," said Jorgen. "How is it possible?"

"It's just devastating to imagine," agreed Xander.

"Why?" asked Derek.

"Why, Howard Longyear is the one who discovered how to time travel," said Jorgen, "although it was his descendants who commercialized it."

"Really?" said Neill. "That's fascinating."

Neill needed a minute to let that information sink in. What did that mean to him? It was a lot to wrap his mind around.

"Hey," said Derek, "can we see the Chief Kawbawgam statue? I bet Neill would get a kick out of it."

"If you want to," said Jorgen.

"Won't that be cool, Neill?" asked Derek.

"Ye-es," said Neill. "I would love to see it." But statues were not as interesting to him now as the fact that Howard might be tied to his figuring out how to travel back to his own time.

"It's very strange," added Jorgen, "that you come from a time when Howard Longyear died young. Thank God he didn't in ours because he was intent on preserving early Marquette history. Without him, who knows what might have been lost."

"Yes," said Neill, though he was thinking otherwise. Of course, it was wonderful that Howard had preserved Marquette's past, but what about his own past—Neill Vandelaare's past, which had been wiped out by letting Howard live to have a future? How could he explain all that to Jorgen and Xander?

It turned out he didn't have to because Derek said, "It's not completely good that Howard lived. You see, if Howard doesn't die, then Neill never gets to be born."

Jorgen and Derek looked at each other strangely, then laughed. "How can that be? Neill is here before us, isn't he?"

"Yes, I am," said Neill, "which confuses me. You see, my great-great-grandparents only met as a result of Howard's death. But in this alternate time I'm in, my great-great-grandmother married Howard, which means my great-grandfather was never born. So, you see, if Howard doesn't die, ultimately, I'll never be born."

"Well," said Jorgen, "that's true in your time technically, but not in this one. It's a known fact that you can't really change the past. So when you went back in time, you didn't change the past—you created an alternate version of it."

"I don't understand," said Neill.

"What I don't understand," Derek interrupted, "is why if you people have known about time travel for a while...."

"We've known how to do it for about forty years now," said Xander.

"Then," said Derek, "why didn't you go back in time to stop the volcano from erupting?" Derek asked.

"That's what I'm saying," said Xander. "You can't change the past. You can only create an alternate version of it."

"So Neill can't go back and drown Howard to set things right?"

"Definitely not," said Jorgen. "Besides, that would be immoral."

"I don't understand," said Neill. "So there's a second past then?"

"Exactly," said Jorgen. "Probably many versions of the past. In fact, some people after the deluge did time travel back to before the volcano erupted and managed to stop it, or at least that's what they told us they were going to do. If they succeeded, they have created an alternate time they are living in now where Marquette never flooded. They could not change the future, but they could create a new future. Sadly, they never came back so we can only speculate what became of them."

"But then why didn't you guys yourselves time travel so you could live in a better future too?" Derek asked. It was a good question. Neill was rather surprised Derek was understanding this time travel dilemma so well.

"Because the government quickly made time travel illegal, other than for a few," said Jorgen.

"Yeah, we even have one of the early time travel devices down in the museum," said Xander, "but if the government found out we had it, we'd probably have to relinquish it. No one knows we have it because it was found in an old safety deposit box when I was groping in the ruins of the First National Bank. I probably should report it...."

"Really?" said Neill. "It didn't get ruined in the deluge?"

"Well, physically it appears fine, but whether or not it actually works is another thing," said Jorgen. "We wouldn't dare try to use it. The death penalty has been issued to anyone who time travels other than a few TTC agents who have special permission."

"What is TTC?" asked Derek.

"Time-Travel Certified," said Jorgen, "and there are only a handful of them—maybe twenty at the most, who sort of police the universe."

"But if you can't change the past, only create new versions of it, why does the government care if people time travel?" asked Derek.

"Taxes," said Xander. "It's all about money. People might try to disappear into a new time and take with them all their money, and then the government would lose out on revenue. Another problem early on was people returning from the past with large numbers of coins they sold as antiques on the black market."

"Wow," said Neill. "I never would have thought of doing something like that."

"Yes, so while Longyear Legacies started out as a sort of vacation time-travel company, the government quickly regulated it, even took it over, so that now it's a government agency and located in DC—obviously, it can't be located here or it would be underwater too. Plus, Canada has made all time travel illegal and we're part of Canada now."

"That's a shame," said Neill. "Time travel might be used for good."

"It's not a shame," said Jorgen. "Time travel destroyed the US economy, resulting in the Economic Crisis of 2109-15, and that led to World War III, or so they called it, but it was mostly fought with

currency, not weapons. During the crisis, the Southern states seced-
ed from the Union, and Russia invaded China, and well, when the
oceans rose, a lot of Europe ended up submerged. Once London
went underwater due to climate change, the stock market pretty
much collapsed. There's nothing left of the Netherlands now—all
underwater—and parts of Great Britain too. And then when Upper
Michigan got wiped out, the US government was too bankrupt to
do anything to help so it sold much of the Great Lakes region to
Canada."

"Wait. You're saying all that happened because Longyear
Legacies invented time travel?" asked Neill.

"Yes," said Xander. "Even the flooding of the U.P. You see, it
was time travelers from the future who came to this time to mine the
Great Lakes. They had already mined them in their own time and
exhausted all the resources, so they had the brilliant and fatal idea
to travel back in time to mine what they had already mined when it
was still here, only they didn't realize how the lakebed was different
in this time so they made mistakes that resulted in the flooding."

"So if Longyear Legacies didn't invent time travel, the U.P.
wouldn't be flooded?" said Neill.

"Exactly," said Xander.

"This is making my head hurt," said Neill. "So ultimately, because I saved Howard Longyear's life, World War III started and the
United States split in two and then sold part of its land to Canada,
including the flooded U.P.?"

Xander and Jorgen did not deny the statement.

Neill felt like the weight of the world had fallen on his shoulders. Jorgen, seeing how agitated Neill was, said, "Let's take a break
and go show you some of the Marquette treasures we saved. You
might find that interesting, and you've had enough information to
take in for one evening."

"Okay," said Neill, sighing. He was devastated by what he had
just heard and did need a breather.

"I'm ready," said Derek, pushing his now-empty trout loaf tray
away.

Chapter 4

A MINUTE LATER, XANDER HAD CLEANED off the table and put all the food trays in some sort of dishwasher. Then he and Jorgen led Derek and Neill back into the main part of the basement where pancake breakfasts and church bazaars had given way to preserving Marquette's past.

"It's rather a mess," said Xander, clapping his hands to make the lights come on. They were so bright that it took everyone's eyes a moment to adjust. "For the longest time now, we've just been collecting things and putting them in here."

Glancing about, Derek and Neill could see the basement was very crowded, with only narrow pathways weaving around stacks of materials. It was like being in an antique shop, though many of the items were larger and tended more to be outdoor objects than the typical interior furniture in most antique shops.

"Unfortunately," said Xander. "Very few items have been properly restored from the water damage they experienced. Anything wooden rotted and was unsalvageable, but this room is temperature and humidity regulated to protect everything we preserved as much as possible."

Neill stood there and stared, his eyes taking in a great deal, but not recognizing much of what he saw.

"Did you save any records?" he asked. "I see some books back there, but what about things like the birth and death records from the courthouse?"

"No," said Xander. "Those were all ruined. Some things at the courthouse were in vaults, but even there, the water seeped in, or it will if we open the vaults that weren't compromised. We don't have the equipment yet to raise an entire vault up above water to salvage it. Fortunately, most of those records were on the Internet or in our computer systems when the flood happened. The digital revolution in your own time preserved many things that would have been lost otherwise."

The basement's vastness and the number of items in it made it difficult for Neill to focus on any one item at first. Then Jorgen said, "The Kawbawgam statue is over here," and he led the way through stacks of metal boxes, garden gnomes, and cemetery stones. Mailboxes, a fire hydrant, and the peace globe from Harlow Park stood beside city Christmas decorations, an old DVD player, and several electronic-looking things Neill didn't recognize that he figured had been invented after 2021. The collection appeared to have no rhyme or reason. "Why'd you preserve that?" he could not help asking, pointing at the giant lion's head drinking fountain he remembered from Presque Isle Park.

"It's part of history," said Jorgen. "Everything we can save is worth saving."

"Over here," Xander said, beckoning with his hand. They followed him around a pile of metal boxes that towered over their heads until they came face-to-face with a life-size statue of Chief Kawbawgam. The nineteenth-century Ojibwa chief was dressed in his long coat and hat and holding the hand of a little girl, just like in a photograph Neill had seen many times.

"Yup. That's it," said Derek. "You must have had a hell of a time getting it here."

"It wasn't too bad," said Xander. "We have pretty good excavating equipment."

"Unfortunately, the Father Marquette statue didn't fare as well," said Jorgen, gesturing to the monument they could just glimpse behind another stack of boxes. "I wish we had just left it alone. The head broke off and we don't know where in the lake bottom it rolled off to, and we couldn't fit it in the museum here with the pedestal, so we had to leave that behind, but even a headless statue is still worth preserving."

Neill shook his head. He had to hold back his tears to think what had become of Marquette. He was happy to see Chief Kawbawgam had gotten his statue after all, but what did it matter now, two hundred years after it was built, if no one was left to see it?

"Over here we have the sign from an Italian restaurant," said Xander.

Neill followed him and saw, propped up on a shelf, a neon-looking sign that looked like it would never light up again, yet the writing on it—"Villa Capri"—was plainly visible.

"Ever hear of this place?" asked Xander.

"Sure. My parents and I used to eat there all the time," said Neill.

"Really?" said Jorgen. "Do you recognize what it's sitting on?"

"It looks like a bar from a tavern," said Neill.

"Yes, it's the bar from the Vierling Restaurant," Jorgen replied.

"Hey, what's this?" asked Derek, drawing their attention to a glass display cabinet against a wall.

"Oh, those are various examples of electronics from the past," said Xander, stepping up next to him. "These mostly aren't important to Marquette's past per se, but they are still examples of things people would have used back in the day."

Neill stepped over to look at them. Many of them looked familiar.

"What's that?" asked Derek, pointing at one.

"It's a cassette recorder," said Neill, who recognized it because his father had had one, even though they were long out of date by the time Neill and Derek were born.

"There's a laptop," said Derek, pointing at another item. "I recognize that."

"Do you know what this is?" asked Xander, pointing at another item — a small red camera-shaped piece with a little lever on the side and two glass sections that jutted out to put your eyes against.

"No," said Neill and Derek both.

"It's called a View Master," said Jorgen. "I would think you'd know it. I think it's late twentieth century."

"A little before our time," said Derek. "I was born in 2002, and I think Neill was too."

"I remember my mom talking about those," said Neill. "I think she had one when she was a kid. They had comic strip slides or something like that which you inserted in them so you could see comics in 3-D."

"Sounds right," said Jorgen. "We haven't found any of those slides, though, that would fit. I think we found that in the Marquette Regional History Center's storage section. Unfortunately, most of what was there was ruined before we could get to it."

"What about this thing?" asked Derek, pointing at a gold-colored dial a little smaller than a cell phone.

"Oh," said Jorgen. "Yes, that's what we were talking about. It's one of the Longyear time dials."

"A time dial?" said Neill. "How does it work?"

"Well, it was used for time travel," said Xander. "It was one, if not the first, model, but I'm not really sure how it worked. I wasn't even born then."

"And you don't know if it works?" asked Neill.

Xander raised his lower lip, as if frowning a bit, and said, "Like we said, time travel is illegal so we wouldn't dare to try it."

"There's something else over here you two might recognize," said Jorgen, drawing their attention away.

Derek turned to follow him, but Neill kept staring at the time dial.

"Didn't you at least check to see if it still worked?" Neill asked Xander.

"Xander, where is that movie reel?" asked Jorgen, calling to him.

"Coming," said Xander, and he brushed past Neill, ignoring his question, to join Jorgen.

"Oh, here it is," said Jorgen a moment later. Neill could hear Jorgen and Xander telling Derek something, but Neill was still staring at the time dial, nearly pressing his nose up against the glass case to try to read what it said. There was definitely a dial, and a little pointer, like the hand of a watch in the center, but it was pointing to the year 1800 where a 9 would normally be on a wristwatch. Then halfway between where the 10 and 11 would be, it said 1850, and right where the 12 would be, it said 1900. Then where the 3 was it said 1600 and the 6 said 1700. Obviously, it ran from 1501-1900 since the 12 wasn't 1500, but 1550 was about halfway between where the 1 and 2 would be.

"Neill, come see this!" called Derek.

"Neill," Xander added, "you'll definitely want to see this!"

Neill didn't want to take his eyes off the time dial, but he turned and walked over to them.

"It's an actual old movie reel," said Derek, "from that murder movie filmed in Marquette—I can never remember the name of it."

"*Anatomy of a Murder*," said Xander.

"Yeah, that one," said Derek.

"And here we have a movie poster from it that all the stars signed," said Jorgen, motioning to the wall where the poster was in a glass frame.

"Cool," said Derek, reading the signatures. "Lee Remick, James Stewart, George C. Scott....afraid I never heard of any of them."

"They were all big stars," said Neill. "You must have seen *It's a Wonderful Life* on TV at Christmas. Jimmy Stewart was in that."

Derek just shook his head. Sometimes Neill had to wonder about the cultural illiteracy of his contemporaries.

"Here's one of the gold lamps that used to be in front of a bank downtown," said Jorgen.

Neill and Derek walked over to it. Derek didn't remember it, but Neill did. It was from Louis G. Kaufman's expensive First National Bank, which had been part of the Flagstar Bank family in Neill's time.

Jorgen and Xander continued to lead their guests through the pile of mementos. There were many more items, but most of them dated to the last hundred years, the future compared to Neill and Derek's time, so the items were not of as much interest to them. Many of the items and their uses had to be explained to them by Jorgen and Xander, which left the boys' heads swimming. This lesson in Marquette history between 2021 and 2142 left them very confused.

Finally, Jorgen noticed Derek starting to yawn.

"You must be exhausted," said Jorgen.

"Yes, I am," Derek admitted. "After all, Neill and I were up early this morning, and kayaking for eight or ten hours or whatever it was does tend to wear out even a strong guy like me."

"I'm sorry," said Xander. "We get so few visitors that I guess we got a bit carried away in our enthusiasm to show off our treasures."

"No, not at all," said Neill. "It was all very interesting. We appreciate you sharing it all with us."

"Is there somewhere we can crash?" asked Derek.

"Crash?" asked Xander, looking at Jorgen in confusion.

"He means," said Neill, realizing they didn't understand Derek's twenty-first century slang, "is there somewhere we can sleep tonight?"

"Yes, we have a spare room," said Xander.

"But what will you do here in our time?" Jorgen asked them. "You can't stay here long. You're undocumented. We'll have to bring you to Toronto or at least notify the Canadian government so someone can come interview you."

"Interview us?" said Neill.

"Yes, because you are time travelers," said Jorgen. "As we said, time travel is illegal in this time. Granted, you didn't do it intentionally, so I doubt they'll give you the death penalty—maybe not even a prison sentence—but I'm sure the authorities will have some questions for you."

"Is…is the death penalty possible?" asked Derek, surprised by the remark.

"The government is very strict," said Jorgen. "But since you did it accidentally, they'll probably be lenient."

"But do you have to turn us in?" asked Derek.

"Yes, or we'll get in trouble," said Xander. "No one can go about these days without being tracked."

"Tracked?" said Neill.

"Yes," said Jorgen. "There are too many illegal immigrants in the country now. Everyone has a chip in their left index finger that can be scanned and tracked to ensure they are legitimate Canadians."

"No one's putting a fucking chip in me!" declared Derek, his nostrils flaring.

"How about," said Neill, knowing how belligerent Derek could get when he was tired, "we talk about it in the morning. Then you both can tell us what you think is best for us to do."

"All right," said Xander, who looked a bit intimidated by Derek's outburst. "I can show you to your room, but I will have to report you. I should have done that already, but I admit I got a bit side-tracked by the pleasure of having guests."

Neill was tempted to threaten that if they were reported, he would tattle on them about having the time travel device they hadn't shared with the authorities, but he was too tired to fight with anyone tonight. In the morning, he thought he might be more persuasive.

"We totally understand," Neill simply replied. "I'm sure the government will do its best to help us return to our time then."

"As we said before," Jorgen replied, "you can't go back in time."

Derek looked like he wanted to argue, but Neill put his hand up on his big friend's shoulder and said, "Derek, let's talk about it in the morning."

Derek's eyes were flaming, but he did not object.

"I should be heading home myself," said Jorgen to Xander.

"Oh," said Xander. "I thought you'd stay like usual."

Jorgen gave him a funny look.

"We're not taking your bed, are we, Jorgen?" asked Neill.

"Well," said Jorgen, "there is only one bed and one spare room, so yes, but it's okay. My wife will want me home anyway."

"Are you sure? It's a long way back to L'Anse," said Neill. "We can sleep on the floor."

"You'll have to anyway," Derek told Neill, "because I'm taking the bed."

Neill wasn't going to argue. He just wanted to lie down and be alone with his thoughts.

"All right," said Xander. "Well, thanks for coming, Jorgen. I'll contact you tomorrow."

They all took the elevator back to the main floor, and then Jorgen said his goodbyes and turned to climb up the tower by himself. Derek wanted to go with him to check on his kayak, but Jorgen promised to check that it was tied tightly to the dock so it would be safe for the night.

Once Jorgen disappeared up the tower steps, Xander led Derek and Neill down a hall to a spare bedroom. As stated, there was only one bed in it, and it was a twin. Xander explained that what had been the rectory had been badly damaged by the flood and was still being repaired. There was only a small room below what had been the altar, and it contained the one spare twin bed. Neill assured Xander that they would be more than comfortable in the cramped surroundings. After Xander adjusted the heat—Neill asked for a blanket, but Xander explained blankets were germy and needed to be washed, and modern heating systems were regulated to ensure body comfort throughout the night without physical coverings—Neill and Derek thanked him and said good night.

Derek took one look at the bed and said, "That thing's too small for me. My legs will hang over the side and I might roll out of it. You can have it."

Neill just looked at Derek for a moment, trying to think where to begin.

"What's wrong?" asked Derek, seeing the troubled look on his face.

Seriously? thought Neill. *What is not wrong?* Then he took a deep breath and said, "Derek, we have to escape from here."

Chapter 5

EREK HAD LOOKED HAGGARD A moment before, but now his eyes popped open.

"What? Escape?" he said. "I thought you were all, 'Oh, we'll talk about it in the morning'?"

"I thought you were all, 'No one's putting a fucking chip in me,'" Neill replied. "How are we going to avoid that if we don't escape?"

"I figured I'd get a good night's sleep," said Derek, "so I'd be well-rested to kick some ass tomorrow if anyone tries."

Neill sighed and sat down on the bed. "Derek, we need to leave tonight, while Xander's asleep."

"And go where?" asked Derek. "All we have is a kayak and no idea how many miles we'll have to paddle to get anywhere."

"No, not leave in the kayak," said Neill. "We need to get back to 1900."

"But how? The dolmen's underwater," said Derek, so exhausted that he slumped down against the wall as he spoke.

"We'll use the Longyear Legacies time dial," Neill replied.

"What?"

"The time dial. The one in the glass case."

"I thought Xander said it didn't work."

"He said he didn't know if it worked or not. He was afraid to try. We have to steal it and try to get it to work. It's our only hope of getting back to 1900. Even if it turns out the Canadian government is all warm and fuzzy and doesn't want to put chips in us, do you really want to live in this war-torn, economic, and global-warming disaster of a future?"

"No," said Derek, shaking his head.

"Then help me steal the time dial. Then we'll take off in the kay-ak before Xander can come after us. You can paddle while I try to figure out how it works."

"If Xander comes after us," said Derek, "I'll break his skull."

"No, let's not get violent," said Neill. "I tell you what—let's nap for a couple of hours while we wait to make sure Xander is asleep. Then we'll make a break for it."

"All right," said Derek, yawning. "I could use a nap. You just wake me up when you're ready to go."

"Okay. I'll figure out our next move while you sleep," said Neill, although he was exhausted himself.

"You do that," said Derek, lying down on the floor.

Neill got up to turn off the light, but not seeing a light switch and then remembering what Xander had done, he clapped his hands and the room went black. Feeling his way back to the bed, he heard Derek already snoring.

Neill let his friend sleep, realizing Derek was the brawn while he was the brains of this operation. Derek would need his strength to paddle them out of the place before Xander discovered they had stolen the time dial while Neill figured out how to use it. Neill knew they'd have to flee once they stole it even if they didn't set off any alarms. He hadn't seen any security cameras, but he had no idea what kinds of security systems existed in 2142. Too bad he didn't know how to use the time dial so he could transport them back to the past right away. Even if they didn't steal the time dial, they had to get out of here. For all he knew, Xander or Jorgen had already reported them to the authorities. Someone might arrive tonight to interrogate or even imprison them. He and Derek would have to take their chances with escaping and figure out how to use the time dial later.

Since he had lost his cell phone in the lake and he had no wristwatch, Neill had no idea how much time had passed. He just sat on the bed with his back up against the wall, knowing if he lay down, he'd likely fall asleep. He started thinking about everything he had been through in the last few weeks, and he tried to envision what he should do going forward. Would he be able to fix things if he did return to 1900? What would he do when he got there? How would he explain his disappearance to Howard? Should he try to kill Howard—would that cause 2021 to revert to the version he had known? He hated the thought of killing anyone. He considered he might be able to get Derek to kill Howard, but he'd still be morally responsible for it. And not only was murdering Howard reprehensible, but it would not guarantee that his great-great-grandparents would come together. No, instead of murdering Howard, he would have to figure out how to introduce his great-great-grandparents and make them like one another. But they hadn't gotten together until 1903—would he have to stay in the past for three years before he could ensure everything was back to normal?

And what if he still failed? Then it would be pointless to return to his own time. In that case, could he find peace living in 1900 and the many years that he would live? He'd have to live through two World Wars and the Great Depression, and even the Spanish influenza, which given that he had been living through the coronavirus pandemic and only just gotten his second vaccination shot before going up to the Club for the summer, seemed like the scariest event to face. And how weird would it be if he befriended his great-great-grandparents and then watched his great-grandparents being born and growing up and then saw his grandparents born before he died an old man before his own parents were born. It was just too surreal—too hard to wrap his head around. Well, at least he would be long dead by the time he would be born.

And if he was able to return to his own time, how would he explain where he had been? People must be missing him by now—he had been gone for about three weeks. They were going to wonder what had happened to him. His poor parents must be hysterical with worry if not grief, and after seeing how hard his father had taken Uncle Chad's death, to cause him such additional pain made Neill's heart ache.

He began to tear up at the thought of his parents. He felt like Dorothy in *The Wizard of Oz*, just wanting to go home. At least Dorothy had had the ruby slippers. She'd always had the power to go home, even if she hadn't known it. Neill wished he had such power. He might soon have a time dial, but even if that got him back to 1900, only returning to the dolmen could probably get him to 2021 since the time dial only worked for the years 1501-1900. Different time dials must have been made for travel to different time periods. And since the dolmen had not taken him and Derek where they had wanted to go this time, it seemed unpredictable whether he would ever be able to return home.

Finally, unable to continue worrying about how this adventure would turn out—thinking of it as an adventure did make him feel better about it; it was something he could tell his grandchildren about someday, though he doubted anyone would believe it—he figured a couple of hours must have passed, so he got up from the bed, knelt down on the floor beside Derek, and shook him.

"Derek, wake up."

"I am awake," said Derek.

"Didn't you sleep?"

"A little, but I've been awake for a while. I was just about to wake you. I figured you must be sleeping."

"I didn't sleep," said Neill, "but I can't stand waiting any longer. Let's get going."

Derek stood up and reached for the shoes he had taken off at some point.

Neill didn't turn on the lights. He didn't want to arouse suspicion. He groped his way in the pitch black to the door and gently opened it. A soft light greeted him. He could see small lights along the floor, like those along the aisle of a movie theater. He was grateful for this aid to his vision, although it would also make them more visible.

"Lead the way," Derek whispered.

Neill quietly started down the hall, easily recalling the route Xander had brought them along, for despite some construction, the cathedral's layout was still largely how Neill remembered it. Eventually, he found the stairs—he feared taking the elevator would be too noisy—and he and Derek descended into the basement. After a minute, they were back in the large gathering space that had been turned into a storage unit.

"This place is a mess," whispered Derek. "Do you remember where the time dial was?"

The room was very dark because it was crammed full of so much stuff. The few dim lights along the wall were largely blocked by the towering boxes and larger items that had been salvaged from Marquette's past.

Neill didn't say anything, just motioned for Derek to follow him as he led the way between winding stacks of boxes.

"Wait up," said Derek. "I can't see you."

Neill walked backward a few steps, and then Derek put his hand on Neill's shoulder so he wouldn't lose him. They proceeded, and after a couple of wrong turns, they came to the glass cabinet. It wasn't lit up at all, and Neill was pleased that no alarms went off when he touched it. He slid his hand along the glass until he found an indented handle that showed it had a sliding door.

"Do we have to smash it?" asked Derek.

"No," said Neill. "There's a door. Just be patient."

Neill's eyes were adjusting now to the dim light so he could see the outlines of the shelves, but he could not see the objects sitting on them well enough to tell which was the time dial. He reached in and fondled several objects with his fingers before he found one that felt like it was the right size and shape.

Clasping the object in his hand, Neill pulled out his arm, not realizing the dial was sitting on some sort of little book or pamphlet, which he pulled forward as well. The book fell as Neill's fingers fumbled to retain a hold on the time dial.

"Shh!" warned Derek as the book fell, banging against the glass case before hitting the floor.

"Sorry," said Neill, holding the object up to his face to ensure it was the time dial.

Derek bent down to grab the book. He was about to return it to the case when he saw Neill looking at the time dial and said skeptically, "That's going to help us travel to 1900?"

"I hope so," said Neill, confirming it was the item he sought. "We don't have any other options."

"Any idea how it works?" asked Derek.

"There's a dial on it for different years, so I imagine we have to point the dial to that year, but it's too dark in here to see the writing on it, and I don't want to try and get us stuck in the wrong year."

"Yeah. Let me put this book back and shut the case so no one will hopefully notice it's gone."

"I'm surprised there's no alarm," Neill said, just happening to glance at the book Derek was holding. Then he exclaimed, "Wait!"

"What?" whispered Derek, alarmed that Neill had spoken so loudly.

"That book," said Neill. "Let me see it."

Derek handed it to him. Neill saw it was quite a small book, small enough to fit in a pants pocket, not more than three-by-four inches. It was hardcover, though, and sturdy. But what struck Neill most was that in the dim light he could just make out on the cover, because of its gold lettering, that the title said, *Journal of Howard Longyear*.

"Oh my God," Neill said, opening the journal. "It can't be a coincidence."

"What?" asked Derek.

"This journal. It was with the time device and says it belonged to Howard Longyear."

"So?"

"I wonder if…here, hold this." Neill handed Derek the time device so both of his hands would be free to examine the book. He quickly flipped the journal open to a few pages from the beginning, but the light was too dim to read by. He did make out the date July 30, 1900, which made him say, "It was written just a few days after I left Marquette—after I would have disappeared before Howard's eyes."

"So?" asked Derek.

"I'll explain later. We have to get going."

"Are you taking that with you?" asked Derek.

"Yeah," said Neill. "We might need it later." He quickly shoved the journal into his pants pocket.

"Let's go up the tower now," said Derek, handing back the time dial to Neill. "Once we're outside, maybe you can see the time dial better in the moonlight, and if not, we can at least paddle out of here so we are far away when the sun rises."

"I hope so," said Neill, wondering just how quickly they would be picked up on a scanner the way Jorgen had first noticed them. Beginning to fear being caught, Neill tried too quickly to slide shut the glass case and it jammed. Giving it a shove to make it close, he made it jiggle and an item on the top shelf tumbled off and smashed onto the floor, making what seemed like an excruciatingly loud noise in the silence.

"Shit!" said Derek. "Let's get out of here."

Derek started back down one of the narrow alleys between all the artifacts. Before Neill knew it, his friend was out of sight. Neill tried to follow him, but he soon realized he didn't know where he'd gone.

"Derek, where are you?" he whispered, tightly clutching the time dial while trying to adjust the book he'd stuck in his pants.

No answer.

"Derek!" Neill called louder, almost in his normal voice.

"Over here," said Derek. Neill could tell he was right in front of him, but on the other side of a pile of stuff. Neill turned to the right, thinking it would take him around the pile, but instead, it sent him down a long path and finally to a pair of stairs leading out of the basement.

"Derek, where are you?" Neill called again.

"Over here!" said Derek.

This time, it sounded like Derek was behind him. Neill turned around and saw Derek right outside the piles of artifacts, around the corner from the stairs.

"Are these the stairs to the tower?" Neill asked, not wasting time on reprimanding his friend for getting separated from him.

"Looks like it," said Derek.

But they weren't the tower stairs, which they found out once they had gone up them. They led upstairs to the main floor, the vestibule, but from there, they easily found the staircase up the tower.

Finally, they were just starting up the tower's stairs when they heard a door open.

"Who's there?" shouted Xander. His voice revealed he was at the far end of the vestibule.

"Go!" whispered Derek, pushing Neill up the stairs.

They rushed up the stairs, not moving very quietly since the stairs were old and creaky.

"Stop!" shouted Xander. Neill was sure Xander had heard them go up the tower and was pursuing them, but Neill didn't stop until he got to the top of the stairs. Then he pushed open the hatch to the top of the tower and emerged outside. Immediately, Neill was stunned by the bright light—a full moon. For a second, he saw the moonlight shining on Lake Superior. It was surreal to be up in a tower looking out at the lake like this, but there was no time for further admiration of the night's beauty. Derek was coming through the open hatch now.

"Stop!" shouted Xander from below.

"I'll stop him," said Derek, half-jumping through the hatch. He quickly turned around to close it, then stood on top of it. "Can you see the numbers on the dial now?" Derek asked Neill.

"Yeah," said Neill, walking over to the arched window to see better.

By now, Xander was pounding on the hatch. But then he stopped. They could hear him talking to someone and giving his location. Obviously, he was calling for help from one of his cronies.

"Derek!" shouted Neill, looking out at the raft. "The kayak's gone!"

"Gone!" shouted Derek. In his surprise, he thoughtlessly stepped halfway off the hatch for a better look. It was the wrong move. With a mighty thrust, Xander popped open the hatch as Derek lost his balance and landed on the tower floor.

"Stop, you trespassers!" shouted Xander, bursting out of the hatch.

"Trespassers?" said Derek, jumping around. "You're a thief. You or your friend stole my kayak!"

"You're undocumented!" declared Xander, stepping forward with a laser gun in his hand. "We had no choice. We could get in trouble for not turning you in."

Before he could complete the sentence, Derek lunged forward, knocking the gun from Xander's hand and kicking it behind him.

"Don't come any closer," Derek warned Xander. "No one's putting a chip in me, and if you try, you'll feel the weight of my fist."

Xander looked at Derek, then backed up a step, realizing he was no match for his adversary.

"The authorities will be here within minutes," Xander stated. "They'll come in their velocitizers and tranquilize you. Don't think your brute strength can save you."

"Maybe not," said Neill, "but this time dial might. Show us how it works."

Xander's eyes grew large when he saw the dial in Neill's hand. "You have no right to take that!" he declared.

"Show us how it works," Neill repeated.

Xander laughed. "Even if I knew how to use it, I wouldn't risk going to prison for life by showing you."

"If you dare to tell anyone we were here," Neill replied, "you'll go to prison for keeping it a secret from the Canadian government. I'll make sure the government knows I was only able to use it because you were hiding it!"

"You wouldn't dare!" said Xander. "I'll kill you first!"

He lunged toward Neill, but Derek was too fast for him. He reached out and grabbed Xander by the throat. Xander's feet left the ground as Derek flung him up against the tower's frame. "Tell us how the time dial works," he repeated.

Xander's eyes started to bug out from the pressure.

"Derek, he can't speak!" Neill exclaimed.

Derek grabbed Xander under an armpit with his free hand, then released his other hand from Xander's throat to the other armpit.

"Tell us how it works," Derek repeated, effortlessly holding the man two feet off the ground.

"I don't know!" cried Xander, rubbing his throat.

"Tell us," said Neill, suddenly having an idea. "We can take you with us if you want." Neill wasn't sure they would take him, but it didn't hurt to bargain. Xander couldn't be happy in this forlorn place. He probably wanted to leave as much as they did.

"I'm not stupid enough to do that," Xander replied. "You'll be hunted down no matter where you go. The authorities won't let you get away with this."

"Derek, I'm going to turn the dial," said Neill, stepping up beside him. "I don't think we have any other choice. Wherever it takes us will be better than here."

"No!" shouted Xander. His hand reached out and knocked the time dial from Neill's hands. It went flying out the arched window but, fortunately, landed on the raft. Derek and Neill both jumped through the arched windows to grab it, Derek dropping Xander to the floor in the process. But Xander was faster than they would have thought, and soon all three men were kneeling on the floor of the raft, wrestling for the time dial. Finally, Derek saw Neill was firmly grasping the dial, so he grabbed Xander by the leg and, with a quick wrestling move, got him in a headlock.

"Go ahead, Neill. Turn the dial," said Derek.

Neill crawled over to Derek. "We need to be touching each other so we travel together," he replied.

"What about this guy?" asked Derek. "I can't let him go...or can I?"

Derek looked out at the lake.

"No. I can't swim!" screamed Xander, reading Derek's mind. Derek began to pull him toward the raft's side.

"Can't swim?" said Derek. "When you live in Waterworld? That's the stupidest thing I've ever heard, and here you claimed you aren't stupid."

"Derek, the dial moves," said Neill. He had been unable to resist turning it. "I don't think it does anything though just by turning the dial. I changed it to 1900."

"How does it work then?" asked Derek.

"You idiots!" said Xander. "You're so primitive."

"Primitive?" said Derek.

"It's simple voice-activated technology," said Xander. "They even had that technology back in the twenty-first century."

"Oh," said Derek and bent backward a little—just enough, since Xander was still in a headlock, for Xander's feet to move out over the lake. Xander began to flail about as he became suspended in the air.

"Seems like it's pretty primitive of you not to be able to swim," said Derek. "Even we could do that in the twenty-first century." He released Xander from the headlock.

"No!" screamed Xander, plunging into the lake.

Derek walked back to Neill and put his hand on his shoulder. "Tell it to do something."

"Alexa, take us to 1900," said Neill, half-laughing as he used the name of his parents' Echo Dot.

"My name isn't Alexa," said a computer-generated male voice. "It's Howard."

"Holy shit!" said Derek.

"Howard," said Neill, now grinning, "take us to 1900."

"Your wish is my command," replied the time dial.

As Xander struggled to pull himself back up onto the raft, he saw his adversaries disappear.

Part IV

Chapter 1

"AAAAHHHHHH!" NEILL SCREAMED AS HE felt himself falling. Reaching out, he grabbed onto a bar as he fell past it and soon found himself dangling in the air, just a foot from the cathedral tower.

"Neill!" Derek shouted.

Neill looked up and saw Derek on a platform above him, looking down.

"Neill, are you okay?"

"Help me!" cried Neill.

"Just let go," said Derek. "You'll be okay."

"Let go?" Neill repeated.

"Yeah. You're only about five feet from the ground."

Neill looked down. It was dark out, but he could faintly see the sidewalk below him. He still felt leery about falling that far, but Derek was up a good thirty feet above him—there was no way he could reach down and grab him. They appeared to be on some sort of wooden scaffolding. Derek was on a platform while Neill was hanging from a two-by-four built along the side of the scaffolding. Neill looked down again and dimly saw another two-by-four a few inches above his feet. He swung his feet up onto it. Then he was able to crawl down the scaffolding to the sidewalk.

Derek, seeing Neill was safe on the ground, called, "Hold on. I'll be right down." He proceeded to climb down a ladder on the front of the scaffolding.

By now, Neill could see they had successfully traveled back in time. Looking up, he saw the cathedral towers looked flatter, without their painted domes and nowhere near as tall. He knew the cathedral had partially burned in 1935 and the towers he had known all his life—the same towers that had been poking above the lake in 2142—were constructed after that fire. Now he was staring at the cathedral's original towers, those erected in the 1880s, which told him this time was somewhere between 1880 and 1935, and hopefully, was the year 1900.

And then, as Derek descended the ladder in his shorts, sandals, and T-shirt, Neill realized they had a problem.

"Dude, I think we made it," said Derek, reaching up his hand for a high-five as soon as his feet touched the ground. Neill half-heartedly raised his hand, but as he withdrew it, he said, "But we have another problem."

"What's that?" asked Derek.

"You're going to get arrested for indecent exposure wearing those shorts."

"Oh," said Derek. "I hadn't thought of that."

"I wish you had told me you were going to pull that stunt of coming back in time with me," said Neill. "I would have told you to get some period-appropriate clothes."

"Don't get snippy with me," said Derek. "I've been through enough in the last couple of days."

"I know," said Neill, not wanting to push his luck with this larger, less predictable version of his friend. Besides, even though it had been Derek's choice to travel with him, he felt it was his fault they were in this predicament to begin with.

"Where's the time dial?" asked Derek.

"Oh," said Neill, looking around in a panic. He was quickly relieved to find it lying on the sidewalk, but when he picked it up, he discovered it had landed on its face. The glass was smashed and the dial looked dented. He didn't dare turn the dial to see if it still worked. Not wanting to worry Derek—it had only had a time range of 1501-1900 anyway—Neill stuck it in his pocket and said, "Got it." Then he felt his pocket to make sure he still had Howard's journal. Fortunately, they hadn't landed in the lake again or the time dial would have been ruined like his cell phone had been.

"What do we do now?" asked Derek.

"Figure out where we can find some clothes for you," Neill replied. Since it was still dark, no one was likely to see them, but Neill could see a glimmer of dawn in the sky. It must be close to 6 a.m.

"Where?" asked Derek. "Are we going to break into someone's house?"

"No, we'll get caught. We'll find a men's clothing store."

"And break in there?" asked Derek.

"No, we can't do that."

"We have no money," said Derek. "You got a better idea?"

"But we can't be stealing," said Neill. He had never stolen anything.

"We stole the time dial, didn't we?" said Derek.

"That's different," said Neill, realizing he wasn't as moral as he had thought. "It was a matter of life or death."

"So is my getting arrested for indecent exposure," said Derek. "If we end up in jail, we won't be able to find Howard Longyear or do whatever you think necessary to get you back to your own time."

Neill didn't know what to say. Derek was right. He had always been a law-abiding citizen, but desperate times called for desperate measures.

"We can head downtown," said Neill, "but what if someone sees you on the way? There might be early risers about now."

Derek sighed and raised his head to stretch his neck.

"Hey!" he suddenly said.

"What?" Neill asked.

But rather than answer, Derek was climbing back up the scaffolding, and a second later, a thick white sheet came floating down.

"I'll wrap that around me until we find me some clothes," said Derek.

Neill didn't argue. Derek wrapped the sheet around him, then pulled it up so there'd be enough material to flip over his shoulder like a toga. His hairy legs were still bare from the knees down, but it was a definite improvement by Victorian standards.

"I hope this works," Neill said.

"Well, maybe people will think I'm a ghost and run when they see me coming," said Derek.

"Don't count on it," Neill replied.

"We'll find a clothing store," said Derek. "There has to be one on Front or Washington Street. And it's not like they have security alarms in this time."

"I don't know," said Neill. "I think they might."

"I'm not worried," said Derek. "I just hope we can find something that fits me. Weren't people shorter in 1900? Finding something to fit someone who's six-foot-four won't be easy."

Great, Neill thought. *How many stores will we have to break into just to find him a pair of pants?*

Neill wasn't sure they should walk down Baraga Avenue since it was a main street, so they went down Fourth Street for a block—either way they had to go past the jail, which meant the police might spot them—then on to Spring Street to approach Front Street from the back. When they were a block from Front, Neill realized Getz's Department Store, newly opened, was on the corner. In Neill's time, Getz's was the finest men's clothing store in Marquette, so he figured it would be their best hope now. However, as they were about to cross the street to try to break in Getz's back door, they saw the back door fly open and a man run out. He started in their direction, but upon seeing them, he turned and ran down an alley. Suddenly, a middle-aged police officer came running around the corner. He stopped to look at Neill and Derek and said, "Did you see anyone come out of that store?"

"Yes, Officer. He went that way," Neill replied, pointing toward the alley behind the store.

"Thanks," said the officer, giving sheet-clad Derek a strange look, but apparently deciding he had more urgent business.

The officer took off after the apparent burglar, leaving Getz's back door wide open.

"That was easy," said Derek, running over to the back door.

"What if there are other criminals in there?" asked Neill.

"Don't worry. I can handle them," said Derek.

"What if the police officer comes back?" asked Neill.

"Did you see the gut on him?" asked Derek. "Don't worry. I can handle him too. Come on."

Derek went into the building. Neill could see he had little choice but to follow. The lights were turned off, but enough light was coming through the front windows for them to find their way through the main display room where assorted pants, shirts, suits, ties, and other men's garments were arranged to advantage.

"Here we go," said Derek, looking at a rack of pants. He began pulling off pairs and holding them up to his waist to see how long they were.

"What size do you wear?" asked Neill.

"Thirty-four long, thirty-two waist," said Derek.

Neill started to help his friend, but there were no sizes on the pants in the places he was used to.

"These look like they'll fit," said Derek, who quickly whipped off his toga sheet and pulled the pants up over his bathing suit shorts. "Yes, these fit. Neill, you should find some new clothes too. Something classier so we're taken seriously in this time."

"That's not a bad idea," said Neill, who knew his hiking clothes were not appropriate for calling on the Longyears in town or for finding a decent office job if he were to be stuck in this time forever.

After about five minutes—they had no time to be fussy—Derek and Neill had both found new pants, shirts, ties, jackets, and caps. Neill quickly changed out of his clothes, other than the modern underwear he had gotten from Derek, which he wasn't about to part with, even if one pair would not last for long. He carefully put the journal from Howard Longyear in the inside pocket of his suit coat, but the time dial was too bulky and would look awkward, so he put it in his pants pocket, the bulge of which would be hidden by the end of his suit. He took a few seconds to admire himself in the mirror as Derek fiddled with his tie, and then finally Neill had to help him with it. Altogether, despite their unfamiliarity with such garments, Neill had to admit they looked rather dapper and should fit right in with the late Victorians on Marquette's streets.

They were just about to exit the back door when they heard a voice in the back. "Mr. Getz, I'm so very sorry I didn't stop to close the back door." It was the police officer they had previously seen.

"It's okay, Officer McCarey. I appreciate your efforts. I'm just glad you nabbed him. I can tell you Harry Cumming won't be working here again."

"I still think you should press charges," said Officer McCarey.

"No, he has a wife and children to feed, and I'd feel responsible if he ended up in jail while they starved. I got his key from him—that's enough."

While this conversation was ensuing, Neill and Derek had been slowly moving toward the front door, hoping to escape out of it. Only, it was locked. Derek was messing with the bolt when Mr. Getz shouted, "Officer, someone's in here!"

"Are you open?" asked Neill, spinning around.

"What?" asked Mr. Getz.

"Aren't you open?" Neill repeated. "The door wasn't locked, and we thought we saw lights on."

"No, no," said Mr. Getz. "We don't open until nine o'clock."

"I'm sorry," said Neill. "I thought it was still early, but we saw someone inside, so we figured you must be open."

"Officer McCarey," said Mr. Getz, turning to the officer, "Harry Cumming must have unlocked the front door too."

"Did you men see anyone suspicious looking around here?" asked Officer McCarey, staring at them but apparently not recognizing them from earlier.

"No, we just got up early and were walking downtown," said Derek. "We apologize for intruding."

"It's all right," said Mr. Getz, "but we don't open until nine."

"My apologies," said Neill. "We'll come back then."

"Good day," said Derek, stopping to tip his hat—Neill was surprised he would think to do something so old-fashioned—and then he opened the front door, which he had fortunately managed to unbolt without anyone noticing while Neill was speaking.

"Good day," Mr. Getz replied.

Neill and Derek walked out to the sidewalk and leisurely strolled up Front Street past the store's windows. Every second, Neill feared the officer would come running out of the building to shout, "Stop thief!" Derek had left the sheet in a corner of the store, so Neill would not be surprised if the officer figured out who they were, plus Neill's hiking clothes were on top of the sheet.

But by the time they reached Washington Street, no one had started in pursuit of them.

"Let's go this way so we're out of sight," said Neill, turning left on Washington just to be safe. It was still early and few people were out to take notice of them. They made another turn up the hill on Third Street, then waited until they got to Ridge to turn east toward the Longyear Mansion.

"That was quick thinking on your part," said Derek, "to pretend we had just come into the store."

"Thanks," said Neill, "but you were the one who got the door open. Otherwise, my story would have quickly fallen apart."

"Yeah," said Derek, "but it's your honest demeanor that saved us. I'm so tall I thought for sure that cop would recognize us from earlier."

"You know what?" said Neill. "I think that cop was my great-great-grandfather. Mr. Getz called him Officer McCarey. My great-great-grandpa was Patrick McCarey, and he was a police officer at one point, I believe, and later a prison guard."

"I thought he was a carpenter," said Derek.

"No, that's a different great-great-grandpa. That's Will Whitman. He's the one who married Margaret Dalrymple, the one we have to stop from marrying Howard. Will and Margaret's son, Henry Whitman, will marry Beth McCarey, the daughter of Officer McCarey. They'll be my great-grandparents."

"I don't know how you keep all that straight," said Derek. "I can't even remember my grandparents' first names most of the time."

"Well, my parents are addicted to genealogy, and our family has been in Marquette since it was founded," Neill replied, "so I know my family history pretty well."

"I guess it's a good thing you can keep it straight," said Derek, "so you know what you have to do to fix the past."

"Yeah," said Neill. "If I can."

"So where are we going?" Derek asked.

By now, they were crossing Front Street again and about to walk past the Methodist Church.

"To the Longyear Mansion," said Neill. "We have to go way down to the end of Ridge and then over to Arch, and then you'll see the Longyear Mansion in all its glory."

"In all its glory?" said Derek.

"I promise you, it's like nothing you've ever seen in Marquette before," replied Neill.

"You forget," said Derek, "the Longyear Mansion was always in Marquette in my time. I used to mow the lawn there."

"Oh, yeah," said Neill. "Sorry."

"That's okay. Let's just hope they let us in. Why do we have to go see Howard anyway?"

"I want to know how he reacted to my disappearing before his eyes. It must have shocked him, and I need to know if he told other people about it. I want to make sure people aren't out looking for me. And I need to talk to him about some things."

"Are we going to knock him off?" asked Derek. "I mean, he's supposed to be dead, right?"

"Dead, yes," said Neill, "but we aren't going to kill him. I know if he lives, the 2021 I knew will never be the same, but that doesn't matter so long as my great-great-grandmother marries my great-great-grandfather instead of Howard. Otherwise, my family won't exist when I return to 2021."

Derek sighed. "It's all so complicated."

"It is," said Neill. He really wasn't sure what he hoped to accomplish by finding Howard first. But he worried that if Howard just happened to see him around town, he might flip out. Better that he immediately find Howard and learn what he had told people; then he could try to convince him to keep his mouth shut, or make up some rational explanation so Howard wouldn't be totally weirded out and any rumors he might have already started could be stopped. Howard had seemed like a rational person, someone who could be reasoned with. Neill wondered if he might even feel out Howard to see if he could tell him the whole truth and get him to promise never to marry Margaret Dalrymple. But did rational people believe time travel stories? Neill doubted it, but all he could do was try. Otherwise, his own time would remain altered.

And then, Neill had an alarming thought. If he did change the past back to what it was so he could return to his own time, what would Derek do? A Derek already existed in his own time, so could this Derek come back with him? Would that even be possible since if he reversed the past, this Derek wouldn't even exist—or would he? After all, Neill realized, he had already changed the past, yet he still existed. It was complicated, like Derek said.

"We'll turn here," said Neill as they reached Cedar Street. Derek had been strangely quiet as they walked, taking in all the grand old Victorian houses and perhaps noticing which ones were different from his own time. Neill thought maybe Derek did have some interest in history. Maybe that was what had motivated him to time travel with him. Neill wondered if he would ever understand this version of Derek. Whenever he started to feel comfortable with him, like he would have with the Derek he had grown up with, this Derek would do something to make Neill realize they were two very different people. And then he remembered how Derek had kind of blurted out things to Xander and Jorgen that he shouldn't have. Neill hoped Derek would have more discretion in this time, especially now that the Longyear Mansion stood before them.

Chapter 2

"This place looks a lot ritzier than when I used to mow the lawn," said Derek. "They've obviously kept up the place better in this time."

"It's also completely new by comparison," Neill reminded him.

The gate into the Longyear property now stood before them. Derek was surprised there was no gatekeeper, but Neill reminded him it was Marquette, so even millionaires were safe. They unlatched and opened the pedestrian gate, walked through, closed it behind them, and entered the grounds. Derek looked around with interest, having been here before, but more than a century in the future. Neill, although he had spent two weeks with the Longyears, also found himself again marveling at the property's size. The gardens looked expertly landscaped and manicured, reflecting the genius of Frederick Law Olmsted, and then, there was the daunting mansion before them.

A gardener was busy in the yard and spotted them as they walked toward the house, but he said nothing. Neill did not recognize him, but he wondered if the man ignored them because he recognized him from his earlier stay at the mansion.

Neill still wasn't sure what story he would tell the Longyears to explain his previous disappearance—it might depend on who he ended up talking to—but he felt comfortable enough to ring the bell, while hoping Derek would be on his best behavior.

"Let me do the talking," Neill told Derek while they waited for the door to be answered. "And go along with whatever I say."

"No problem," said Derek.

Neill hoped it wouldn't be a problem.

In another moment, Franklin, the butler, opened the door. He may have been surprised to see Neill, but he was a professional, so no one would have known it. He simply said, "Good day," and waited to know their business.

"Is Mr. Howard in?" Neill asked.

"I am afraid he is out of town at the moment, sir," said Franklin. "Would you like to leave your card?"

"Ah...I'm afraid I don't have a card with me," Neill replied. "Are any of the other family at home?"

"Whom may I say is calling?" Franklin asked, being properly formal despite having previously made Neill's acquaintance.

"Ah...Neill, but they know me as John."

"John Neill?" said Franklin.

"Sure," said Neill, feeling it might be awkward to use his real last name. After all, what if something happened that would cause him to end up in the history books? People in his version of 2021 might find it suspicious that the Neill Vandelaare they knew had been a friend of Howard Longyear in 1900—how would he ever explain that? After all the trouble this time traveling had already caused him, Neill wasn't about to publicize his adventures when he returned to his own time.

"Mr. Longyear," Franklin was saying while these thoughts ran through Neill's head, "is at his office, but I will see if the mistress is available to receive you."

"Thank you," Neill replied.

"Won't you step inside?" asked Franklin, gesturing for them to move into the entry hall.

"Thanks," said Derek.

Once they were inside the house, Franklin shut the front door and said, "Follow me." He led them into the octagonal hall with its giant glass dome.

The second they entered the room, Derek exclaimed, "Holy cow!" He stared up at the ceiling until Neill elbowed him. Then they followed Franklin down a hall and into what Neill knew was the drawing room.

"You weren't kidding that these people have money," Derek whispered to Neill.

"Please wait here," said Franklin, and then he turned and walked backward out of the room. When he had passed over the threshold, Franklin took the handle of each French door in one of his hands and closed them, leaving Derek and Neill alone.

Derek started wandering about the room, whistling as he admired the expensive wallpaper, velvety chairs, and fine mahogany furniture. "Man," he said, "I want to get to know this Howard dude."

"I'm bummed Howard isn't home," said Neill. "I wonder where he is."

"At least you get to talk to his mom," said Derek. "What's she like?"

Longyear Mansion circa 1898, Drawing Room North

Drawing Room West

Drawing Room Southeast

"She's kind," said Neill, "but a bit too into Christian Science for my taste. She's always spouting off her views about how good health is all a state of mind."

"Isn't it? I mean, look at the muscles I have," said Derek. He lifted up his arm to flex, but with a Victorian suit on, there wasn't much to see. At least he didn't rip his shirtsleeve. "It's because I have a good attitude."

"Really? Even after dating Miss Allison Negativity?" asked Neill.

"Well, I guess by coming to the past with you," said Derek, "I've removed the negativity from my life, right? So, that makes me healthier than ever."

"I guess," said Neill.

"So, what are you going to tell Howard's mom?" asked Derek, plopping himself down in a chair. Neill was relieved there was nothing nearby for Derek to put his feet on.

Before Neill could answer Derek's question, the French doors reopened and Mrs. Longyear entered the room.

"John, I'm so surprised to see you," she said, coming forward and giving him her hand in greeting.

"It's a relief to see you, Mrs. Longyear," he replied. "You and your family were so kind to me that I've come to give you some explanations I feel you deserve."

"We are relieved to know you are okay. We were so worried about you." Her eyes drifted over to her seated visitor, and Neill's eyes followed hers.

"Thank you," said Neill. "This is my brother, Derek." He turned and gestured to Derek, with a waving motion that warned Derek to stand up in the presence of a lady.

Derek looked momentarily puzzled, but as Neill continued gesturing behind Mrs. Longyear's back, he finally got the idea. He put his hands on the arms of the chair as if to push himself up, but Mrs. Longyear said, "Please, stay seated," and crossed to the sofa. She seated herself and then nodded at Neill, as if giving him permission to do the same. He perched on the front of the chair beside where Derek sat.

Mrs. Longyear did not speak—she appeared to be waiting for further explanations. Neill was still uncertain how to begin the conversation, but finally, he said, "I'm sure you're wondering what happened to me."

"Yes. Howard said you just vanished."

Mrs. Longyear said this so simply that Neill did not know how to reply at first. She did not seem surprised by the idea.

"Ye-es," said Neill. "Sort of."

"He said one minute you were with him," Mrs. Longyear continued, "and then he turned away just for a minute and you were gone. He tried to find you. He thought maybe you'd had a memory lapse and gotten lost in the woods. He and Santinaw searched for you for hours."

Neill breathed a sigh of relief. She apparently thought he had just gotten lost, but somehow he doubted Howard thought the same. He was sure he had vanished right before Howard's eyes. Perhaps Howard had been afraid of being thought crazy himself so he had tried to make Neill's disappearance seem plausible. In any case, Neill felt grateful that Howard had kept his secret.

"Yes," said Neill. "You will remember I was experiencing some memory problems. Well, once Howard, Santinaw, and I reached the dolmen, I suddenly felt strange—ill—and then things started coming back to me. I don't know what came over me—it was like a panic attack, and I don't remember the experience very well. I just know I suddenly found myself running through the woods, as if trying to reach somewhere I couldn't quite name."

"I see," said Mrs. Longyear, pinching her skirt nervously. "And did you find that destination?"

"I did," said Neill. "I think I instinctively remembered in which direction our family farm lay. I—well, remember how my pants looked like they had been burnt off when I was found?" He was making up his explanation as he went along.

"I remember hearing that, yes," said Mrs. Longyear, "but I didn't think it polite to question."

"I apologize," said Neill. "I only mention it because I remembered I had been in a fire. You see, our family property is very close to the Huron Mountain Club's property, and in the middle of the night, our home went up in flame. I must have inhaled a great deal of smoke and gotten confused, and that's how I ended up wandering about in the woods; I got lost and ended up on the Club's property. I must have tripped over something—after all, it was dark and the fire happened at night. Apparently, I knocked myself unconscious, and then I was found by Hugh and Santinaw at the Club."

"I see," said Mrs. Longyear. "I can't imagine how terrifying that must have been—the fire, I mean."

"Yes, and it happened in the middle of the night," said Neill, almost enjoying making up details since Mrs. Longyear's face expressed compassion and, more importantly, belief in his story. "I must have been completely disoriented by the smoke and the shock."

"I can understand," she replied. "I can't imagine what you went through."

"Anyway," said Neill, "when I went to the dolmen with Howard, I had a strange feeling, like I remembered something, and it caused me to bolt through the forest before I even really knew what I was doing. All that time when I was having memory issues, I was blocking out the horror of what had happened, and then I suddenly remembered and needed to know desperately what had happened to my family."

"How terrifying for you!" exclaimed Mrs. Longyear.

"It really was," said Neill.

"And did you find your family?" she asked.

"Yes, he did," said Derek, grabbing Neill's hand as if overcome with emotion. Neill was surprised. He had no idea Derek could be such a ham. Trying to restrain his laughter, disguising it as emotion, Neill replied, "I found my brother." And he turned sideways in his chair to put his other hand on Derek's. "Only Derek and I survived."

"What about your parents?" asked Mrs. Longyear, though she knew the answer.

"Gone to the Lord," said Derek, looking reverently up at the ceiling.

Neill cleared his throat, as if to tell Derek to shut up.

"I'm so very sorry," said Mrs. Longyear. "Such a tragedy."

"Yeah, we had a sister who died too," said Derek, obviously not taking Neill's hint.

"Oh, how horrible," said Mrs. Longyear. "It seems like there's been so much tragedy lately, first poor Hugh drowning, and you and Howard having to witness it, and now for you to remember this tragedy as well."

"It has been devastating," said Neill, trying to sound appropriately sad. "You can't imagine how much it hurts to lose your parents. Somehow you always know that day will eventually come, but you can never prepare yourself for such a loss. I'm just grateful that Derek survived so I'm not completely alone in the world."

"And were you there, Derek, at the property when your brother returned?"

"Yes," said Derek. "I was making do living in the chicken coop. It was all that was left on the property."

"You were sleeping with the chickens?" said Mrs. Longyear, shuddering. "How inconvenient. And will you rebuild your home?"

"Well, we haven't quite decided on that yet," said Neill. "And now that I've had a few days to accept my loss, I convinced Derek to come with me to Marquette to thank you for everything you did for me. Plus, I knew Howard would be worried about me. I've told Derek how intelligent Howard is, so we're hoping he can give us some advice about what to do next."

"Howard is a smart and a good boy," Mrs. Longyear replied, "and I'm glad you think so highly of him, though perhaps Mr. Longyear or I would be better suited to give you assistance."

"We don't wish to impose," Neill replied.

"It's no imposition. Helping others is the Christian way. We can't have the two of you sharing a chicken coop. You'll stay with us until we can determine what is best to be done for you."

"Thank you, ma'am," said Derek. "You have no idea how horrible it has been for me. When Neill showed up, it was a true godsend."

"Yes," said Mrs. Longyear, looking on him with sympathetic eyes before turning her attention back to Neill. "And so, is Neill your real name?"

"Yes," said Neill. "It turns out my father's name was John, which is why it seemed familiar to me, and I agreed to using it at first when the Allens' housekeeper suggested it."

"That makes sense," said Mrs. Longyear.

"And your name is Derek?" Mrs. Longyear asked Neill's alleged brother.

"Yes, ma'am," said Derek.

"I have never heard that name before," she said.

"It's German," said Neill. "Our mother was German."

"Oh," said Mrs. Longyear. "Are you related to the Blemhubers? They are German I believe, and they have property near the Club."

"No," said Neill. "We don't know any of our mother's family. And our father was of English descent. His people came over on the *Mayflower* way back."

"Very respectable," said Mrs. Longyear. "The Longyears are German, but I'm of old New England Puritan blood myself."

"Interesting," said Derek, nodding his head as if enthralled by this information. Neill could not help thinking his friend really should have been an actor.

"And so, what is your surname?" asked Mrs. Longyear. Neill had told Franklin his name was John Neill, but he had only gone along with that to alleviate initial confusion. Still, he did not want to show up in the history books as Neill Vandelaare in his own time, so he thought about saying "Whitman," his mother's maiden name, but then he might have to explain how he wasn't related to the Whitmans now living in Marquette.

Mrs. Longyear's face began to express curiosity at Neill's silence. "Are you having another memory lapse?" she asked.

"I—um," Neill fumbled.

"It's Jackson," said Derek, using his own last name. "We're Neill and Derek Jackson."

"Jackson," said Mrs. Longyear. "I believe there are some Jacksons in Marquette, though I don't know them."

"Yes, I have some distant cousins here, but I don't really know them," said Neill, not wanting to continue the topic and needing to get to the purpose of their visit. "When do you expect Howard to be home?" As kind as Mrs. Longyear was, he knew Howard was the only one who could truly help them.

"He's up at the Club still looking for you," said Mrs. Longyear. "Plus, I think he wanted some time alone in the haunts he and Hugh used to frequent. He is mourning his friend terribly, you know, even though I have explained to him that there is no such thing as death."

"I'm sure it's hard for him," said Neill. "Even if we see our loved ones in the next life, we miss them in this one."

"That is true," said Mrs. Longyear. "But he plans to return to-morrow. I'm sure he'll be overjoyed to know you are safe."

"Oh, good," said Neill. "I wish we could tell him sooner so he could quit worrying."

"He'll know as soon as humanly possible," said Mrs. Longyear. "Meanwhile, I'll have Martha show you to a guest room with twin beds since I imagine you boys, after being separated for so long, will want to stay together."

"Thank you," said Neill.

Mrs. Longyear rang a bell. Then, while they waited for Martha, she said, "You both look exhausted. Why don't you go rest now and Martha can call you when it's time for lunch."

In another minute, Martha was leading Neill and Derek upstairs. They wouldn't be sleeping in a chicken coop tonight, and after all the paddling and not getting much sleep in 2142, a Victorian featherbed sounded delightful.

Chapter 3

DEREK AND NEILL WERE RELIEVED to find themselves alone in the guest room. It had already been a long day, given that they had barely slept the night before. Derek immediately lay down on the bed and shut his eyes. Neill was surprised by how nonchalant Derek was about everything; he had just tagged along on Neill's mission like it was a great adventure, and he seemed unconcerned about how he would get back to his own time. Neill didn't have the heart yet to tell Derek he feared the time-travel device was broken.

In a few minutes, Derek was snoring. Unlike his friend, Neill had not slept at all in that pathetic little guest room in St. Peter's Cathedral, and yet he was wide awake compared to his companion. Still, it wouldn't hurt him to rest a bit. He took off his suit coat so he wouldn't wrinkle it and laid it over a chair, but as he did so, he felt Howard's journal in the pocket. Instantly, he knew he had something more important to do than sleep.

Quickly retrieving the journal from the inside jacket pocket, Neill sat down with it on the bed. He was dying to know what it said, and he hoped it would somehow help him talk to Howard since it might tell him how Howard had responded to his disappearance. Neill opened it to the front page and saw the first entry was dated July 25, 1900, the very day after Howard had led him to the dolmen, where he had disappeared before Howard's eyes. But Neill was intensely disappointed to find that while Howard had clearly recorded his thoughts that day, he had written the entry in another language, one Neill did not know. He thought it might be Latin. Neill knew a few words of Latin since he had been raised Catholic, and he had studied French in high school, so he was able to pick out a word here or there, but he did not know it well enough to understand full sentences. Frustrated, he started turning the pages, only to discover the next entry was written in yet a different language, one with a strange alphabet, like it was Russian or something, and then the next entry, the one he had before noted was from July 30, was written in some sort of numerical code.

"Howard, why?" Neill gasped with frustration. But he thought he knew why. Howard had not wanted anyone else to read or understand the journal. He obviously had something to hide—perhaps a fear for his own sanity after witnessing how Neill had disappeared. A couple of pages farther in, Neill saw a drawing of the dolmen—a sure sign Howard had been trying to figure out what properties the dolmen had—and then there was a series of strange letters in yet another language Neill wasn't sure he'd seen before, but he thought they might be Sumerian or Phoenician or some other ancient language since it looked like something he'd seen in a book before, perhaps in a photograph of cuneiform tablets. As Neill kept turning the pages, he discovered Howard had written rather sporadically, sometimes days apart, sometimes months apart. In 1905, Neill came to an entry in another strange code, but this entry also had mathematical equations written, with some scribbled out and then arrows to indicate the equations continued on other pages, as if Howard had been trying to figure out something, only whatever it was, it wasn't just algebra or simple equations. It seemed more like a formula, like something Einstein might have written. After that, there were many more entries, but often years apart, until the journal ran out of pages. The last entry was dated August 9, 1945.

Even though Neill didn't understand a word of it, he was fascinated by the journal. What had Howard been trying to figure out? Obviously, it had something to do with the dolmen. Could the mathematical equations be a formula for time travel? After all, Neill thought his college physical geography professor had said Einstein's theory of relativity had an aspect of time travel to it. Was he remembering that properly? He wasn't sure. It had all been rather over his head. He'd had a hard enough time just keeping the various climate zones straight. His mind wasn't configured to understand anything as cerebral as Einstein's discoveries.

There was only way to find out what the journal said—to ask Howard. Neill hoped Howard would understand it—after all, he had written it, but he had done so mostly in the future. Neill was surprised that Howard had known so many languages. He had skills beyond what Neill had realized from knowing him for only a couple of weeks. He was beginning to understand why Hugh had practically hero-worshiped his friend.

But to get Howard to tell him what the journal said, Neill would have to explain how he came to possess it—a journal from the future. But maybe that wouldn't be so difficult. After all, the journal showed that Howard was trying to puzzle out how Neill had disappeared. Maybe he didn't figure it out until 1905 or 1906, but he had already been working on the problem for the last few days, and he knew the languages in the journal. In this very house there must be another journal like it with only the first few entries written in it.

If Howard figured out how time travel works, thought Neill, *even if he hasn't figured it out yet in this time, we can use this journal to trigger his thoughts, and then maybe he can help me get home.* Was it possible? Neill sure hoped so. In fact, he felt determined again—and hopeful that his return home could happen with Howard's help.

Neill began mentally outlining all the possible ways he could approach Howard. He was grateful, from what Mrs. Longyear had revealed, that Howard had not been completely truthful in describing his disappearance, but Neill knew he would still have some explaining to do to Howard. It wasn't just that he had to explain he had time traveled—he had a feeling from the journal that Howard might have already figured that out, or at least guessed that Neill had gone through a portal or something similar. What would be harder would be explaining that he had come back to 1900 to try to change the past back, and that Howard was central to that effort since he should be dead.

As these thoughts flooded Neill's mind, he waffled between fear, anxiety, and hope. The easiest option was to quit trying and stay in 1900. After all, just trying to fix the changes he had made to the past had a terrible potential to make things worse. For all he knew, he might have already changed the future again simply by stealing clothes from Getz's or lying to Mrs. Longyear—who knew how fickle fate or time was? And Neill knew he could never intentionally cause Howard to die, so no matter how close he got to reversing what he had already done, the past could never be exactly the same again.

Neill was still caught up in these thoughts when someone knocked at his door. Neill sat up on the bed and said, "Come in." The door was opened by Martha, who announced that dinner was served. Neill thanked her and said they would be down in a minute. Once Martha left, Neill shook Derek awake. Then he put back on his suit coat and waited for Derek to finish yawning and stretching before he put on his own. In another minute, they were headed downstairs.

Mrs. Longyear and all her children were gathered in the dining room. As soon as Neill and Derek sat down to eat, they found themselves playing twenty questions with the inquisitive children. Jack especially seemed delighted to see them. Marveling at Derek's size, he asked him if he played football, followed by other sports-related questions.

Mrs. Longyear tried to get Jack to stop pestering Derek, but when Derek bent his arm to bring his fork to his mouth, in the process, nearly popping his jacket sleeve with his large bicep, Jack exclaimed, "You're a veritable Sandow!"

"Who's Sandow?" asked Derek.

"Who's Sandow?" repeated Jack. "Why, he's the strongest man in the world!"

"John, remember your manners," said Mrs. Longyear, but the other children also now expressed surprise that Derek should be ignorant of the famous Sandow. "Even his stomach has muscles on it!" Jack told him.

"Mr. Sandow's displays of his figure are indecent," Mrs. Longyear told her son. "He is not a proper topic for dinner table conversation."

"Yes, Mother," said Jack. "But I want to grow up to be as strong as him."

"Then," said Mrs. Longyear, "you must remember that muscles are mind forces, so there is no need to praise someone's physical strength. It is their mental strength and their connection with the God-force that deserves the praise. Obviously, Mr. Jackson here" — she was referring to Derek — "must have great mental powers that have made him such a strong and healthy specimen. If you focus on your mental acumen, you could grow up to be just as big and strong as him."

Neill could not help smiling at this statement. Derek might have muscles, but he doubted they reflected his intellectual or spiritual efforts. But Neill could not blame Mrs. Longyear for spouting off her Christian Science beliefs; he recalled how she had told him on his previous stay with the family that they had given her great comfort when she had lost her son, John Beecher Longyear, at just fourteen months, back in 1884. He also recalled from reading about the family history in his own time that when Mrs. Longyear had died, she had left this very house to the Christian Science Church — largely because Christian Science had further comforted her when Howard had drowned. Neill was glad she would not have to go through that grief now; whatever her religious beliefs, no mother deserved to lose a child.

After lunch, Jack and Rob wanted Neill and Derek to go outside and throw the football with them. Neill had noticed that Helen, Abby, and even fourteen-year-old Judith all had eyes for Derek, so they agreed to go outside and watch. In his own time, Neill had been used to being in Derek's shadow with the other sex, and he saw it would be the same here. But he did enjoy talking to the Longyear children; they shared a lot of stories with him about Marquette—stories that now made a lot more sense to him since he had his memory back and could remember who most of the people they talked about were in Marquette's history. He gathered all sorts of interesting tidbits from them about historical people from town benefactor Peter White and snooty Horatio Seymour, who didn't think the Longyear children of a good enough class to associate with his children since his uncle had been Governor of New York, to Alfred Swineford, who had owned *The Mining Journal* and become Governor of Alaska, and the Blackmores, about whom they seemed to have nothing good to say, claiming Mr. Blackmore had cheated their father out of some real estate. Neill tried to remember it all, thinking how delighted his parents would be with such stories if he ever saw them again and dared to tell them of his adventure.

The afternoon passed pleasantly. When Mr. Longyear came home, he was surprised but pleased to see Neill and learn he had recovered his memory. He welcomed Derek graciously, and told the alleged Jackson brothers they were welcome to stay until they figured out their future and that he would be happy to assist them however he could. Neill was grateful since he had no idea how they would support themselves otherwise; he felt any future decisions hinged on his upcoming conversation with Howard.

After supper, they all played games in the parlor until bedtime. Finally, Neill and Derek said goodnight to the family and made their way to their room. "I could get used to living like this," said Derek when they had crawled into their beds.

"Don't get too used to it," said Neill.

"Why?" asked Derek. "Those girls seem to like me. I could end up marrying one of them and living happily ever after like a prince."

"Girls like the Longyears don't marry boys like us," Neill said. "We're the common herd."

"Speak for yourself," said Derek. "Plenty a girl from a wealthy family has married a ne'er-do-well because he was handsome or manly, and I'm both."

Neill laughed. "Really? A *ne'er-do-well*? I'm surprised you even know that word."

"Hey, I'm picking up on this Victorian slang pretty quickly," Derek replied.

"Whatever," said Neill, laughing and tossing a pillow at him. Derek tossed it back, and then Neill turned out the light. He was exhausted, but after a few hours, he woke and lay there in the night worrying about the future. He didn't like Derek's last comment about marrying one of the Longyear daughters. He knew all three of them would grow up to be married, and no Derek Jackson was in their family histories. Would Derek's romantic interests mess up the future even more? Perhaps he would have to kill Derek and Howard both to return the future to normal. Of course, he would never do that, but Derek could quickly become a major problem for him. He was already surprised the Longyears were so accepting of his coarseness.

Chapter 4

A T BREAKFAST THE NEXT MORNING, Mrs. Longyear said Howard would be returning that evening. Neill did not know how he would control his nervousness for that long, but the answer came when Mrs. Longyear invited Derek and Neill to join them for their Christian Science services since it was Sunday. The services were held in their home and attended by a few neighbors who also subscribed to their beliefs.

"We hope to build a church of our own eventually," Mrs. Longyear said, "since we are starting to outgrow the parlor."

Neill had to admit he was surprised by how many people did come to the service. It was less structured than the Catholic Mass he had grown up attending. Passages were read from founder Mary Baker Eddy's *Science and Health*, which to Neill sounded like a jumbled text purposely written to sound smart while saying almost nothing, but it could simply have been that he was too worried about what he would say to Howard to focus on the message. He was concerned Derek would fall asleep during the service, but Derek, who was sitting beside Abby, was too busy trying to get her attention, and more than once, Neill heard her giggle, but fortunately, Mrs. Longyear did not seem to notice.

After the services, they had a light lunch. Jack invited Derek and Neill to bowl with him in the Longyears' private bowling alley and that consumed much of the afternoon. Howard was returning on *The City of Marquette*, a boat owned by Mr. Longyear that made trips a couple of times a week back and forth from the Huron Mountain Club to transport members. It would not arrive in Marquette's harbor until suppertime. Mrs. Longyear had decided to hold supper for Howard, so they had lemonade and snacks on the veranda in the late afternoon to tide them over.

The Longyears kept asking Derek and Neill questions about the fire and their future plans, which the alleged brothers replied to the best they could, trying not to contradict what they had already said. As suppertime approached, Mr. and Mrs. Longyear went inside to their own activities while the children and Derek and Neill went outside to watch for *The City of Marquette* to sail into the harbor.

"I'll walk down to the harbor to meet Howard," said Neill not long before the boat was expected.

"I'll go with you," Derek replied, not at all thrilled by the idea of being left alone with these strangers he had to keep up a façade for.

"That's not necessary," said Helen. "Mother will send the carriage for him."

"No, I want to be able to apologize to him privately," Neill replied, hoping that would stop anyone from accompanying him.

"Well, if you want to," Abby said. "But wait until we see the boat coming. Then you can have walked down there by the time he disembarks."

"That's okay," said Neill. "Derek and I need to stretch our legs and we have some things to talk over so we'll leave now."

The older Longyear children accepted this. Rob wanted to go with the Jackson brothers, but his siblings told him he had to stay and wash up for supper, which could be a time-consuming task for the small boy.

Neill and Derek promised to be back as soon as possible with Howard. Once they left, they were relieved to be alone for a little while, though they knew a difficult conversation awaited them. Neill planned to tell Howard the truth of what had happened to him—what else could he do since Howard had witnessed his sudden disappearance? Neill thought that way Howard, Derek, and he could make sure they had their story straight for Howard's family.

By the time Neill and Derek reached the bottom of the Hundred Steps, *The City of Marquette* was steaming into the harbor. A few minutes later, the young men were at the harbor themselves and could see the pleasure boat held less than a dozen people. Neill did not recognize any of the passengers except Howard, but as the boat pulled up to the dock, he heard a woman call out, "Hello, Neill and Derek!"

Neill just about fell off the dock into the lake when he saw who was shouting his name.

"Allison!" exclaimed Derek.

Neill couldn't say anything. He was in too much shock as the boat was tied to the dock.

"Wow!" said Derek, stepping up to Allison as Howard handed her out of the boat. "What happened to you?" He was referring to her pink dress, the height of late Victorian fashion, as well as her absence of black eyeshadow, multiple piercings, and the usual air of disdain.

"What are you doing here?" Allison replied, equally surprised to see Derek. "I didn't know you were here or that you would know I was coming."

"I didn't know," Derek replied. "Why did you follow us?"

By now, Neill was beside Allison, filled with questions and barely remembering Howard was there. Fortunately, *The City of Marquette*'s other passengers had quickly said goodbye to Howard and headed for home, eager for their suppers after the long journey. Howard was too busy speaking to his fellow travelers to listen to his new friends' conversation, but he raised his eyebrows at the sight of Neill.

"I didn't know I was following you, Derek," said Allison. "I didn't know you had come." Then she looked around as if to make sure no one could overhear, and half-whispered, "I came because of Neill's email."

"Wha-at—wait…!" said Neill, beginning to understand.

"Neill, you look like you've seen a ghost," said Howard, now stepping up to them since they were the only people still standing on the dock. "I'm sure I looked the same way when you disappeared."

Neill didn't know how to respond. How would he explain all this to Howard—all this he was still trying to figure out? And what had Allison told him? How was it possible she was even here?

"Relax, Neill," said Howard. "Allison told me everything. I admit I had a hard time believing it at first, but you did disappear before my very eyes, and then she appeared before them. The two of you have made believers out of me."

"But," said Neill, frantically recalling what he had told Allison in his email—he had told her he had time traveled, but he had hardly told her *everything*, "let me get this straight…."

"Oh, wait," said Allison, seeing some workers who had come onto the dock staring at them because of their surprised expressions and tones.

Howard, sensing her concern, took her arm and said, "Let's go where we can talk in private."

"Good idea," said Derek.

"Howard, this is our friend, Derek," said Allison as Derek turned and used his imposing body to lead the way past the dock workers, silencing them from making any inquiries.

Once they had walked a few feet from the lake and listening ears, Neill stopped and said to Allison, "So, you did get the email I sent you? But I got a message saying it wasn't deliverable."

"What email are you talking about?" Derek asked.

"I emailed Allison while I was at the restaurant downtown where Allison works."

"But why would you email her when you were right there with her?" asked Derek.

"What restaurant?" asked Allison. "I don't work in a restaurant."

"Hold on," said Neill to Allison; then he turned to Derek and explained, "I emailed the Allison who lives in my version of 2021. This is that Allison, not the Allison from your version of 2021."

"Oh," said Derek, taking a moment to wrap his brain around that. "Wow, that makes a lot of sense. I mean, it explains a lot." He stopped to look at Allison, his eyes traveling up and down her. "I mean, you look beautiful—I never did like your nose ring."

"Thank you," said Allison, "and I would never be caught dead with a nose ring. So, am I right that you're not the Derek I know?"

"Yes," Neill answered for him. "This is the Derek from the altered version of 2021 that I told you about in my email. He knows a very different version of you."

"But I like your version better," Derek told Allison, smiling in a way that made Howard tighten his grip on her arm.

"This is very confusing," Allison replied.

"I am quite baffled by it all myself," said Howard. "I think I understand what happened, but I'm not clear on some of the details."

"I'm not completely clear either," Neill said. "I mean, I understand what has happened, but not how any of it is possible. Let me start at the beginning with what happened to me so everyone is on the same page."

"Okay," said Derek, "but we should head back to the mansion so Howard's parents don't wonder what became of us."

They all agreed to this and started walking toward Front Street to head back to the Longyear Mansion. Neill then launched into his explanation, with Derek adding in some details when Neill got to the part where he had met him. Howard kept shaking his head through it all. Neill, however, avoided mentioning that Howard was supposed to drown with Hugh, and while he explained that when he got back to 2021, he realized he had changed the past from things like the ore dock not being in the harbor, he did not give all the details or what he thought had caused them to change. When Derek tried to insert further explanation, Neill shot him a look that said, "Shut up," and then added, "There's more we can get into later, but for now, that's it in a nutshell." He figured Howard had enough to wrap his head around without needing to know he should be dead at this moment. If the need presented itself, Neill could always explain more to Howard, though he still wasn't sure he should. He also wanted to know what Howard's journal said, but he could see Howard was already feeling overwhelmed, so he would have to wait for the right moment.

"That," said Howard when Neill had finished, "is the most incredible story I've ever heard. It makes *Gulliver's Travels* seem boring. Tell me more about 2142."

"I really don't know much more about it," said Neill, who had also omitted mention that Howard's descendants had invented time travel devices. "First, I want to understand how Allison got here and the two of you met."

Howard looked at Allison, apparently feeling she would be better at explaining it all.

"Well, Neill," said Allison, "if anyone else had sent me an email like the one you did, I would have thought they were completely nuts, but when I got it, you had been missing for a couple of weeks. Search parties have been out looking for you at the Huron Mountain Club, and your parents have been just crazy with worry."

"I was afraid of that," said Neill. "Did you tell them what happened to me after you got my email?"

"No," Allison replied. "But I had spoken to them the night before I got it, so I knew how worried they were. I didn't want to upset them by telling them about the email in case it was a cruel prank. I thought about going to the police, but something told me first to see if it could be true—that you could have touched a dolmen and been transported back into time. I wanted to ask Derek to help—I even tried to call him, but he was off on some forestry program mission and must not have had good cell coverage. After a little thought, I decided I would just have to try to help you myself. Then, I figured if I were traveling back to 1900, I would have to look the part, so I dug out my dress from when I played Cecily Cardew in *The Importance of Being Earnest* and stuffed it into my backpack. Next, I drove up to the Huron Mountain Club and told the gatekeeper I was a friend of yours. I explained I had received an email from you the morning you disappeared that said where you were going. The gatekeeper called your boss, who met me at the Clubhouse. When I told him you had gone to the dolmen, he pulled out a map and showed me where it was. He said we would go search there in the morning. Then he brought me to an empty worker's room where I could sleep."

"That was all very brave of you," said Neill.

"What was braver," Allison replied, "was that I didn't want your boss to think I was nuts or to see me disappear before his eyes if I touched the dolmen, so I set out at the first sign of daylight before anyone else was up. When I reached the dolmen, I quickly changed into my dress and then touched it, and voilà, suddenly I was in 1900."

"You must have been shocked," said Neill.

"Not as shocked as I was," said Howard.

Allison laughed. "Howard looked like he was going to have a heart attack when he saw me."

"Well, you would too if Aphrodite suddenly appeared to you," said Howard.

"Aphrodite?" said Derek.

"Yes, the goddess of love and beauty," Howard replied. "Who else could I think she was when she made such an entrance?"

"It was rather embarrassing actually," said Allison. "For some reason, my hat caught on fire. A total loss, but fortunately, Howard grabbed it and stamped it out before it caught my hair on fire. He's such a hero."

"The least I could do," Howard replied, his eyes looking more than fondly at her.

"It took quite a bit of explaining to get Howard to understand who I was," said Allison, "and how I had time traveled and that you had done the same. Plus, he had to catch me up on how he had met you and what had happened to you in his time."

"I'm just glad you trusted me," said Howard, "because I didn't know what to think. It's still all hard to believe, even though everything that the three of you have now explained does seem to make sense."

"What I don't understand, though," said Allison, "is that once I arrived here, Howard and I waited all day for you, Neill, to appear at the dolmen, too, since you said in your email you were going back the next day. Did you return in the middle of the night?"

"No," said Neill. "Derek and I did go to the dolmen, but for whatever reason, it sent us to the year 2142 instead of 1900. And then when we stole the time device, it brought us to 1900, but by the cathedral, where we were in 2142, rather than at the Huron Mountain Club."

"Oh, that makes sense," said Allison.

"It's so amazing to think someone invented a time travel device in the future," said Howard. "I kind of wondered if that was what happened to you. I knew you didn't have a time machine like in H. G. Wells' novel, but I wondered if that weird rock-like device you picked up was some sort of time travel device."

"I don't think my cell phone could have done it," Neill replied. "I think the dolmen just has some magical powers."

Howard squished his lips together and sort of shook his head, like he had something to say but wasn't sure he should. He started to ask, "Cell phone? What—"

But Allison interrupted by saying, "Howard, tell them about your own discovery."

"What discovery?" asked Neill.

"Well," said Howard, relegating the cell phone question to the back of his mind, "after you disappeared, I was a bit scared of the dolmen. You'll remember Santinaw was there with us when you disappeared. Being part Chippewa Indian, he was convinced an evil manitou must reside in the dolmen, so he refused to go anywhere near it. I told him that was all nonsense, but he asked me how else it could be explained. I didn't know. Then he warned me we were never to speak of it again in case the manitou became angry and made us disappear as well. But, of course, I couldn't restrain my curiosity. The next day, I went back and dared to touch the dolmen myself, only nothing happened."

"That's what I don't understand," said Allison, "how Neill and I could travel in time through the dolmen but Howard couldn't."

"Maybe it only works one way, like back to 1900 but not forward," said Derek.

"No," Neill replied, "because I went forward to your version of 2021, remember?"

"Oh, yeah," said Derek. "Weird."

"I'm not sure," said Howard, "but I might have found the answer."

"What do you mean?" asked Neill.

"When I went back to the dolmen," said Howard, "I noticed that when I touched the stone, it wasn't really smooth. After a little while, I realized something was inscribed on it, but that years of weather had made it unreadable to the naked eye, so I went back to our cabin and returned with some paper. I was going to do a rubbing like people do to old gravestones. I was just about to start when Allison showed up. Then after she explained everything to me and I realized she didn't really understand how it worked either, I did the rubbing. I discovered there definitely had been some writing on it."

"What did it say?" asked Derek.

"That's what I want to find out," said Howard. "I couldn't read it. The writing must be hundreds or even thousands of years old."

"Then how will we figure out what it says?" asked Neill.

"Don't worry," said Howard. "I love languages, and I've studied hieroglyphics and other forms of writing, so I think we should be able to decipher these, but we'll have to identify the language and find a book or professor of ancient languages to explain it for us."

Neill felt deflated by this statement. It seemed so difficult, if not impossible.

"Maybe the writing explains about the time travel," said Allison, sounding intrigued. "Then we could figure out how to return to our time, Neill."

"Howard!" screamed a little boy up ahead on the sidewalk.

"What do we do now?" asked Derek, realizing they were just a block from the Longyear Mansion and Rob was running toward them.

"Just please keep quiet about everything, Howard, until we figure it all out," pleaded Neill.

"No problem," said Howard. "I'll play along." Then he reached down to grab his little brother, who ran to him with open arms, and swung him up on his back.

"Who's she?" asked Rob, riding piggyback and staring at Allison.

"Allison, this is Rob. Rob, this is Allison," said Howard. "Come on, Rob. I'll give you a horsey ride." And Howard galloped down the hill with his brother to the mansion's gate.

"Do you think he'll keep quiet?" asked Derek once Howard was out of hearing range.

"I think so," said Allison. "Howard seems like a good guy, and he knows what you told his family, so I'm sure he'll play along."

"I just hope he can help us figure out how to get back to our time," said Neill.

"What about Derek, though?" asked Allison. "He's not from our time. How will we get him back to his version of 2021?"

"Don't worry about me," Derek told Allison. "I'm content just to get to know you better. I had no idea you were so beautiful."

Allison looked a bit irritated by this remark.

"You are very different from the Allison in Derek's time," Neill told her.

"And the Derek in my time is very different from you," Allison told Derek, implying his remarks were too personal.

"What did I say?" asked Derek, lifting up his hands in surprise.

"Nothing, shh," said Neill since they were now at the gate.

"But how are we going to explain Allison to the rest of the Longyears?" asked Derek.

"You forget," Allison replied, "that I'm an actress. Allow me to practice my craft."

Chapter 5

A S SOON AS THEY ENTERED the house, Rob tore off somewhere, while Mrs. Longyear greeted Howard. After kissing his mother, Howard said, "Mother, look who I met at the train station."

"Hello," said Mrs. Longyear, greeting Allison with puzzled eyes.

"Hello, Mrs. Longyear," Allison replied. "It's such a pleasure to meet you. Howard has told me so much about you."

Mrs. Longyear took the hand Allison extended and shook it.

"You have me at a disadvantage," Mrs. Longyear replied.

Allison laughed. "Oh, I'm so sorry. I'm Allison, Neill and Derek's sister."

"My," said Mrs. Longyear, "your mother must have had the three of you close together."

"Oh, I assure you I'm older than I look," said Allison. "I'm twenty-three. But I'm flattered that you think I look as young as my brothers—it's the Dove beauty cream I use."

She giggled in a way that made Neill nervous.

"But I thought Neill and Derek said their sister died in the fire," said Abby, who had stepped into the hall while Allison was speaking.

"Oh, that was our little sister," said Neill, suddenly remembering the story he and Derek had made up.

"I'm not surprised they didn't mention me," said Allison. "They haven't seen me since I left for Bryn Mawr when I was eighteen."

"What's Brinmar?" Derek whispered to Neill.

"A woman's college," he whispered back.

"How wonderful that you went to Bryn Mawr," said Abby. "I am going to go to Smith in the fall."

"That's grand," said Allison. "Yes, we are fortunate to have a wealthy aunt who believes in women's education, so she paid for me to go to school there. After I graduated, I began studies in medicine at Harvard. I plan to be the next Dr. Quinn."

"Who is Dr. Quinn?" asked Abby.

"You know, Dr. Quinn," said Allison, smiling as if enjoying the joke. "She's the famous medicine woman of the Wild West."

"I'm afraid I've never heard of her," Abby replied.

"Really?" said Allison, as if shocked.

"But I do think women should be doctors and lawyers and anything they want to be," said Abby.

"Abby," Mrs. Longyear reminded, "we are Christian Scientists, so we do not put our trust in doctors and worldly medicine. We believe in the body's ability to heal itself through the power of the mind and belief in God."

Allison stared at Mrs. Longyear like she was some sort of religious quack. Neill, however, could not help thinking it took a quack to know one since Allison knew nothing about medicine.

"Regardless," said Mrs. Longyear, her polite nineteenth-century manners taking over, "it is very impressive for a young lady to be so accomplished."

"Thank you," said Allison. "Like Abby here, I do believe a woman is just as capable as a man of doing anything she puts her mind to."

"Unfortunately," said Neill, playing along to help keep Allison's story believable, "so did our aunt to the extent that she didn't really like boys. She didn't leave any money for Derek and me to do anything except keep working on the family farm."

"I assure you," said Allison, turning to Neill and Derek, "that once my practice becomes successful, I will help you boys. That's why I came home after you wrote to me about the fire. Of course, I was devastated by the loss of our parents, but I think it's time you boys did bigger and better things."

"I think your brothers are very fortunate," said Mrs. Longyear, "to have an elder sister who takes such an interest in them. I agree it's about time women help their brothers rather than it always being the other way around."

"I'm so glad we see eye to eye," said Allison. "I just know we're all going to be great friends."

Neill felt she was really laying it on too thick now.

"Mother," said Howard, "you don't mind if Allison also stays with us for a little while, do you?"

"No, of course not. We have plenty of room," said Mrs. Longyear. "But where is your luggage, dear?"

"Oh, I travel light," said Allison.

"But all the way from Boston in only the clothes you're wearing?" asked Abby, looking horrified.

"Unfortunately," said Allison, "my trunk was stolen on the train, somewhere around Chicago. I suspect Al Capone was involved."

"Al who?" asked Abby.

"He's a gangster in Chicago," Neill explained, although he didn't think Al Capone would be famous for a few more decades. Allison might be a great actress, but she was no great historian. "Anyway, we are glad you are here, sister."

"Yes, and the girls and I can take you shopping for some new clothes," Mrs. Longyear said.

Allison appeared downcast at this. "Unfortunately, all my money was in my trunk. I can't afford to buy any new clothes."

"That is too bad," said Mrs. Longyear. "But I'm sure we can help you regardless. It's our Christian duty to aid others in need."

"We don't like taking charity," Neill replied.

"Nonsense," said Mrs. Longyear. "You have all been through a horrible ordeal in losing your farm and your parents. It's the least we can do. As you can see, God has provided us with more than enough, so allow us to do unto our neighbor."

"You're very kind," Neill replied.

"Yes," said Allison. "We greatly appreciate it."

"Thanks a lot," chimed in Derek.

"We will consult with Father, too," said Howard. "Maybe we can find you some work until you're all ready to go East."

"Your father has already suggested he could help us," Neill told Howard. "He's been just as kind as your mother."

"I don't want to go East," Derek said. "The Northwoods suit me just fine."

"Do you like working in the woods?" asked Howard. "We own many forestry and logging properties. I'm sure we could find work for you. Dad can always use another big, strong worker."

"I would love that," Derek replied. "I like to keep in shape," and he flexed his pecs, though it was barely perceptible beneath his layers of clothing, but the smile he gave Abby made her blush.

Neill, trying not to roll his eyes, said, "I also would like to find a job to pay my expenses."

"Well, we'll see what we can do," said Howard, "but let's get Allison settled in now. I'll show you to your room, Allison."

"Howard, put her in the room next to Derek and Neill," said Mrs. Longyear. "It's empty and has an adjoining door. That way the Jackson family can stay together."

"Thank you, Mrs. Longyear, for your hospitality," Allison told her hostess, curtseying awkwardly, unsure how else to take her leave. Then Howard and Abby led the way upstairs with the three alleged siblings following. Meanwhile, Mrs. Longyear returned to whatever wealthy ladies of leisure do.

Neill was hoping to explain more to Howard, but Abby remained with the boys after Allison was shown to her room, and then she invited them downstairs for more lemonade on the veranda. Neill found he had to follow the rest back downstairs and make trivial conversation with everyone, none of which was helping him solve the mystery of how to get back to his own time. Worse, Neill noticed Howard seemed captivated by Allison, as did Derek, so he feared the two would become rivals. Every time Howard said something, Derek would say something to one-up him, and at the same time, Abby seemed to be trying to flirt with Derek and vice-versa. Neill felt irritated by it all. He wanted to get Howard alone so he could tell him about the journal, but no one seemed interested in solving the mysteries of time travel when the opposite sex was around. Meanwhile, the other Longyear children floated in and out, and Mr. Longyear became acquainted with Allison. Neill began to wonder if he'd ever get a moment alone with Howard.

Soon, everyone assembled in the dining room for supper. As they ate, Mr. Longyear was all business, discussing with Derek what position he might like working in the woods since the Longyears owned a lot of land and had forestry operations. Neill, when asked about his own possible occupations, remarked that he thought he might be good at bookkeeping. Mr. Longyear had no openings for a bookkeeper but promised to ask among his friends and business associates to try to find Neill an office position downtown. Given that Allison was a lady, no one considered she should seek employment. However, she said, "I don't want to be separated from my brothers after all we've gone through. Will Derek have to go stay at a logging camp or somewhere like that?"

"We log in the winter," Mr. Longyear explained. "It's easier to transport logs out of the woods in winter on sleighs. No, I'll try to find him work that allows him to come home every day or at least most of them."

"And," added Mrs. Longyear, "you will all stay with us until you've saved enough money to get your own place or you decide to return East."

And so it was all settled, at least in the eyes of the Longyear family, minus Howard, who knew far bigger concerns were at stake than finding employment for the alleged Jackson siblings.

Not until late that evening, after the family had gone to bed, did the three friends from two different versions of 2021 have the opportunity to talk alone with Howard. He came to the boys' room, where he also found Allison.

"I'm glad you're still awake," he said. "I didn't want to disturb you, but I also know we can't talk in front of the rest of my family. If my siblings overhear us, especially Jack or Rob, they might start talking about time travel around town, and the last thing we need is for people in Marquette to think the Longyear family crazy."

"We understand," said Neill. "But I was starting to worry we'd never get to talk with you."

"No need to be concerned," said Howard. "We'll figure out how to get you back to your own time. That's why I brought this with me." Howard opened his suit jacket and pulled out a large rolled-up set of papers that had page numbers in their corners. He laid them out on Neill's bed, piecing them together.

"These are the rubbings I did at the dolmen," Howard said. "I needed several pieces of paper to get all the detail. As I said before, you can see they look like runes, but I'm not sure what they mean. I recognize some of the symbols from books I've read about ancient languages, but there are too many for me to translate easily."

"What kind of ruins are they?" asked Derek. "Egyptian?"

"No," said Howard. "Egyptians wrote in hieroglyphics."

"And they're *runes*, not ruins," Neill told Derek. "They're the language or symbols that Europeans mostly used before they adopted the alphabet."

"Yes, our alphabet is Latin-based," said Howard. "Runes were used by people in the British Isles or by the Norse or Vikings before they adopted that alphabet."

"So we don't know who made them?" asked Derek.

"I suspect they were made by Viking travelers," said Neill. "We know the Vikings had colonies in Greenland, and some historians, or pseudo-archeologists anyway, believe they settled in North America and maybe even ventured into the Great Lakes."

"I remember learning something like that in high school," said Allison. "I think the Vikings even had a settlement in Newfoundland or somewhere around there."

"Maybe," said Howard. "After all, a Viking runestone was found in Minnesota recently that suggests Vikings were there in—I think it was the 1300s or 1400s—but others say it was a forgery. There have been lots of forgeries of runes and other ancient artifacts in recent years. In the Lower Peninsula, someone has been making a whole bunch of fake ones and passing them off as real."

"Really?" said Derek. "Why would someone do that?"

"To become famous," Howard replied, "or to make money selling fake ancient artifacts to gullible people."

"Well, someone had to make these," said Allison. "There's no doubt they are very old. They must have been made before the French came to the Great Lakes in the seventeenth century."

"Yes," said Howard. "I don't know how long it would take to weather the dolmen, but probably several centuries. You can tell from my rubbings that the writing is very rough and worn in places to the point where I'm not sure how accurate the shapes of the runes are. I don't see how anyone could have faked this. I suppose it could have become weathered enough in 100 years or so, but until iron ore was discovered in the Upper Peninsula in 1844, hardly any white people were in the area, and I can't imagine why the few British fur traders or French voyageurs who were here before that would have wanted to fake ancient runes."

"Could they be Native American?" asked Derek.

"I hadn't thought of that," said Neill. "Who are we to say Europeans and not Native Americans made these?"

"I suppose it's possible," said Howard, "but I've never heard that Native Americans used runes. I know the Chippewa used pictographs, but they were more like hieroglyphics and written on birch bark. Still, we might consult Chief Kawbawgam to see if he can tell us anything about them."

"What about Santinaw?" asked Neill. "He already knows what happened, and we don't want too many people finding out."

"If I told him they were from the dolmen, I think he'd refuse to look at them," said Howard. "Besides, I'm pretty sure they are of European origin."

"I think we have to be careful whom we ask for help," said Allison. "Since these runes were on the dolmen, they might be instructions about how to use it to time travel."

"Yes, we don't want to mess up time even more by letting other people time travel," said Neill. "I've made a mess of things already."

Howard looked curiously at Neill, but before he could ask what Neill meant, Derek said, "How will we figure out what these ruins mean?"

"First," said Howard, "I think we should go to the library to see if we can find a book on runes. That might help us translate them."

"Do you really think they'd have such a book at the library?" asked Neill.

"We won't know until we go and look," Howard replied. "We have quite an impressive library in Marquette for being such a small city."

"Okay," said Neill. "It's worth a try."

"I'd also like," said Howard, "to figure out how the time travel device you found operates."

"I'm not sure it still works," said Neill. "I dropped it and smashed the glass on its face."

"You did?" said Derek. "You didn't tell me that."

"I didn't want to worry you," Neill replied.

"Even so," said Howard, "maybe we can take it apart to figure out how it was made and then fix it."

"That's a good idea," said Allison, "but are you very mechanical?"

"Dude," Derek broke in before Howard could answer, "you live in 1900. I'm from the twenty-first century and I couldn't fix anything like that. I can't even figure out how to fix my laptop."

"What's a laptop?" asked Howard.

"I'll explain it to you later," Neill replied. "Derek, let's let Howard try. What can it hurt?" He went over to the closet where he had hidden the time dial beneath some spare pillows. "Here it is," he said, handing it to Howard.

"Interesting," said Howard, looking at it and then turning it over. "I do know how to take apart a pocket watch and put it back together. This looks kind of similar. It can't be that much more complicated, can it? I even fixed our phonograph last year when the table wouldn't go around. But the real question is: What is the device connecting to that makes the time travel itself possible?"

"Connecting to?" said Allison.

"Yes, some force in the universe like an ether that allows you to step into another dimension."

"Oh, like a wireless connection," said Derek.

"Sort of," said Howard. "Do you have wireless telegraphs in your time? I know people have been trying to figure out how to invent them."

"Derek meant a wireless internet connection," Neill replied.

This comment led to questions from Howard and a shared effort on Allison, Neill, and Derek's part to explain what a computer was and how to access the internet using Wi-Fi. They made a muddle of the explanation since Howard had never conceived of a computer, but he was fascinated by the idea. Finally, he drew the analogy that using the time travel device was sort of like connecting to a wireless signal to look up things on the internet, only you were turning a dial on a time travel device to connect with some sort of physical but invisible energy or ether source that would allow you to access another dimension. For all his lack of knowledge about twenty-first-century technology, the three friends realized Howard was far more scientifically inclined than they were.

"I think what you're saying makes sense," said Neill, "but I don't know how we will ever figure out how to tap into that...ether."

"Neither do I," said Howard, "but if we can't figure it out, maybe we can find people more knowledgeable than us whom we can trust to keep your secret."

"Like who?" asked Allison. "Like scientists?"

"Sure," said Howard. "There must be some scientist who knows something about time travel and if it's even real."

"Is Einstein alive yet?" asked Derek.

"I think he's just a little boy in 1900," Allison replied.

"Actually, I think he's about our age," said Neill, "but I doubt we could ever contact him."

"What about H. G. Wells?" asked Allison. "Howard, you said you read *The Time Machine*."

"Yes, but it's just a story, not a scientific treatise."

"But what if H. G. Wells knows stuff about time travel he didn't want to put in his book because it would be giving too much away?" said Derek.

"Doubtful," said Howard.

"Maybe there's a scientist at NMU who can help us," said Allison.

"What's NMU?" asked Howard.

"Northern Michigan University," said Derek in a tone that suggested Howard must be an idiot not to know that.

"Derek," said Neill, "remember that Howard isn't from our time. Howard, NMU is what Northern Normal School will be named in our time."

"Really, the normal school will become a university?" Howard replied.

"Yes, but not until the 1960s I believe," said Neill.

"Well, I don't think there are any scientists at Northern Normal in this time," said Howard. "It's just a teaching school right now, and it only opened last year. Maybe someone there knows basic chemistry or biology, but there are no physicists."

"Then where will we find one?" asked Allison.

"Howard, do you know anyone at Cornell who could help us?" Neill asked.

"Hmm," said Howard. "Maybe there is someone, but I don't know them. I'm studying forestry, not physics, though all forms of science do interest me."

"I still think we should contact Einstein," said Allison.

"How would we even find him?" asked Neill. "We only know he lives in Germany somewhere. There's no GPS or Wikipedia or anything like that in 1900 to help us track him down."

"Who is this Einstein?" asked Howard.

"He's the smartest man who ever lived!" Derek exclaimed.

"What did he do that made him so smart?" Howard asked.

Allison and Derek looked at each other. They weren't sure.

"Didn't he invent the bomb?" said Derek.

"I think his theories were used to create the atomic bomb," Neill replied.

"A bomb? He sounds dangerous," said Howard.

"No, he was brilliant," Neill replied, "but he had no control over how his theories were used. He's best known for his theory of relativity. I think that's the $E=mc^2$ equation, but I can't remember what it stands for other than I think the E is for energy."

"Oh," said Allison. "I think the m is for mass."

"That's more than I know," said Derek. "I was never into school much."

Howard waited for more information, but his new friends just stared blankly at him.

"Well," Howard said finally, "it's getting late, and I think we're all agreed that our next move is to go to the library tomorrow to see if we can find a book on ancient runes, and maybe even one on time travel or physics."

"Sounds like a plan to me," said Allison.

"I can't go," said Derek. "I'm going with your dad tomorrow to find a job. Besides, I hate libraries. You guys can go and let me know what you find."

"And I told your mom I would go shopping with her and your sisters," Allison told Howard. "Besides, it will seem suspicious if we all go off to the library."

"Okay," said Howard. "Just Neill and I can go. Well, I better get back to my room."

"Howard, thank you for all your help and kindness," said Allison, getting up and crossing the room to hug him. He seemed surprised when she wrapped her arms around him.

"Good night," Derek said, stepping toward Howard as if to claim Allison as his territory.

"You better hang onto the time travel device for now," Howard said, handing it back to Neill. "I don't want my siblings to catch me with it."

"Okay," said Neill. "Good night."

Howard said goodbye and closed the door behind him.

"Don't get too attached to him," Derek told Allison as soon as Howard started down the hall.

"Why?" Allison asked.

"He's not like us," said Derek. "And you'll only break his heart if you return to 2021 and he's in love with you."

Allison frowned and said, "I'll see you boys in the morning." Then she passed through the adjoining door into her room.

Neill could see Derek looked irritated, but saying nothing, he went to hide the time travel device back in the closet. When he turned around, Derek was getting undressed.

"I'm so tired," said Neill.

Derek didn't reply, just changed into his nightshirt.

"At least we got some ideas for how to get back home, though," said Neill.

"We'll see," said Derek, crawling into bed. "Good night."

"Good night," said Neill, deciding it best not to discuss matters further. Derek was obviously not in a good mood. Neill went to bed worried that Derek's interest in Allison and jealousy of Howard would interfere with him getting back to his own time, but despite his anxiety, it had been an exhausting day, so he fell asleep seconds after his head hit the pillow.

Chapter 6

THE NEXT MORNING, DEREK WAS up early and went off with Mr. Longyear, who said he would find work for him on some of his properties. Allison graciously accepted Mrs. Longyear, Helen, and Abby's offer to take her shopping downtown, even though she protested she had no money. "You are our guest, dear, so let us treat you," Mrs. Longyear insisted. The rest of the children planned to enjoy a beautiful summer day outside, leaving Howard and Neill the opportunity to go to the library without anyone questioning them.

Before leaving for the library, Howard rolled up the paper rubbings he had made at the dolmen and hid them inside his suit. Neill hid a small notebook in his inner coat pocket, along with a few pencils so they could take notes. He also had Howard's journal in the pocket. He was hoping today would give him the opportunity to talk to Howard about it and explain to him why he had traveled back to 1900—Howard understood Neill had been trying to get back to his own version of 2021, but he did not yet know that would require reversing certain events that had already happened in 1900. Neill was not looking forward to the difficult conversation, but he was determined to have it.

"I don't know how lucky we'll be at the library," said Howard, once he and Neill had passed through the Longyear estate's front gate and were out of the hearing of his nosey siblings' ears, "but hopefully we'll find something—if not a book that can decipher runes, maybe an idea of whom we can approach for further help."

"It's bizarre to think those runes could have something to do with time travel," Neill replied. "They have to be hundreds or even thousands of years old. It's hard to fathom that people in the past could have understood time travel when we don't."

"We don't know that ancient peoples did," said Howard. "Those runes just might mark who was buried under the dolmen or state something like 'Thor was here.' They may have nothing to do with time travel."

"True," said Neill, "but the legends say Atlantis was highly advanced, so who knows what the ancients might have known that has been lost to us, and since the dolmen itself is clearly connected to time travel, I hope those runes provide us with answers."

"If not," Howard replied, "our next task will be to see if we can figure out how that time travel device you brought with you works."

Neill didn't like the thought of that. The time travel device made him nervous because he had stolen it and Xander and Jorgen had said time travel was forbidden in their time. Plus, some people in their time apparently did know how to time travel, so Neill was concerned some version of the time travel police might come after him and Derek or even after Allison. If that happened, how would they defend themselves against twenty-second-century weapons? They might be arrested or even eliminated. Neill shuddered just to think about it. It was bad enough he felt like he was trapped in a sci-fi film. He didn't want to be in a horror film too. Just stealing the time travel device had been difficult for him since he'd always had a big dose of Catholic guilt. He had not stolen anything since he was four years old when he had taken a pack of bubble gum from the checkout aisle at Econo Foods. His mother had made him return it and tell the store manager what he had done, leaving him feeling like a criminal. Now he had stolen not only a time travel device but clothes from Getz's, and both weighed on his conscience.

"Howard," Neill said, "I didn't mention it before, and I don't know what other choice Derek and I had, but when we first arrived back in this time, Derek was in modern clothes and I was wearing the hiking clothes you gave me. I knew people would think we looked strange, so we broke into Getz's and stole these clothes we've been wearing."

Neill said it in such a mournful tone that Howard could not help but laugh. "I've been meaning to ask you where you got those clothes," he replied.

"Well, I don't know what else we could have done. I was afraid Derek would be arrested for indecent exposure since he was only wearing his swimsuit and a T-shirt, though that would be perfectly acceptable in our time. I knew we couldn't show up at your house like that."

"My sisters," said Howard, smiling, "would probably faint if they saw a half-naked man, so I'm glad you did what you had to do."

"Still, it was wrong," Neill replied, "and I feel bad about it. I want to make it right somehow, but I don't want you to have to loan me the money to repay Mr. Getz, and I can't go confess it and risk being arrested."

"Well," said Howard, "you said you wanted to get a job. Why don't we go to Getz's after we finish at the library and see if Mr. Getz will give you one?"

"What if he doesn't have any openings available?" asked Neill.

"My father and I are very good customers of his," Howard replied. "I'm sure if I tell him you're my good friend, he'll find something for you."

"Oh, that would be wonderful," said Neill. "Then I can take the money for the clothes out of my earnings and send it to him with an anonymous letter explaining what it was for and apologizing for his trouble."

"That would be fine, I think," said Howard. "Anyway, we're almost at the library."

In his mind, Neill had envisioned them walking to the Peter White Public Library on the corner of Ridge and Front Streets, which had been there since 1903 he believed, but now he recalled the day of the Fourth of July parade when he had felt something was missing on that corner, though he couldn't remember what then. It took him a minute now to realize they were going to the earlier version of the library, which had been founded in 1891. Howard led them down to Washington Street and to a sign on the Thurber Block that proclaimed it was the home of the library.

"It looks so small," Neill could not help remarking as they entered. And it was small by Marquette's twenty-first century standards, yet it housed thousands of books.

"It has outgrown its space," said Howard. "My parents just donated land on Front Street for a new one to be built. Mr. White tried to get Andrew Carnegie to fund a new library for us, but he said—"

"Shh!" shooshed the librarian.

"Sorry," said Howard, now whispering. "Mr. Carnegie said this was Peter White's town, so he had to do it himself, and my parents agreed to help the cause."

Neill looked about, seeing only a few tables and chairs for patrons to sit at and very few books, but Howard whispered that the collection was in the back and you had to ask the librarian for what you wanted. The librarians didn't want just anyone going into the stacks and mixing up the books.

"Weird," said Neill, thinking how such an arrangement spoiled all the fun of browsing. "Everyone here might overhear what we're looking for."

"It's okay," said Howard. "The librarian knows I'm interested in geography. She won't think anything of it."

Howard stepped up to the librarian's desk, while Neill stood slightly behind him.

"Oh, Mr. Longyear, I didn't realize it was you," said the librarian who had just shooshed them. Now her face lit up. "I didn't know you were back in town. How is Cornell?"

"Hello," Howard said. "It's good." He was clearly not interested in young women fawning over him, although Neill could see the librarian, who had to be twenty-five—an old maid in this time really and clearly too old for Howard—was eager to converse with him. But Howard was all business and stated he was looking for a book on runes. When she said she did not know what runes were, Howard was forced to spell the word and explain it. She then asked him a series of rather stupid questions, which Neill thought was just her way to prolong the conversation so she could flirt with Howard. Finally, Neill said, "Excuse me, but we are in kind of a hurry."

The librarian gave Neill an irritated glance but said, "I think I know the book you want." Neill felt relieved when she turned to enter the stacks. When she returned with three books in less than two minutes, Neill was sure all her questions had only been a form of flirting. He felt a bit jealous then. He could see Howard was good-looking, but he didn't think he was that much better looking than himself. *It must be his money*, Neill thought.

Howard thanked the librarian and took the books. One was on ancient languages, one on the Vikings, and one actually on runes. Howard and Neill walked over to the empty table in the corner farthest away from any other patrons.

After they sat down, Howard opened the book on runes while Neill opened the one on ancient languages. They didn't think the book on the Vikings would be much use to them. After a few minutes of paging through the volumes, Howard came to a chart that showed various runes and their meanings.

"I think this is it," he whispered, his eyes poring over the chart.

"Does it match the runes you found on the dolmen?" asked Neill.

"I don't know," said Howard. "There appear to be different types of runic scripts—they're all called Futhark, but they're broken into the categories of Elder, Anglo-Saxon, and Younger. They date from different time periods and cultures. Some have been found in England, others in Friesland and Scandinavia."

"That's interesting," said Neill. "My great-grandfather Vandelaare came from Friesland. It's part of the Netherlands."

Howard didn't reply. He just kept flipping through the book. As Neill watched him, he realized Howard hadn't really heard him or he would have wondered what he meant by "cool." He remembered how "cool" had confused Hugh. Poor Hugh. Neill felt guilty that they hadn't been able to save him, and yet who knew what further mess would have resulted for the future if they had?

Neill turned his eyes back to his own book, but while it talked about Greek, Latin, Hebrew, and Egyptian hieroglyphics, it contained nothing about Norse languages or runestones. Setting it aside, he picked up the book about the Vikings, but he quickly realized it said nothing about them settling in North America, so it wouldn't be much use to them either.

After another minute, Howard whispered, "It's going to take a long time to try to figure this out, and I don't want to draw attention to us, so I'll check out this book and we can go."

"Okay," Neill replied.

Howard closed the book, got up, and pushed his chair under the table. Then he walked up to the desk. Meanwhile, Neill grabbed the other two books and followed him. After the librarian stamped Howard's book, and Neill handed her back the two they didn't need, they wished her a good day.

"Stop by anytime, Mr. Longyear. I'll be happy to assist you further," she replied.

"Thank you," Howard said and quickly turned to the door with Neill close on his heels.

"I hope this book has the answers," said Howard once they were outside.

"So do I," said Neill, looking around to make sure no one was close enough to hear their conversation. "I hope the runes you found will tell me how to get back to my own time."

"Do you want to go to Getz's now?" asked Howard.

"Sure," said Neill. They turned east toward the lake, then right to go down Front Street. Since the sidewalks were largely empty of people, Howard felt free to say, "There's one thing I don't understand."

"What's that?" asked Neill.

"Why everything was different when you went back to 2021. You said it was different, but you didn't really tell me how."

Neill started to sweat. Here was the opportunity he had been looking for, but he didn't know if he had to the courage to say what he needed to.

"I apparently changed something in 1900 when I was here before," Neill said.

"Yes, I understand that," said Howard, "but what did you change? And how was the future different as a result?"

"It's a long story," said Neill, seeing the sign for Getz's just down the block. "Let me tell you after we visit Getz's. I think you'll want to sit down for it."

Neill looked pointedly at Howard as he spoke. When Howard saw the serious look on Neill's face, it made him jerk back his head with surprise. Neill doubted Howard could guess what he meant—that Howard should be dead—but he felt bad to leave his friend in suspense. Still, here at Getz's he had another, and easier, wrong to right.

"Let's see if I can get a job," said Neill, "and then I'll explain everything to you after."

"All right," said Howard, though he sounded nervous about it.

They opened the door and entered the store. A couple of women were browsing, likely looking to buy something for their husbands. A clerk was helping one of the women. No one else seemed to be inside. Then the other lady, who had not seen Howard and Neill enter, went up to Neill to ask if he could help her find something; she obviously thought he worked there. Before Neill could explain he did not, she said she was looking for a tie for her son for his twenty-first birthday. Neill wasn't sure he could help, given he knew nothing about men's fashion in 1900, but between him and Howard giving her their opinions, she was able to choose one she seemed pleased with. By that point, the clerk had finished with the other customer, and he happily rang up the woman's purchase. She left the store smiling while Howard asked the clerk if they could see Mr. Getz.

"Mr. Longyear, I didn't know you were back in town," said Mr. Getz, suddenly appearing from the back room. "Or that you were such a good salesman. I overheard you helping out that customer."

Howard smiled and shook Mr. Getz's hand. Then he introduced Neill, and Mr. Getz thanked them for aiding his customer.

"I'm glad we could help," said Howard. "In fact, Neill here is looking for employment and was hoping you might have an opening."

"Actually, my other clerk is just out sick today," said Mr. Getz. "Usually, we can easily handle the clientele, so I don't need another salesman."

"Oh," said Neill, sounding disappointed. "Thank you anyway."

"Not so fast," said Mr. Getz. "What I do need is a bookkeeper for the rest of the summer. Are you qualified for that?"

"I think so," said Neill. "I'm very good at math."

"Is your handwriting legible?" Mr. Getz asked.

"Yes, I believe so," said Neill.

"Show me," Mr. Getz replied, and he motioned for Neill and Howard to follow him into a large back room, which housed both an office and inventory. Mr. Getz led them to a desk. There he picked up a pen and dipped it into an inkwell, then handed it to Neill. Neill was grateful he had dipped it in the inkwell because he would not have thought to do so and would have made himself look ridiculous. Mr. Getz handed Neill a piece of paper and dictated a sentence complete with some prices in it for Neill to write. Neill did as he was told, finding the pen awkward to hold, so he wrote a bit slowly to ensure accuracy. When he finished, he handed the paper to Mr. Getz.

"Very nice," said Mr. Getz. "I dislike a hand that is flowery in its script—it's hard to read. Your writing is very legible."

Neill was surprised, knowing how inferior his writing was to Howard's beautiful penmanship, so he thanked Mr. Getz for the compliment.

"Can you start tomorrow?" asked Mr. Getz.

"Yes, thank you," said Neill, smiling.

"Be here at nine. You'll work until five with a half-hour for lunch. I may also have you help with the customers when the clerks are at lunch or it gets busy."

"I'll be happy to do that," Neill replied. But he was happier to be a bookkeeper because he was already plotting how he could slip money from his pay into the cash register and then write it in the ledger as if the clothes he and Derek had stolen had simply been sold all along.

"Very good. I'll see you tomorrow then, Mister.... I didn't get your name."

"Jackson, Neill Jackson," said Neill.

"I'll see you tomorrow then, Mr. Jackson," said Mr. Getz, shaking his hand.

"Thank you, sir," said Neill. "I promise I'll be on time and you won't be disappointed."

Mr. Getz smiled and nodded. Howard and Neill then found their way back out to Front Street.

"I'm very happy for you," said Howard, patting Neill on the back once they were on the sidewalk.

"It wouldn't have happened without your help," Neill replied. "I think everyone is so awed by you Longyears that they are afraid to tell you no."

"Maybe," said Howard, "though sometimes I wish I could walk around town anonymously. Anyway, let's get back to what we were discussing earlier. Why do you think everything in your time changed?"

"Like I said," Neill replied, "I think you need to sit down for this one, or at least, we need to go somewhere very private."

"All right," said Howard, turning south. "Let's go get some lunch at the Hotel Marquette."

"No, more private than that," Neill replied.

"Hmm," said Howard, looking puzzled. "Is it something bad you have to tell me?"

"Kind of," Neill said, though he imagined Howard would consider being alive a good thing. "I guess it depends on how you look at it."

Chapter 7

Howard decided to lead Neill down to the lakeshore near the harbor. For a moment, Neill was afraid Howard would suggest they go to the boathouse where his canoe was stored. If Howard wanted to go out on the lake, Neill would refuse. That was the last place he wanted to be when he told Howard he should have drowned. Fortunately, Howard turned south toward Gaines Rock and strode along the beach, away from the industrial blight along the lakeshore, which in Neill's lifetime had been replaced by the bike trail and the gentrified Founders Landing neighborhood.

"Okay," said Howard finally, once they were past the bustling harbor and away from where anyone could hear them except the seagulls, "tell me what's so important."

"It's not easy to tell," Neill warned.

"I've already gathered that," said Howard, walking beside Neill along the beach.

"Well," Neill said, carefully choosing his words as he stared out at Lake Superior, "you asked what happened that caused everything in 2021 to be different when I returned."

"Yes," said Howard.

"What happened is I changed something while I was here in 1900."

"You've said that," Howard replied, "but you haven't said what you changed."

"Because I'm not sure you're going to like it," Neill replied.

"Just tell me," Howard said, stopping to stare Neill in the eye.

Neill also stopped. Wanting to get it over with now, he maintained eye contact with Howard and said, "It's about the canoeing accident."

"You mean Hugh drowning? I knew it. He wasn't supposed to drown. I just—I feel—so responsible," said Howard, and he began to tear up. Neill reached out and put his hand on his shoulder.

"It's not that," said Neill.

Howard wiped his eye with his hand and said, "Sorry. I just feel it was my fault. He looked up to me and I should have watched out for him better."

"There was nothing you could have done," Neill replied. "The truth is…well, Howard, you were both supposed to drown."

Howard said nothing for a second, then "What?" as a look of astonishment spread across his face.

"In the original version of 1900," said Neill, "I wasn't there to save you. You and Hugh both drowned that day."

Howard stepped back like someone had struck him. Then, slowly, he began to grin, and after a few seconds, he let out an awkward laugh.

"I don't believe it," he said, as if trying to convince himself Neill was joking, but Neill could see the truth was slowly sinking into his friend's brain.

"I'm sorry," said Neill. "I wasn't sure I should tell you, but…."

Howard's face screwed up as if he were overcome with emotion. Turning away, he started traipsing up the beach.

"Howard, wait!" Neill said, swiftly following him. "Howard, I…I'm sorry." He reached out and put his hand on his friend's shoulder, stopping him. "Maybe I'm selfish to tell you, but now you can understand why I feel so desperate—why I risked coming back to this time again."

"Because you want me dead?" asked Howard. "Is that it? If I were dead, you think everything would be normal for you again?"

"No," said Neill. "I want you to know because…well, so we can figure out a workaround so you can be alive, but my time can still be close to normal."

"How?" asked Howard. "How is that possible?"

"I don't know if it is," said Neill, "but let me explain why it matters to me—why what has changed is so important."

"Just what did change?" asked Howard slowly, staring out at Lake Superior's waves, still trying to take it all in.

"When I got home," said Neill, "your house was still in Marquette."

"What's so strange about that?" asked Howard, turning toward him.

Neill explained that in the original version of 1900 when Howard had drowned, his family had been so distraught that they had moved to Massachusetts and taken their mansion with them.

Howard laughed. "Wow. But I wouldn't put it past my parents to do something like that. Still, I don't see why that matters so much to you."

"It's not the house moving that matters to me," said Neill, "though it was strange your house was still in Marquette. What was so hard for me was that my family was gone."

"Where did they go?"

"Well, they weren't exactly gone. They didn't exist. They had never been born."

"What?" asked Howard.

"They were never born because I found out you married my great-great-grandmother instead of the man she was supposed to marry."

"Are you telling me?" asked Howard, raising his eyebrows in disbelief, "that I'm your great-great-grandfather?"

"No," said Neill, shaking his head. "You and my great-great-grandmother had other children. But because she married you instead of my great-great-grandfather, my great-grandfather was never born nor were any of his descendants."

"Who is this woman I married?" asked Howard.

"Margaret Dalrymple," said Neill.

"I never heard of her," said Howard, shaking his head.

"She lives here in Marquette. She's sixteen I think. I guess you just haven't met her yet. But that's the thing. As long as you don't marry her, maybe she will marry my great-great-grandfather, and then everything in my time will be fine."

"Oh," said Howard, his face reflecting that his mental faculties were working overtime to figure this out. "I guess...well, I guess I can just promise not to marry her. That doesn't seem difficult, especially since I don't even know her. Do you really think that's all it's going to take?"

"Well..." said Neill. "Well, for my family anyway."

"So there's something else?" asked Howard, sighing with exhaustion.

"Yes," said Neill. As he started to reach into his suit pocket, Howard turned and walked toward a small clump of trees.

Neill followed, pulling Howard's journal out of his pocket.

"It's about time travel itself," he called after Howard.

Howard had come to an overturned tree on the beach. He sat down on it while Neill approached.

"Time travel?" said Howard.

"Yes, and it's time travel specifically relevant to you," said Neill. "You see, when I was in the future, I learned that your descendants invented the time travel device I used, or so I was told, but when I stole the time travel device, I also stole this journal."

He held out the journal to Howard. Howard looked surprised when he read the title.

"This is my journal! Did you steal this from my room? But how did it get so beat-up looking?"

"No, I got it from the future," Neill repeated.

"But I just wrote in this book this morning," said Howard. "Why does it look like a train ran over it?"

"It's just old," said Neill. "In 2142, it was 242 years old. That's why it looks that way."

"Let me see it," said Howard, reaching out and taking it in his hands. He opened it and carefully began to flip the decaying pages.

"Here's what I wrote this morning," he said, "only...but...but I wrote that you and I were going to the library this morning. It doesn't say that. I don't understand."

"Because," said Neill, "it contains what you would have written if I had not returned to your time. Now that I've brought it back from the future, this time is an alternative version of the one when you originally wrote it."

Howard looked doubtful.

"Turn a few more pages and you'll see what I mean," said Neill.

Howard silently turned the pages, his face expressing astonishment as he saw entries dated into days, months, even years that he had not yet lived.

"I can't believe it," said Howard.

"But you do, don't you?" said Neill. "I mean, you believe I've time traveled, so shouldn't you believe I could bring your journal back from the future?"

Howard kept turning the pages. "I don't even know what some of this means," he said, looking at a diagram of some sort of mechanical equipment, "and what's all this math?"

"That's the thing," said Neill. "I think you were so astonished that I disappeared at the dolmen that you began to study it, just like you are now. I think maybe in this journal you write about how you already solved what the runes said, and eventually, you figured time travel out, and that…I'm just guessing here, but maybe your descendants used what you wrote in this journal to create time travel devices, one of which I used to get back to this time."

"This is like something out of a novel," said Howard. "It's stranger than anything H. G. Wells has written."

"Sometimes truth is stranger than fiction," said Neill.

"Yes," said Howard. "I doubt H. G. Wells could have made up something as convoluted as this."

"Then you do believe me?" asked Neill.

"I guess I have to," said Howard, looking up at him. "The proof is in my hands. This is my own handwriting."

"What about how you wrote in different languages, or some sort of code?"

Howard flipped through a few pages. "I definitely wrote this since it's my handwriting and I know most of these languages. I think here," he said, staring at a page, "I used some sort of code, but I bet I could easily figure it out since I wrote it, even if I wrote it in the future."

"Then," said Neill, fearing the possibility was too good to be true, "do you think you could read this journal and find out from it how I can get back to my own time?"

"Maybe," said Howard, "provided we don't change the future further."

"Meaning?" asked Neill.

"Meaning I have to make sure I don't marry this Margaret Dalrymple you're descended from."

"Right," said Neill.

"All right," said Howard. "Then I guess we know what we have to do. Maybe in the long run, this will all turn out for the good, other than Hugh having died. After all, I'm happy to still be alive, and I'm sure my parents would rather not have to move their house."

Howard's tone seemed more lighthearted now, which relieved Neill. He knew it had to be a shock for Howard to find out he should be dead. But Howard seemed resilient, like he was more interested in what could be in the future and what they should do next than pondering what might have been.

"Let's head home," said Howard, standing up. "We have some runes to translate, and I have this journal to read too."

"Okay," said Neill.

They started down the beach, each caught up in his own thoughts for a minute or two until Howard said, "You know, even if you hadn't told me all this, it's unlikely I ever would have married Margaret Dalrymple."

"Why?" asked Neill. "Historically…if that's the right word… you did."

"Because now there's another young lady I'm interested in," said Howard.

"Who?" asked Neill. "Is it a young lady you met at Cornell?"

"No," said Howard. "Now it's my turn to say something you might find shocking. Is Allison your lady friend?"

Neill laughed. "Allison? No. Why? Are you interested in her?"

"Only if you aren't," said Howard. "I wouldn't want to steal my friend's fiancée."

"Fiancée!" said Neill. "Definitely not. Allison and I are just friends."

"That's what I thought," Howard replied, "but she obviously cares about you since she was willing to risk time traveling to find you."

"She's a really good friend," Neill said. "Almost like a sister."

"What about Derek?" asked Howard. "Is she interested in him?"

"Not the Derek in my time," said Neill. "But the Derek in this time with us, I don't know. In his version of 2021, he and Allison were dating, but they weren't getting along very well. She was very different from the Allison you've met. I can't imagine this Allison would be interested in him."

"But I think he's interested in her," Howard replied.

"I think he just likes to flirt," Neill replied so as not to get Howard worked up. "I know he's maybe said some things to try to flirt with her, but I think Allison would find him a bit too crude."

"I see," said Howard. "Do you think she could grow to like me?"

"I have the feeling she already does," said Neill. "In fact, I was surprised by how willingly she took your arm when we walked to your house. She's a rather independent young woman, and she's told me before that she doesn't understand how girls can throw themselves at men, especially when the guys don't treat them well. I was rather surprised to see she was being so friendly with you."

"I want to be more than her friend, though," said Howard.

Neill kind of smirked, wondering how that could work out.

"You understand," he said, "that Allison will want to go back to 2021 with me, right?"

"Yes," said Howard. "You're right. She and I can have no future."

"If you two got together," Neill replied, "I have no idea what strange shifts that could make in the future."

"That's true," said Howard. "But just the fact that I'm alive is going to make shifts in the future from what you've said."

"Well, not major ones so long as you don't invent a time machine or marry Margaret Dalrymple."

"But my parents' house will still be in Marquette in your time."

"I wouldn't mind that," said Neill, though it still bothered him. He knew somehow it wasn't right, but....

"Uncle Chad!" Neill gasped.

"What?" said Howard.

"Never mind," said Neill, realizing he had to think this one out more. After all, Uncle Chad had lived in an apartment in a house on the property where the Longyear Mansion had been. If the mansion had never been moved, Uncle Chad wouldn't have had that apartment, and then maybe he wouldn't have tripped over that rug and broken his foot and then gotten the blood clot and then he'd still be alive. Maybe Howard being alive was a good thing after all. Maybe when he returned to his time, Uncle Chad would still be alive!

"What are you thinking?" asked Howard, noting Neill's silence.

"Nothing," said Neill, not ready to share such a dramatic hope. "I think my brain is exhausted after everything."

"Mine too," said Howard. "Besides, we should get back. My mother and the girls might be home by now."

"You don't know Allison," said Neill. "She never met a mall she didn't like."

"What's a mall?" asked Howard.

Neill laughed. "It's a place you go shopping. I mean that Allison is quite the shopper."

"I see," said Howard. "Well, that's okay. My mom can afford to buy her whatever she wants."

Neill was struck by how generous the whole family was. "You've all been very kind to us," he said. "I will miss you all when I get back to 2021."

"It's kind of you to say so," said Howard, "but before you can miss us, we have to figure out how to get you back there."

Chapter 8

WHEN NEILL AND HOWARD GOT to the Longyear Mansion, the first thing Howard did was hide the book about runes and his journal from the future under his coat. Then he entered the house and took them to his room. Fortunately, no one was around to question why his stomach looked flat and distorted when he entered the house. He buried the books in a bottom drawer of his dresser where prying siblings' eyes would not find them.

It was past lunchtime now, but the women had not yet returned from their outing, probably having dined downtown, so Howard and Neill went into the kitchen where the cook found them some leftovers. They had just finished their meal when Allison returned with Mrs. Longyear and Howard's older sisters. His other siblings had been out playing in the yard but came inside when they saw the carriage return.

The afternoon was taken up by Howard, Neill, and Allison being called upon to entertain the children. Howard wanted to investigate the book about runes, but he knew if he hid in his room, questions would be asked, so several vigorous games of lawn croquet were indulged in until a final tournament ensued. Allison and Neill, having never played the game before, were soon eliminated. They sat in the shade, far enough from the others that they could talk without being overheard. Allison began telling Neill all about the beautiful things Mrs. Longyear had bought her. She was deep into a discussion about furbelows and other female frippery when Howard joined them, having also been eliminated from the competition.

"I told you, Howard," Neill said, interrupting Allison's description of her new dress.

"Told him what?" Allison asked.

"I told Howard," Neill replied, "that you never met a mall you didn't like."

"I'm not that bad, am I?" asked Allison, laughing at herself.

"I would like to see one of these malls from your own time," said Howard. "Neill was trying to explain them to me."

"Yes," said Neill. "I wish I had a photograph of one."

"Oh, I have one," said Allison. "Remember, Neill, we took that picture of us in front of the Christmas decorations at the Westwood Mall a couple of years ago. I think that photo is still on my cell phone."

"Cell phone?" asked Howard. "Neill mentioned that earlier. Do you mean a telephone?"

"Yes," said Allison, "kind of, but it's a cellular phone."

"But how can you take photographs with a telephone?"

"It's not really a telephone," Neill said. "It isn't connected to a wall and doesn't have a cord. It uses a cellular signal that connects to a cell tower or a satellite in outer space. It's like a mini-computer—you can do all kinds of things with it: call people, check your email, and take photographs."

"Amazing," said Howard, who remembered their earlier explanations of computers and email. "I'd like to see one of these cell phones."

"I can show you mine," said Allison. "It's in my room, and then I can show you the pictures of the mall too, if the battery hasn't gone dead yet. I brought the charger, but I doubt there's anywhere in this time to plug it in."

"Shh," Neill warned, seeing Abby approaching.

"I'll show you later," Allison whispered to Howard.

"Show him what, dear?" asked Abby.

"The beautiful things your mother bought for me," said Allison.

"Oh, Howard," said Abby, sitting down with them, "we saw her try them on at the store. That green dress really brings out her eyes. She looks so enchanting in it."

"I'm sure she does," said Howard, gazing at Allison. Neill could see the adoration in his eyes. When Abby giggled, Neill knew she had also noticed her brother's attraction to Allison.

The other Longyear siblings now joined them, having completed their game. Judith had won, to Jack's chagrin since they had been tied until the final play.

"We should go in to change for dinner," said Howard.

"Yes," Helen agreed.

"Allison," said Abby, "you should wear your new green dress to dinner so Howard can see it."

"If you think so," Allison replied.

"I would love to see it," said Howard as they stood up, and then he offered her his arm to lead her into the house.

As the rest of the Longyears followed behind them, Abby held back to say to Neill, "My brother seems quite taken with your sister."

"I've noticed," said Neill.

"You don't need to worry," Abby replied. "Howard is a gentleman. Mother has lectured him and all of us on morality and relations with the opposite gender."

"I wouldn't expect anything else," said Neill.

"But would you be in favor of such a match?" asked Abby.

"I would leave that completely up to Allison," Neill replied.

"But aren't you her oldest brother?" asked Abby. "Or is Derek?"

"It doesn't matter," said Neill. "Allison is old enough to make her own decisions."

"That's very modern of you, Mr. Jackson."

"I try to be open-minded," he replied, smiling because Abby had no idea just how very modern he was.

"I've never seen my brother so taken with a young woman before," Abby continued.

"But would your parents approve?" asked Neill. "You know my family is relatively poor. Wouldn't your parents want a more advantageous match for their son?"

"My parents are not snobs," Abby replied. "They will want Howard to do what will make him happy, so long as he chooses a wholesome girl."

"You don't have to worry about that," said Neill, knowing what Abby's veiled Victorian language meant. "Allison can be a little flamboyant, I admit, but I assure you she is a good girl. She's been saving herself for a gentleman like Howard."

"She seems to have a good heart," said Abby. "I can see how attentive she is to you and your brother, though I imagine that's to be expected since you recently lost your parents."

"Yes," said Neill, almost having forgotten about his fictional dead parents. God, he hoped Howard was right and that his promise not to marry Margaret Dalrymple meant his real parents were alive again in their own time. Also, he wondered now that no one had been surprised that he and his alleged siblings weren't all wearing mourning clothes, but he decided not to bring that up. He had no desire to wear mourning. If asked, he could just say they couldn't afford it. "Should we go inside?" he asked Abby.

Unsure what propelled him to it, Neill offered her his arm and led her through the door. Hopefully, she did not read too much into it, especially since Derek seemed to be the one interested in her. But Neill knew Abby was to marry Alton Roberts according to the Longyear family tree—and divorce him one day also. Maybe she would be happier if she did marry Derek, though he couldn't imagine she would ever want to, and he had interfered enough with the past. From here on, he had to focus on returning to his own time and let other matters take their course as they would.

Chapter 9

NEILL WENT UP TO HIS room to change for dinner. Earlier, Howard had loaned him some suitable clothes for all occasions. He was glad to find Derek in their room, sitting on the bed and removing his shoes.

"Hello, Neill," said Derek when he entered.

"Did you just get home?" Neill asked, closing the door.

Derek laughed. "Home? I wish I had a home like this, but yes, I just got here. Mr. Longyear brought me back."

"Did he find you a position?" asked Neill, beginning to change his clothes.

"Oh, yes," said Derek. "I went out with one of his men on the train up to Ishpeming and we spent a few hours looking at some property just west of there. I'm going to be helping with some surveying, or 'landlooking' I think Mr. Longyear called it. You know, measuring property, determining the value of the timber on it, that kind of stuff. It pays well too. Twelve dollars a week. Isn't that hilarious? I was making more than that per hour at Rocket's. But Mr. Longyear's manager—I guess that's what you'd call him—told me that was a good starting wage in this business."

"Well, I'm glad you'll be earning money," said Neill. "Meanwhile, I found a job at Getz's. I'm going to be a bookkeeper and maybe help out on the floor with the sales once in a while. I forgot to ask what I'll be paid, though. Anyway, I'll use the money to pay for the clothes we took from there."

"I guess we're off to a good start then," said Derek. "Maybe we can get our own place soon. I don't want to freeload off the Longyears; they've done enough for us."

"Yeah," said Neill, sitting down on the bed in his underwear, suddenly feeling depressed at the thought of staying long enough in this time to get their own place.

"What's wrong? You got a job; that's a good thing," said Derek, reading his face.

"I just really miss my parents," said Neill. "I don't want to get a place of our own and live there. I want to go home."

"Well, you can't do that until you figure out how to time travel back there," said Derek.

"I know," said Neill.

"Did you have any luck at the library?"

"We found a book on runes, but figuring them out seems pretty complicated. Howard checked it out and said he'd have to study it, but we were busy all afternoon. It's hard because we don't want his family to know what we're doing, so we don't have many opportunities to be alone and try to figure it out."

"You'll figure it out if it's meant to be," said Derek.

"I gave Howard the journal too," said Neill. "It turns out it's mostly written in other languages and code, so he said he could read some but not all of it. Still, since he basically wrote it, he thinks he can figure it out."

"Good. I almost forgot about the journal. Was he surprised?"

"Yes, especially after I also explained to him how he was supposed to drown and everything else."

"How did he take it?" asked Derek.

"He was shocked at first, but he seemed okay once I explained it all. He promised me he wouldn't marry my great-great-grandmother, so when I get back to my time, hopefully, most things will be normal again."

"How long do you think it will take for him to figure out the journal and the runes?"

"I have no idea," said Neill. "That's why I feel depressed."

"Well, we'll just have to make the best of it here until then. It's not really that bad," said Derek. "I wanted an adventure after all."

"I suppose," said Neill, "but I never asked for one."

"No, but maybe it's a gift in its own way," Derek replied. "Think how much you're learning about history, and we never would have met each other otherwise."

Neill was rather surprised by his friend's positive outlook. This Derek had seemed harder, tougher, more negative back in his version of 2021. Neill was starting to think now that Derek's attitude had largely been due to the way Allison treated him and not having any good job prospects since he hadn't finished high school. He seemed like he was enjoying this adventure in the past.

"I suppose," he said. "Anyway, I guess we better get changed for dinner."

"I don't have anything to change into," said Derek. "No one in this house wears my size."

"Well, the Longyears will understand," said Neill. "I can try to find some more clothes for you at Getz's tomorrow when I go to work."

"Thanks," said Derek. "Though, I don't think I'll ever get used to things like changing for dinner. The Longyears are kind people, but this place is really too fancy for me. I think the novelty of it is starting to wear off. I'd rather just be out in the woods and maybe have a little cabin of my own."

"I doubt Helen or Abby would settle for that," Neill teased. "Even their 'cottage' at the Huron Mountain Club is fairly grand."

"I wasn't serious before about those girls," said Derek. "I know better than to think one of them would ever be interested in me. I know I was kind of flirting with them, but…well, what do we have in common? How could they ever understand a guy like me from the future, and how would I go about telling them I came from the future or keeping it from them all those years?"

"True," said Neill. "Howard doesn't seem too concerned about that, though."

"What do you mean?"

"He has a crush on Allison. Of course, he already knows we're from the future, but still, if Allison wants to go back with us to—"

"Oh," said Derek.

Neill saw the crushed look on his face, but asked anyway, "What's wrong?"

"I was thinking maybe Allison and I…well, who better since we're from the same time, sort of?"

"Not really," said Neill. "Allison will want to go back with me to our time. Don't you want to go back to yours?"

"But if you go back to your time," said Derek, "won't that somehow affect my time? And I can't go with you back to yours. It would be too weird being in a time where there's another Derek who looks just like me."

"I guess," said Neill.

"I was hoping maybe Allison would just stay in this time. I'm kind of thinking I want to stay here. It wouldn't be bad. We may have to stay here anyway."

"I'm not staying here if I don't have to," said Neill, pulling up his pants and buckling them.

"I kind of like it here," Derek replied. "There are a lot of advantages to this time. I never liked all those electronic gadgets. I liked being out in the woods today, and I like using my hands. I'm a big, strong guy, and I like doing physical activities, but in our time, it seems like it's all about being smart with computers and stuff. Unless you're into sports, which I always thought rather pointless, being strong doesn't mean much, but in this time, it does."

"I can see why you'd feel that way," said Neill. He was glad to see Derek was enjoying his time here; he rather envied him since it was amazing to be in another time. He wished he could enjoy it more, but all he could do was worry about getting back to his family. As he asked Derek more about his day and saw his enthusiasm for the work Mr. Longyear would have him do, Neill wondered how easily he could reconcile himself to this time if he had to stay here, but he felt like not getting to see his parents and sister again would make any happiness in 1900 impossible.

Soon, the two new friends were heading down to supper. Derek's enthusiasm continued, and during the meal, he talked about his workday and Mr. Longyear discussed Derek's future duties. Mrs. Longyear, Allison, and the older Longyear girls also discussed their shopping trip, and Neill told how he had gotten a job at Getz's with Howard's help. Throughout the meal, Neill could not help noticing how Allison's new green dress really did bring out her eyes, and that Howard kept sneaking peeks at her.

After dinner, Mr. and Mrs. Longyear adjourned to the drawing room, he to read *The Mining Journal* and she to read the works of Mary Baker Eddy. The younger children decided to go out and play more croquet while Abby and Helen chose to go for a walk. That left Howard and the Jackson siblings alone. Before separating from the rest of the Longyears, Allison made a point of saying she would like a good book to read, so Howard suggested he show her around the library. Neill suspected Derek wanted to join Helen and Abby, despite his saying he knew they weren't for him, but he followed Neill, Howard, and Allison.

Once they were alone in the library, Allison sat down at a table and told Howard, "I brought my phone with those pictures you wanted to see of the mall."

"Oh, great," said Howard, sitting down across from her.

"I think we have more important things to discuss while we're alone," Neill said. "Howard and I found a book on runes at the library."

"Yes, but I haven't had a chance to look at it," Howard said as Allison retrieved her phone from a hidden pocket of her dress.

"It'll only take a minute to look at the photos," said Allison, about to turn the phone on.

"Wait a minute!" Howard said, so excited he grabbed the phone from Allison's hand. "This is that weird rock we found at the dolmen!"

"Weird rock?" said Derek. "It's not a rock. It's plastic or metal or something."

"But isn't it what we found at the dolmen, Neill?" Howard asked, turning it over. "I remember it had this weird button-thing on it. So, this is a telephone?"

Neill leaned over to get a better look. "It's a cell phone," he clarified. "What we found was my cell phone. When I came through the dolmen, I must have dropped it the first time, and we found it just before I went back through to 2021. But I lost mine in 2142 in the lake."

"So this is Allison's telephone?" said Howard. "There's more than one of these things? You mean to say someone manufactures these?"

"Yes," said Allison. "Several companies, actually. There are numerous brands of cell phones."

"Allison and I have the same brand," Neill added. "That's why they look similar. It's a rather cheap brand, but several more expensive kinds are made by different companies."

"Do you have one too, Derek?" asked Howard.

"No," said Derek. "Not the same brand. I have an iPhone, but I left mine in the truck before Neill and I kayaked to the dolmen."

"So, just to be clear," asked Howard, "you didn't have one with you when you time traveled here?"

"No," said Derek.

"Why do you ask, Howard?" Neill asked.

Howard was too enthralled to answer as he ran his fingers over the cell phone in admiration. "I never imagined anything so small could do so much."

"You haven't even turned it on yet," said Allison, and she showed him which button to press. Then she explained about swiping the screen to unlock it. Howard did so, and then his thumb inadvertently hit the photo button. He was surprised when it flashed.

"What was that?" he asked, jumping back.

"You just took a photo of the desk," Allison replied.

"Just like that?" he asked.

"Yes, just like that," she replied.

"And you can telephone people with it too?" Howard asked.

Neill and Derek, tired of standing, sat down in a couple of more comfortable chairs off to the side of the desk.

"Yes," Allison continued, "though the battery will need to be recharged soon. It's at less than 50 percent."

"What does that mean?" asked Howard.

"It means," said Derek, "that when the battery dies, it won't work anymore unless you have an electrical outlet to plug it in."

"Our house has electricity," said Howard.

"And I brought the charger cord," said Allison.

"Yes," said Neill, "but I suspect your electric sockets don't match up with what we have in the twenty-first century."

"Then how do we keep it from dying?" asked Howard.

"We can't," said Derek, "other than to turn it off to delay the need to charge it."

"How do we turn it off?" asked Howard.

Allison took the cell phone from him and showed him. "But I thought you wanted to see the pictures of the mall?" she said.

"I did," said Howard, "but we better conserve its charge."

"Why? What good is it to us?" asked Allison, addressing Neill. "We can't get an internet connection or anything here."

"That's true," Neill replied.

"But I think these cell phones have something to do with how you time traveled here," Howard stated. "I mean, you and Neill both had a cell phone when you touched the dolmen. When I tried to time travel by touching it, nothing happened, and I think that's because I didn't have a cell phone."

"But a cell phone isn't a time travel device," said Neill.

"Maybe not," said Howard, "but maybe something in it triggers something in the dolmen that makes the time travel happen. Maybe there's something in the time travel device you stole in the future that works similarly. If we were to take the cell phone and time travel device apart, we might find something similar in them that will tell us how this whole time travel thing works."

"Wow," said Derek. "That's mind-blowing!"

"It is," said Neill, "but, Howard, maybe you already figured it all out and wrote about it in your journal we brought back from the future. Couldn't we just find the answers there to make it work?"

Howard thought about that for a second. "First off," he said, "I'm kind of afraid to look at that journal. I don't understand all the code it's in, and while I'm sure I could figure it out, it might take a while. Secondly, I'm uncomfortable reading what the future has in store for me, and third—"

"But the future is different now than what it was back then," said Allison, putting her hand on his arm as if to comfort him, "because now you know us."

"Yes," said Howard, hesitantly putting his hand over hers, for he was a gentleman and did not want to seem forward, "but that's also part of my point. I never saw the time travel device because you didn't come back to the time when I wrote that journal, though perhaps later I invented it...but I think you said my descendants actually invented it."

"True," said Neill. "I think you figured out time travel in that other time, but it probably did take you longer since you didn't have us come back and bring the time travel device."

"Exactly," said Howard.

"So, what do we do then?" asked Derek, not quite following the conversation.

"Allison," said Howard, clearly getting excited, "would you mind if I took your cell phone apart?"

Allison looked unsure and turned to Neill to see what he thought.

"I don't see why not," Neill said to her. "I mean...."

"But what if you break it?" Allison asked Howard.

"I'll do my best to be careful," he said.

"But those electronic things are complicated," said Derek. "You need to be like a rocket scientist to put them together. They're not as simple as things in this time."

"I like putting things together, though," said Howard. "I can't learn if I don't try."

"I don't think they're that complicated," Neill replied, "but there are lots of little bits and pieces in them. They're like a whole computer in a phone."

"Yes," said Allison. "If you lose one piece or put it in wrong, I might not be able to use it again."

"You won't be able to use it anyway once the battery dies," said Derek.

"Maybe I can figure out how to recharge it," said Howard, still completely clueless about how complicated twenty-first century technology was compared to that of his own time.

"What if you can't figure it out?" asked Allison.

No one said anything for a minute.

"Are you telling me I might never get back home?" said Allison, the gravity of this possibility sinking in for the first time. "What will my mom do? She'll be so worried."

"She probably already is," said Derek.

"Aren't you worried about getting back to your time?" she asked Derek.

"Nah. No one in my time cares about me. I haven't seen my dad in years and my ma is dead. And my girlfriend, well...."

Allison looked like she was about to cry. Howard handed her his handkerchief.

"This is difficult for all of us," Neill told her. "I'm sorry I got you into this mess."

"It's not your fault," she said, sniffling a bit as she wiped her eyes. "You're my friend, and I thought I was helping you."

"I'm afraid I've made a mess of everything for all of us," Neill replied.

"Not me," said Derek. "I'm enjoying the adventure."

"And I," said Howard, "would be dead if you hadn't come to this time, Neill."

"I'm glad you're not dead, Howard," said Allison, taking his hand.

"So am I," said Howard, "and regardless of what happens, I'm glad to have known all of you, and if things don't work out so you can go home, Allison, I want you to know you can stay here with my family. I'll make sure you're taken care of." He squeezed her hand and looked into her eyes.

"Oh, geez," said Derek, looking at Neill like he wanted to gag. Neill couldn't help smiling. He was sorry to have upset Allison, but Howard's 1900 protective gentleman act, sincere as it was, seemed over the top to him and Derek.

"Allison," said Neill, seeing Howard's words had calmed her down, "I think if we can figure out what the time dial and the cell phone have in common, maybe we can figure out how to get back to our own time, so will you let Howard take your cell phone apart?"

Allison didn't reply but handed the cell phone to Howard.

"Do you know anything about their inner workings?" Howard asked Neill while he turned it over in wonderment.

"No," said Neill. "I'm afraid none of us is very mechanical."

"Still," said Howard, now realizing what he might be getting himself into, "since the three of you at least know how they work, you might be better at trying to take them apart and comparing them to the time travel device. Meanwhile, I could work on translating the runes or my journal."

All three time travelers hesitated in agreeing to this, but before they could answer, the library door opened.

"There you all are," said Mr. Longyear, suddenly appearing before them. Allison quickly grabbed the cell phone from Howard and stuffed into her pocket, hoping Mr. Longyear didn't see it.

"We were just talking about books," Howard said.

"Did you find one you want to read, Miss Jackson?" Mr. Longyear asked.

"No, actually, Howard has recommended so many that I haven't decided," Allison replied.

"What can we do for you, Father?" Howard asked.

"Your sisters are back from their walk," said Mr. Longyear, "so we thought we'd all go sit out on the veranda and have ice cream. It's a beautiful evening."

"Good idea," said Derek, standing up.

"Somehow, I knew you wouldn't be opposed to the idea, Derek," Mr. Longyear said.

Derek led the way to the door, and as he passed Mr. Longyear, the older man put his hand on Derek's shoulder and walked down the hall with him.

"I think your father likes Derek," Allison said to Howard.

"I know," said Howard, but he was more concerned about the mystery they had to solve, so he whispered to her, "Make sure you hide the cell phone in your room where no one will see it."

"I will," she promised.

"Don't worry, Howard," said Neill. "We'll do our part. You just get those runes translated."

"I'll do my best," said Howard, and then they all made their way to the veranda where the servants were already carrying out dishes of ice cream to the family.

Chapter 10

ONCE NEILL AND DEREK HAD retired to their room that evening, Neill found his mind spinning with trying to figure out how to return to his own time. Derek stripped down to his underwear to sleep—he refused to sleep in a Victorian nightshirt—while Neill kept talking about what the runes might say. Then Derek lay down on his back on his bed and closed his eyes. He had not said a word in reply to Neill.

"Do you think that's possible?" Neill asked, concluding his speech.

Derek did not reply.

"Are you even listening to me?" Neill asked.

"Not really," Derek replied. "It's been a long day and all this worrying isn't going to get you home."

"What do you mean?"

"I mean," said Derek, "neither you or me, and probably not Allison, is smart enough to figure it out. You'll just have to let Howard see if he can."

"But what about the time travel device and cell phone? We should take those apart to see if they're similar."

"You'll never figure that out," said Derek. "I don't even know how you'd get the cell phone apart. You'd need a special tool."

"You don't sound like you care if I go home," Neill replied.

"I want you to if that's what you want," said Derek, "but I'm kind of concerned what it will mean for me. If you change back your version of 2021, what is there for me to go back to?"

"I'm not sure," Neill said, sitting down on the bed. "But we won't—"

"What if my version no longer exists, so I cease to exist?" asked Derek.

"Hmm," said Neill. He hadn't considered that. But after a moment, he said, "My version of 2021 no longer exists, but I'm still here, so if your version changed, wouldn't you still be here too?"

"Maybe," said Derek, "but how is that possible? How can it be that your parents never existed because some ancestor of yours didn't marry another, but you still exist?"

"I don't know," said Neill. "I guess it's because the version I lived in did exist once; it's still part of the historical record even if it isn't the same anymore."

"Wait!" said Derek. "That's what Xander and Jorgen said, I think. Didn't they say something about there were always different timelines, or…. No, it was that you create a new timeline when you change the past!"

"Yeah," said Neill, trying to remember. "I think they said something like that, but I didn't really understand what they meant."

"I think it means…" said Derek, pausing to gather his thoughts. "What if you didn't really change the past when you saved Howard from drowning? What if, instead, you just created a new version of the past, which created a new version of the future, but your version of the future still exists? That would mean if you could go back to your version of 2021, everything would be normal!"

"Yeah!" said Neill, jumping up with excitement. "And that would mean your time exists too, so you could also go back to it."

"If I wanted to…."

"What do you mean?"

"I'm not sure I want to go back," said Derek. "I like it here. But don't worry about me. Just figure out how to get back to your own time."

"Yeah. I just don't know how."

"I don't think you have to reverse the past," Derek replied. "Just…well, create a bridge to that past so you can get back there."

"Yeah," said Neill. "Yeah, that makes sense!"

"It's like you need a…what's the word…a portal, no, a wormhole, so you can get back to it."

"A wormhole?" said Neill.

"Yeah, like on that TV show *Stargate*. The Stargate connects them to different planets so they can travel from one to the other easily, but you need one that connects us to different times, and then you just dial the right coordinates to get there."

"I never watched *Stargate*," said Neill.

"Well, I did. I used to watch it all the time when I was in elementary school."

"Can you explain it to Howard?"

"I think so," said Derek. "But right now I need some sleep."

"Tomorrow?" asked Neill.

"Tomorrow night after work," said Derek. "Hey, I think Allison used to watch it too. Maybe she could explain it to Howard tomorrow. That way you won't have to wait."

"Okay," said Neill. "I'll talk to her in the morning. I have to work too, but maybe she can get time alone with Howard tomorrow to explain it to him. Then he can…well, figure out how to make a wormhole."

"Oh," said Derek.

"What?"

"Well, I doubt making a wormhole is easy. You probably need some big equipment for that. And I don't think anyone has actually ever done it. I don't even think we know if wormholes are real. They might just be a theory."

"Still," said Neill, thinking Derek seemed a lot smarter than he let on sometimes, "if Howard could figure it out from reading his journals, or if the runes hold the key…?"

"Those are big ifs," said Derek, yawning. "I'm sorry. I'm beat. Just be patient. It must be possible somehow since we've already time traveled to different times. You just have to hang in there until we can figure it out."

"Yeah," said Neill. "I just hope it doesn't take years."

"Worrying about it won't help," Derek advised, rolling over onto his side. "Just take it one day at a time. Now, can you turn off the light?"

"Sure, just a minute," said Neill, quickly changing into his nightshirt and then flipping off the light switch. "Good night."

Chapter 11

I N THE MORNING, HOWARD STOPPED by Derek and Neill's room before breakfast. Neill told him Derek must have already gone downstairs to eat because his bed was empty when Neill woke. Neill was about to head downstairs himself so he could get to Getz's before it opened.

Neill also explained he hadn't looked at the time travel device or cell phone the night before because he didn't have any tools to open them with. At that point, Allison heard Howard's voice and unlocked her door to enter the boys' room. After greeting Howard, she said to Neill, "Howard and I can work on trying to get them apart today while you and Derek are at work."

"I don't think that's a good idea," Howard told Allison. "It wouldn't be decorous for you and me to be alone together."

"Why not?" asked Allison.

"You are not related to me," said Howard. "You shouldn't be alone with me without the protection of one of your brothers."

"Protection?" Allison let out an unladylike snort. "They're not even my brothers."

"Still," Howard replied, "my mother would be very upset if we were to be alone together. It would be better if I try to take the devices apart myself. I can go find some tools without raising suspicion since I live here, whereas you are guests."

"I think Howard is right," said Neill. He stepped over to the bedside table to retrieve the time travel device for Howard. Meanwhile, Allison went into her room to fetch her cell phone to give Howard.

Once Howard had both instruments in his hands, he turned them over and realized just how difficult they would be to take apart.

"I have another idea," said Neill, "but it's kind of complicated to explain. Allison, Derek reminded me that on the TV show *Stargate* they used a wormhole to get from one planet to another. I was thinking maybe we also need a wormhole to get back to our correct time. Derek reminded me that when we were in the future, Xander and Jorgen told us that when you cause something to happen outside of the historical time stream, you don't really change the past; instead, you create a new timeline. That means Howard doesn't have to die for us to return the past to how it used to be."

"Thank goodness," said Howard.

"And hey," Neill continued, "I just realized, even though I was in a different version of 2021, when I emailed you, you were still in the version I had come from, so the past didn't really change after all. So, all we need to do is figure out how to open a wormhole to our own version of 2021."

"Oh, Neill!" said Allison. "You're right! Though, I have no idea how to create a wormhole."

"What's a TV show?" asked Howard, still trying to catch up with what they were talking about.

"Howard, I can explain it all to you," said Allison. "But you will have to spend time alone with me."

"But how?" asked Howard, looking astonished. "I respect you far too much to jeopardize your good reputation."

"Just leave that to me," said Allison. "Neill, you better get going or you'll be late for work."

"Okay," he said. "Good luck, Allison."

"I'll go hide these in my room," said Howard, referring to the time travel device and cell phone, "and then meet you downstairs."

They parted, and although they all saw each other at breakfast a few minutes later, they could not say much more to each other. Derek had already left with Mr. Longyear, and Neill quickly ate so he could get to work on time. As they ate, Helen said to Allison, "We were hoping you would like to go on a picnic with us today."

"I'd love to," said Allison. "Howard, will you be going?"

"Certainly," he said, although he shot Neill an apologetic look, as if to say now his plans to work on the time device were ruined. Neill, however, knew Allison would figure out how to find time to explain wormholes to Howard. Once he understood those, it might get them a step closer to returning to their own time.

Soon, Neill was walking to Getz's. His strong work ethic made him want to be on time, and like most people, he was a little nervous about his first day at work. He made it there with only a minute to spare, but Mr. Getz greeted him cordially, and the other clerks were friendly as they explained the business to him. Mr. Getz showed him the ledgers and what needed to be done. Neill immediately saw how much work bookkeeping would be without a computer or spreadsheets that automatically calculated totals. The store didn't even have a pocket calculator. He'd have to do all the math in his head or by hand on paper. He was good at math, so he could do that, but it was just all so much more time-consuming than he ever could have imagined. He wondered if he would be working at Getz's the rest of his life if he and his friends couldn't figure out how to get him back to his own time.

Chapter 12

DEREK DID NOT RETURN HOME for supper that evening. He and a fellow worker, as Mr. Longyear explained, would be spending a couple of nights at the Breitung Hotel in Negaunee. That would make it easier for them to do some survey work on the western end of Marquette County. Howard, Allison, and Neill all exchanged frustrated glances at this announcement. Neill also felt irritated that by the time he had gotten home from work, he'd had to change for dinner so he'd had no time to ask Allison or Howard if they had made any progress on learning more about the dolmen and its runes or how he might return home.

However, dinner conversation revealed that while Allison had gone on the picnic to Presque Isle Park with the rest of the family, Howard had stayed home, claiming he had a headache.

"I hope your headache is better now," Mrs. Longyear said to Howard. "I don't understand why it tormented you for so long. You know headaches are a state of mind that we can easily heal by changing our thoughts."

"I think I was just tired," replied Howard. "I didn't sleep very well last night."

"How well we sleep is also related to our thoughts," said Mrs. Longyear.

"Son," asked Mr. Longyear, "is something bothering you that you didn't sleep?"

"No," said Howard, then added—Neill could tell he was trying to come up with a plausible excuse to evade his parents' curiosity, "well, maybe I've been thinking too much about poor Hugh. I do miss him."

"I can understand that, Howard," said Mrs. Longyear, "but you know you will see him again in the next life."

"I know," Howard replied, "but I'm still young. I expected we would be friends for a long time, and now it could be fifty or more years before I see him."

"Time is eternal," said Mrs. Longyear. "Trust me, fifty years will go very quickly. Your father and I can't believe how old we are already, and once you are with Hugh in the Lord's presence, it will seem like your separation never took place."

"I hope so," Howard replied.

"Recovering from a loss just takes time," Mr. Longyear added, more direct in his speech than his wife. "Your grief will lessen as time goes by. After all, it's only been a few weeks since Hugh's passing."

"Mother," said Abby, "we should go call on the Allens. We haven't seen them since the funeral."

"That's true," said Mrs. Longyear. The conversation then turned to deciding when would be a good time to visit the grieving family.

"I'm sure," Helen said, turning to Neill, "that Mr. Allen will be happy to hear you've regained your memory. I know he appreciates what a good friend you were to Hugh in the short time you knew him."

"If I had really been a good friend," said Neill, "I would have tried harder to save him." Now that he realized he had not changed the past but created a new version of it, he would have liked to have seen Hugh and Howard both live.

"Don't blame yourself," Howard replied. "There was nothing we could do. Hugh simply disappeared under the water. We had no way to find him."

"Surely, the Allens don't blame you," said Mrs. Longyear. "Mrs. Allen expressed to me how glad she was that you and Howard survived."

"Still," said Neill, "it is hard to accept that you've survived when another is gone."

Although he did not say so, Neill felt a little guilty that he had not thought much about the Allens since the funeral. In truth, he had been so focused on trying to figure out how to get back to his own time that he hadn't given much thought to anyone else's feelings. Now, thinking of the grieving Allen family, he felt acutely how much he was still grieving the loss of Uncle Chad, though it had been eighteen months since his passing. One reason he wanted to get home was he knew how hard it had been on his father to lose his brother, and he did not want to put him through the grief of losing his son as well. *I never should have gone up to the Club this summer*, he thought. *I should have stayed home and spent more time with my dad. After all, now I realize how quickly you can lose someone you love.*

"I think we should go back up to the Club this weekend," said Mr. Longyear, changing the subject. "It would do us all good to get away."

"I want to go stay up there by myself," said Jack.

"That's not going to happen," his father replied.

"Why not?" asked Jack. "You let Howard stay up there by himself."

"Howard was trying to find Neill after he disappeared, and besides, your older brother is a grown man. You are not."

"I'm almost eleven," protested Jack.

Mr. Longyear simply glared at his middle son.

"You might get eaten by a bear," Rob told his brother.

"I'd shoot the bear," Jack replied.

"You aren't shooting any bear until you're at least twelve," Mr. Longyear replied.

"I'm a good shot," said Jack. "Ask Howard. He's seen me shoot."

"*Howard!*" exclaimed Mrs. Longyear, her eyes growing huge. "Howard, did you let him shoot a gun?"

"I stood behind him and held onto it," said Howard, "and we only shot at a tree."

"I hit the tree, though," said Jack.

"A tree is a lot easier to shoot than a wild animal," Helen told Jack.

"Why?" asked Rob.

"Because a wild animal is moving," Mr. Longyear replied. "Anyway, that's enough talk of shooting. No more."

"But I want—" began Jack.

"No more," repeated his father, looking him in the eye. "Do you understand, sir?"

"Yes, sir," Jack replied, lowering his head from his father's piercing gaze.

The servants now came in to collect the dishes.

"Are we not to have dessert?" Mr. Longyear asked.

"Oh, no," said Mrs. Longyear. "I've had too much as it is."

"I don't need any," Howard said. "Allison, would you like to go for a walk?"

Neill caught Mrs. Longyear's look of dismay at this request. Allison also saw it and quickly replied, "Yes, if my brother will come with us."

John Munro Longyear and Mary Beecher Longyear

Mrs. Longyear's alarm changed to a look of relief. Neill suspected she trusted in her son's morality, but perhaps not yet Allison's.

"I'll be happy to go and keep my sister company," Neill replied.

"Can I go too?" asked Jack.

"No," said Mr. Longyear. "We're going to Stafford's to get ice cream."

"Me too?" asked Rob.

"Of course," said Mr. Longyear. "Anyone who wants to can join us."

"Not me," said Mrs. Longyear. "I have to watch my figure."

"That's why we'll walk there," Mr. Longyear told his wife. "A walk will counterbalance the ice cream."

"Thank you, but you go with the children," Mrs. Longyear replied. "I'm almost done reading *Science and Health*, and I want to finish it this evening."

"You've read it many times," her husband reminded her. "I'm sure Mrs. Eddy would understand if you put it off another night."

"You know this is a new edition," Mrs. Longyear stated, as if that made finishing it that evening imperative.

"Very well," said Mr. Longyear. "I'm sure the children and I do not wish to interfere with your spiritual welfare."

"I'm ready whenever you are, Howard," said Allison, wishing to relieve the strained environment she felt whenever Mrs. Longyear's obsession with Christian Science became the center of conversation.

In another minute, Neill, Howard, and Allison were out the front door and heading down the driveway to Arch Street.

"So, what's the latest news?" Neill asked his friends once they were out of the hearing range of the mansion's open windows.

"I didn't have a chance to talk to Howard at all since he stayed home from the picnic," said Allison, sounding perturbed.

"I'm sorry," said Howard, "but I just couldn't bear wasting the day when I could be trying to translate those runes."

"I suppose spending the day with me would have been wasting it," Allison replied. Her tone surprised Neill.

"I want to do everything I can to help you get home," Howard replied, boldly taking her hand in his.

His affectionate move quickly silenced Allison.

"Well, did you have any success?" Neill asked Howard.

"Not exactly," Howard replied, "but I made some progress with translating the runes. Some of them are very confusing, and I can't find anything equivalent to them in the book from the library. I know they say something about Wotan, or Odin, as most people pronounce it today."

"Odin, the Norse god?" asked Allison, expressing the surprise Neill felt.

"Yes," said Howard. "It makes me wonder whether the dolmen is some sort of religious altar. The book also talks about magical charms associated with Odin, so I wonder if the inscription on the altar is some kind of charm. So far, I know it begins with something like, 'Here is Odin who knows…' but then there are some words I haven't made out yet."

"That's disappointing," said Neill.

"But fascinating too," said Allison. "What do you think Odin knows?"

"I have no idea," Howard replied. "I believe Odin was supposed to know everything. I can't quite remember how it goes, but I think in Norse mythology, he gave up an eye in exchange for getting to drink water from a magic well that allowed him to obtain all knowledge. There's a book of Norse myths I read when I was a kid that must be in the house somewhere—maybe John or Judith has it now. I'll have to look in their rooms for it when they aren't around so no one suspects anything."

"Well, besides trying to keep translating the runes," said Neill, "what do we do now?"

"Should we take apart the cell phone and time travel device still?" asked Allison.

"I don't know," said Howard. "I can't even imagine how to get the cell phone apart without breaking it, and the time travel device is one solid piece of copper shaped to surround the entire device, so there's no way to get inside to see its mechanisms. It's very frustrating."

"We know the cell phone is able to trigger time travel somehow," said Neill, "so I think we should just leave it alone in case we figure out the message from the runes and then can use it. We don't want the battery to die in it."

"It's bound to, though," said Allison, "if we don't figure things out in the next day or two."

"True," said Neill.

"I'll just keep working on it," said Howard. "There must be some way."

"What about your journal from the future, Howard?" asked Neill. "Did you read any more of it?"

"No," said Howard. "I was too caught up in trying to translate the runes."

"But I'm sure you figured out time travel in the future," said Neill, "or at least in the alternative future I stole it from. Maybe the answer to the runes is in the journal. Maybe you figured out the inscription in the future too."

"Maybe," said Howard, "but...."

"But what?" asked Allison.

"But I don't know if I want to read that journal. I'm not sure I want to know what could become of me."

"But that's a different future," Neill reminded him. "That future in which you wrote it didn't include me showing up again in 1900, and Allison wasn't in that time either, so that future isn't necessarily what your future will now be."

"But it's the future in which I married your great-great-grandmother," Howard replied. "You don't want me to marry her, but what if I read in there something about our relationship that makes me fall in love with her and jinx the whole thing."

"I doubt that," said Neill, laughing when Allison's eyes grew wide at the thought. "The journal isn't very long and looks like it mostly has mathematical equations and such in it. I think you must have used it solely to write about your scientific pursuits, not to recall your love life."

Howard smirked, as if he knew Neill was correct, but he still felt resistant.

"Howard," asked Allison, "what are you really afraid of?"

"I just don't want to know the future," he said. "It's hard enough knowing I should be dead."

"But it's not like that," said Neill. "Like I already told you, Jorgen and Xander said when you alter the past, you don't really change it; you just start a different past that runs parallel to the old one."

"Oh, right," said Howard.

"So that means, the version of 2021 that I came from still exists. I just created a new version of it that I went to after I saved you from drowning."

"Cool!" said Allison.

"Then," said Howard, thinking too hard to be concerned about Allison's strange expression, "whatever the journals reveal about my future doesn't mean that is my future?"

"Exactly," said Neill, glad Howard had got it.

"Wow," said Howard. "In some ways, that sounds really complicated, but in other ways, it simplifies things, especially since you don't have to try to change the past again then. You just have to get back to your own time."

"Yes!" said Neill, excited that Howard understood. "That's why we need a wormhole."

"What exactly is that?" asked Howard.

Allison explained to him about how in the *Stargate* TV show, they used a wormhole to travel from one planet to another, and that you could probably also use one to travel from one time to another.

"That makes sense," said Howard, "but how do we make one?"

"That's the problem," said Allison. "No one ever has; in fact, it's just a theory, so no one is even sure a wormhole can exist."

"You're awful smart for a girl," said Howard.

Allison raised her eyebrows. If Neill or Derek had said that to her, Neill knew she would have said they were sexist, but after a second, Neill could see she was accepting that Howard was a product of his time.

"Anyway, I need some time to wrap my head around all this," said Howard, "but I think a wormhole must be possible because how else could you have time traveled so far? Obviously, the dolmen must be some sort of gateway or must open up a wormhole, and the cell phone or time travel devices are maybe like keys to unlock the gate into the wormhole."

"But the time travel device doesn't need to work in conjunction with the dolmen like the cell phone. It seems to be independent of it," Neill said.

"True," Howard replied, "and the time travel device is definitely broken. When everyone was at the picnic, I examined it and tried to turn the dial on it, but it is smashed beyond repair. I don't think it will work at all, so all our hope lies in the dolmen."

"And in your journals," said Neill.

"Ye-es," Howard replied.

"Howard," said Neill, "you need to read those journals. They could be the solution to all of our problems."

"Maybe to yours," said Howard. "They could be the start to mine."

"But I already explained to you that they don't hold the answers to your definite future," Neill said.

"Still," said Howard, "reading them is like eating the apple in the Garden of Eden. I could suddenly know things it might be better for me not to know."

Allison squeezed his hand, sensing his fear. Returning the pressure, Howard leaned over and gave her a kiss on the cheek. Neill thought how people would sometimes brave everything for love. Would Howard overcome his qualms about forbidden knowledge out of love for Allison so she could get home safely?

"This is all so complicated," said Howard, "but I'll keep working on the runes, and if we go up to the Club this weekend, we could explore the dolmen some more. After the part of the translation where I was stuck, the runes did say something like 'Here is' or 'Here is buried' so there must be something there that we missed."

"*Buried*?" said Neill. "But the dolmen is on top of a rocky outcropping on Mount Huron. How could something be buried beneath it?"

"I don't know," said Howard, "but something must be buried under it or close by. Maybe something magnetic or electrical that might trigger your cell phone to open up the wormhole that makes time travel possible."

"Howard!" someone shouted, interrupting their conversation.

Turning, they saw Rob running toward them. The three of them had turned down Cedar Street to Michigan and then walked toward Front Street. They had now turned onto Front and walked to Arch.

Meanwhile, the rest of the Longyear family, minus its matriarch, had made their way down Ridge Street to Front where Rob had spotted them. The Longyears had set out just five minutes after them and walked three blocks less.

"I guess we'll have to pick up this conversation later," Howard said to Allison and Neill.

"Come have ice cream with us!" Abby called to them.

Howard waved at them, and in a couple of minutes, the two parties had united and started down Front Street together in the direction of Stafford's.

Neill was frustrated by the interruption, but he realized there was little more they could discuss that evening. He wished Howard would just read the journal, but at least he was making progress on the runes. And when Rob grabbed his hand, asking him what kind of ice cream he wanted, Neill decided being in this time wasn't so terrible, provided it would only be for a little while longer.

Chapter 13

FOR THE REST OF THAT week, Derek stayed at a hotel in Negaunee while he worked with some of Mr. Longyear's other employees on the west end of the county. Meanwhile, Neill kept busy working at Getz's. He spent the evenings playing croquet, or on hotter days, using the family's private bowling alley at the back of the Longyear property. The Longyear children were surprisingly skilled bowlers.

Neill wasn't able to get time alone with Howard, but because of their adjoining rooms, he and Allison were able to talk in private, and then she would update him on Howard's continuing attempts to translate the runes. By this point, Neill could see Allison was totally smitten with Howard. Whenever Neill was alone with her, she was always relating some joke he had made or remarking how kind he was to his sisters. She also thought Mrs. Longyear was starting to warm up to her, though Neill was not so sure. Mr. Longyear definitely seemed oblivious to the romance brewing between his oldest son and houseguest.

When Neill finally asked Allison how serious she was about Howard, she admitted she was falling in love with him. When he asked her if she planned to return with him to 2021, she was noncommittal.

"What about your mother?" he asked.

Allison paused, then said, "It'll be hard, but she'll get by without me."

Neill was shocked by this response. She had seemed so broken up about not seeing her mother before.

"It will be devastating to her," said Neill, "not to know what became of you."

"I know," she replied, "but the worst is probably over for her now that I've been missing for several days."

Neill was surprised she sounded so casual about it. He had been missing longer, yet he constantly thought about how devastating it must be for his parents, especially after the loss of Uncle Chad.

"You barely know Howard," Neill told Allison. "Is he really worth deserting your mother over?"

"Brian will look after her," Allison replied. "She's been dating him for a while now, and it's getting pretty serious."

Neill wasn't sure what Allison considered "a while." Her mother had met Brian through an online dating site. He was from Gladstone, more than an hour away from Marquette. They had only started to see each other in person that spring after they had gotten their COVID-19 vaccinations. Neill could not imagine how a short-time boyfriend was expected to make up for a daughter of nineteen years.

"I don't think you're thinking this through," Neill told Allison.

"What's there to think through?" asked Allison. "I love Howard, and I know he's a gentleman and will take care of me."

"Couldn't you find a gentleman in our time?" Neill asked.

"Who, Neill?" she replied. "Who is there but you? And I can't marry you; you're like my brother."

"What about Derek?"

"The Derek from our time is a good guy, but he and I don't have the same interests or goals. It would never work. And the Derek from the alternate 2021…well, I could never love someone who had dated that nasty other version of me."

"But," said Neill, "don't you worry that Howard's rather sexist; I mean, maybe not intentionally, but because of the time he's from."

"Sure, now and then he says something a bit demeaning to women," Allison replied, "but he doesn't know he's doing it, and when I point it out to him, he acts surprised to realize I'm right, and then he tells me how refreshing my perspective is. He says he hates when he sees his sisters acting like they have to be less smart because they are women. He even supports a woman's right to vote."

Neill didn't know what more to say. He liked Howard. He was sure Howard would make a great husband for Allison. If Allison loved him, who was he to say they couldn't be together? It was just the time difference he had difficulty getting over. And look at Derek; he seemed happy to be off working with Mr. Longyear. He wasn't concerned at all about getting back to his own time. Both of his friends astounded Neill, especially since he felt nothing in his own life would be right until he got home.

"Don't worry about me, Neill," said Allison. "I know you would miss me if you went back to our time, but I have to do what feels right for me. Until recently, you've acted like time travel only made a mess of things because you thought you had changed the past. Now that we understand you didn't, we need to see being here as an opportunity. That's what I'm doing, and frankly, you could enjoy your time here more."

Neill couldn't argue with that. Someday, he might see this all as a great adventure. Maybe he should take advantage of it while he was here? But knowing his parents were worrying made him feel that was almost impossible.

On Thursday evening after dinner, Neill and Allison accompanied Howard, his parents, and Helen and Abby to the Allens' home to pay a call. Neill had struggled with trying to think what to say to the grieving family, but he was not at all prepared to see them all sitting glumly in their parlor dressed in black. He had only met Mrs. Allen and the other Allen children at Hugh's funeral, but he knew if Hugh were still alive, he would be aghast at their somber demeanors. Mrs. Longyear embarked on a speech about how Hugh was still alive and his parents just had to be patient until they could see him again. The Allens were polite in their responses, but Neill doubted they found any comfort in the visit.

"At least they know we care," said Mr. Longyear as they walked back to the mansion. "That's the important thing. For them to know they aren't alone in their grief. Hugh was a special boy, and we will always miss him."

Neill noticed Howard tearing up at these words. When Neill patted him on the shoulder, Howard whispered, "It should have been me. I wish you had saved Hugh and not me."

Neill could not help realizing how fragile life was. He remembered that fatal day when Uncle Chad had called him in desperation. He'd gotten a blood clot, and in great pain, had called his nephew, probably because Neill's number was the first contact that came up on his phone. Before Neill or the ambulance could arrive, Uncle Chad had dropped dead. Just calling a minute or two sooner could have made such a difference. The same was true with Hugh. If, once he was in the canoe, Neill had just paddled faster toward Hugh and

Howard, everything might have been different. Hugh would still be alive, and who knew what wonderful things he might have done? A minute or two sooner and Uncle Chad might still be alive, and then Neill would not have to feel such guilt over not getting there in time, and his father would not be so depressed now. For all Mrs. Longyear's talk of eternal life, Neill felt little consolation in knowing he would be parted from those he loved for decades before he joined them, and then, only if eternal life were real. He had his doubts.

Chapter 14

NEILL HAD BEEN LOOKING FORWARD to Derek returning to Marquette for the weekend, assuming he would go up to the Club with them, but he quickly realized a quick weekend excursion to the Huron Mountain Club was not possible in this time. There was no train yet that went to Big Bay, much less the Club, and no automobiles, and to try to travel overland was a two-day journey. The only way to get there was by boat, and that took a good chunk out of the day. They would spend most of Saturday traveling, so they wouldn't just turn around and go back on Sunday to ensure he and Derek could be back to work on Monday. Instead, they would stay a few days.

Then Mr. Longyear said Derek wouldn't be going because he needed to continue the surveying work in West Marquette County. Neill felt irritated over this since Mr. Longyear had initially assured them Derek would be able to stay with them at the mansion. But then Mr. Longyear said Derek had volunteered to stay in Negaunee and work on Saturday. That meant he would not be around even on Friday evening before they left for the Club. Neill wondered if Derek was trying to avoid him and Allison. He didn't understand why his friend would. He tried to tell himself Derek wasn't essential to the effort to get him back to his own time so it didn't matter, but the truth was Neill found he was missing the new version of his old friend.

Neill had to do some convincing to get Mr. Getz to let him off for a few days so he could go to the Club. These late Victorians had no real concept of a weekend. They usually worked at least half-days on Saturday. Nor did they know how to do things quickly since they didn't have the technology for it. Neill was so used to living in the fast-paced twenty-first century that he found it all very frustrating. Mr. Getz begrudgingly gave him the time off because the Longyears were his valued customers, but if he hadn't, Neill had considered quitting; getting back to the dolmen was the only thing that really mattered to him at this point. He promised Mr. Getz to work extra if needed when he returned, but he secretly wondered if he would return; it all depended on whether Howard, Allison, and he figured out how to time travel back to his own time that weekend.

Once they arrived at the Club, Howard, Neill, and Allison found it hard to get away from the rest of the family. It was late Saturday and would be dark soon after they reached the Club, so nothing could be done about the dolmen that evening. They had a late supper, then joined some of the other Club members at a bonfire where they roasted marshmallows and sang camp songs until well after midnight.

Sunday morning, they slept in, then had a huge pancake breakfast. Mrs. Longyear insisted on having a private Christian Science service, which mostly comprised reading Mary Baker Eddy's *Science and Health* and then discussing it. Neill and Allison said little, but politely listened, and it did give them time to digest their breakfast before they all went swimming that afternoon at the younger children's urging. Once thoroughly soaked, they followed that activity with rowing across Pine Lake and having a picnic lunch on the other side. The afternoon was filled with a long family hike, a return to the compound, and general merriment as they cooked dinner. More singing around a campfire followed until they all fell asleep, happily exhausted.

All except Neill, who kept wondering when he, Allison, and Howard would get to the dolmen. Neill and Howard were sharing a room with Jack and Rob, and by bedtime, Neill was despairing that he'd be stuck having another day of family time. But once the younger boys fell asleep, Howard whispered to Neill that they would get up at daybreak before anyone else was astir and head for the dolmen. Neill was concerned Allison wouldn't accompany them, so although Howard thought it risky, he went to the girls' room and knocked on the door. After Abby answered, he apologized for disturbing them and asked to speak to his sister. Allison answered the summons by talking to him in the hall in her nightgown. After Neill explained the plan, she promised to do her best to join him and Howard in the morning.

Once Neill went to bed, he was afraid he wouldn't wake in time, which caused him to lie awake for what seemed an eternity, but at some point, he finally fell asleep.

Neill woke to see the first glimmer of daylight in the sky, and then he heard movement.

"Howard?" he whispered.

"Get up," Howard whispered back.

A few minutes later, both were dressed and waiting outside for Allison. They stood to one side where no one could see them. After a few minutes, when they were beginning to think they'd have to go without her, they heard the back door open, and then Allison was with them.

Without a word, the three scurried toward the woods. They waited to speak until they were far enough away not to be overheard. Then Howard said he had left a note on the kitchen table stating that they had gone out for an early walk. Hopefully, everyone would just assume the young lovers wanted time alone, with their chaperone, Neill, of course.

Howard brought the dolmen rubbings with him, hoping to finish the translation. He had figured out all but one word that he thought he must not have copied properly. He also brought the book on runes, but Neill noted Howard had not brought his journal from the future.

"I wasn't completely accurate earlier in what I thought the rubbings read," said Howard as they trudged through the woods. "I know now that it begins, 'Here lies the eye of Odin,' but what follows isn't as clear. It says something like 'By which all *blank* are known,' but I can't make out the word that fills in the blank."

"What do you think it might be?" asked Allison.

"I don't really know," Howard replied.

"Maybe it's wisdom?" said Neill. "By which all wisdom is known."

"No," said Howard. "That seems like the obvious wording, but I'm sure it's not that. It doesn't resemble the word for wisdom or knowledge or anything similar."

"Do you still think it means something might be buried beneath the dolmen?" asked Allison.

"I still don't know how that can be possible," said Neill. "Isn't it all solid rock under the dolmen?"

"It looked that way to me," Howard said, "but I could be wrong. I don't know what else 'the eye of Odin' could mean unless it's the dolmen itself. We'll just have to investigate the ground when we get there."

"What if it's a treasure?" asked Allison. "Will we be able to keep it?"

"A treasure would be exciting," said Howard, "but I doubt it's that. It's supposed to be Odin's eye."

"It can't be a real eye," said Allison. "It would be all moldy or decayed by now."

"I suspect the phrase is metaphorical," said Neill. "Aren't jewels sometimes known as the eye of something? It could be a diamond or a ruby."

"Oh, yeah, it could be like a detachable eye made out of a jewel," said Allison. "Kind of like the detachable eye the three witches have in *Macbeth*, or was that in the Perseus legend?"

"Like in *Clash of the Titans*?" asked Neill. "The Stygian witches have an eye."

"Oh, yeah," said Allison. "I don't really remember much about that film; I was too distracted by Harry Hamlin's hotness."

"Who's Harry Hamlin?" asked Howard, sounding jealous. "Is he a beau of yours?"

"Oh, no," said Allison.

"He's a movie star," said Neill.

"What's a movie star?" asked Howard.

"Someone who acts in movies," said Allison. "You know, moving pictures. An actor like in a stage play, but instead in moving pictures."

"Oh," said Howard. "And you know this *Harry* personally?"

"I wish," said Allison.

Neill laughed and replied, "Harry Hamlin is old enough to be your grandfather." Then he turned to Howard and said, "You have nothing to be jealous about. She's never met Harry Hamlin and never will."

"I hope not," said Howard, reaching out to take Allison's hand.

"Don't worry, Howard," she replied, letting his fingers curl around hers. "You know how I feel about you."

"And you know how I feel about you," Howard replied.

The conversation now dwindled as Allison and Howard seemed content to hold hands in the early morning sunlight that seeped between the trees. Neill was tired from not sleeping well and anxious to get to the dolmen, so he didn't much feel like talking.

"Well, we're almost there," Neill finally said when they reached Mount Huron. "Hopefully, the mystery of Odin's eye will soon be solved."

Neill felt grateful for the cool morning breeze as they started climbing up the fifteen-hundred-foot mountain.

After a few hundred feet, Allison said, "I know you want to get home, Neill, but it's such a beautiful day, and everything is so very green; don't you think it's a blessing for us just to be here in this moment?"

"Yes," said Neill. "I am anxious to get home, but you're right; after all I've been through, I'm lucky just to be alive and have two good friends to help me."

"And to be surrounded by God's beauty," said Allison. "During the pandemic, I've sometimes wondered if God even exists, but how can we doubt it when we see the magnificence of the creation?"

Neill looked around, admiring the tall pine trees, the blueberry bushes now bearing fruit, the magnificent blue sky with barely a cloud, and the overwhelmingly lush green foliage everywhere. He had scarcely noticed any of it since he had begun his worrisome quest to return home, but Allison was right—there was beauty everywhere. He just hoped she was correct that it was all a reminder that God was in charge.

"Whatever happens," Howard said, "it will all be well. God is watching over us and works all things for our good when we trust in him."

Neill was not so sure about that after what he'd experienced in the last couple of years. First, Uncle Chad had died so unexpectedly, and then the pandemic had begun and it was still continuing, despite people being vaccinated; more than 600,000 Americans had died to date, plus nearly 4 million people worldwide; and then last summer there had been the race riots and all the political turmoil, and to top it all off, he had mysteriously time traveled here and seen Hugh drown. How could he believe in a God who ordered the world when he was surrounded by such chaos? He knew people said God worked in mysterious ways, but if that was the case, he wished the great mystery of life's meaning would be solved—though today he would settle for a solution to this time travel mystery.

"There it is," said Howard, pointing up to the dolmen as it came into view.

"It seems strange," said Allison, "that such a small thing can have so much importance to us."

"It's not that small," said Neill as they drew closer. "It's not very tall, but I remember someone telling me that top stone weighs seven hundred pounds."

"If that's the case, we'll never be able to dig under it or move it," said Allison.

"Derek claimed a couple of guys his size could have moved it," said Neill.

"I have no doubt Derek is a fine physical specimen," Howard replied, "but I doubt we could move it even if he were with us."

By now, Howard was beside the dolmen. He knelt down and began running his fingers over the carvings, which had become faint from years of exposure to Mother Nature's elements.

"Which rune is the one you can't make out?" asked Allison, taking the cell phone from her pocket and setting it on the ground so they'd have it if they needed it later, but also to ensure she didn't get transported in time by accident.

"That's what I'm trying to figure out," Howard replied. He retrieved the rubbings from inside his jacket. Neill held onto the library book, ready to search inside of it as needed.

Several minutes passed as Howard tried to line up the rubbings he had made with the stone to determine where the rune he hadn't been able to translate was located. Then he did a fresh rubbing and compared it to his earlier rubbing as Allison and Neill anxiously watched.

"That's it!" he exclaimed after a minute of contemplation. "See where this part of this letter jags outward? I missed that when I did the earlier rubbing."

"But what does it mean?" asked Allison, looking at the paper.

"Hopefully, we'll know in a moment," said Howard. "Neill, let me see the book." Neill handed it to him, then waited breathlessly as Howard flipped the pages back and forth in his quest for a translation. After scanning a page, his eyes would start to light up, but then he would frown and flip to another page, and then his brows would raise, followed by him frowning again.

Finally, excitement gleamed in his eyes. "Eureka!" he cried. "I think that's the most appropriate word for this discovery. That word I couldn't read means *eons* or *ages*—periods of time. That's what it means."

"So, what does the whole quote say then?" asked Allison.

Howard looked again at his original rubbing, where he'd written his translation, then read:

> "Here lies the eye of Odin
> By which all ages are known."

"All ages," said Neill. "That makes sense—ages are like time periods. It must be a reference to time travel. It's saying that Odin's eye has the ability to see into all periods from history, just like I've been able to travel to different time periods."

"Yes, that makes sense," said Allison.

"But what or where is the actual eye?" asked Howard. "And how do we know that seeing all times in history is the same as traveling to other times?"

"I don't know," said Neill, "but let's look for other clues. None of us at first noticed the faded runes on the dolmen, so maybe there are other things we've overlooked."

"Maybe there's something like a secret latch," said Allison. "Maybe it'll flip open and the eye will be inside."

"No," said Howard, running his hand over the top stone. "This rock is solid. I don't think it opens or slides or does anything like that."

"What about the smaller stones holding it up?" asked Allison.

Neill got down on his knees opposite the side of the dolmen where Howard and Allison stood. He began looking carefully at one of the three smaller stones that made up the pedestal the larger stone rested upon.

Howard bent down to examine the supporting stone nearest him, and Allison did the same with the remaining one.

Neill was just about to say he had found nothing when Allison suggested they try to slide the stones sideways.

"We don't want to knock over the dolmen," Howard replied. "If the big rock falls, we'll never be able to lift it to rebuild it. It would be a shame to have that happen."

But Neill paid him no heed. The rock before him had a pointy top and was not very level beneath so that when he tried, using incredible effort, it moved just slightly, almost as if rotating. Suddenly, they all heard a jarring sound.

"Watch out, Neill!" warned Howard. "If the large stone falls, you'll crush your hand!"

But Neill wasn't watching; he was listening. "Didn't you hear that?" he asked.

"Hear what?" asked Allison.

"It was like a scraping or opening noise," he replied, and then he put his head almost under the giant supported stone and looked up.

"Oh, wow!" he said.

"What is it?" asked Allison.

"It's a door. When I moved the stone, it pushed open a sliding door on the bottom. It's hard to see, but…" He reached up as Howard and Allison kneeled down to see what he was doing. "There's something in here."

Neill had his hand up inside the stone, through the open door.

"What is it?" asked Allison.

"I don't know," said Neill. He couldn't reach it easily, so he crawled backward, then lay down on his back and slid himself under the stone as if he were a mechanic under a car.

"Be careful," said Howard.

Neill reached up and this time was able to grab whatever was inside the stone. He felt some sort of base and then a globe of some sort that was cold to the touch. The base felt metallic while the globe felt like glass. Gently, he wrapped his hand around the back of it and started to push it toward him until he could get it far enough over the opening to grab it with his other hand. There was barely room under the stone for him, much less the object, which was shaped like a giant glass ball. He had to scoot himself out with his hands behind his head and try to set it down behind him. Then he pulled himself out from under the dolmen. Once the space was clear, Allison bent down and drew the strange device forward.

"Be careful," Howard repeated, but Allison managed to pull it out without trouble. In another second, she was standing up and placing the device on top of the dolmen.

"Why, it's like a snow globe," said Neill, "but without the snow."

"Or like a witch's crystal ball," said Allison.

"But what is it?" asked Neill, thinking it looked very complicated—the base seemed to have buttons all around it.

"Why, obviously," said Howard, "it's Odin's Eye."

Chapter 15

"I**T MUST BE A TIME-TRAVEL** device," said Neill, staring at what Howard had just dubbed Odin's Eye, "especially with all those buttons and controls all around it."

The globe itself was about six inches tall. The base was about three inches high at the center where it supported the globe, but it sloped down so that it was only about an inch high at the very ends, which had made it easy for Neill to grasp. All about the base in a circle were little buttons, about six rows of them, shiny gold buttons like one would see on a very small pocket calculator. Each button had upon it a letter or number or rune—Neill wasn't quite sure what they were. Some levers and other small instruments were also sporadically spread around the base.

"It's so strange-looking," said Allison. "How old do you think it is?"

"I don't know," Howard replied. "I imagine it dates back to the Vikings. They must have brought it here, although I never heard that the Vikings had technology like this."

"No, me neither," said Neill, thinking it resembled something out of a science fiction or fantasy film, maybe something from the Victorian steampunk genre.

"I wish we knew how to make it work," said Allison.

"I'm afraid to touch it," Neill replied. "Pushing any one of those buttons might transport us to another time."

"I don't think it's that simple," said Howard. "I think some of these buttons contain whole formulas or mathematical calculations or codes, strings of codes. I think they have to be combined in some way to make it do different things."

"Sort of like a sentence?" asked Allison.

"Or maybe like html code," said Neill.

"What's that?" asked Howard.

"Computer code," said Neill. "Code that makes computer programs work."

"Like your cell phone?" asked Howard.

"Yeah, something like that," said Neill.

"But I don't understand," said Allison, "if this is a time-travel machine, how were we able to travel without it with only cell phones on us?"

"We don't actually know if the cell phones are what caused us to time travel," Neill replied.

"No," said Howard, "but I suspect maybe the energy or frequency or something magnetic in your phones somehow interacted with energy coming from this device, which triggered the time travel."

"What energy?" asked Allison. "It's not doing anything."

"I think it is," said Howard. "Don't you see that glow in the globe?"

"I thought that was just pink glass," said Allison, looking closely at the glass, which had a sort of foggy or frosted pink tinge to it.

"I don't think so," Howard replied. "I think it's sending out some sort of signal or frequency."

"Like a satellite that connects to cell phones?" asked Neill.

"Perhaps," said Howard, who by now understood probably as much as Neill or Allison about how cell phones operated from the inadequate descriptions they had given him.

"But how will we figure out how it works?" asked Allison.

"Give me a minute," said Howard, slowly rotating the base of the globe with his hands as he examined the buttons.

Neither Allison nor Neill knew what Howard intended to do, but they waited anxiously.

"I think," said Howard, after a couple of rotations of the globe, "that if we touch this button," and he pressed it down before his friends could stop him, "and this button, we may get some answers."

"Oh, Howard, be careful!" exclaimed Allison as his finger pressed down the second button.

Suddenly, the globe lit up. Although the three friends were all standing on a different side of it, each saw a clear picture inside the globe of a natural forest scene very like the place in the forest where they were currently standing.

"That definitely turned it on," said Neill.

"It's like a computer," said Allison. "It's always been on, just asleep."

"Yes," said Howard, "which is why your cell phones may have been able to communicate with it; we just don't know what commands they were giving each other, and those commands must have determined where in time you traveled."

"Look!" said Allison as a deer walked across the wooded scene on the globe.

"Is it like a camera?" asked Howard.

"I don't know," said Neill. "I thought we were supposed to see different time periods in it."

"But if it's just showing us a place here in the woods, we would never know," said Howard. "I mean, these woods couldn't have changed that much over the years, not compared to if we were seeing different scenes of Marquette as the city developed."

"Push another button," said Allison.

Neill wasn't sure that was a good idea, but he also found he couldn't resist his own curiosity, so he did not protest when Howard pressed a third button.

Suddenly, the scene changed. This time, the globe truly did resemble a snow globe. Where there had been a wooded forest was now a great glacier, and it was snowing out.

"Is that the same place?" asked Allison.

"I think so," said Neill. "At least it could be. It could be during the Ice Age."

They stared at the scene for a few minutes to see if it would change on its own or anything would enter the scene like the deer had earlier, but no activity commenced. Finally, Howard said, "I'll try another button."

This time, they saw trees again, but the trees were sticking up out of water like the area had been flooded. Only the top few feet of the tallest trees were visible.

"That place must be a century from now," said Neill, "or maybe later. Maybe it's after 2142 and the water is beginning to recede."

"Or it could be after the glacier started to melt and before the water from the Ice Age receded," said Howard.

"True," Neill replied.

"But what's the point of all this?" asked Allison. "We might be seeing different times in history, but how do we know which times they are or how we can get back to 2021?"

"We?" said Howard, looking at her. "I thought you wanted to stay here with me."

Neill raised his eyebrows. "Allison, are you seriously thinking of staying here? Derek has been saying the same thing to me."

"I told you before that I did," Allison replied, looking like she was afraid of upsetting Neill.

"But you barely know each other," Neill said. "You only just met a few days ago."

"I can't explain it, Neill, but…well, I love Howard. I know it's sudden, but he's like no one I've ever met before."

"I feel the same way," said Howard, putting his arm around her as he addressed Neill. "I've never felt so much love for someone, and since Hugh died, I've learned how fragile life can be. We have to take our happiness when we find it, so I've asked Allison to be my wife."

"Your wife!" exclaimed Neill. "What will your parents say?"

"We haven't told them yet," said Howard, "but they'll learn to accept it. They like Allison."

"We only just decided it the day before yesterday," said Allison, "before we came here. We wanted to tell you first, but we haven't had a chance yet, and this morning…well, we know how upset you are that you can't get home, Neill. We thought you had enough to worry about without wondering whether I would come home with you."

Neill didn't know what to say.

"Anyway, we can decide all that after we figure out this machine," Allison said. "Howard, hit another button."

Howard did as she said, but Neill wasn't ready to move on yet from the discussion.

"Allison, have you really thought this through? I mean, it would mean staying here in 1900."

"Look," said Allison, pointing at the globe. It had turned once more to a wooded scene like the first one they had seen, but this time, people were walking through the woods—Native Americans, about half-a-dozen of them.

"That's definitely the same scene as we first saw. I recognize that big tree," said Allison.

"And it definitely has to be a scene from the past," said Howard. "There are no bands of Chippewa dressed like that in these woods, not anymore. That could be from a hundred years ago or more."

"How do we figure out what year it is?" asked Allison.

"I don't know," said Howard. "So far I've only tried the buttons in this top row." He pointed at the globe's base. "Maybe these bring the time period into view and the ones below actually transport you to that time."

"Maybe," said Neill. "But I don't understand how we can know for sure...unless we experiment...and I'm not sure that's a good idea."

"Neither do I," said Allison.

"Do the buttons actually mean something?" asked Neill. "Are those runes on them also?"

"I think so," said Howard. "A couple of them look familiar, but I can't say for sure."

"Well," said Neill, "if those Native Americans were from 1800, maybe one button is for 1900, and one for 2000, and...."

"I don't think they go up in hundred-year groups," said Howard. "Besides, I was only guessing the Native Americans could be from 1800. They would certainly have to date back a few decades."

"What increments do you think the buttons are in?" asked Neill.

"I don't know," said Howard. "One row could select the century, another the decade, another the year, or they could be different versions of the same year, plus, have you noticed that when you have traveled, it's never been in one-hundred-year increments? It's always been 121 years apart. From 1900 to 2021 is 121 years, and then to 2142 is another 121 years."

"That's true," said Allison. "I wonder why."

"Maybe it works not in 121 but in eleven-year segments," said Neill. "After all, eleven multiplied by eleven is 121."

"True," said Howard.

"So maybe the Native Americans were in 1779," said Allison, subtracting 121 from the current year.

"That's a logical assumption," said Howard, "but we just can't know for sure. And what would be so special about the number eleven?"

"I don't know," Neill admitted.

"I think the only solution," said Howard, "is to bring it home with us so we can study it further. Using the book about runes, maybe we can translate the symbols on the buttons."

"Maybe," said Neill, "by looking in your journal, you could find out if you already figured out a translation."

"Maybe," said Howard, sounding less than enthusiastic about the idea.

"Howard," said Neill, "I don't understand why you're so resistant to read your journal; you know it must have the answers I need to get home."

"Maybe," Howard repeated, not committing to anything.

Neill could feel anger rising into his face, and Allison must have noticed it because she said, "Neill, we don't want to make any rash decisions. Howard and I both want you to get home safely, but it's been a long morning and we've hardly slept, and I am starving for my breakfast. I think we should head back to the cottage and take this with us. We can figure it out later."

"I agree," said Howard, smiling at his beloved in appreciation of her peacekeeping efforts.

"Fine," said Neill, frustrated but realizing Allison was right. He had hoped they would find something today, and they had, which meant he was a step closer to going home, but this device looked downright complicated, and he feared it might be days, weeks, months, or even years before they understood it.

"Okay," said Allison. "Now that that's decided, how will we hide the globe from Howard's family?"

"If you two can distract my family when we get back," said Howard, "I'll sneak it in through the back door of the cabin. I can hide it under my bed. No one will spot it there. In fact, I'll wrap it up in my clothes in my luggage to protect it from being damaged."

"Okay," said Allison. "Just be super-careful with it. If you break it, we're doomed."

"Doomed?" said Howard, surprised by her word choice.

"I mean, it's our last hope."

"No," said Neill. "You have your cell phone. If we just touch the dolmen with it…."

"Too risky," she replied.

"Plus," said Howard, "now that we've removed Odin's Eye, I don't think the cell phone will work with the dolmen. In fact, I think the cell phone must have triggered Odin's Eye somehow, so we can maybe use the cell phone and this instrument without needing the dolmen."

"That makes sense," said Neill, "and if we remove it, no one else will ever have to face the shock and confusion I experienced just by touching the dolmen."

"Not in this time anyway," said Howard.

"What do you mean?" asked Neill.

"Let's just get moving back to the cabin," said Allison. "I'm starving. Howard can explain whatever he means on the way back."

"I'm afraid to carry it," said Neill. "What if I drop it?"

"I'll wrap it in my sweater," said Allison, removing the light sweater she had worn because the morning had been cool. "It's quite heavy," she added, picking up the instrument as she wrapped her sweater around it.

"I can carry it," said Howard, relieving her of the burden, which did weigh a good ten pounds. "You carry your cell phone. You don't want to carry both and risk triggering the time travel activity."

"Right," said Allison, retrieving her cell phone from where she had placed it on the ground. "Thanks for the reminder."

Carefully, slowly, they now started to descend Mount Huron.

After a minute, Neill asked Howard, "What did you mean by 'not in this time anyway'?"

"I meant, we're removing it from this version of 1900, but it would still exist in your version of 2021 and the alternate version, just not in the future years attached to this timeline."

"When I get back to my time then," said Neill, "I'll remove the Odin's Eye in my time frame."

"That might not be such a bad idea," said Howard.

"I wish we knew who put the instrument in the dolmen," said Allison. "It sure doesn't look like something the Vikings made."

"I wish it came with an instruction manual," Neill replied.

"Don't worry, Neill. We'll figure it out," Howard stated.

Neill didn't respond. A thousand questions ran through his brain as he tried to imagine what this instrument might do, how it might be operated, how it could have been made, and who had made it, but none of those questions would have easy answers unless Howard read his journal, and for whatever reason, Howard did not want to do that.

Allison's stomach growled, causing Howard to laugh, and soon they launched into a discussion of what they wanted for breakfast; even Neill joined in. They all seemed to need a mental break from the mystery of the dolmen and how and why the strange device they knew as Odin's Eye had been buried beneath it.

But lingering in the back of Neill's mind was Allison's remark that without it, they were doomed. He seemed to remember the Norse gods had been doomed to face Ragnarok in the end. He hoped he would not share a similar fate.

Chapter 16

NEILL, HOWARD, AND ALLISON MANAGED to get back to the Longyears' cabin without incident, and since the family was down at the lake swimming when they returned, Howard was able to get into the cabin and hide Odin's Eye without being seen. The rest of that day and the next were spent with the family, relaxing and enjoying summertime activities. Howard, Allison, and Neill had no chance to discuss further the mysteries of time travel. Howard, however, successfully hid Odin's Eye in his luggage and carried it back to Marquette on Wednesday when they returned to town.

That same evening, now back in their old rooms, Neill visited Allison privately by using the door connecting their rooms. Derek was still staying in Negaunee and wouldn't be back until Friday, so Neill took the opportunity to talk to Allison.

When he knocked on her door, she was just about to crawl into bed, but she answered the door and let him in when he asked if he could talk to her.

"I'm really tired, Neill," she said, sitting down on the bed.

"I know," said Neill, "so am I, but I want to know if you're serious about marrying Howard and staying here when I return home."

She sighed, scooted back against the headboard, and pulled her legs up to her chest.

Neill sat down in a chair across from the bed.

"You don't sound very sure," he said in response to her sigh.

"How can anyone be sure about such things?" she replied. "I know I have very strong feelings for Howard. I never met anyone I felt this way about before."

"But what if you met someone back in our time that you might love?"

"And what if I don't?" she replied. "Why should I throw this away? I've waited a long time and never found anyone in our time, and Howard is everything I've ever looked for in a boyfriend."

"But what about your mom?" asked Neill.

"I already told you she and Brian will probably get married. She'll be okay."

"The poor woman already lost her husband. How do you think she'll feel losing her daughter?" said Neill, unable to understand Allison's attitude when he was so concerned about his own parents being worried about him.

"I don't know. I imagine it will be difficult for her, and under normal circumstances, I would never hurt her, but who's to say I wouldn't end up moving away anyway? Then I wouldn't be with her."

"At least she could come visit you and she would know you are okay. How am I supposed to explain to her that you time traveled and decided not to return. You know I can't do that."

"I know, Neill. You don't have to. No one knows where I went. They won't even necessarily realize I went looking for you."

"It's going to be hard enough to explain where I've been all this time," said Neill.

"What if you just told the truth when you got home?"

"And have the whole world start experimenting with time travel? Look at the mess it's already made for us. I don't think that's such a good idea."

"But couldn't you just tell your parents?" Allison asked.

"No," said Neill. "My father is a pretty rational person. I'm not sure he'd believe me. My mom might, but...."

"What if you had proof you could bring back to them?"

"Like what?"

"Like information from the past they can verify," said Allison. "Maybe stuff about your family they didn't know but you could somehow prove. You told me earlier you met some of your ancestors when you first got here. Why not get to know those ancestors better and learn more about them? I bet your parents would be fascinated by that. I know how obsessed they are with local history and genealogy. I've always rather envied you in that way since my family isn't from Marquette, but you have all kinds of roots here. I would think you'd be thrilled to be back here in the past, but all you can think about is getting home."

"Because I don't want my parents worrying about me," Neill replied.

"You can't stop them from doing that, Neill. You need to enjoy your life, no matter what situation you find yourself in. That's what I'm trying to do. I love every moment I get to spend with Howard. He's so smart, and such a gentleman, and has such good energy. I've never met anyone as charismatic as him. He doesn't let things worry him like you do, or most people do."

"He's worried about reading his journals," Neill replied, not sure he liked being compared to Howard.

"I know," said Allison, "and I'm going to work on him there. But for the most part, he's seeing your time travel experience as an opportunity to learn new things. You need to see it that way too, even if you learn something different than he does."

"Is that what you're doing?" asked Neill. "Taking advantage of the opportunity to stay here?"

"Maybe," said Allison, beginning to yawn. "Neill, I'm just too tired to talk anymore, and you have to work at Getz's tomorrow. Let's call it a night. We can talk about it more tomorrow."

Neill inhaled and exhaled through his nose, trying to stay calm. He knew Allison was right. He couldn't decide for her if it were right or wrong for her to stay. All he could do was be patient and try to enjoy this experience until he was able to go home himself.

"All right, Allison," he said. "Good night."

"Good night, Neill," she replied as he stood up to leave. "Don't worry. It will all work out somehow."

Chapter 17

THE WEEK THAT FOLLOWED WAS disappointing to Neill. He simply went to Getz's each morning and then came back to the Longyear Mansion in time for supper. Derek worked out of town all week so Neill did not see him, and Allison carried on her romance with Howard, which made Neill irritated since he feared it was distracting Howard from figuring out how time travel worked. Neill began to feel hopeless that he would ever go home again. He remembered what Allison had said about how he should take advantage of being in this time, but he just could not seem to work up any enthusiasm about it.

When the next Friday came, Mr. Longyear announced that Derek was going to Wisconsin on some business for him next week. Neill felt disappointed that his friend had become so involved with the Longyears to the point of not having time for him. Derek hadn't even come home the weekend prior, although he had initially said he would. Neill knew this Derek wasn't the Derek of his own past, but he still felt like he was his friend. However, both Allison and Derek seemed more interested in this time than helping him return to his own time.

Friday night, Neill went to bed feeling highly depressed and frustrated. He also felt overly tired from working hard all week since the store had been doing inventory. He hoped this weekend Howard and he could make some progress on figuring out how the strange time machine contraption worked, provided they could get time alone without Howard's family interfering.

That night, Neill didn't sleep well at all. He drifted off soon enough, but he woke within a couple of hours and could not fall back asleep. He tossed and turned, worrying about his family; he wondered how his parents were coping with his disappearance, wondered how Allison's mom was coping with her loss, and wondered if the pandemic had gotten worse or if COVID-19 had all but disappeared now that most people had been vaccinated. And he worried about what he would do if he ever did get home; how could he ever explain his absence all these weeks?

Finally, after an hour or two, Neill was more exhausted than when he went to bed, and frustrated that he could not fall asleep, so he resorted to what he always did to try to fall asleep—counting. It didn't matter what he counted. Mostly he counted years, thinking about historical events as he came to the year they happened—33 AD when Jesus likely died; 180 AD when the Roman emperor Marcus Aurelius died; 312 when the Emperor Constantine converted to Christianity; 476 when the Roman Empire fell; 622 when Mohammed fled to Medina; 800 when Charlemagne was crowned Holy Roman Emperor; 1066 when William the Conqueror had invaded England; and so on. He was approaching the Renaissance when he finally drifted into sleep.

And then in a dream he saw Uncle Chad. His uncle was walking down the street—down Ridge Street, which wasn't so odd since he had lived on that street, but he was dressed in clothes similar to those Mr. Longyear wore. At first, Neill couldn't believe it was Uncle Chad—wasn't he dead? How did he get back to 1900? But Neill was certain it was his uncle, and then he ran toward Uncle Chad, and he stopped in front of him and asked him what he was doing there. "I always wanted to be Victorian," said Chad, "so I've come to visit you and all our Victorian ancestors." "Oh, Uncle Chad!" Neill cried, overcome with emotion, and he lunged forward to hug his uncle. Just as his arms folded themselves around his uncle's figure, however, he found his arms were empty. One moment he had been convinced that death was not a real thing, and in the next, his uncle was gone and he was waking up sobbing, practically wailing because his uncle was dead and he knew he would never see him again. And then Neill got a grip on himself. Allison was in the next room, and he did not want to wake her up.

Neill sat up and found a handkerchief. He blew his nose several times and then wiped his eyes. Then he went to the bathroom and washed his face and hands. A minute later, he crawled back into bed, still feeling like crying. His throat was parched from the sobs, so he got up again and got himself a glass of water. Then he felt calmer and lay back down. He thought about the dream and how good it had felt to see Uncle Chad again, and how his uncle had looked so happy to see him and so excited to be there in 1900.

"It wouldn't be so bad at all if Uncle Chad were here," Neill told himself. "Then I could survive being stuck in 1900."

Neill remembered then what Uncle Chad had said in the dream about wanting to be Victorian. Uncle Chad had loved the Victorian period. He had purposely lived in a house on the Longyear property because he had loved the era so much, and especially the elegant Longyear Mansion. He would have done almost anything to have been here inside the Longyear home, associating with the family. And he had also said he wanted to see his own ancestors.

What an idiot I am, thought Neill. *I have seen my ancestors—at least Cordelia Whitman and Margaret Dalrymple, who will marry Cordelia's grandson Will. Oh, and I've also seen my great-great-grandfather Patrick McCarey, whose daughter Beth will marry Will and Margaret's son Henry. Henry and Beth were my dad's grandparents. He knew and loved them. They won't be born for a few more years, but I bet my dad and Uncle Chad both would have loved to be here in 1900, to be with their ancestors whom they only knew from the stories of their mom and grandparents. And here I am in 1900 for real, but all I can do is moan and groan that I can't be back in 2021. I'm kind of like Dorothy at the end of* The Wizard of Oz *when she tells Aunt Em how some of Oz was beautiful, but all the time, all she kept telling everyone was how she wanted to go home, and finally, they sent her home. No one is sending me home, though. At least not yet. Dorothy was lucky because in the later Oz books, she got to return to Oz again and again, and she finally moved there with Aunt Em and Uncle Henry. I guess Dorothy just didn't appreciate Oz enough the first time, so she had to go back there again, but I doubt that will happen to me. If I do get home, I'll never risk returning to 1900, so I better see all of it that I can while I can.*

Neill lay there in bed, feeling better now. He'd heard that sometimes the same things keep happening to people until they learn from it the intended lesson. He had kept being stuck in the wrong times, but what had he learned from it? Pretty much nothing so far. He had to admit that. He had been so busy trying to control everything, to right the mistake he had unintentionally made of saving Howard's life, that he had completely ignored the opportunities of this experience. Allison had already told him that, but it had taken seeing how excited Uncle Chad was to be in 1900 to fully realize the opportunity he had.

As the morning sun started to filter through the window, Neill remembered it was Saturday, so he had all day to enjoy himself, to explore Marquette and maybe to meet more of his relatives from 1900. He would learn all he could about them. He wasn't sure if what he learned from them would include whatever it was the Universe might want him to learn, but maybe the whole lesson intended for him was just to embrace the opportunity.

"Whatever the lesson may be," Neill told himself, "I know one thing; today, I intend to have a wonderful day."

Howard and Allison seemed surprised when Neill told them he had plans that morning. He wasn't quite sure what those plans were, so he did not elaborate on them. Allison even asked him not to be mad at them, but he assured them both he was not. He just wanted some time alone to think. *And enjoy myself*, he thought. He would see what the day presented to him, and tell them later how he had fared.

And the day appeared willing to help him. As Neill turned from Arch onto Cedar Street, he saw Peter White approaching from the opposite direction. Mr. White looked to be in a jovial mood this morning, his face lighting up when he saw Neill.

"Hello," Mr. White said. "I hear you've regained your memory and been reunited with your siblings."

"Yes," Neill replied. "I always suspected I was from the Marquette area, and now I know my family lived on a farm near the Huron Mountain Club."

"That's what Mr. Longyear told me when I saw him the other day. I'm very sorry about your parents, but I'm glad you found some answers to your dilemma."

"Thank you," said Neill. "I appreciate how you tried to help me."

"My pleasure," said Mr. White. "I'm glad it worked out for you. And where are you off to this fine, sunshiny morning?"

"I'm not sure," said Neill. "It's such a beautiful day I just thought I'd go for a walk."

"Well, you must enjoy it. Our summers are far too short here," said Mr. White. "Not that I'd want to live anywhere else. When I was a boy, I wanted to see as much of the world as I could. I never would have guessed when I first came to help found this town at age nineteen that I'd stay here all my life."

"It must be surprising to you how Marquette has grown since then," Neill replied.

"Yes," said Mr. White. "Actually, I've been thinking about that a lot lately since I'm one of the last early settlers still alive and last year was Marquette's fiftieth anniversary. I've been thinking I should write a history of Marquette, but I'm afraid I'm just not a writer."

"I like writing," said Neill. "My father was always writing, so I think I inherited a little of his talent."

"Would you consider writing a history of Marquette?" asked Mr. White.

"I don't know," said Neill, his mind suddenly racing at the thought, "but it sounds like an important project." He had wanted to visit his ancestors, but he had not known what excuse he could use to get inside their homes. Now he might have an excuse. He could interview them and some of the other early settlers about Marquette's past, all the while pretending he was writing a history book. Just think of the information he could preserve for Marquette—things no one knew in 2021 because they had never been written down. He could change that...or could he? Wouldn't that be altering the past, or toying with it in some unorthodox way? Well, he could figure that out later. He didn't have to share his notes with posterity. He just wanted to get to know the fascinating people from this time better.

Mr. White had continued talking to Neill while all these thoughts were racing through his mind. Now, refocusing on the conversation, he heard Mr. White say, "If you have time, of course."

"Sure," said Neill, not knowing what he was agreeing to.

"Wonderful," said Mr. White. "I know they would love to meet you. It's this house right here."

Mr. White turned and walked across the street, then up the front walk of the house that in his time Neill knew as the Jopling home. He seemed to recall Peter White's daughter had married a Jopling. Was that where they were going?

"I'm sure they'll have plenty," said Mr. White. "They always make a big breakfast and won't mind having another guest."

"I already ate," said Neill, "so I won't impose on them, though I wouldn't mind another cup of coffee."

Mr. White laughed. "Who does mind another cup of coffee?"

Neill followed Mr. White to the door and waited while he knocked, all the while trying to remember which Joplings would have lived here in 1900.

A servant girl let them in, but in another second, a female voice called out, "Uncle Peter, come in here." Mr. White led Neill into a dining room where a relatively young man and woman were dining with a middle-aged woman and a young boy of about seven.

"Hello, everyone. Sorry I'm late," said Mr. White, sitting down at the table. "I've brought a friend with me, Mr. Neill Jackson. I hope you don't mind."

"Oh, no, we have plenty of food," said the young man—well, maybe not that young. From the looks of him, Neill would have guessed he was forty.

"Thank you," said Neill. "I'm much obliged." He had never said that in his life, but it somehow seemed appropriate.

"You're welcome," said the older woman. "It's a pleasure to meet you."

"Same here," Neill replied. "Mr. White tells me you are his relatives, but I'm afraid I already forgot how."

The group then explained to him all their connections to one another. It took a while for Neill to sort it out, but he had listened to his parents and their friend, Mr. Tichelaar, go on and on about Marquette history, so he was able to piece it all together and remember it. Mr. White had married Ellen Hewitt, the daughter of Dr. Morgan Hewitt, which Neill already knew. Dr. Morgan's other daughter, Mary Hewitt, had married Henry Mather. Mr. Mather had died some years back, but Mrs. Mather, née Hewitt, was the older woman at the table—Neill guessed she was about sixty. Her daughter, Bessie, was the mistress of the house, and her husband was Mr. James Jopling. The little boy was their son, Richard Mather Jopling. They also explained that Mr. Jopling's brother, Alfred Owen Jopling, had married Peter White's daughter, Mary, who had passed away. Neill had heard all these names before and had some jumbled recollection of them, but he had forgotten the Jopling brothers had come from England, so he was surprised by Mr. Jopling's English accent.

Mr. and Mrs. Jopling and Mrs. Mather were charming and friendly while young Richard was restless and, after eating his toast, quickly sent off to play. Neill was finding it hard to concentrate on the conversation because he kept thinking how his father would have loved to be here to talk to these people. He wanted to remember every word, but he knew he would not remember most of it. Then Mrs. Mather said something that recalled to Neill's mind what his father considered one of the great mysteries of Marquette history.

"Aren't you all related somehow to the novelist Constance Fenimore Woolson?" Neill asked.

This led to another complicated family history lesson, but yes, they were. Henry Mather's brother Samuel L. Mather had married

Georgiana Woolson, Constance Fenimore Woolson's sister, which meant they were related to her not by blood but by marriage. "She is Kate Mather and Samuel Mather, Jr.'s aunt by blood, and a sort of step-aunt to their half-brother William Gwinn Mather," said Mrs. Jopling, who was Samuel Mather, Jr.'s first cousin.

"I love her novel *Anne*," Neill replied. He had never read the book, but it seemed the polite thing to say, and he had heard his father talk about Miss Woolson ad nauseam. "I know she also wrote some short stories set in Marquette, but I've always wondered if she ever visited here."

The Joplings looked blankly at each other. "I think so," Mrs. Mather finally said, "but I'd have to double-check with Samuel or Will."

"I believe she did also," said Mr. White, "though I don't recall seeing her here. I did meet her in Italy. I just happened upon her by chance one day, I think it was in Florence, and she looked so like her niece Kate that I knew it must be her and introduced myself. We were quite struck by the coincidence of meeting so far from home and recognizing each other."

"So, Mr. Jackson, are you interested in literature?" asked Mrs. Mather.

"Yes, somewhat," said Neill, "but my father was more than me. He was a great reader. I'm more interested in history myself. Mr. White has suggested I write a history of Marquette."

"That would be a wonderful undertaking," said Mrs. Mather. "My father was instrumental in founding the Cleveland Iron Company, so I came here just a few years after Peter. The city has changed so much since then that it would be good to document the changes before they are forgotten."

"I agree," said Neill. "Even in my short lifetime, I can't believe how things have changed."

"Imagine how I feel then," said Mr. White, pushing back his chair. "Well, I do need to get to the bank before the morning is over."

"But it's Saturday, Uncle Peter," Mrs. Jopling protested.

"A banker's work is never done, my dear," he replied.

"I'll walk with you," Neill said, still thinking he might go visit some of his relatives. The Joplings made him promise to return soon so they could share with him more of their memories for his history of Marquette. Obviously, they had decided he was the one to write the book. Neill doubted he really would; he hoped not to be in 1900 long enough to write a book, but he promised to return.

"We'll be sure, Mr. Jackson," added Mrs. Jopling, bidding them goodbye at the door, "to check with our cousins about whether Miss Woolson ever visited Marquette and let you know."

"Thank you," said Neill.

"Neill is staying with the Longyears," said Mr. White, "so it will be easy to get a message to him."

"Oh, no," she replied, smiling. "He has to keep his promise to come back if he wants that information."

Mr. White and Neill laughed and thanked her for her hospitality, then started down the front path to the sidewalk.

"They were all so nice," said Neill as they turned back onto Cedar Street.

"Are you serious about writing this history of Marquette?" Mr. White asked.

"Yes," said Neill. "Mr. Getz says that since fall is coming, my hours will be reduced so I'll need something to occupy my time."

"Writing a book will certainly do that," said Mr. White. "Well, if anyone knows Marquette's history, it is me. Why don't you come over some evening next week and interview me?"

"I would love that," said Neill as they turned onto Ridge Street and headed west. As they walked, Neill looked at the relatively new homes that had seemed so ancient in his time. Even after all these weeks, he still marveled at the tall Kidder home and the Peter White house, both of which had been replaced by flat, one-story smaller homes in the mid-twentieth century and which remained in his own time. Looking at them now inspired his next question.

"Who else would you recommend I interview?" Neill asked. "Will the Kidders know much of Marquette's past?"

"They've been here for quite some time," said Mr. White. "It wouldn't hurt to talk to them. This big house next to theirs belongs to the Spears."

"Yes, I know," said Neill. "It was built by…by Colonel…." Neill was racking his brains.

"Colonel James Pickands, yes," said Mr. White. "But they moved in before the plaster dried, so his wife got sick and died. Terrible tragedy. Caused him to leave Marquette and sell the house to Henry Thurber. Thurber didn't live here long, though, before he sold it to Frank Spear."

Neill recalled hearing from his father about Mrs. Pickands dying because of wet plaster. Mr. White began telling him about all the other people who had lived along the street—the Balls, Merritts,

Breitungs, Rankins, and so many more whose names Neill had heard but did not know much about. As they came to St. Paul's Episcopal Church, Mr. White waved at a man coming out of a brownstone house across the street. In another moment, Neill recognized him as Dr. Dawson, the doctor who had examined him the day he had woken from his concussion in the Allen house. Dr. Dawson stopped to ask how he was and to discuss the weather with Mr. White for a moment, and then Mr. White mentioned that Dr. Dawson's father-in-law, Mr. Adams, was also a Marquette pioneer.

"My father-in-law," said Dr. Dawson, "loves to talk about the old days, and so does my brother-in-law, Will Adams. I have an appointment to get to, but feel free to go in and visit with them."

Mr. White agreed to step inside with Neill for a moment to introduce him to the family, but then he had to get to the bank. Before he knew it, Neill was left alone inside the Adams family's parlor, holding a conversation with Mr. and Mrs. Adams, their daughter, Mrs. Dawson, and Will Adams, their adopted son who suffered from ossification. Will's body was slowly turning to stone, so he was in a wheelchair. He could not move his legs and had difficulty moving his arms, but he was full of life—life that just wasn't able to make him mobile. When Neill had been about eleven or twelve, he had gone to see Mr. Tichelaar's play about Will Adams at Kaufman Auditorium. He had been quite taken with the young man who could quote Dickens and ran his own magazine despite his disabilities, so he was thrilled to meet Will in person.

But Will was less interested in talking about himself than encouraging his father to tell stories about Marquette's early days. Before he knew it, Neill was listening to Sidney Adams recall how Chief Marji Gesick had befriended him when he first arrived in Marquette and helped him overcome the weakness in his body. "Those Indians know their herbs and medicines," he said. "Not like these quack doctors who run around selling patented medicines they claim are based on old Indian recipes."

"Oh, Sidney, don't get started on that," said Mrs. Adams.

"Well, it's true," said Mr. Adams. "I wish James"—he meant his son-in-law, Dr. Dawson—"would spend more time talking to the local Indians and less time giving people morphine. We should get an Indian medicine man in here to see if he can help Will."

Neill didn't know what to say to all of this, and he could see the remark perturbed Mrs. Adams, so he turned to Will and said, "As Mr. White told you, I want to write a history of Marquette. Since I know you're a prolific writer, I was wondering if you had any advice for me."

Will laughed or tried to—the sound came out of his throat but his facial expression looked half-frozen. "Get a good artist to do the illustrations," he replied. "I'm sad to say most people are philistines and won't pick up a book without pictures. You also want to put lots of gossip and scandal in it so they'll keep reading."

"Oh, Will, you're so cynical," said his sister.

"You know it's true, Bertha," Will replied. "Why, look at Oscar Wilde. You know people won't admit to reading his books, but I guarantee you the scandal helped his book sales, even if people read them under their bed covers."

"I don't know about that," said Bertha.

Unable to resist, Neill asked, "What scandals have there been in Marquette?"

Will laughed as if to suggest there had been plenty.

"Let me see," he said, as if ticking them off on the fingers he could not move, "there's the Methodist minister who stole the building funds for the church, and then the things they say about Robert Graveraet, and—"

"Will, that's enough," his mother interrupted. "You know gossip is wrong."

Will's eyes smiled. "That's funny, Mother, considering that both of the things I just mentioned happened before I was born, so I must have heard them from you and Dad."

Neill tried hard to repress a laugh, only a small sound slipping out.

Mrs. Adams frowned, but she did not know how to reply in her defense.

"In any case, Will," said Mr. Adams, "there is a difference between gossiping within the family and printing gossip in a book. Mr. Jackson, I suggest you do not mention any of those items in your history of Marquette."

"Yes, sir," said Neill politely, though he was aching to know more.

"Well, I hope someone still buys it then," said Will. "Like I said, look at how popular Oscar Wilde's name is now."

"It's indecent what that man did," Mrs. Adams replied. "Please quit speaking of him."

"Regardless, he was a brilliant playwright," said Will. "I wish I could write like him."

"You would do better than use him for your model," said Mr. Adams. "Let's not discuss that man any further."

"Would you like to write a play?" Neill asked Will, knowing full well that one day Will would write one that was performed all over the U.P.

"I have already written a few," said Will, "but they are short things. What I would really love to do is write an operetta, something in the style of Gilbert and Sullivan."

"That would be wonderful," said Neill, who wasn't even sure who Gilbert and Sullivan were, but he felt he should encourage the young man. It seemed so strange to be sitting here, talking to someone so famous in Marquette history, and see he was just a few years older than him. He wondered if Will's physical impediments were holding back the full genius of his creativity, or if it were the impediments that drove his perseverance. He didn't dare ask, but he felt so privileged to be talking to him.

Finally, Will said he needed his nap. Neill thanked the Adamses for having him, and when asked, he promised to call again.

"Will gets a lot of visitors," Mrs. Dawson told Neill as she walked him to the door, "but few people really appreciate his quick wit and interest in literature. I could see his eyes light up from the interest you showed in him."

"I think he's fascinating," said Neill. "I wish I had his talent."

"I'm sure you will write a wonderful history of Marquette," Bertha replied.

"Thank you. I'll try," said Neill, but as he walked away, he felt like such an impostor. He would try to write down everything people told him, but he doubted he'd ever write a full history book. The best he could hope to create was notes that would probably remain unpublished, but he still felt it would be important to write them down.

It was after two o'clock now, so while Neill had considered going to visit his four-greats-grandmother Cordelia Whitman, he also felt like he'd already learned a lot of Marquette history and should write it down before he forgot it. He also wanted to make the most of his time when he visited his ancestors, so he decided to think about what he wanted to ask them before he met with them. He'd have to figure out how to ask the more personal questions without revealing he was their descendant. He decided to return to the Longyear Mansion for now and write up his notes before supper. Then he would set out to meet his ancestors tomorrow.

Chapter 18

W HEN NEILL RETURNED TO THE Longyear Mansion, Franklin told him Mrs. Longyear had gone to a meeting, Mr. Howard was in his room, and Miss Allison and Mr. Howard's siblings had gone out for a walk. That was perfect as far as Neill was concerned because he would have time to go to his room and write up a storm. He had seen his father do that plenty of times, and now and then, he'd had to do it for a college paper. He was a good writer, but until now he'd never felt passionate about it.

Neill decided just to write up notes for now rather than full paragraphs. The notes would then remind him of everything and he could rework them later. The main thing was to get everything down on paper. He found his memory had already failed him on a few details, so he also made a list of clarifying questions to ask the Joplings and Adamses when he saw them again.

Once his notes from the day were complete, Neill began making a list of all the relatives he wanted to visit. It was hard to fathom just how many different ancestral branches of his family he could talk to, all on his paternal grandmother's side since his mother's family had left Marquette in 1876 and his paternal grandfather's family were from other parts of the U.P. But his grandmother, Ellen Whitman Vandelaare, was descended from a slew of early Marquette ancestors. Her parents, Henry and Beth Whitman, would not be born yet in 1900, but their parents were alive in this time. Beth's parents were Patrick McCarey and Kathy Bergmann. Patrick was the officer Neill and Derek had met at Getz's. Kathy's mother, Molly Bergmann Montoni, was still alive; she had come to Marquette the very first year, so he would definitely want to talk to her. Both Patrick and Molly had been immigrants from Ireland, while Kathy's father had come from Germany. Neill knew the family did not know where in those countries they had come from, so he wanted to find out. And then on Henry Whitman's side, there was Henry's mother Margaret Dalrymple, whom he had met at Cordelia Whitman's house. Margaret was alive in this time, as were her parents, and her future husband, Will Whitman. Both of Will's parents were dead, but his grandmother Cordelia was another early Marquette settler alive in 1900. He couldn't wait to speak to all of them.

Once he had a list of relatives, Neill began writing down questions to ask them such as "Which part of Ireland did you come from?" and "What was the journey to Marquette like?" But he only got half-a-dozen questions written when someone knocked on his door.

After hiding his lists and notes under a book on the desk, Neill answered the door.

"Franklin told me you were back," said Howard, slipping past him into the room. "I have something interesting to tell you."

"What?" asked Neill, closing the door.

"It's about Odin's Eye," said Howard, sitting down at the desk while Neill sat on the bed.

"Okay," said Neill, "but should we wait for Allison?"

"No. I made the discovery this morning so I already told her."

"Did you figure out how I can go home?" Neill asked.

"No," Howard replied, "but I think I'm closer."

"Did you read your journals?"

"I started. I'm sorry it's taken me so long, but they're in different languages and codes, and some took a while to decipher. They reveal that the future version of me figured out something I was just starting to guess might be the case. I'm happy my future self was able to confirm my guess was right."

"But what is it?" asked Neill.

"It's that," said Howard, pausing to be dramatic or give the news the full importance it deserved, "time travel is definitely not random."

"Don't we already know that because we found Odin's Eye?" asked Neill.

"We assumed it wasn't, but now I've figured out why it isn't," Howard replied. "It's because your time and my time and these other times are all different. We're in different time streams, not all in the same one, like you said Xander and Jorgen explained to you. In your original time, the version of Odin's Eye under the dolmen must be set to 1900. That's how you were able to travel to this time and also why Allison traveled to this same time. In my time, however, the version of Odin's Eye under the dolmen is set to 2021, as we discovered when we found it. That means, if you had left this time again, you would have traveled to 2021. However, when you changed 1900, you caused your version of 2021 to alter so you went to the right year but a different version of it. Does that make sense?"

"I think so," said Neill, "but it still doesn't tell me how to get back to the first version of 2021 that I came from."

"I know," said Howard. "We still have to figure that out, but isn't it interesting that the time travel devices are consistent in that way?"

"Yes, I guess so," said Neill. "I don't really understand how it helps us, but hopefully it will."

"It definitely will," said Howard, "because now we know for sure we can set them to go to a certain year, even if we don't know how to get a specific version of that year."

"Wait," said Neill. "What about when Derek and I went to the future? How do you explain that?"

"Because the version of 2021 you were in had a version of Odin's Eye that was set to 2142 rather than 2021."

"Okay, but then why didn't Allison also go to 2142?"

"Because," said Howard, starting to sound impatient, "she didn't come from the second version of 2021. She came from the original one that you came from, so she would also go to 1900. Do you understand?"

Neill felt his head hurting, but he said, "Yes, I've got it."

"Here," said Howard, turning to the desk and grabbing a piece of paper. He began drawing a diagram to illustrate how the time travel worked. Neill got up from the bed and stood over him, watching. After a minute, Howard showed him the diagram, which reflected what he had just said. Neill looked it over, and after Howard answered a couple of more questions, it made sense to him.

"What we need to do then," said Howard, "is figure out how to get you from this version of 1900 to your starting point version of 2021." He drew a broken line from 1900 to the original 2021.

"And how do we do that?" asked Neill.

"I think," said Howard, "we would have to open up what you and Allison called a wormhole. Think of it as like a secret passage from one place to another."

"Yeah," said Neill, getting excited by the analogy. "It's like in *Clue* when you take the secret passage from one room to another and basically jump across the whole board."

"What's *Clue*?" asked Howard.

"It's a mystery game where someone has been murdered—Mr. Body—and all the players pretend to be different characters like Miss Scarlett or Professor Plum and try to figure out who committed the murder."

"Kind of like Sherlock Holmes?" asked Howard.

"Exactly," said Neill. "There are clues, and you have to go from one room to another through the hallway to find the clues in the different rooms, but it takes a long time to get from some rooms to others unless you take the secret passageway. Think of it like being here in your house in the drawing room and wanting to go to the sitting room, which is way on the other end of the house. You'd go through a secret panel in the wall that would take you there instantly rather than having to walk through the usual hallway."

"Sounds *cool*," said Howard, smiling at how he had picked up some of his twenty-first-century friends' slang. "I wish when Mr. Charlton designed this house, he had included some secret panels."

"Maybe he did and you don't know it," said Neill, "which reminds me that I definitely have to include Mr. Charlton among the people I interview."

"Interview?" said Howard.

"Yes. I met Mr. White this morning and he put the idea into my head that someone should write a history of Marquette, and then he took me over to the Joplings' house and then to the Adamses' house, so I spent most of the day talking to them and asking them questions about Marquette's past. Tomorrow, I plan to do more, including visiting my ancestors without letting them know I'm asking them questions because I'm their descendant. Writing a history book about Marquette is the perfect excuse to get to talk to all these people."

"That's a good idea," said Howard.

"Well, it will give me something to do while you keep trying to figure out how to get me back to my time."

"True," said Howard. "I am sorry it is taking me so long."

"I understand," said Neill, although he didn't totally. "I'm sure it's complicated, and I wish I knew how to help. I want to get home as soon as possible because my family must be worried sick about me, but until then, I can make the most of my time here by learning more about my ancestors."

"I imagine it might take more than a little longer," Howard replied. "Maybe weeks or months."

"I'm hoping for days," said Neill, "though I know that's unreasonable. But I don't like imposing on your family by staying here."

"My family likes having you here," said Howard, "but I'll do what I can to make it as fast as possible."

"If I can help at all, let me know," Neill replied.

"I will. The main thing I need to do is finish translating and reading my journal. I admit it is taking me longer than it should because I still find it scary to read."

"Just remember it reflects a different future from the one you can create. Those pages don't reflect your fate or destiny."

"I know," said Howard. "I'd much rather be writing a history of Marquette, though. That sounds like an interesting project, even though my family are relative newcomers here compared to your ancestors."

"Yes, your parents came in what, the early 1870s?"

"I think my dad came in 1873," said Howard, "and my mom was here a few years earlier."

"Well, one of my ancestors, Molly Bergmann Montoni, came when the town was founded in 1849, and Cordelia Whitman came a few years after that."

"I'm almost jealous," said Howard. "That's a long time ago."

"Only fifty-one years for you," said Neill, "but in my time, it's 172 years. Molly Bergmann Montoni is my three-greats-grandmother, and Cordelia Whitman is four-greats."

"Wow," said Howard. "I don't even know the names of my ancestors that far back, though I know my mother's family, the Beechers, go way back in New England. The Longyears were originally from Germany."

"Well," said Neill, "my parents are genealogy nuts, so they drilled all this into me at a young age."

Just then the doorknob turned, causing the young men to fear someone had overheard their conversation.

They were both surprised when Derek entered.

"Hello," he said. "I didn't know if anyone was here."

"I thought you were going to be gone all week?" said Neill.

"I'm going to Wisconsin on Monday," said Derek, coming into the room and sitting on the bed across from Neill to take off his shoes, "but I thought I'd come back for the weekend—well, what's left of it. I did work most of today."

"I'm glad to see you," said Neill. "I've missed you."

"I've missed you too," said Derek.

"It's almost suppertime," said Howard, "so I should go change. I'll see you both downstairs. Good to see you, Derek."

"You too," Derek replied.

Howard left, shutting the door behind him. Neill sat down again in the chair at the desk and hid Howard's time travel drawing under the same book where he had hid his notes in case a maid or anyone else entered the room.

"How have you been?" Derek asked, standing up to change his clothes for dinner.

"Good," said Neill. "Getz's has been slow, so I'm working less, but Howard is making progress in understanding time travel, so I'm hopeful I can go home soon."

"That's good," said Derek, undoing his shirt buttons.

"What about you?" asked Neill. "Do you want to go back to your time, or come with me to mine?"

Derek frowned. "I don't think I'd be comfortable in your time considering I'd have a Derek double there."

Neill stood up, realizing he should also change for dinner. "What will you do then?" he asked, taking off his suit jacket and beginning to unbutton his own shirt.

"I'm going to stay here," said Derek. "I rather like 1900, and I think I have reason to stay."

"I hope you don't still think one of Howard's sisters might marry you," said Neill.

"No...actually, I've met someone."

"What do you mean?" asked Neill, changing his shirt. "Like a romantic interest?"

"Yeah," said Derek. "Her name is Betty and she works at the Breitung Hotel in Negaunee where I've been staying."

"But you've only known her for what—a week or two?"

"I think that's enough," said Derek. "She's nineteen and really pretty. She has the most stunning blue eyes of any girl I've ever seen. I think she has a really good figure, too, from what I can tell beneath all those clothes. Plus, she's an orphan and a hard worker."

Neill kind of grimaced and shook his head.

"What?" said Derek.

"None of those things is a good enough reason to marry her."

"I think she has all the qualities I want in a wife," Derek replied. "She's a hard worker and would take good care of me, and she has no one to look after her. I want to protect her and make her life easier."

"That's noble of you," said Neill, realizing being a young single working woman in 1900 probably wasn't the easiest life.

"Even if she decides she doesn't want me," Derek said, "you know I wasn't happy in my own time. Allison and I don't have any future together there, and I have a chance to start over here. This time isn't so bad. Mr. Longyear is paying me well. Soon I'll be able to afford a house with running water and electricity, and in a few years, maybe I can even afford a car. It's not like this is the Stone Age."

"Still, it's a big adjustment," said Neill.

"Well, the culture shock is mostly over for me," said Derek. "It can only get better as things progress."

"That's true," said Neill, pulling up his pants. "I admit I'm kind of enjoying 1900 myself now." He then told Derek about his history project.

"See, Neill, there's a reason for everything," Derek replied.

"I don't know about that," Neill said. "I still feel like everything that has happened has been kind of random, but Howard has figured out there's some logic to the time travel. I'll explain it all to you after dinner. In any case, I realize even if the universe is chaotic and bad things happen, all we can do is make the best of it."

"That's a good attitude to have," Derek replied. "Are you ready to go down to dinner?"

"It's the only attitude I can have," said Neill, grabbing his suit coat. "I really miss my uncle Chad. Remember, I told you how he died. He would have loved to see 1900, so I should take full advantage of this experience."

"I think," said Derek, patting Neill's shoulder while opening the bedroom door, "that this is the first time since I've met you that you've been happy and excited rather than worried."

"Really?" said Neill. "I guess you're right. Today is the first day I feel lighthearted since this whole experience began."

"Well, we better get to dinner," said Derek, leading the way into the hall.

"Okay," said Neill, "but later, I want to hear all about blue-eyed Betty."

"Oh, you will," said Derek.

Chapter 19

NEILL SPENT THE REST OF the weekend doing activities with the Longyears, but on Monday, he was eager to continue his Marquette history project by interviewing his ancestors. He decided to begin by visiting the McCareys since his father and grandmother had always wanted to know where Patrick McCarey came from and even the Bergmann family tree had been a mystery to them, unlike the Whitman family's since their genealogy could be traced back to early New England and then the Middle Ages in England.

Neill's father had pointed out the McCarey house in South Marquette to him many times, so he knew where to go, but it was quite a walk from Ridge Street. Neill didn't mind walking, but he hated sweating, and wearing layers of Victorian clothes was not conducive to staying cool. Wanting to make a good impression rather than arrive a sweaty mess, he decided to take the streetcar as far as he could. He learned from Howard that if he got on the streetcar at Arch Street, he could take it to the Hotel Superior in South Marquette. He'd still have to walk several blocks from there, but Neill had only seen the fabled hotel in the distance when he was downtown, so he decided he wouldn't mind walking from there.

After breakfast, Neill walked down Arch Street to the streetcar stop. Once aboard, he rode to Front Street and then downtown to Baraga Avenue. He traveled West on Baraga to South Third, then further south up the hill to Fisher Street, then Champion, and then on Blemhuber to the Hotel Superior. The McCareys lived on Division, which crossed Blemhuber but was still several blocks away. Regardless, Neill disembarked at the Hotel Superior. In Neill's time, the hotel was considered one of Marquette's great lost buildings, but it still appeared in its full glory in 1900 despite its financial problems. First opened in 1891, its owners had spent years struggling to promote it as "the queen of northern resorts." After failing to attract enough clientele to make it viable, it was leased to a Chicago businessman. Even with an orchestra brought from Chicago, the hotel's economic woes continued, and Neill knew it would soon cease operations altogether and be torn down in 1929. Therefore, he could not pass up this opportunity to see it.

The Summer Streetcar

Neill wandered about the beautiful gardens and peered up at the hotel with its three soaring towers that gave it a castle-like façade. Then he walked up the front steps onto the large veranda, not as large as that of the Grand Hotel on Mackinac Island, but certainly trying to compete with it. After walking the length of the veranda and nodding politely to the various guests relaxing on it, Neill entered the lobby and marveled at the beautiful interior, the height of Victorian elegance. Unable to resist, he then entered the dining room. He'd already had breakfast but could not pass up a chance to dine there, so he ordered coffee and a sweet roll. He people-watched the wealthy late Victorians in their elegant clothes dining around him, while above him were a hundred rooms, only half of which were filled with the well-to-do and those seeking the health benefits of Marquette's fresh air and the cool breezes blowing off Lake Superior.

The Hotel Superior

As Neill finished his meal, however, he began to feel nervous about his upcoming visit to the McCareys. He needed a little extra courage to leave the hotel, but eventually he did, bidding it adieu, thinking how thrilled Uncle Chad would have been to visit it. He would have analyzed and commented on every aspect of its Victorian grandeur from the potted plants to the exquisite curtains. Neill felt a little teary-eyed at the thought. Not wanting to cry in public, he took a last sip of coffee, then paid the bill, and focused on the next part of his mission.

Leaving the hotel behind him, Neill walked east a bit on Blemhuber to Division Street. Then he started south down the hill, and soon the McCarey house came into view. The simple two-story home could have fit inside the Longyear Mansion's tower and could hardly compare to the Hotel Superior, but Neill thought it had a homey look those structures lacked.

As Neill approached the house, a couple of boys were running about in the yard. He guessed they must be his great-grandmother's older brothers, though he could not remember their names. When they said hello, he asked, "Is this the McCarey residence?" Being told it was, he asked if their parents were home. "Our father is at work," the younger boy replied. "My mom and grandma are inside," replied the other.

Neill felt momentarily dejected. He had not considered that Patrick McCarey would be working, but he still wanted to meet the rest of the family. Before he could step up on the porch, the younger boy ran inside shouting, "Ma, there's a man out here to see you!"

Neill followed him onto the porch but not inside. He heard a woman reply, "Jeremy, you don't need to shout at me," and then she came to the door and said, "Hello. How may I help you?"

Neill recognized her instantly from the only photograph he'd ever seen of her—it must have been taken about this time. It was his great-great-grandmother, Kathy Bergmann McCarey.

"I'm Neill Jackson," he replied. "I'm writing a book about Marquette's history, and Mr. Peter White suggested I talk to Mrs. Montoni. He said she was one of the first settlers here."

"Oh," said the woman. "That's my mother. I'm Mrs. McCarey."

"It's a pleasure to meet you," Neill replied.

"I'm flattered Mr. White remembers us," said Mrs. McCarey, "though he and Mother did both arrive in Marquette that first year. Won't you come inside?"

Neill followed her into the house, freaking out to think she was his great-great-grandmother and in another moment he would meet her mother. She led him into the dining room where Molly was sitting. No one in Neill's family knew Molly's maiden name, but they knew she had married Fritz Bergmann before arriving in Marquette. She'd had two children, Kathy and Karl Bergmann, with him. Then he had died and she'd married a Mr. Montoni, whom family tradition said was abusive to her. After he died, she was apparently content to stay a widow. Neill could not believe she was sitting there at a table before him.

"We just finished breakfast," said Kathy, for that is how Neill thought of Mrs. McCarey, "but I'd be happy to get you some coffee."

"Thank you. That would be very kind," said Neill, fighting to hold back the tears coming to his eyes as Molly turned to look at him.

"And who is this?" asked Molly. Neill was surprised by her voice. She had a lilting Irish accent, despite her years of being married to a German and then an Italian husband, and living in the United States for more than half a century.

"I'm Neill Jackson," he replied, reaching out to shake her hand. He had expected a very old woman, but she seemed youthful and full of life. Quickly doing the math, he realized she couldn't be much more than seventy. "You must be Mrs. Montoni," he said.

"Yes. To what do I owe the pleasure?" she asked as he released her hand and took a seat across from her.

"Mother," said Kathy, "Mr. Jackson said Mr. White told him to come talk to you. Mr. Jackson is writing a book about Marquette and wants to interview you about Marquette's history."

As Kathy spoke, she went to the kitchen counter to pour Neill a cup of coffee and bring it over to him. "There's sugar on the table," she said, "and I can get you some cream if you like."

"Thank you," he said, looking about at the simple kitchen complete with a hand pump at the sink.

"I'm honored that you're interested in anything I can tell you," said Molly. "Peter knows more about Marquette history than I do, given that he's been more involved in making it, but I'll be glad to tell you what I know."

At that moment, a baby started crying. "Oh, dear," said Kathy. "Michael has been so fussy this morning." She set the cream on the table and excused herself, leaving Neill alone with Molly. For a moment, he recalled his great-grandmother had had an older brother named Michael—he had grown up to become Monsignor McCarey. Neill felt overwhelmed with delight at remembering this and being here with his family.

"What do you want to know?" asked Molly, waking Neill from his revery.

"Oh, so many things," said Neill. "I hope you don't mind if I have a lot of questions."

"No," said Molly. "I'll help you all I can."

What followed may have been the most exciting conversation of Neill's life. Molly told him all about how she had been working as a maid in Boston when she met her German immigrant husband Fritz and they had moved to Milwaukee. Fritz had struggled to find good work and they hadn't liked the city, so in the summer of 1849, they had decided to come to Marquette when it was first being built. Molly told Neill about the cholera epidemic and how Peter White had helped to nurse the sick that first year. She shared her memories of Chief Kawbawgam, the Harlows, the Everetts, and so many other early Marquette families, including her dear friend Clara Henning, who had died so young. Neill had had no idea she had been friends with Clara, who was his four-greats-grandmother on the Whitman side. When he asked Molly more questions, she told him how she had been like a second mother to Clara's daughter, Agnes, after her mother died, especially since she didn't get along with her new stepmother, Sophia. Then she described Agnes' wedding to Jacob Whitman, most memorable because the night of their honeymoon, in 1868, Marquette burned to the ground. "Poor Agnes and Jacob are both gone now, just like Clara," she said, adding with a hint of humor in her voice, "The good die young while the wicked like me live on."

Neill was tempted to ask Molly more about her family and his other relatives, but he did not want to appear nosey, so he asked her some questions about Marquette history. She recalled the first horrible winter when the settlers almost starved to death. "The supply ship was late, so Fritz and I and a group of others who had come from Milwaukee started walking back there to spend the winter when a messenger came after us to say the ship had come in. It was like a Christmas miracle." And then she recalled the first train in Marquette, the locations of different early businesses, being a member of Marquette's first literary society, the saloon her second husband Montoni owned, and what the first St. Peter's Cathedral had looked like before it burned down.

By then, Kathy had returned to the kitchen, so she added in a comment now and then. The morning passed so quickly that soon Kathy was asking Neill if he would stay for lunch. He did not wish to impose, but when both women pressed him, he agreed. They were so insistent, pushing food on him just like his grandmother, Ellen Whitman Vandelaare. He thought how she would have been perfectly at home here with her own grandmother and great-grandmother, women she'd never had the chance to meet and heard little about from her own mother. Neill again had to hold back tears as he thought what it would have meant to his grandma to be here.

Soon, the rambunctious boys from outside—Frank and Jeremy, ages twelve and nine respectively, as they informed him—were seated at the table beside him, eating sandwiches and asking him personal questions he tried to answer. They weren't interested in Marquette's history, but they were very curious about the inside of the Longyear Mansion when they learned he was staying there.

"No wonder you are a friend of Peter's," said Molly. "You know all the rich people in town."

"I'm hardly rich myself," said Neill, and when they questioned him about his family, he told the made-up story of the fire in which he had lost his parents.

"Tragedies happen even to the best families," said Molly, "but if you are hardy, you can survive anything."

"You have to have *sisu*—that's what our Finnish neighbors call it," added Kathy. "It means guts or gumption. You have to be tough."

"Fires are terrible," said Molly. "I know that well after having lived through the 1868 fire, and there have been plenty of other bad ones in Marquette, but let me tell you, the potato famine, now that was something to live through. You boys," she said, addressing her grandsons and Neill both, "have no idea how fortunate you are to live in this prosperous country. I do miss the Emerald Isle, but I thank my God every day that I came to the United States."

Neill tried to ask Molly about the potato famine, but she wouldn't say much beyond, "It was terrible," and "I don't want to give the boys nightmares." Finally, Kathy said, "Mother won't give us any details. The only person she's ever talked to about it is my husband, Patrick, and only because he came here from Ireland himself."

"Only another Irishman or Irishwoman can understand," said Molly.

"Mother, we're all Irish," Kathy replied.

"Only part-Irish," said Molly, "and you've never set foot there. But what about you, Mr. Jackson? You have a look of the Irish about you."

"Yes," said Neill, "I'm part Irish."

"Did your parents or grandparents come from Ireland?" asked Molly.

"No, much farther back than that," he said.

"Do you know which county they came from?" Molly persisted. Neill was amused by the question since the only way he could know was if she told him.

"No," he said. "I wish I did. What part of Ireland did you come from?"

"County Kerry," said Molly, satisfying his curiosity.

"Mother says it was beautiful," Kathy added.

"Aye, so very beautiful," said Molly. "More sparkling green than anything here in Upper Michigan, though it is beautiful here too, and like I said, I am glad to be here."

"Did you leave your family behind?" Neill asked.

"No, my parents came with me," said Molly.

"And what were their names?" asked Neill, hoping she would not think the question too personal since it was vital information from his perspective.

"Daniel and Katy Moynihan," she replied. "We arrived in Boston, and they stayed there with my siblings, but I fell in love with Fritz and went with him to Milwaukee and then here."

"Mother named me for my grandmother," said Kathy, "but my father liked Kathy over Katy."

Neill was thrilled. Now he knew Molly's maiden name, her parents' names, and where in Ireland she came from. With that information, he might be able to trace his Irish ancestry further.

"And what about your husband, Mrs. McCarey?" asked Neill. "What part of Ireland did he come from?"

"Patrick's like Mother, I'm afraid," said Kathy. "He won't talk much about Ireland. He's never told me."

"He has his reasons," said Molly.

"He's told Mother all his secrets," Kathy explained to Neill. "The two of them are as thick as thieves."

"Some of us have good reason to keep our secrets," said Molly. "Most people here consider themselves Americans, but there are several people from England in this town, and the English can't always be trusted."

"What does that mean?" asked Neill, thinking Mr. Jopling had seemed trustworthy.

"You clearly don't know your Irish history if you don't understand why I have no fondness for the English," said Molly, her eyes sparking.

"Oh, Mother," said Kathy, "you just said a little while ago how Clara Henning was the best friend you ever had, and she was English."

"She was American. There's a difference. Her ancestors left England centuries ago."

Kathy frowned and finished her cup of coffee, then said, "Well, excuse me, Mr. Jackson, but it is Monday, so I have to finish the washing."

"I should really help her, Mr. Jackson," said Molly, as her daughter stood up. "But it's a been a pleasure talking to you, and I wish you much luck with your book."

"Mother, you can sit," Kathy replied. "I can get the boys to help me."

Molly gave her a look as if to suggest she was crazy.

"I won't have those boys hanging up my unmentionables to dry," Molly said. "Please excuse us, Mr. Jackson. I'm sure you know a woman's work is never done. I may be an old lady, but I'm no lady of leisure like your Mrs. Longyear."

Neill suspected Mrs. Longyear would not appreciate the comparison, being far more down to earth and constantly occupied than Molly might think. However, he sadly realized it was time to go, so he thanked the women for the coffee and lunch, said goodbye to the boys, and started toward the front door. Something stopped him, though, and he turned around to ask, "Mrs. McCarey, do you think your husband would be willing to talk to me some time?"

"Oh, I don't know," she said. "He's fairly a newcomer to Marquette. Been here less than twenty years. I don't know what he could tell you, and he's busy working all the time. It's surprising how much crime there is in a town this size."

"I see," said Neill. "Well, thank you anyway." And he took his leave.

Neill hated to walk away without permission to return to talk to Patrick McCarey, but it was understandable they did not think Patrick could tell him much about Marquette history, and it did not sound like he would want to share his past. Patrick McCarey had always seemed like a rather mysterious ancestor to him, and it looked like he would remain that way. But if he had time, Neill thought he might try again someday, and he had plenty of other people to interview. Besides, he was thrilled just with the priceless family information he had gained today.

It was now almost two o'clock, and Neill was content with what he had accomplished for the day. He dearly wanted to talk to the Dalrymples, Cordelia Whitman, and maybe Will Whitman, but he also wanted to write down what he had learned. Plus, it was a hot day, and by the time he had walked uphill on Division Street, he was more than sweaty enough. He was so tempted to take off his jacket and roll up his shirt sleeves, but he was afraid that would be too scandalous—Officer McCarey might arrest him then, and as much as Neill wanted to talk to him, he knew he had to find a better way to get his great-great-grandfather's attention.

So, Neill hopped back on the streetcar and rode it to Arch Street, noticing so many things as he went through the downtown that he had still not noticed before and that were so different from how Marquette looked in his own time. Hotels, businesses, churches, houses—he had a treasure trove of details he could spend the rest of his life documenting if he stayed in this time. He would rather return to his own century, but it was sad to think when he did, he would have only scratched the surface of the knowledge available to him about Marquette and his family's past.

Once back at the Longyear Mansion, Neill was greeted on the veranda by Abby and Allison. They said they were just going to have some lemonade if he wanted to join them. He thanked them and promised to be back in a few minutes. He was thirsty, but first he wanted to go upstairs and wash off the sweat clinging to his body. He would have rather written down his notes than drink lemonade, but he didn't want to be rude. He also felt like he needed time to absorb everything he had learned.

Truth be told, when he got to his room, he sat down on his bed and had a little cry, which surprised him, but he was so glad to have talked to Molly and Kathy and to have met his great-grandmother's brothers. He felt happy, wistful, homesick, and just too many emotions to describe any of them accurately. Meeting his ancestors felt like he had gained a piece of himself that had always been missing, though he had not known it was lacking until now. It was simultaneously a feeling of completeness and sadness to know he might never see them again.

Once he got ahold of himself, Neill washed up, changed his shirt, and went down for lemonade. Sitting on the veranda, he tried to make small talk with Allison and all the Longyear siblings, though he noticed Howard was very silent. Neill suspected Howard had read more information in his journal that might be troubling him.

"Allison, how much longer do you think you'll be staying with us?" Helen asked as they enjoyed a cool breeze off the lake. "Don't you have to get back East soon?"

"Yes," said Allison. "Howard and I just talked about that this morning. Classes resume at Cornell and the medical college at Harvard on the same day. Howard has offered to accompany me back East."

"I wish I could go with you," said Abby, "but classes don't start at Smith until September so I have a couple of more weeks."

"What about you, Neill?" asked Helen. "Will you and Derek be going back with your sister?"

"I don't know," said Neill. "I think Derek really likes working for your father and wants to stay here in Upper Michigan. I haven't decided for myself. If I do stay, Derek and I will get a place of our own so we don't impose on your family any longer."

"It's no imposition," Abby said.

"We like having you here!" said Judith.

"I appreciate all your kindness," Neill replied, "but I've stayed long enough. And without Howard here to keep watch over his sisters, it would be indelicate for me to remain."

"You're so old-fashioned, Neill," said Helen.

"Besides, I can protect my sisters," said Jack.

"As can our father," Abby told her younger brother.

"I think you should come with us, Neill," said Howard. "You could stay with me at Cornell and go to school there. You're more than smart enough, and I'm sure if my father put in a good word for you, they'd admit you."

"We'll see," said Neill. "I'll think it over."

"Well, we'll be leaving Saturday," said Allison, "so you better think fast."

Neill was surprised by this statement. Why hadn't they told him this sooner? Of course, Howard had to return to Cornell, but there was no reason Allison had to leave. What kind of plans was she really making? He'd have to wait to find out later.

"Excuse me," Howard said, "but I want to collect some of my books so I don't forget to bring them back to Cornell. I better do it now before I forget. Neill, would you mind helping me?"

"Sure," Neill said, imagining Howard just wanted to talk to him in private. "I'll see all of you at dinner."

Neill stood up and followed Howard inside. Howard kept his lips sealed until they reached his room. Then he shut the door and said, "Allison and I are going to take the train East, or pretend to, so no one will suspect anything."

"You're not really going back to Cornell?" asked Neill.

"Maybe," Howard said, "depending on what I learn between now and then. Of course, Allison isn't going back to school since she concocted that whole story about attending medical school at Harvard, so we need to figure out what you and she will do. Maybe you can find somewhere in Ithaca to live while I attend school there, or maybe I'll figure out how to get you back home before then."

"Don't we need to go back up to the Club to do that?" asked Neill.

"No," said Howard. "The dolmen doesn't actually have anything to do with time travel. It's all done through Odin's Eye. We should be able to transport you from anywhere, though if I transported you from Cornell, you would end up at Cornell in your own time. Is there a Cornell in your time?"

"I think so," said Neill. "I've never been there, but I've heard of the school."

Howard looked surprised that Neill seemed almost unsure. "Cornell is one of the top schools in the country," he said.

"And it probably is in my time too," said Neill, "but I went to Northern Michigan University, which grew out of the Normal School here. My parents couldn't have afforded to send me to Cornell."

Howard frowned.

"What's wrong, Howard?" asked Neill. "You don't look very happy. I'm not trying to put down Cornell."

"It's nothing," Howard replied.

"Do you really think you'll be able to send me home?"

"I am pretty sure I will," said Howard. "At least, I'm sure I can figure out how it would work; I made a big discovery today that made it all seem clear to me. It might still take me a little longer to work out the details, though. I'm not sure I can make it work without the help of a lab, which is why I want to be at Cornell."

"I trust you will figure it out," said Neill. "You obviously did in another time based on the journals you wrote and what I learned when I was in 2142."

"Yes, I figured it out then, but it took me many years," said Howard, "not a few weeks."

"Well, I'll have to be satisfied with however long it takes," said Neill, patting him on the shoulder to show his appreciation, though he'd much rather have waited in Marquette than Ithaca to get back to his own time. He had no ancestors in Ithaca.

"Thanks, Neill," said Howard, sitting down on the bed. "I just hope figuring it out is the right thing to do."

"It is for me," said Neill. "I know Allison and I will both be grateful."

"What if Allison decides not to go home with you?" asked Howard, looking up at him.

Neill sat down in an easy chair and asked, "Is she planning not to?"

"She doesn't know," Howard replied. "She's said that if Derek is going to stay, there's no reason why she can't."

"There is a reason," said Neill. "Her mom must be heartbroken that she's gone, just like my parents. If I return to our time but she doesn't, how will I ever explain it to her mom?"

"It seems," Howard replied, "like you and Allison are both good at coming up with stories to cover the truth."

"What does that mean?" asked Neill, feeling he was being accused of something.

"Nothing. Just that you've had to play roles to hide that you are time travelers, so I'm sure you can find a way to hide the truth from people in your time."

"I suppose we'll have to," said Neill. "No one will believe the truth after all."

Howard sighed and stared at the floor. He looked like he had the weight of the world on his shoulders. Neill didn't know how to comfort him, so he said, "I better go change for dinner, and I want to write down some of my notes from meeting my family members today, unless you seriously need help with your books."

"No," said Howard, not looking up. "Go ahead."

Neill went to his room, shut the door, and sat down at the desk. He felt frustrated again about the time travel situation, but he knew he had no control over when he would get to travel or if Allison or Derek would accompany him. He thought it best to focus on writing down his notes. He was writing them because family was important to him, but he realized not everyone felt the ties that bind as strongly as he did.

Chapter 20

T HE NEXT MORNING, NEILL SET off for the Dalrymples' house. He had consulted the *Polk City Directory* for Marquette to find out where they lived. He knew Charles Dalrymple, his three-greats-grandfather, had been a carpenter and often would live in one house while building another, then move into the new house and sell the old one, then start building another house to move into, all while building other people's houses. Consequently, the Dalrymples had moved about many times over the years. Neill could not begin to remember the locations of all of their houses. This year, he found, they were living on Michigan Street over by the corner of Fifth. It was quite a walk there, but no streetcar ran in that direction, so he had to walk.

This morning, Neill expected a similar situation to yesterday—that Charles Dalrymple would be at work, so he would only find his wife, Christina, at home and possibly the children. And Neill was almost correct in this assumption.

After knocking on the Dalrymples' front door, Neill waited a moment until it was opened by Margaret. Her eyes expanded to twice their size when she saw him.

"Hello, Miss Dalrymple," he replied. "Do you remember me?"

"Yes, John, right?" she said.

"No," he replied, and quickly explained that he had now regained his memory and that his name was Neill Jackson.

"That's so interesting and romantic," she replied. The word "romantic" immediately reminded Neill of her crush on Howard Longyear, so he thought it best not to mention he was now staying with Howard's family.

"It turns out I'm from Marquette," he said, "and Mr. White has encouraged me to write a history of Marquette, so I am interviewing early residents."

"You're awful young to be writing a history book, aren't you?" asked Margaret.

"I'm almost twenty," he replied.

"Oh, you must be really smart then," she replied. "I have always liked clever men, probably because I'm Scottish and the Scottish are very clever. Are you Scottish?"

"Yes, a little," he replied, knowing all his Scottish blood came from his descent from her.

"A little bit?" she replied. "What else are you?"

"Irish, English, Germ—"

"I can't marry an Englishman," Margaret interrupted. "My grandfather would be appalled."

Neill couldn't help wondering what it was everyone had against the English. Well, he knew, but it was strange he kept finding people who disliked them given that most of Marquette's founders were of English descent, via New England.

"Well," said Neill, "in any case, I was wondering if I could speak to your parents about their memories of Marquette."

"My parents aren't home," said Margaret. "My father is working, and my mother went to pay calls with my sister Sarah, and my brother Charles is playing next door. It's just me and my grandpa here. I had to stay home to keep an eye on him because he's not very good at walking now."

Her grandfather? What was his name? Neill couldn't remember.

"Is your grandfather's memory still good?" Neill asked.

"Oh, yes," said Margaret. "He knows all about Bonnie Prince Charlie and Mary, Queen of Scots, and Robert the Bruce, and Sir William Wallace, and everything there is to know about the Dalrymple clan's history."

"Can I talk to him?" asked Neill, less interested in Scottish than Marquette history, but Mr. Dalrymple might tell him something of his Scottish ancestors.

"I can ask him," Margaret replied. "Wait here."

She left Neill standing on the front porch with the door wide open. He could hear her talking to her grandfather, but he could not make out the words. Then she hollered, "Come in, Mr. Jackson!" so he entered the house and shut the door behind him.

By then, Margaret had returned to the hall. She took him by the hand and led him into the parlor to meet her grandfather.

"Hello, sir," said Neill to the elderly man, who looked like he must be ninety. His skin was weathered and he had an almost snow-white beard. But his eyes sparkled with life when he saw Neill, suggesting his mind was still good, even if his body was failing him.

"Hello, laddie," he replied.

Surprised to be called such a thing, Neill said, "I'm Neill Jackson, and I'm writing a book about the history of Marquette. I wondered if I could interview you for it."

"Certainly," said Mr. Dalrymple. "Sit down."

Neill found a chair and explained he would take notes as they talked, which Mr. Dalrymple said was fine. Then Neill asked him for his full name.

"Arthur Charles Dalrymple," he replied. Instantly, Neill recalled that was the name he had seen in a family tree and on the gravestone his father had shown him in Park Cemetery. "But before we go further," said Mr. Dalrymple, "are you related to Henry Jackson and his wife? She was a good Scotswoman, though I can't remember her first name now. Henry wasn't Scottish, but her first husband was of the name of Stewart. Any relation?"

"No, I'm afraid not," said Neill, loving the old man's accent, which was Scottish in origin but had been diluted by growing up in Nova Scotia. It reminded him of his father's trying to imitate a Scottish accent whenever he would point out something was Scottish, adding, "and if it ain't Scottish, it's cra-ap."

"Sad story about Mrs. Jackson," Mr. Dalrymple continued. "She got run over by a drunk driver when she was trying to cross Washington Street."

"A drunk driver?" said Neill, surprised since he didn't think anyone in Marquette even owned an automobile yet. "When was that?"

"Oh, let's see. Must be a few years ago now. It was on Decoration Day. The driver was coming in his horse and carriage from the doings they were having to remember the soldiers. They hit her and just kept going. So tragic and irresponsible."

"How terrible," said Neill, surprised to think drunk driving had existed in horse-and-buggy days.

"I knew her quite well," said Mr. Dalrymple. "All we Scots used to stick together, you know. Her daughter married a Swiss man—funny since my son Charles married a woman from Switzerland too—quite a group of them in Ontario. But her other children all married Scots. Let's see. There was her son William Stewart; he's still around—owns a livery stable. And the daughter who married a Swiss man—Joseph Zryd, that was his name—he plays the violin beautifully—they had a daughter who married William McCombie.

And William McCombie's brother Daniel married a Rutherford—I think she was a cousin of some sort—a granddaughter of Mrs. Jackson too. The McCombie brothers are both carpenters. They work sometimes with my son Charles. Yes, there has been quite a community of Scots here, though most of us are getting older now and the younger generations are marrying whomever they want—that's Americans for you—they want to forget their roots and pretend to be all the same nationality."

"Not me, Grandpa," said Margaret. "I want to marry a Scot, preferably an earl."

Arthur Dalrymple laughed and said to Neill, "Maggie used to want to marry a prince, but I told her Scotland hasn't had a prince since Bonnie Prince Charlie. Those Hanoverians stole the throne, and today all the British princes are more German than Scottish or English."

"That's why I changed to an earl," said Margaret. "I couldn't marry someone English."

"Well, I don't know where you're going to find a laird of any kind around here," said her grandfather.

"You said the Earls of Stair are Dalrymples," Margaret reminded her grandfather, "which makes them my distant cousins, so they would be perfect."

"Yes," said her grandfather, "but unless you go to Scotland, you won't likely find one of them."

"Well, if I must marry an American, there's always Howard Longyear," said Margaret.

Neill considered pointing out that Howard had English blood in him, as well as German, but he decided to focus on Mr. Dalrymple, so he asked him, "What made you move to Marquette?"

Mr. Dalrymple explained how the family had come to Marquette to work after migrating to Chicago from Ontario. They had gone to Chicago to find work because the city was being rebuilt after the great fire of 1871 and carpenters were in high demand. He had moved to Ontario in his youth, but he had been born in Nova Scotia, and his father had been born in Scotland. Whenever Neill tried to ask Mr. Dalrymple questions about Marquette, Margaret would interrupt or Mr. Dalrymple would go off on some tangent about Scotland or Nova Scotia. Neill found neither Mr. Dalrymple nor Margaret were much good as sources of Marquette history, but regardless, he was enjoying his interaction with them. They were his family members after all, and he couldn't help noticing that some of Margaret's mannerisms, including her flair for the dramatic, rather resembled those of his sister, Madeleine.

Just before noon, Margaret's mother and sister Sarah returned home. Mrs. Dalrymple looked rather annoyed to see Neill there, though she was polite. Sarah proved to be as inquisitive as Margaret and immediately began asking Neill questions about himself.

"Isn't he handsome, Sarah?" Margaret asked her.

"Now, girls, none of that," Mrs. Dalrymple reprimanded. "Mr. Jackson, will you be staying for dinner?"

"Oh, thank you, but I'm afraid not," Neill replied, sensing she did not want him to stay. She clearly had housework to do, and he realized he was in her way. He felt bad that his own ancestor would feel annoyed by his presence, but he had intruded into her home so he understood. He was curious to know more about her own Swiss ancestry—he recalled her maiden name had been Zurbrugg, and he wanted to ask how she and her husband had met, and so many other questions, but he didn't know if he'd ever get the chance now, especially if he ended up leaving Marquette with Howard and Allison on Saturday.

"Come again," said Margaret as she showed Neill to the door. He was almost afraid she would want to walk him home, which could have been a disaster since she'd learn he was staying at the Longyear Mansion. By now, Neill understood it wouldn't matter if she did marry Howard Longyear, but he still couldn't imagine how Howard, in any time, could be interested in such a talkative and romantically unrealistic young girl. That said, there had to be something attractive about her for his own great-great-grandfather to marry her. Neill could only think Margaret would do a lot of maturing in the next three years before she got married.

Neill was hungry since he hadn't had lunch, but he also knew Cordelia Whitman's house was just a few blocks away and walking downtown or back to the Longyear Mansion to get something to eat would be out of his way. He feared Cordelia might be napping if he called after lunch, given she was not that many years younger than Mr. Dalrymple, so he took his chances and walked to her house now.

He was hardly prepared for the reception he received. After knocking, Neill waited only a few seconds before Cordelia flung open the door with a smile on her face and said, "Why, Will, I didn't expect to see you today!"

Neill didn't know how to respond. She thought he was her grandson. Did he look like his great-great-grandfather?

"Um," he said, "Mrs. Whitman, I'm sorry, but I'm Neill Jackson."

"Neill Jackson?" she replied, peering at him over her spectacles. "I'm afraid I don't recall ever meeting you."

Neill launched into an explanation of how he had visited her previously with Mr. White, but at the time, he had thought his name was John.

Cordelia just laughed and immediately understood her mistake.

"My eyesight isn't what it was," she admitted, "but still, you are very like Will. The same height and build, and there's something about your nose and cheekbones…. I'm surprised I didn't notice the resemblance when you were here before, but then you were with Mr. White, so I saw you in a different context, I guess."

"Yes," said Neill, still stunned by the mistake she had made. He recalled his father telling him how once his great-aunt Eleanor had told him he looked like her father, Will Whitman. Neill's father had said he could never see the resemblance until he was in his thirties and got his first pair of glasses. When he had looked in the mirror, there he saw staring back at him his great-grandfather. *People do say I look like my father*, Neill thought, *so I guess I could look like Will also.*

"How rude of me to keep you standing on the porch," said Cordelia. "Please come inside. I was just going to make a sandwich for dinner. Would you like to join me?"

"That's very kind of you," he said. "I'd love to if it's not too much trouble."

Neill could see it was a bit of trouble, though Cordelia said it wasn't. She had a hard time carrying some of the heavier things to the table like the jar of pickles, which she couldn't even get open, but Neill opened it for her and helped her with some other things. He sensed that unlike Christina Dalrymple, she felt it a relief and pleasure to have him there.

As Neill helped Cordelia make sandwiches, he told her his fake story of how he had regained his memory, and then about his Marquette history project, which instantly sent her off reminiscing about Marquette's early days. She talked about the boarding house she had operated, all the years she and her family had been involved in the local Methodist church, her views on temperance, including how she hoped someday Prohibition legislation would be passed, and also why women should be allowed to vote. Then she talked about her childhood growing up in New York and what Methodist meetings had been like there and how her grandfather's drinking problem had hurt the family fortunes, causing him eventually to convert to Methodism.

It was quite the rambling conversation, but Neill let her talk, asking her a question now and then to bring the subject back to Marquette so he didn't seem too eager to learn about her family.

"I'm very proud of my family," Cordelia said at one point. "Why, we've been involved in almost every major event in this country, not the least of which is the growth of the iron ore industry here in the Lake Superior region, which is why my father was intent on coming here. He wanted to start his own forge, but he ended up working with Mr. Harlow instead. My grandson Jacob fought in the Civil War. We didn't have any relatives in the Spanish-American War or the Mexican War, but my father fought in the War of 1812 and his father and both grandfathers fought in the American Revolution."

"Yes, I knew that," said Neill before realizing such a statement was a slip up on his part.

"You did?" said Cordelia. "How could you know that?"

"Um, I think Mr. White told me," Neill replied, "or maybe it was Mrs. Montoni. She told me about the Hennings. Your sister married a Mr. Henning, right?"

"Oh, yes," said Cordelia, not finding Neill's excuse odd at all, and then she was off talking about her sister Sophia and her brother Darius, who had been an Indian scout; that made her recall that she had an ancestor who had been killed by Indians in King Philip's War. Neill had never heard of King Philip's War, which surprised Cordelia. She informed him it had been a major uprising of Native Americans against the Puritan settlers of New England in the 1670s.

"Oh, yes," she said, "as I told you, my family has connections to almost all major events in American history." Neill wasn't sure King Philip's War counted as a major event, but he realized he was no expert on colonial history.

"We go way back in Connecticut and Massachusetts on different sides of the family," Cordelia continued. "One of my ancestors was even accused of witchcraft during the Salem Witch Trials, though she lived in Andover. Most people don't know a lot of other people were accused not just in Salem but throughout Massachusetts and Connecticut. It was just horrible," she said. "Makes me glad to be a Methodist and not a Puritan, though I do admire my Puritan ancestors for coming to this country."

"I can't imagine being hanged as a witch," said Neill, thinking he was fortunate to have time traveled to 1900 and not 1692 Salem; if he'd been discovered to be a time traveler then, he'd have probably been burnt at a stake. "What was her name?"

"Oh," said Cordelia, "you would ask me that."

"Was it Brookfield?" asked Neill, knowing that was Cordelia's maiden name.

"No, it was on my mother's side of the family, but her mother's mother's side, I believe. Oh, dear, I can't remember. It will probably come to me in the middle of the night."

Neill did not press her further. But he filed away the information for future investigation. His father would be very interested and probably could find the information through some online genealogy website.

When they finished lunch, Neill helped Cordelia clean off the table. He offered to wash the dishes for her, but she said no, that she would do it after she had a little nap.

"Can I do anything for you before I go?" asked Neill, thinking how she reminded him of his own grandmother and Great-Great-Aunt Eleanor whom he had known as a small child.

"No, Sylvia or one of the boys will be over later to check on me."

"Who's Sylvia?" he asked, not recalling the name.

"My granddaughter, Jacob's daughter. She has her hands full with her own children, but she usually stops by when she can. Sometimes I think it's just to get away from her husband, though. I tried to tell her not to marry him; he's a good-for-nothing—just recently got fired for stealing from his job at Getz's; he never holds down a job for long, but I probably shouldn't be talking about her business to strangers."

"I'd love to meet her," said Neill, "and her children."

"If you do, don't tell her I told you all that. Anyway, she rarely brings the children. She usually leaves them with Will or Clarence. They can be unruly, so she always worries they'll break something."

"I see," said Neill. "And where does she live?"

"Oh, just a few blocks away," said Cordelia.

Since Neill had not found any other Whitmans in the city directory, he realized his great-great-grandfather Will must live with Sylvia and her husband.

"What is her husband's name?" asked Neill.

"Cumming," Cordelia said. "His family isn't old Marquette like ours, so I doubt you'd want to talk to them."

Neill did want to talk to Sylvia and her brothers, if not her husband, but he did not press Cordelia further. He could see she was tired. He could find out the Cummings' address in the city directory.

"I'll be going then," he said reluctantly. "I hope you have a good rest."

"Thank you," Cordelia replied. "It was pleasant having someone to eat dinner with. Being an old lady who lives by herself can get lonely."

Neill said goodbye, but Cordelia insisted on walking him to the door, though she was clearly tired. She stood at the door and was still waving when he looked back a block later. He again had that feeling he'd had the day before of wanting to cry. He hoped he would see Cordelia again. Maybe he would visit her some evening when her grandchildren might be there.

Neill understood now that knowing more about the dates when his ancestors were born or where they came from or even their parents' names were not the things that really mattered. What mattered was what he had inherited from them—and not titles or castles, like the dream of being royal or connected to famous people—but how he had inherited personality traits, beliefs, hopes, dreams, and mannerisms—those were his true inheritance that had made him part of a family chain—and God willing, someday he would help to continue it.

Overall, it had been a most satisfying day. Neill also appreciated that it was cooler today as he walked back to the Longyear Mansion. He couldn't wait to get to his room and write down his family history directly as he'd heard it from the mouths of his ancestors.

But he had only been sitting and writing for a few minutes when someone again knocked on the door. Neill quickly hid his paper under a book and said, "Come in!"

"Neill," said Howard, quickly entering the room and shutting the door behind him, "I need to talk to you."

"Okay," Neill replied, turning in his chair.

Howard sat down on the bed and, raising his eyebrows with excitement, said, "Neill, I believe I've figured out how to get you back to the twenty-first century!"

"Really?"

"Yes. I know how to get Odin's Eye to work with Allison's cell phone to trigger the right path to be created."

"You mean the wormhole?" Neill asked.

"Sort of. Not exactly, but I'm pretty sure it will work. We just need to gain a little velocity to make it happen, and I think that can be done on a train."

"A train?" said Neill, not understanding.

Howard began a discussion of physics that included something about how velocity was needed to trigger their passage through the wormhole once the Odin's Eye opened it. Neill did not understand why velocity was needed when it hadn't been before, but it had something to do with the need to create a type of shortcut to Neill's original time. Neill really didn't catch 90 percent of what Howard said, but it didn't matter; he was just relieved that Howard thought it would work.

"How did you figure it out?" he asked, amazed.

"It's in my journal," said Howard, "and may I say there is a lot of other stuff in there that horrifies me."

Howard went on to explain more, citing scientific theories and mathematical equations that might as well have been Greek to Neill. But Neill couldn't resist saying, "Wow!" when Howard mentioned how his journals revealed that in the 1920s he had spent time working with Albert Einstein. Neill found that amazing, but what Howard and Einstein had discussed all went over Neill's head. Nothing much about time travel made sense to him. He was just grateful it made sense to Howard.

"But to get to the point," said Neill, "you can get us home?"

"Yes," said Howard. "I think if we get a private car on the train, we—meaning you, me, and Allison—can use Odin's Eye to make it happen."

"And just what will happen?"

"When the train is at full speed, I'll enter in the combination needed to suck us through a wormhole to 2021."

"Us?" said Neill. "Are you going too?" Neill was in total shock at this development.

"I want to be with Allison," Howard replied, "and I don't know how to make it work so only the two of you can go since you won't know how to operate Odin's Eye by yourself and we have to be touching it to make us enter the wormhole."

"You don't think Allison and I are capable of it if you show us what to do?" asked Neill.

"I don't think we want to take a chance of something going wrong," Howard replied. "If somehow you ended up in the wrong time, you wouldn't know how to get where you want to go from there.

"And we'll just disappear from the train?" asked Neill.

"Yes. If anyone sees us, which we'll make sure doesn't happen, it will seem like we disappeared, but actually, we'll go through the wormhole and end up wherever the train track was in the twenty-first century—somewhere in Wisconsin most likely, but once there, we can figure out how to get back to Marquette."

Neill looked skeptical. He was glad Howard had found a solution, but he wasn't sure he wanted to disappear on a high-speed train.

"Are you sure you want to go too, Howard?" he asked, imagining the issues that might result from Howard traveling to the future.

"As I said," Howard replied, "there are some really terrible things going to happen in the future if I stay in this time and live until 1965 like you told me I would. I'm not sure I want to live through World War I, the influenza of 1918, the Great Depression, or the atomic bombing of Japan."

"I see," said Neill. "But do you think 2021 is any better?"

"Well," said Howard, "I know you told me one day about the coronavirus, but it doesn't sound as bad as the 1918 influenza."

"But the coronavirus pandemic isn't over yet," said Neill. "Most people were getting vaccinated when I left, but they were still worried about getting it."

"I'll take my chances so I can be with Allison," Howard replied. "That's the most important thing. After losing Hugh, I realized how precious life is and we have to take our chances for happiness while they last."

Neill didn't really understand love, having never experienced it yet, so he wasn't going to argue. He just asked, "Will we arrive there in 2021 in August on the same date as we leave here?"

"Yes," said Howard, "and who knows what's happened since you left your time. By now the pandemic is probably over."

"I hope so," said Neill, "but who knows what other horrible things will happen in my time, and what if you decide you want to go back to your own time but you can't?"

"Oh, but you see, I'll have the Odin's Eye, or I can go to the dolmen in your time, where there's another Odin's Eye, and that will bring me back to 1900, just like it brought you and Allison here from 2021."

"That's true," said Neill.

"But I don't intend to come back," Howard stated. "I intend to be with Allison."

"It will be difficult for you to live in another time," said Neill.

"Not any harder than it's been for you," Howard replied.

"I don't know about that," said Neill. "I at least knew my history and had some idea of what to expect. You have very little conception of what the twenty-first century is like."

"It sounds amazing from what you and Allison have told me," said Howard. "I want to see it for myself, and since Allison has decided she can't abandon her mother, if I want to be with her, I have no choice."

"What about your parents? Won't you miss them?"

"Of course. I love them, but they will have my brothers and sisters to console them, and like I said, I can always come back. Maybe Allison and I will even decide to come back permanently someday. Or we can come and go as we please. It would be like if the year 1900 is our summer home and 2021 is our winter home."

"I don't know," said Neill, shaking his head. "That's a big maybe. And what about Derek? Aren't we going to invite him to come with us?"

"I sent him a private message this morning while you were out," said Howard, "so we should hear from him tomorrow, but I suspect he's going to stay here."

"I think so too," said Neill. "He thinks he's in love with some woman named Betty who works at the Breitung Hotel."

"Well, men make sacrifices for the women they love," Howard replied, smiling like a lovesick fool.

"I guess," said Neill, wondering if someday he would ever feel the same way. First, he'd have to meet the right woman. "So, when is this going to happen?"

"Saturday," said Howard. "I've already booked a private car to take us as far as Chicago. We'll need a good speed, so we'll wait until we're in Wisconsin and the train is moving rapidly to try it. If it doesn't work, we'll go on to Cornell since I'll be starting college again the week after, and then we can figure out what to do from there, but I'm pretty confident it will work."

"It is wonderful you figured it out, Howard," said Neill. "I really appreciate all the effort you've put into trying to help me."

"You're welcome," said Howard. "Let's just hope it works the way I think it will. Anyway, I'll leave you be for now. I promised my brothers I'd bowl with them this afternoon. They've been complaining that I've been spending too much time locked up in my room this summer, especially since they know I'll be leaving in a few days."

Neill's face dropped. Saturday was only four days from now, and he'd barely started on his history project. Plus, he was supposed to work at Getz's the rest of the week. He hated to do it, but in the morning, he would go tell Mr. Getz he had to quit. He didn't want to lose any opportunities to interview more historical people of importance.

"Have you visited all your relatives?" Howard asked, seeing Neill's expression.

"Most of them," said Neill, "but I'd like to talk to some other people in Marquette too."

"Good," said Howard. "My siblings and I will take you around and introduce you to some people. We'll make the most of these last days."

"Great," said Neill, trying to sound enthusiastic, but he was nervous the time travel would not work, and he did not want to get his hopes up too much.

"Well, I'll see you at dinner unless you feel like bowling," said Howard, getting up from the bed and tapping Neill on the arm.

"No thanks," said Neill. "Maybe this evening, but first I want to get my notes organized of what my family told me today."

"Okay," said Howard. "I'll see you later."

Once Howard had shut the door behind him, Neill found his mind spinning.

Velocity. Einstein. Something about density and energy and, of course, a wormhole. It's unbelievable. I wouldn't believe any of it if it weren't happening to me. I wish my and Allison's cell phones hadn't died on us. Imagine if I could have videotaped all this. But it's probably better that we keep it to ourselves. We don't want time travel to fall into the wrong hands.

Now that he was about to go home, Neill felt like he could begin to appreciate what an adventure it had all been. *Maybe someday I'll even wish I could do it all over again. But for now, I'm grateful that I might finally be going home.*

Chapter 21

THE NEXT THREE DAYS TURNED out to be among the happiest of Neill's life. His hopes were high that he'd return home, yet he remained focused on enjoying every moment of late Victorian Marquette just as Uncle Chad would have wanted.

Howard was as good as his word, telling his sisters he had yet to visit many of their neighbors that summer and convincing them to form a party to pay calls on some of Marquette's most notable residents. After Neill telephoned Getz's and explained to his employer that he was quitting, which Mr. Getz was fine with since business was slowing down, Neill found himself inside the parlors of the Balls and Charltons, Spears and Kaufmans. Of course, he, Allison, and the Longyears visited Peter White and the Joplings again and some other families Neill did not recall ever hearing about from his parents or any Marquette history book. He gladly soaked up every minute of priceless conversation.

The Longyear children often laughed at Neill on the way to and from these visits because he would stop to stare at buildings, trying to imprint on his memory every inch of 1900 Marquette. He was especially fascinated by the exquisite and decorative buildings that no longer existed in his time, such as the Wilkinson Block on the northeast corner of Washington and Front Streets, which had been replaced by a modern glass and steel bank long before he was born. And then there was the Ely School on Bluff Street. Howard told him all these buildings had been designed by Mr. Charlton, who had been the architect for the Longyear Mansion. Neill even got to see Dandelion Cottage in its original location behind St. Paul's before it had been moved farther down Arch Street in 1992, an event his father remembered. Even the horses, wagons, and streetcars were wonders to him, and the Lower Harbor was a great industrial railroad mess of astonishment to him. It was all Neill could do to rein in his enthusiasm. Even though he'd been in this time now for the better part of a month and a half, he realized he had only begun to appreciate it.

But there was one place he really wanted to see. Friday morning before breakfast, Neill confessed to Howard his seemingly impossible desire. "You see," he said, "I grew up in the Robert O'Neill Historical Home. Mr. O'Neill won't even be born until 1904, but his house is that big brownstone on Ridge that belongs to his great-aunt, Carolina Smith. Do you think there's a way we could convince Mrs. Smith to let me inside?"

"Hmm," said Howard. "None of us like Mrs. Smith. We could ask Mother, but I doubt she would agree to call on Mrs. Smith and drag us along. Let's ask my sisters to see what they suggest."

After Mr. and Mrs. Longyear left the breakfast table, Howard broached the question to Abby and Helen.

"Neill would like to see the inside of Judge Smith's house. Do you think we could pay a call there?" he asked.

"And see that old biddy, Carolina Smith?" asked Helen, shocking everyone at the table, for the Longyear children were rarely anything but well-mannered. "Not on your life."

"Helen," Howard reprimanded her, while nodding his head toward their younger siblings to warn she was setting a poor example.

"Well, you know she is a nasty woman," said Abby, defending her sister.

"That word is just as bad as the one Helen used," Howard replied, but then he smiled and said, "Not that I couldn't come up with a few choice ones for her myself."

"Mrs. Smith isn't nice," Neill agreed. "When Mr. White was trying to help me recall my memory, he took me there because I thought the house seemed familiar. She basically yelled at him. But still, I've always admired the house and would love to see inside it."

"I'd love to see the inside of it too," said Allison, who understood what the Longyear sisters did not—it was the home Neill had grown up in, and he wanted to see it in all its Victorian splendor. After all, his parents operated it as a historical home, and she had been inside it herself countless times.

"Jane is a sweet girl, despite her mother," Abby said, "and she had a baby last spring. I've been feeling guilty that I haven't called on her. She's a few years older than me, but she's always been friendly to me."

"So you'll call upon her?" asked Howard. "Is she living with her mother?"

"Yes, she and her husband recently had a new house built and will be moving in next month, I believe," said Abby, "but she should be at her parents' house now. Of course, we'll have to go downtown to buy a present for the baby, but then we could go pay a visit."

After a little discussion, it was decided Neill and Allison would accompany Abby and Howard in paying a call. The rest of the Longyear children had plenty of excuses for not seeing Mrs. Smith.

Once they finished breakfast, the four designated visitors walked downtown to find a baby gift, and then they returned to Ridge Street and stopped at the Smith house.

They had great good fortune, for Judge Smith was at the courthouse and Mr. Hampton, Jane's husband, was at his law office, while Mrs. Smith was off bullying some church committee. All that meant Jane was home with just the baby and servants.

Jane seemed surprised to see them, but she welcomed them into the house. Abby and Allison immediately began cooing over the baby, remarking how adorable he was. Neill realized once his mother used the baby's name that he was Mark Hampton, who would one day inherit this house and marry Eliza Graham—the beautiful young woman the teenage Robert O'Neill would be desperately in love with. Robert O'Neill had hated his second cousin Mark Hampton as a result. But it would all work out. Mark would be killed in World War I, and after many years, Eliza would marry Robert. Neill knew all this from Mr. O'Neill's autobiography. He had never liked Mark based on what Mr. O'Neill had written about him, but now staring at the little baby in his crib, Neill only felt sorry for Mark, conscious of the fate that awaited him in war-torn France.

"Jane," Howard said once all the cooing was over, "Neill is very interested in architecture. Would you give us a tour of the house so he can see all its splendor?"

Jane laughed and replied, "Despite my mother's efforts, our house is nothing compared to yours, Howard, but I'll be happy to give you the tour."

"I can stay with the baby for you," Abby offered.

Jane consented to this, telling Abby to call for her or the maid if she needed anything. Then she led Howard, Allison, and Neill through the house, from dining room to butler's pantry, upstairs and downstairs through the bedrooms, and best of all, to the exquisite library. Neill was delighted to see the library very much resembled the one he had grown up with, though the 1900 version's wallpaper was brighter and there were far less books, most of them having been acquired after bookworm Robert O'Neill owned the house. *I should tell my parents to rename the house the Carolina Smith Historical Home*, Neill could not help thinking, for the O'Neills had changed very little of it during their many years in the house before passing it on to Neill's family. But Mr. O'Neill had become a famous author, and that is why people came from all over the world to visit the house. However, Neill now understood just how important Carolina Smith's taste had been to making it the home it was, and he had a newfound respect for her, even if he still didn't like her.

But Neill was most interested in when the house had belonged to his ancestors, the Hennings, who had built it and later sold it to the Smiths. He asked Jane several questions about what was original to the house and what her mother had changed. Jane seemed surprised by the specificity of his questions and could not answer many of them. The Smiths had bought the house in 1876 and she had been born in 1877, so she did not remember what it had looked like when bought, though she did remember many of the changes made in her childhood and shared those with Neill. In his brain, Neill filed away information about everything from carpets and wallpaper to lighting fixtures and drapes. He wished he had a cell phone to take pictures with or had asked Howard to bring his new Kodak, but he realized taking interior pictures of someone's home would have been the height of rudeness. His memory would have to suffice.

Eventually, the tour ended, and then Jane looked at the clock and remarked that her mother should be home any time now. She asked them if they would like to stay for lunch, but they all knew she was only being polite and could see she was nervous about her mother finding them there.

After Abby reluctantly handed baby Mark back to his mother, with a few last-minute coos, and Neill and Allison profusely thanked Jane, they left her to her last moments of domestic bliss, promising to call again once she was settled in her new home. All but Abby knew they would never keep that promise, but Jane seemed happy to think she would be friends with the Longyears once out from under her mother's yoke.

It was Friday afternoon now, and the last day before Howard, Allison, and Neill would leave on the train for their presumed trip back East. As they walked home, Abby announced that she had a surprise for them. Her mother had ordered a picnic lunch be packed, and Mr. Longyear and Derek were coming home early from work, so they could all take a boat ride out to Partridge Island for a picnic.

Neill was delighted, but also a tad worried. His ancestor Madeleine had nearly drowned in Lake Superior on a canoeing trip to Partridge Island. Fortunately, she had made it ashore, but she had used the event to fake her death and elope with her boyfriend. Not until Neill's mom had come to Marquette to do genealogy research, which was when she met his father, had anyone known Madeleine had lived, much less had descendants, Neill's mom being one of them. Neill also recalled—he could never forget it when he looked at Lake Superior—that Howard was supposed to drown in the lake. He had a dreadful foreboding about the trip.

But a beautiful sunshiny day, with sun sparkling on Lake Superior's surprisingly calm waters, and the general joviality of the Longyears, soon dispelled Neill's fears. They had a wonderful picnic, they enjoyed the beauty of the cliffs at Presque Isle, and they enjoyed the cool air blowing off the lake. Neill even got to inspect the place where the dance pavilion had once stood. Mr. Longyear explained he'd had it constructed in 1894 so people could come over to the island for parties, but this proved somewhat impractical, so in 1898, he'd had it transported in winter over the ice to Presque Isle Park. Neill could not help marveling at the ingenuity of these Victorians to move entire buildings. Perhaps moving the dance pavilion had inspired Mr. Longyear's idea to move his mansion to Massachusetts, only in this version of 1900, it did not look like that would happen.

It was almost dark by the time they arrived back in Marquette's harbor. With great joy, Neill took in the sight of Marquette rising up on the hills above Iron Bay, noting how different and yet similar the skyline looked from his time. The Savings Bank was still a major building to see from the harbor, but there was no white Presbyterian church tower or the imposing Landmark building in sight. In the far distance, Neill could glimpse the Hotel Superior, and the towers of St. Peter's Cathedral stood out, despite not yet having the colored domes they would sport after the 1935 fire. Neill felt it was good to be in Marquette, no matter what year it was. He could feel the pride and affection his predecessors had for his hometown, and his heart rose up with love for Marquette, a love his parents had helped to instill in him, and a pride at all that Marquette's residents had done over the years to keep their city vibrant and beautiful—even with the ugly industrialism of the Lower Harbor. By Neill's time, the Lower Harbor would be transformed into a beautiful park and marina. He just hoped future generations would love Marquette as much as he did, and protect it from the results he had seen in a different version of its future. Thankfully, if what Howard said was true, he would return to a 2021 no longer aligned with that version of a Marquette yet to come.

Despite Howard, Allison, and Neill having to get up early in the morning for their train trip, no one seemed ready for bed. Plus, they returned earlier than they had thought since sunset was earlier as the late summer days got shorter, so they sat out on the veranda, had ice cream, and talked for a long time about Marquette and how it had changed just in the time since the Longyears had first arrived there. Neill, listening more than talking, realized how much he was going to miss this family that clearly loved one another and had so willingly opened their arms to him and his alleged siblings. The Longyears were one of a kind, and Marquette had been blessed with them. It would never again know, not just a mansion, but a family like the one who lived on the top of the hill between Ridge and Arch Streets.

Longyear Family on veranda, circa 1898
Left to Right seated: Howard, Mrs. Longyear, Robert, Helen, Grace
Tibbitts (cousin), Jack. Floor: Abby, Ajax (dog), Judith,
Railing Harry Burrall (cousin)

When bedtime finally arrived, Neill and Derek stayed up late talking about Derek's future. Derek announced that he had asked Betty to marry him, and she had said yes. They were going to keep their engagement a secret until next month when her aunt and uncle visited from their home in Calumet since she wanted them to be the first to know. But Derek told Neill now so he would know he would be all right here after he left.

"I'm really happy for you, Derek," said Neill, hugging him. "You've proven yourself a remarkable young man, and I'm really proud of you. I wish you all the happiness in the world."

"I'm proud of you too," Derek replied. "I wouldn't be this happy if I hadn't met you and taken a chance by coming here. You were kind of a worry wart at first, but now you've become very mellow."

"Because I'm going home I guess," said Neill.

"It's not just that," said Derek. "You've learned to go with the flow. That's not always easy to do, as I know because I had to learn the same thing. Back in my own time, I was trying to force my relationship with Allison, and we were both miserable as a result. I had to keep looking until I found what made me happy, and now I have, thanks to you."

Neill was touched by this remark. This time travel business, stressful as it had been, had resulted in several good things for several people. He felt so content that he had the best sleep of his life.

Chapter 22

AFTER MANY GOODBYES AT THE depot, Howard, Neill, and Allison embarked the next morning on the train. So the family would not be suspicious, they planned to switch trains when they reached Ishpeming, where Howard had arranged for them to have a private car. Mr. Longyear had joked about how much Allison's trunk weighed as he had helped her unload it from his carriage onto the train. "It's a wonder I have any money left," he said, "after all those dresses my daughters insisted on buying for you."

"You've all been so generous," said Allison, kissing him on the cheek, which quickly shut him up. The truth was that what made it so heavy was the Odin's Eye was wrapped carefully in it. Three other precious items also accompanied them: Allison's cell phone, hidden carefully inside her dress, and Neill's history notes and Howard's journal, tucked away in Neill's small carry-on bag. Howard also had a trunk filled with clothes and books for appearance's sake, realizing he would have to leave it behind as Allison and Neill would have to do with all their belongings save the most important ones.

Once on the train, Allison, Neill, and Howard had a million thoughts running through their heads, but they said little to each other since they did not want the other passengers to hear them. When they disembarked at Ishpeming, they had to locate Allison's trunk, which for a moment seemed to have been lost, alarming them, but they managed to find it and get it placed in their private car on the new train even though the porter insisted it should go in the luggage car and would only inconvenience them when they had to change trains in Chicago.

Howard, gentleman though he was, quickly explained to the porter in the politest terms possible that he was Howard Longyear and the porter should trust that he knew what he was doing. Of course, he knew the porter was only trying to be helpful and they would never make it to Chicago if all went well. The porter, realizing he was talking to his superior, even if he were twice Howard's age, shrugged his shoulders and walked away, leaving Neill and Howard to carry the trunk into the private car.

Once the three friends were alone, Howard explained there would be a few stops on the way, causing the train's speed not to accelerate enough for their experiment, but Howard said they should reach the speed needed between Green Bay and Milwaukee. He cautioned they should not take the Odin's Eye out of the trunk until they departed Green Bay to avoid anyone accidentally seeing it, and once they did remove it, they would have to act quickly. But they still had a few hours before they would reach Green Bay, so they did their best to relax and discuss what they might expect from the time-travel experience and once they were in 2021.

"I still don't understand one thing," Howard said. "I get how the Odin's Eye works and why and how we will make this happen—"

"That's more than I understand," Neill said.

"What don't you understand, Howard?" Allison asked.

"Who created the Odin's Eye and put it there in the first place."

"Who do you think did?" Allison asked.

"Well, it is very advanced technology, so it seems strange to think Vikings created it."

"Yes," Neill agreed, "but the runes on top of the dolmen clearly stated it was there, and the runes must have been made by Vikings."

"Maybe they were faked," said Allison. "Do you think they could have been carved more recently?"

"They were pretty weathered," said Howard, "but I have no idea how long it would take for them to reach that weathered state. Maybe they were a forgery, though who before our time would have been able to forge them? There were no Finns or Swedes or anyone likely to understand runes in the Upper Peninsula until a few decades ago. Maybe a British or French explorer made them, but even then, they'd only be a couple of hundred years old, though I suppose they could become that weathered in that amount of time."

"It is very mysterious," said Neill.

"I hesitate to think it was the Vikings, though," said Howard. "That doesn't make sense to me."

"Because of the advanced technology?" asked Allison.

"That and because Odin's Eye also used Arabic numerals," Howard replied, "and they clearly relate to the current calendar we use, which is all based on the idea that Jesus was born in the year zero or one. The Vikings were not Christians. At least I don't think the Vikings became Christian before the late 900s, but whoever created Odin's Eye was clearly Christian or at least used the Christian calendar."

"Well, when did the Vikings first reach North America?" Neill asked.

"Oh, later than that," said Allison. "I think we learned in school that they came around the year 1100."

"So the dolmen must date from then," said Neill, "unless someone else knew how to create runes and place the Odin's Eye there, and if that person or persons weren't Vikings, wouldn't they have named the machine after something other than a Norse god?"

"That's a good point," said Howard. "I guess I'm convinced then that Vikings did visit the Huron Mountains, make the dolmen, and place Odin's Eye there, and it must have been Vikings or at least some other group of Christians that created the eye."

"Maybe the Byzantines made it," said Neill. "I remember my dad telling me that in the church of Hagia Sophia in Constantinople, there is graffiti carved somewhere by a Viking. The Byzantines might have had the ability to make such a device. After all, the Caliph Haroun al-Rashid had a clock made that he sent to Charlemagne about the year 800, and the Byzantines traded with and lived close to the Muslim nations, so they might have had the technology."

"Or the Vikings got the device from the Byzantines," Howard replied, "and the Byzantines got it from someone in the Arabic world."

"But the Arabic world doesn't use the Christian calendar," said Neill. "They date their history from Mohammed's journey to Mecca in 622, so if the Odin's Eye used that calendar and it was set to 1900, I should have ended up in the year 2522."

"True," said Howard. "I'm impressed you know so much about history, Neill."

"My bookworm parents' fault," he replied.

"So that means the Odin's Eye was placed under the dolmen by Vikings," said Allison, "but it could have been made by them or the Byzantines."

"Or at least someone in Christendom," Howard replied.

"Yes," said Neill, "but I suspect we will never know the full truth. Plus, there's the mystery of who changed the settings on the various Odin's Eyes in the various time streams. Why was it set to 1900 in my time, but in your time, Howard, it was set to 2021, and in Derek's version of 2021, it was set to 2142?"

"You're right," said Howard. "That is a real mystery."

"Well, you solved the most important mystery, Howard," Allison replied. "You figured out how to get us home. We can always figure out the other ones later."

"Let's just hope I'm right," Howard replied.

No one hoped that more than Neill.

Nervousness now started to set in, so they talked little, even nodding off to sleep a bit as the train gently jostled their bodies about. Hours passed before they arrived in Green Bay, and then it seemed like forever before they left the depot there.

As soon as the train started moving, Neill wanted to take out the Odin's Eye, but Howard made him wait several minutes until the train picked up speed.

"How will we know when we're going fast enough?" asked Allison.

"By how fast the landscape is moving past," Howard replied. He took out his pocket watch and began to time how long it took them to pass from one telegraph pole along the track to the next, which he said were spaced out about every seventy yards. Neill was impressed that Howard knew this, but Howard had grown up in a train world, not an automobile or airplane one. Finally, after a few minutes, Howard told Neill and Allison to take out Odin's Eye while he continued to monitor the speed. They did so, placing it on the seat between Howard and Allison. Neill knelt down on the floor before it to hold it steady. Allison dug in Neill's bag and got out his history notes and Howard's journal. Then Neill stuffed them inside his coat pockets to make sure they would make the journey with him.

Howard then explained that he was going to enter the year 2021 into the machine and then press a couple of other buttons. Once he pressed the last button—he made sure to point it out to them on the Odin's Eye so they would know it was the last—they would be transported to 2021, a journey he estimated would take about six seconds.

"Neill," Howard said, "you take Allison's hand, and both of you hold onto the machine with your other hands. I'll grab Neill's wrist and use my free hand to push the buttons, and once I push the last button, I'll grab Allison's wrist."

Howard asked if they all understood, and even though they said they did, he repeated the information to be sure. Then he grabbed his pocket watch and looked out the window again. They waited anxiously for him to tell them the moment had come.

"Okay—now!" Howard shouted. Dropping the watch in his lap, Howard grabbed Neill's wrist and rapidly began pushing the buttons, finally saying, "This is the last one."

Instantly, Neill felt himself spinning as he saw Howard grab Allison's wrist. Allison closed her eyes, but Neill had his open as they began to spiral up into the air, all clutching Odin's Eye as its globe began to spin and flash colors. Neill heard Allison scream, probably from fear they would hit the roof of the railroad car, but then a flash of light filled the space. Neill felt himself propelled upward by a great force, as if the train had exploded.

The next thing Neill knew, his body was colliding with a railroad track and he had lost hold of the Odin's Eye, but he still felt Allison's hand in his. Then he felt Howard's strong grip on his wrist, and when he looked up, he saw blue sky and a couple of wispy little clouds floating above him. He realized he was lying on top of the railroad track.

"Everyone okay?" Howard asked. Neill turned sideways to look at Allison.

"Oh, geez," Neill said when he saw Allison smiling at him. "How are we going to explain these old-fashioned clothes? We didn't think of that. We should have changed first."

"Where's my trunk?" asked Allison, sitting up.

"Where's my pocket watch?" asked Howard, rising to his feet.

"Oh, no!" said Neill, seeing the Odin's Eye lying on the track, looking like its globe was cracked.

And then they heard a train whistle.

"Get up!" Howard shouted, jumping to his feet. He reached down to grab Allison's hand and help her stand. He pulled her away from the track as Neill stared and saw an engine coming straight at them. Then he struggled to his feet, tripped over a board in the track, and went down.

"Neill!" screamed Allison.

Quickly getting into a crawling position, Neill got over the rail and then dropped and rolled down a small incline away from the track as Howard and Allison rushed after him and the train began to whiz by.

"Holy cow! I never saw a train like that!" Howard exclaimed, turning to watch it.

"Oh, the Odin's Eye!" cried Allison.

"Oh no!" cried, Howard, suddenly sounding devastated.

They all were on their feet now, staring at the train track, waiting to see if the time travel device had survived.

Once the train had passed, it was clear the Odin's Eye was no more. All that remained was a mess of shattered glass and busted levers. The entire bottom was loose, and the buttons were falling out of it.

For a moment, Neill thought it was a total loss, but Allison, placing her hand on Howard's shoulder, said, "It's okay. We can still use the one under the dolmen in this time if we need to."

"That's true," said Neill.

Regardless, Howard stepped toward the machine and began to pick up the pieces.

"Howard, did you hear me?" asked Allison, walking toward him.

"Yes, you're right," he replied, "but we can't leave the pieces here for someone else to find."

They all agreed with this and began picking up bits of metal and putting them in various pockets of their clothing. The glass they left behind since it looked like nothing more than glass slivers from a smashed Coke bottle. As they picked up the pieces, Howard said, "Maybe this is an advantage since it might give me more insight into how Odin's Eye worked to have these pieces from the inside I couldn't access before. Even if I can't completely put it back together, I'll understand how it was made now."

"What about your journal, though," said Neill. "Doesn't it have that kind of information in it?"

"Where is it?" asked Allison in a panic.

"It's in my suit pocket," said Neill, feeling it to reassure himself.

"But you lost your watch, Howard," said Allison.

"Because it was on my lap and slid off when we began spinning."

"I still have my cell phone," said Allison, feeling where it was hidden inside her dress. Neill knew the battery in it was long dead, but she had hidden the charger in her dress as well. "If we can find some electricity, I can charge it up, and then we can call Derek to come get us."

"How will he do that?" asked Howard.

"In his truck," said Neill.

Howard laughed. "I'm rather looking forward to seeing what it's like to ride in a truck."

"Don't get too excited," said Allison. "It's nothing like that time-travel ride we just had."

They all laughed, and now having retrieved all the pieces they could find of Odin's Eye, they began walking down the train track, expecting to come soon to some outpost of civilization. It wasn't long before they spotted the freeway and on its opposite side off an exit going up a hill was a Taco Bell.

"You're in for the treat of your life!" Neill told Howard when he saw his favorite place to eat.

"What is it?" asked Howard.

"It's a restaurant," said Allison.

"Mexican food," said Neill.

"But I haven't any money," said Howard, "and I don't know if I like Mexican food."

"No worries," said Allison. "I have a credit card."

"What's a credit card?" Howard asked.

"You have a lot to learn about the twenty-first century," Neill replied, patting him on the back. "But first, we have to get past that freeway."

Cars were whizzing along it, and Howard looked terrified at the thought of crossing it, but once Allison stood on the side of the road and drivers saw a crazy woman in a Victorian dress waving at them, they began to slow down and actually came to a stop, letting her run across the road. Howard and Neill quickly followed.

"And I thought we were going fast on the train," Howard said as he saw the cars continue on their journey.

"You haven't seen anything yet," said Neill, starting up the grassy hill to Taco Bell.

In a few more minutes, they were inside the restaurant. When the girl at the counter gave them strange looks, Allison explained to her that they were actors on their lunch break from their play's dress rehearsal. Then Allison looked for somewhere to charge her phone. There was an outlet by one of the tables, which she instantly claimed while Neill ordered a ton of food. Soon trays of chalupas, gorditas, and chili cheese burritos were before them. Howard was hesitant about the food, but having traveled extensively in Europe, he decided to be brave, and he was pleasantly surprised to find it quite tasty.

By the time they were done eating, Allison's phone was sufficiently charged to call Derek. When he answered, he said he'd almost had a heart attack when he saw her number on his phone's screen.

Allison put off telling him where they'd been, but she assured him she and Neill were safe. Derek was overjoyed to hear Neill was with her. She explained they were south of Green Bay, stranded there, and had a friend named Howard with them. Derek only had a truck, but it had little seats in the back. They would be crowded, but he would come get them. He demanded an explanation when he arrived. Allison assured him he'd get one, but she made him promise not to tell her mom or Neill's family he had heard from them until after they had all talked. Derek said everyone was worried sick about them, but he agreed that keeping their secret for a few more hours wouldn't hurt too much. Allison was about to disconnect the call when Neill shouted, "Wait!"

"What?" Allison asked.

"Ask him if the ore dock is still in the harbor," said Neill.

"What kind of crazy question is that?" asked Derek when Allison relayed the message. "Of course it is."

Neill smiled when Allison gave him Derek's response. If his parents were worried about him and the ore dock was still there, he must really be back in his own time.

Allison told Derek she'd text him later about where to pick them up once they figured out exactly where they were.

After Allison hung up, they discussed what they would do in the four hours or so it would take for Derek to reach them.

None of them wanted to draw attention to themselves by sitting around Taco Bell all afternoon. Finally, Neill decided to ask the girl at the counter if there were any clothing stores within walking distance. It turned out there was an outlet mall about two miles up the road, so the three friends headed on foot in the direction the employee gave them.

"I can't wait to get out of this dress," said Allison.

Howard, after seeing what people had been wearing in Taco Bell, remarked how immodest everyone's clothing looked. Allison just laughed. "You'll have to get used to it, Howie."

"Howie?" said Howard.

"Yes, Howie," said Allison. "No one is named Howard in the twenty-first century, at least no one younger than our grandparents' generation."

"And one of the characters on *The Big Bang Theory*," Neill added.

"What's that?" asked Howard.

"A television sitcom," said Allison, "but you're going to have to learn to quit asking what things are except when you're alone with us because people will start to think you're stupid."

Howard understood. After all, if he was smart enough to figure out how time travel worked, he was smart enough to keep his mouth shut around strangers. But it was going to take some doing to fit into this modern period.

When they got to the outlet mall, Howard couldn't believe his eyes. He said he'd been in larger stores, but none so packed with clothing. Allison went off on her own while Neill led Howard to the men's section. Howard absolutely refused when Neill, as a joke, tried to get him to a wear a muscle shirt; Neill had seen a photo of Howard in his sleeveless rowing crew uniform that had made him look quite studly, but Howard was too modest to show off his guns. He finally agreed to a polo shirt, though he felt even that was immodest. He absolutely refused to wear shorts, so they settled for a pair of jeans and some Reeboks.

Howard showing off his guns

Neill opted for shorts and a T-shirt, and he felt a million times cooler once he had shed his Victorian clothes in the air-conditioned mall.

But the biggest shock was when Allison appeared in a tank top and short shorts.

"Where are your clothes?" Howard asked her.

"These are my clothes," she said.

"Those don't even look like undergarments," he replied.

Allison smiled and kissed him on the cheek.

"Don't do that," Howard said, "not looking like that. You'll give people the wrong idea, and I might not be able to control myself."

Allison laughed and led him up to the counter. The salesperson was irritated that they were wearing their purchases, but they pulled the tags off and handed them to her, so she quit grumbling and rang them up. A few hundred dollars on Allison's credit card later and they were ready to go. They left their nineteenth-century clothes in the changing rooms for someone else to dispose of, though they had been careful to collect all the pieces of Odin's Eye from their pockets and place them inside a large handbag Allison also bought. Neill put Howard's journal and his history notes in the handbag as well.

Allison then texted Derek that they were at the outlet mall and told him which exit to take on the freeway. Howard was reveling in the air conditioning, which fascinated him, though Neill couldn't really explain to him how it worked. Neill suggested they all visit the Orange Julius since he was still quite warm. After purchasing their drinks there, they sauntered through the mall. Howard froze in place at the sight of the arcade and then had to go inside and try a few games. Neill was close to exasperated from answering Howard's ten-thousand questions about twenty-first-century technology when Allison's phone rang. Derek was waiting in the parking lot.

They quickly went outside and found him. Derek was overwhelmed with joy and relief to see them and hugged both Allison and Neill tightly. But he only shook Howard's hand while looking at him questioningly, especially since Howard acted like he already knew him. It was going to take some convincing to get Derek to believe another version of him existed, but they had plenty of time for explanations on the long ride home.

Derek was hungry, so they went back to Taco Bell, where no one looked twice at them now that they'd changed their clothes. By the time they got on the road to Marquette, Allison and Neill had decided they could trust Derek enough to tell him the entire story. He asked about a hundred questions in the process and told them they were "bat shit crazy," but eventually, he began to believe them. He also told them no one else would.

"We know," said Neill. "I might tell my parents in time, but—"

"But before you tell anyone," Howard interrupted, "we have to remove the Odin's Eye from the dolmen at the Huron Mountain Club. We need to keep it safe if I need it to return to my time, and we don't want anyone else accidentally transported to the past."

"Good idea," said Allison.

"What will you tell everyone else?" Derek asked.

"How about," said Neill, looking at Allison, "that the two of us eloped and then changed our minds?"

"No one will believe that," said Allison. "Maybe we could claim we were abducted by a human trafficking group and escaped with Howard."

"The police have been looking for you," said Derek, "so that story might just cause more trouble since they'd want to look for your abductors. There are going to be lots of questions."

"We don't have to answer them," said Neill.

"I wouldn't be surprised," said Derek, "if the police aren't tracking your credit cards and cell phone usage to try to find you, so they might already know you've been south of Green Bay."

"Well, then," said Allison, "I guess we can't just pretend we got lost in the woods at the Huron Mountain Club."

"No," said Neill. "I think the best thing we can do is not answer any questions. After all, we've done nothing wrong and it is a free country, so we can go where we want."

"But how will we explain Howard?" asked Allison.

"We won't," said Neill. "Derek, can Howard stay with you until we figure this all out? Explaining Howard might be really difficult, especially around our parents, since he might say something that will make them suspicious. If he stays with you, he can get better acclimated to this time and we can visit him there without raising more questions."

"But I came here to be with Allison," said Howard.

"And you will be, Howie," she said, kissing him on the cheek—they were sitting together in the back of the truck. "But let me go home and see my mom first, and then we can talk about finding a place to live together."

Howard looked shocked at this suggestion. "Live together?" he croaked out.

"Well," said Allison, "we can get married and then find a place to live together."

Howard sighed with relief. As much as he loved Allison and knew he had to adapt to twenty-first-century life, he was not going to live in sin. "It's definitely going to be interesting living in your time," he said.

"It was interesting living in yours," Neill replied. "Just remember it's all an adventure. Even when bad or unexpected things happen, it's an adventure, and we all just have to do our best to go with the flow because, in the end, it will all work out somehow."

Did I get that right, Uncle Chad? Neill thought. He still missed his uncle every day, but he had his parents, sister, and grandparents, so from now on, he would make the most of his life with what remained. Uncle Chad would have wanted it that way.

Author's Note

F OR MANY YEARS, I HAVE said to myself and others, "I wish I could invent a time machine so I could see what Marquette looked like in the past." Then one day, it struck me that the next best thing would be to write a time travel novel. The idea stayed in my head for a while, but I did not get a chance to start writing it until the summer of 2020 when the whole world was enmeshed in the coronavirus pandemic.

As I struggled to decide what time my main character would go back to, I did not realize how my subconscious fears about the pandemic and my grief over the death of my brother in September 2019 were playing into the development of my novel. I knew that to make a good time travel novel, not only would time travel have to happen, but a plot was required. My main character couldn't just go back into the past and tour it; he needed some angst to make the book interesting, and that angst could come from his accidentally changing the past. So I set about trying to figure out what dramatic event in Marquette's past might be changed and tried to envision how Marquette would be different if that happened. I could have chosen from many events, but I had always felt it a shame that the Longyear Mansion had been moved from Marquette, and that never would have happened if Howard Longyear had lived, so a storyline began to develop by my asking, "What if Howard Longyear had lived?"

The decision to use Neill Vandelaare as my main character was a difficult one because he is part of the wide and connected array of characters from my other Marquette novels and short stories. With a few exceptions, those works are realistic historical fiction. To take a character from realistic fiction and suddenly have him time travel would be pushing the boundaries of realistic fiction, yet I decided to do it because, after all, the very world I was living in had suddenly become surreal.

When my brother Daniel was unexpectedly found dead—he had broken a bone in his foot the week before resulting in a blood clot and pulmonary embolism—the shock was so great that I found it hard to believe it was real. Death from a blood clot at age forty-six is very rare. Even months after his funeral, I kept feeling like I was living in some sort of parallel world that was not meant to be, and when the pandemic began less than six months later—an event right out of science fiction films—it made the surrealness even more extreme. Neill's surreal experience of time traveling in many ways makes the world feel turned upside-down for him just the way I was feeling. Since I began writing the novel in late 2020, it was only to be expected I would set it during the pandemic—when for the first time in my life death became as prevalent as it was in Victorian times.

Of course, Neill adjusts to time-traveling at the end of the novel, but will he adjust when he returns to the twenty-first century? Will his family believe him if he tries to tell them the truth of what happened to him, or will they think he is crazy, perhaps suffering from schizophrenia triggered by his uncle's death, the pandemic, or just being lost in the woods? Is it possible the entire experience has only been in Neill's head, like visiting Oz was for Dorothy in the film of *The Wizard of Oz* when she wakes up to find it was only a dream? But in the novel, *The Wonderful Wizard of Oz*, it is not a dream, and in its sequels, L. Frank Baum had Dorothy return to Oz many times, eventually moving there. Will Neill's fate be similar? And what about Howard? The time travel must have happened since he returned with Neill and Allison to the twenty-first century. But what will become of him? Only the future will tell.

Despite the surreal and whimsical nature of this work, I have tried to be historically accurate about as much as possible, from details about the Longyear family to what Marquette looked like in 1900. A few historical tidbits that may interest the reader are worth noting.

The Longyears' son Howard really did drown in Lake Superior along with Hugh Allen, and as a result, the Longyears did move their house to Brookline, Massachusetts. Mrs. Longyear was also a big believer in Christian Science, eventually leaving the Longyear Mansion to the Christian Science Church. Mr. Longyear was a wealthy businessman who at one point owned as much as 3 percent of the state of Michigan's land. The Longyears' daughters, Abby and Helen, later built large homes on the property where the Longyear Mansion stood.

As for Howard, who he would have been had he lived cannot be known, but we know from his journals and the letters and reminiscences of friends and family preserved in the book *The Unfolding Life*, that he was a good, moral boy. He also had a gift for languages. Consequently, I chose to have his gift of language help him with translating the dolmen's runes and writing his journal in codes.

I was unable to find anything about Hugh Allen's character, so the depiction of him is my own invention, but given that he was a year younger than Howard and drowned with him, I think I have developed a plausible character for him.

The events surrounding the drowning of Hugh and Howard are accurate in terms of the trip they made that day. The canoe is described accurately. Howard did bring flowers with him for his mother. The site of the drowning is also accurate based on where Howard and Hugh's bodies were later found, although they were not found for nearly a week. The only major detail I left out was that the young men stopped at Oudotte's to buy a box of crackers and another of ginger wafers. I was unable to determine where Oudotte's was, though it was likely a store on Presque Isle, and including it did not add anything to the narrative.

Abby Longyear Roberts was interviewed on a recording in 1961 in which she states how Howard was her mother's "ideal," an "adored child," and "perfection" while the rest of the children were more like "baggage." She describes how inconsolable her mother was over his death. However, she also suggests that while Howard was a docile and obedient boy, had he lived a few more years to take his life into his own hands and have married, it would have driven Mrs. Longyear crazy. In having Howard fall in love with Allison, I have given him the sort of adult life he was cheated out of. At the same time, his choosing to leave his family for Allison is in some ways equivalent to his death. We can imagine how Mrs. Longyear will react when she does not hear from him after she thinks he has arrived at Cornell. We can only hope Howard will find a way to let her know he is still alive.

Although I tried to find details of the Longyears' servants, none of them, based on perusing the city directories, seem to have stayed with the family long, other than Charles Johnson, who was a helper in 1895 and a gardener in 1901 for the Longyears. Consequently, I made up the names of Martha and Franklin as servants.

I have tried to depict the Longyears in a positive light, and I believe overall they were a happy family by all accounts. Mrs. Longyear tended to be obsessive about her Christian Science beliefs, but according to Abby Longyear Roberts, the Longyears did not push their beliefs on others. The family is kind enough in the novel to take in "John" and later Neill, Derek, and Allison, which I think reflects their actual kindness. In real life, the Longyears' took in Mrs. Longyear's sister Fannie Beecher Burrall, and her three children, Fred, Grace, and Harry, letting them live in the mansion with them. I have omitted the Burralls from the novel since the Longyears are enough characters for the book. However, Grace and Harry can both be seen in the photo included in the novel of the Longyears sitting on their veranda. I also omitted the Longyears' dog Ajax from the novel, who is also in that photograph.

I always have fun trying to mix my fictional characters with historical people so the reader feels like it is all historical and real and has difficulty knowing where the line is drawn. I did that in several places, including referencing myself in the novel as being friends with Neill's father. Later in the novel Arthur Dalrymple refers to Mrs. Jackson being run over by a drunk carriage driver and then lists several of her relatives. Mrs. Jackson is my own four-greats-grandmother and the Dalrymple family is largely based on my own Scottish relatives who lived in Marquette at the time.

The Huron Mountain Club exists as described. It is still a private club to this day. There is a dolmen on top of Mount Huron, and while no one has time traveled by touching it or found a time travel device under it, who placed it there remains a mystery.

Hugh Allen is buried in Marquette's Park Cemetery near his father.

Howard Longyear is also buried in Park Cemetery, the only one of his family laid to rest there. He lies in an unmarked grave.

Tyler Tichelaar
Marquette, Michigan
May 1, 2023

Acknowledgments

THIS BOOK WOULD HAVE BEEN impossible without the sharing of information and resources from many people and from those who took the time to read drafts and listen to me talk about the issues of the plot and characters. My gratitude goes to:

Beth Gruber and Hunter Laing at the John M. Longyear Research Library at the Marquette Regional History Center for all their help with researching the historical facts of this story.

James Harwood for information on the Huron Mountain Club and the dolmen on Mount Huron.

Adam Berger for information on the Longyear family and Huron Mountain Club.

Diana DeLuca and Roslyn Hurley for reading and commenting on early drafts of the novel.

Brandy Thomas for her suggestions on plot development and how to make the time travel seem plausible.

Jenifer Brady for her excellent proofreading skills and enthusiastic support.

Larry Alexander for his invaluable expertise at layout and cover design.

Photo Credits

Marquette Regional History Center – 31, 49, 60, 61, 75, 77, 79, 96, 99, 243, 244, 312, 359, 360, 389

Public Domain, from the book *The Unfolding Life* by Henry D. Nunn – 399

Steve Fine – 196

A Special Request

If you enjoyed this book, please write a book review for it at Amazon, Barnes & Noble, Goodreads, or another bookseller or book-lover website. Authors rely on book reviews and word-of-mouth to sell their books. Readers also rely on reviews to help them make their decisions on which books to purchase and read. Just a couple of sentences from you can have a huge impact. The author thanks you for your time.

Be Sure to Read All of Tyler R. Tichelaar's Upper Michigan Books

IRON PIONEERS
THE MARQUETTE TRILOGY: BOOK ONE

When iron ore is discovered in Michigan's Upper Peninsula in the 1840s, newlyweds Gerald Henning and his beautiful socialite wife Clara travel from Boston to the little village of Marquette on the shore of Lake Superior. They and their companions, Irish and German immigrants, French Canadians, and fellow New Englanders face blizzards and near starvation, devastating fires, and financial hardships. Yet these iron pioneers persevere until their wilderness village becomes integral to the Union cause in the Civil War and then a prosperous modern city. Meticulously researched, warmly written, and spanning half a century, *Iron Pioneers* is a testament to the spirit that forged America.

THE QUEEN CITY
THE MARQUETTE TRILOGY: BOOK TWO

During the first half of the twentieth century, Marquette grows into the Queen City of the North. Here is the tale of a small town undergoing change as its horses are replaced by streetcars and automobiles, and its pioneers are replaced by new generations who prosper despite two World Wars and the Great Depression. Margaret Dalrymple finds her Scottish prince, though he is neither Scottish nor a prince. Molly Bergmann becomes an inspiration to her grandchildren. Jacob Whitman's children engage in a family feud. The Queen City's residents marry, divorce, have children, die, break their hearts, go to war, gossip, blackmail, raise families, move away, and then return to Marquette. And always, always they are in love with the haunting land that is their home.

SUPERIOR HERITAGE
THE MARQUETTE TRILOGY: BOOK THREE

The Marquette Trilogy comes to a satisfying conclusion as it brings together characters and plots from the earlier novels and culminates with Marquette's sesquicentennial celebrations in 1999. What happened to Madeleine Henning is finally revealed as secrets from the past shed light upon the present. Marquette's residents struggle with a difficult local economy, yet remain optimistic for the future. The novel's main character, John Vandelaare, is descended from all the early Marquette families in *Iron Pioneers* and *The Queen City*. While he cherishes his family's past, he questions whether he should remain in his hometown. Then an event happens that will change his life forever.

NARROW LIVES

Narrow Lives is the story of those whose lives were affected by Lysander Blackmore, the sinister banker first introduced to readers in *The Queen City*. It is a novel that stands alone, yet readers of *The Marquette Trilogy* will be reacquainted with some familiar characters. Written as a collection of connected short stories, each told in first person by a different character, *Narrow Lives* depicts the influence one person has, even in death, upon others, and it explores the prisons of grief, loneliness, and fear self-created when people doubt their own worthiness.

THE ONLY THING THAT LASTS

The story of Robert O'Neill, the famous novelist introduced in *The Marquette Trilogy*. As a young boy during World War I, Robert is forced to leave his South Carolina home to live in Marquette with his grandmother and aunt. He finds there a cold climate, but many warmhearted friends. An old-fashioned story that follows Robert's growth from childhood to successful writer and husband, the novel is written as Robert O'Neill's autobiography, his final gift to Marquette by memorializing the town of his youth.

SPIRIT OF THE NORTH: A PARANORMAL ROMANCE

In 1873, orphaned sisters Barbara and Adele Traugott travel to Upper Michigan to live with their uncle, only to find he is deceased. Penniless, they are forced to spend the long, fierce winter alone in their uncle's remote wilderness cabin. Frightened, yet determined, the sisters face blizzards and near starvation to survive. Amid their difficulties, they find love and heartache—and then, a ghostly encounter and the coming of spring lead them to discovering the true miracle of their being.

THE BEST PLACE

An irritating best friend gained during a childhood spent in a Catholic orphanage, a father who became a Communist and went to Russia in the 1930s, and 3:00 a.m. visits to The Pancake House. Such is the life of Lyla Hopewell. But in the summer of 2005, when her old boyfriend Bill has a heart attack, her best friend Bel really gets on her nerves, and Finn Fest comes to Marquette, things will change for Lyla.

WHEN TEDDY CAME TO TOWN

Former U.S. President Theodore Roosevelt was on campaign on the Progressive "Bull Moose" ticket, but his break from the Republican Party had caused him to have many detractors. When a small town Michigan newspaper editor accused him of being drunk while campaigning, Roosevelt decided to make an example of him.

Matthew Newman, reporter for the New York *Empire Sentinel*, should have seen his assignment to cover the trial as the opportunity of a lifetime. But Matthew is also a native of Marquette, Michigan, where the trial will be held. Matthew left Marquette long ago and does not relish returning to deal with a distant sister and her drunkard husband, or to attend his niece's wedding, set for the weekend after the trial begins.

WILLPOWER:
AN ORIGINAL PLAY ABOUT MARQUETTE'S OSSIFIED MAN

There are some stories that deserve to be told. As a young boy, Will Adams' soft tissues were becoming harder, turning him into a living statue. Others faced with such a dark future might have felt sorry for themselves, turning inward. Not so for Will; his disease brought about an amazing creative burst of energy. His true story is as inspiring today as it was more than 100 years ago.

MY MARQUETTE:
EXPLORE THE QUEEN CITY OF THE NORTH
—ITS HISTORY, PEOPLE, AND PLACES

My Marquette is the result of its author's lifelong love affair with his hometown. Join Tyler R. Tichelaar, seventh generation Marquette resident and author of *The Marquette Trilogy*, as he takes you on a tour of the history, people, and places of Marquette. Stories of the past and present, both true and fictional, will leave you understanding why Marquette really is "The Queen City of the North." Along the way, Tyler will describe his own experiences growing up in Marquette, recall family and friends he knew, and give away secrets about the people behind the characters in his novels. *My Marquette* offers a rare insight into an author's creation of fiction and a refreshing view of a city's history and relevance to today. Reading *My Marquette* is equal to being given a personal tour by someone who knows Marquette intimately.

HAUNTED MARQUETTE:
GHOST STORIES FROM THE QUEEN CITY

Founded as a harbor town to ship iron ore from the nearby mines, Marquette became known as the Queen City of the North for its thriving industries, beautiful buildings, and being the largest city in Upper Michigan.

But is Marquette also the Queen of Lake Superior's Haunted Cities? Seventh-generation Marquette resident Tyler Tichelaar has spent years collecting tales of the many ghosts who haunt the cemeteries, churches, businesses, hotels, and homes of Marquette.

Now, separating fact from fiction, Tichelaar delves into the historical record to determine whom the ghosts might be, which stories have a historical basis, and which tales are simply the fancies of imaginative or frightened minds.

Hear the chilling tales of:

- The wicked nun who killed an orphan boy, and how the boy continues to escape from his grave
- The librarian who haunts a local hotel while mourning for her sailor lover
- The drowned sailors who climb out of Lake Superior at night
- The glowing lantern of the decapitated train conductor
- The mailman who gave his life so neither rain, nor sleet, nor snow would stop the U.S. mail

- More ghostly ladies in floor-length white gowns than any haunted city should have

Haunted Marquette opens up a fourth dimension view of the Queen City's past and reveals that much of it is still present.

KAWBAWGAM:
THE CHIEF, THE LEGEND, THE MAN

Today, Charles Kawbawgam, "The Last Chief of the Chippewa," is a legend in Michigan's Upper Peninsula for allegedly living to age 103 (1799-1902). But few know anything else about him beyond his being buried in Marquette's beautiful Presque Isle Park.

Kawbawgam witnessed a period of intense industrial growth and unheralded change for Native Americans. Growing up at Sault Sainte Marie when the area was still claimed by Great Britain, his first memory was of armed Americans coercing his people into ceding their lands to the United States Government. As the son, nephew, stepson, and later son-in-law of Ojibwa chiefs, and in time a chief in his own right, Kawbawgam learned early that he would have to walk a fine line to keep the peace for his people. After temporarily migrating to Canada with other Ojibwa in disagreement with the American government, he returned to the Sault where he was recruited to help found the town of Marquette.

Kawbawgam would preside over an Ojibwa and métis community that helped ensure the white settlers' survival during Marquette's early years, only to be pushed to the city's margins as Marquette grew and prospered. Yet the admiration and affection Kawbawgam won from whites as well as the Ojibwa maintained peace and created a legacy that lives on today. *Kawbawgam* is a story of cross-cultural friendships, survival amid upheaval, and the importance of community and heritage.

For more information about
Tyler R. Tichelaar's Marquette Books, visit:
www.MarquetteFiction.com

And be sure also to check out Tyler's other titles

THE GOTHIC WANDERER:
FROM TRANSGRESSION TO REDEMPTION,
1794-PRESENT

VAMPIRE GROOMS AND SPECTRE BRIDES:
THE MARRIAGE OF FRENCH AND BRITISH GOTHIC
LITERATURE,
1789-1897

CREATING A LOCAL HISTORICAL BOOK:
FICTION AND NONFICTION GENRES

THE NOMAD EDITOR:
LIVING THE LIFESTYLE YOU WANT,
DOING WORK YOU LOVE

KING ARTHUR'S CHILDREN:
A STUDY IN FICTION AND TRADITION

THE CHILDREN OF ARTHUR
HISTORICAL FANTASY SERIES

Arthur's Legacy: The Children of Arthur, Book One

Melusine's Gift: The Children of Arthur, Book Two

Ogier's Prayer: The Children of Arthur, Book Three

Lilith's Love: The Children of Arthur, Book Four

Arthur's Bosom: The Children of Arthur, Book Five

About the Author

Tyler R. Tichelaar has a PhD in Literature from Western Michigan University and Bachelor and Master's Degrees in English from Northern Michigan University. He is the owner of Marquette Fiction, his own publishing company, and of Superior Book Productions, a professional editing, proofreading, and book layout company. He is also the former vice president (2007-2008) and president (2008-2019) of the Upper Peninsula Publishers and Authors Association. Tyler is especially proud to be a seventh-generation Marquette resident.

Tyler began writing his first novel at age sixteen in 1987. In 2006, he published his first novel, *Iron Pioneers: The Marquette Trilogy, Book One*. More than twenty books have followed. In 2009, Tyler won first place in the historical fiction category in the Reader Views Literary Awards for his novel *Narrow Lives*. He has since sponsored that contest, offering the Tyler R. Tichelaar Award for Historical Fiction. In 2011, Tyler was awarded the Marquette County Outstanding Writer Award, and the same year, he received the Barb Kelly Award for Historical Preservation for his efforts to promote Marquette history. In 2014, his play *Willpower* was produced by the Marquette Regional History Center, with assistance of a grant from the Michigan Humanities Council. He has twice been nominated for the Pushcart Prize for his short stories. In 2021, his biography of local Ojibwa Chief Charles Kawbawgam, titled *Kawbawgam: The Chief, The Legend, The Man*, was named a UP Notable Book.

While Tyler also writes on such diverse topics as nineteenth-century Gothic fiction and Arthurian historical fantasy, he remains engrossed in writing about Marquette and Upper Michigan as microcosms for the greater American story. He has many more books in the works.

Visit Tyler at:
www.MarquetteFiction.com.